For Ivan, Jackie and Luke.
So lovely to know you, and thank you all for
all your help over the years.
It's very much appreciated.
Three cheers, Ivan, for becoming a reader again! Well done you!
Joy and Jacqueline

CHAPTER ONE

The night was crisp and cold, the inky black sky spattered with diamond bright stars. Then he saw lights of a different origin, small beams darting and weaving in an uneven path across the fields.

He breathed in and held it. Right on time.

From his lofty position he could see that they were heading for the side of the old building. That was the way he had entered, and he was relieved that they were going to use the same route in. The other entrance was dangerous in daytime, let alone by torchlight.

After a while he heard muffled voices echo upwards.

Waiting wasn't easy, but he knew how to be patient. Many years ago, he had enjoyed river fishing, and now he employed the same strategy, remaining focused and vigilant. The right moment would come, and he would be ready to reel in his prey.

It was over three-quarters of an hour before the perfect moment came and he acted — swift, silent and deadly.

A little later, driving carefully over the fen lanes, he whispered to his passenger, 'So you like dark, dangerous old buildings, do you?' He didn't wait for an answer. 'Well, in that case, you are going to love where I'm taking you now.'

* * *

DI Rowan Jackman looked around the CID room until he spotted the newest member of their team, DC Kevin Stoner.

'Kevin? Would you take this laptop down to IT for me? Orac is expecting it. Give it to her in person, please.'

'Sorry, sir, Orac isn't in today,' Kevin said.

Everyone in the room stopped what they were doing and stared at Kevin.

DS Marie Evans voiced their collective question. 'What do you mean, not in? Orac is always in.'

'Not today, Sarge,' said Kevin, mildly surprised at all the faces turned in his direction. 'I met one of her team earlier who said she hadn't turned up this morning. It's chaos down there apparently.'

Jackman threw Marie an enquiring glance, but she just shrugged and raised her eyebrows as if to say, *I'm as much in the dark as you are.*

Jackman returned to his office, his sanctuary in a frenetic, crime-filled world. It was like no other office in Saltern-le-Fen police station, furnished not with corporate chipboard and steel, but with things he loved, picked up at house-clearances and auctions. He sat down in his captain's chair and considered what Kevin had said. Orac? If it had been any other member of staff, no one would have taken the slightest notice, but in all the years he'd been there, he had never known Orla Cracken (more widely known as Orac), head of IT and undeniable genius, take a holiday or go on sick leave. She seemed to work shifts that encompassed the whole day and most of the night, and whenever you needed her, there she would be, hidden away in her basement kingdom, surrounded by computers and monitors.

'Boss?' Marie stood in the doorway. 'How about I take that laptop downstairs for you? I'll maybe find out what's going on.'

Marie knew more about Orac than anyone. Jackman would not have called them friends exactly, but they certainly had a rapport. Orac's life was a mystery, and the only person she had ever opened up to was Marie Evans. And no matter how eager Jackman was to find out more about the legend in the basement, Marie wasn't telling.

'Yes, do.' He handed her the carefully bagged laptop. 'It's got some pretty sensitive stuff on it, but we're needing to look deeper, that's why I specifically wanted Orac. Still, just make sure whoever logs it in is aware of its importance.'

'The Kirby investigation?'

'I'm hoping this will be the magic bullet that seals his fate. Uniform found it at his grandmother's house, and something tells me that sweet, silver-haired old lady isn't particularly into money laundering.'

'More like Solitaire or Scrabble, I'd say.' Marie looked at the bag. 'I'll take it now. It's a good excuse to get nosey. See you as soon as I've grilled those techies.'

He watched her leave and smiled to himself. They were all still recovering from the aftermath of their last murder case, but in the last few weeks he had noticed a different atmosphere in the CID room, a new energy. The dynamic had altered, and they were adjusting to a new routine. DC Rosie Cohen had left them to care for her baby twins, but her husband DC Max Cohen had returned full time, so that part of the team was still active. And now they had newbie Kevin with them, so along with DC Robbie Melton, and PC Gary Pritchard they were nearly back up to full strength.

He stared at the reports on his desk. The case he had at present was about ready to be handed over to the Crown Prosecution Service, and for once, Saltern seemed more or less at peace. Not that he dared to believe it would stay that way — it never did.

His thoughts returned to Orac. Apart from being one of the most striking women he had ever seen, with her white-blonde hair cut in a kind of GI Mohican style, and those disturbing mirror contact lenses that made her eyes look like sheet metal, she was a closed book. He guessed from her accent that she was from Northern Ireland but other than that he knew nothing about her. He didn't even know where she lived. Indeed, it was rumoured that she never left the

3

basement and probably just hung upside down in a cupboard somewhere. He didn't know if she was married, single or divorced. Jackman sighed. What he did know, as did every other officer and civilian in the station, was that she terrified him. Maybe it was those eyes. Her sheer brilliance? He wasn't sure what caused it, but two minutes in her company caused him to morph into a tongue-tied, red-faced teenager again. Orac knew it too and played on it mercilessly. He was certain that Jackman-baiting was her only true amusement in life. In his time on the force, he'd faced killers and all manner of danger and had shied away from nothing. He had a wonderful partner whom he truly loved, and yet, where that spiky-haired, weird-eyed woman was concerned, he was a wreck.

Jackman pushed aside the funny side of his embarrassing relationship with the IT boss. How very strange it was that he didn't have the slightest idea of where she lived. He knew where all his team had their homes, his superintendent, Ruth Crooke, and even a lot of the civilians that he worked closely with, but not Orac. She generated more whispers and assumptions about her life, past and present, than anyone else at the station. He frowned. And why, when they had no secrets, had Marie never confided in him? That was probably the oddest thing of all. He and Marie had a special bond — after some of the terrible cases they had been through, it was not surprising. They talked openly about everything. Except what Marie knew about Orla Cracken.

He shook his head. This was silly. She had probably broken a tooth and rushed to the dentist, or lost one of those scary contact lenses, or had a family emergency. Not that he knew if she even had family, but no one is an island, she must have someone in her life, on some level. He opened a report. Why speculate when Marie would be back in ten minutes with the lowdown? 'Right, Mr Kirby, let's get back to work and see if we can drive another nail into your coffin, shall we?'

* * *

DC Robbie Melton picked up his phone and a wide grin spread across his face. 'Stella! How are you?'

Stella North, as he'd always known her, now Mrs Stella Chalk, had been his sergeant prior to his transfer to Saltern-le-Fen. She had been shot, suffering injuries that saw her leaving the force that she loved. She was now a farmer's wife, leading a different but very contented life, so there was a happy ending to her story.

'We must meet up, Stel, have a coffee and a catch-up very soon.' They had been the dream team and he still missed her, though he loved working with Jackman and Marie.

'How about later today, Robbie? In fact, could you slip out around lunchtime? I'll come into Saltern and meet you somewhere.'

His smile faltered. Was something wrong? 'Sure. Is everything alright? You haven't had some kind of relapse, have you? There's nothing wrong with Tom, is there?'

'I'm fit as a fiddle, Robbie, and Tom is just fine. Don't fret. I need a favour, and I don't want to talk about it on the phone.'

'Then I'll meet you at thirteen hundred hours at the Cargo Hold in Lemon Alley. Do you know it?'

'Sure. I'll see you then.' There was a short pause. 'And thank you, Rob, I appreciate it.'

'No problem — and lunch is on me by the way.' Robbie replaced the receiver and stared at the phone thoughtfully. He knew that tone of old. Stella was onto something. Why else would she need to meet up at such short notice? And why not ask this favour over the phone, when she knew that he would help her, whatever it was — well, so long as it was legal?

They were friends now, more than just ex-teammates, and always would be. They had both been to hell and back when she was so badly injured, but he was the one who had fallen apart, while Stella found the strength to fight the catastrophe that had befallen her. He heaved in a deep breath and told himself not to revisit those dark days. He was finally happy again. He had a lovely home, work he loved — he would do anything for Jackman and his team — and had a great girlfriend in Ella Jarvis, a top SOCO. He'd bounced back too, finally, but the scars still ached from time to time.

'That's a pensive look, mate.' Max Cohen was staring down at him. 'You okay?'

Robbie plastered a grin on his face and looked up at his colleague. 'I'm good, Max. I was miles away, just wool-gathering.'

'Not enough work to keep us occupied, is there?' He laughed. 'But after that last case, I ain't complaining, that's for sure.'

'Me neither, my cockney friend.' Robbie leaned back in his chair. 'So, how's the lovely Rosie and those beautiful kiddies of yours?'

Max's smile said it all. 'Amazing, that's what. She had doubts that she'd be able to manage the twins, but she's the best mum in the world. And Tim and Jessica are . . .' He waved his arms in the air, struggling for the right words.

'Naughty? Insomniac? In need of having an ASBO slapped on them?' suggested Robbie helpfully.

'I was thinking more along the lines of adorable, or maybe miraculous? But now you come to mention it . . .'

They both laughed.

'I wasn't sure if we'd done the right thing, you know, Rosie giving up the job she loved. . .' Max sighed. 'But it's working, mate, it's working.'

'Glad to hear it.'

'There are days when I know she misses it, but basically she's enjoying being a mum.'

Before they could say more, Marie walked in, a preoccupied expression on her face. 'Uh-oh, the sarge looks worried,' Max said. 'Not a good sign.'

'Hope nothing serious has happened to Orac,' Robbie wondered out loud.

Max returned to his workstation. 'Guess we'll know soon enough.'

Robbie looked at the clock. 10.30 a.m. Another two and a half hours before he was to meet Stella. If she'd turned to him rather than her husband, it had to be that she wanted help from a policeman, which meant trouble of some kind or another. He wandered off towards the corridor and the vending machine. It was going to be a long morning.

* * *

Marie closed the door behind her. Jackman saw her face and knew something was wrong. 'Okay, what's happened?'

'I have no idea, and that's what's so worrying.' Marie sat in the chair opposite him. 'The super hasn't heard from her, and Leon Barras, her second in command, is pretty stressed. Apparently, Orac asked him to be in around eight this morning to help her with some security sweep that they do every so often to check for hacking attempts or any other suspicious stuff. He said that she's really hot on what she calls housekeeping, and never misses a routine check. He's worried sick, Jackman.'

'Common sense says we are all over-reacting. Heavens, she's probably only late in. Three hours is nothing in the grand scheme of things, yet we are all running around like headless chickens.' He tried to sound convinced but did a bad job of it.

Marie looked at him reprovingly. 'You are talking about Orla Cracken. Respectfully, I think you know as well as I do that that's bollocks. Er, sorry, bollocks, *sir*.'

'I'm trying to keep some perspective, that's all.' He grinned at her. 'And I'm struggling.' He looked at her hopefully. 'Can't you tell me just a little bit about that woman? Why are you so secretive about her, Marie?'

'I'm not being deliberately secretive, honestly.' Marie returned his gaze. 'Orac spoke to me twice in confidence, and I wouldn't break a confidence, Jackman, not even for you.' She sucked on her bottom lip. 'Unless she was in trouble, and then it would be different.'

Jackman sighed. He felt excluded, but he also admired her loyalty. 'Okay, but you say Leon is fretting? Well, he's her number-one techie — he must have her private number in case of emergencies? She must talk to him, surely?'

'Oh yes, they talk, alright, like motherboard to mainframe! They don't even speak English, it's technobabble in the extreme! I've heard them, Jackman, and I understood sweet Fanny Adams! I don't think it would enter their heads to ask of each other, "What are you up to this evening?" or mention the weather or the election.'

'Different breed,' muttered Jackman.

'Different species, more like.' She gave an exasperated grunt. 'Are you up to asking Ruth Crooke to access her file and get her address? What if she's had an accident? After all, she is blind in one eye.'

Blind? Jackman had forgotten that Marie had once intimated that she believed Orac to have been blinded in one eye, and that those strange lenses weren't just some weird fashion statement. Jackman bit back the questions that automatically followed and instead said, 'Okay. Good point. No time like the present, I'll go see the super right now.'

He slowly mounted the stairs to Ruth Crooke's office, hoping that she wouldn't accuse him of being ridiculous. With every step he took, he felt less certain of his probable reception. She was not the easiest of women to get along with, even though he was aware that the tight-lipped, acerbic-tongued superintendent had something of a soft spot for both himself and Marie.

He knocked and went inside. He was surprised to see a tall, well-built, fair-haired young man seated across from her at her desk.

'Ah, Rowan, I rather thought I'd see you. I expect you are here for the same reason as Leon.'

He nodded to Leon and took a second chair. 'Well, I know it might seem alarmist, but—'

To his surprise, Ruth shook her head. 'Nonsense. This departure from Orac's normal behaviour is giving me serious cause for concern. The first thing we do is get you round to her home to check it out. Then, depending on your findings, we either heave a sigh of relief, or really start to worry.'

She handed him a sheet of paper, saying, rather cryptically, 'Her address. You should have no difficulty finding it.'

He stared at it: 11C, Heron Court, Trinity Street, Saltern-le-Fen. He looked at Ruth and raised his eyebrows. The police station was in Trinity Street, and Heron Court looked over their staff car park.

'That's right. She couldn't live any closer if she tried. So, it shouldn't take long for you to bring back some answers, should it?' She inclined her head towards the door.

That was the shortest conversation he'd ever had inside that office, and he couldn't help but wonder if she knew an awful lot more about what was going on than he did.

Back in the CID room, Marie looked at the address and shook her head. 'Well I'll be . . .'

He could see her surprise was genuine. So that was not one of the "confidences" that Orac had shared with her. 'Coming?'

'Try and stop me!' Snatching her jacket off the back of her chair, Marie followed him out.

They walked out of the main entrance, along the side of the car park, and into a narrow walkway that led to Heron Court. 'Two minutes from her place of work! How convenient is that?' Jackman looked up at the converted block of flats. It was an old building, quite an ornate piece of architecture, although he couldn't tell what its original use had been. It didn't look like it had been a domestic residence, more some old warehouse or small factory. He noted the rows of beautiful arch-topped windows and the elegant double front door. For a building he saw every day of his life, he knew precious little about it.

Jackman stopped at the front doors and gave them a tentative push. 'Security locked.' He ran his finger down the numbers and corresponding surnames. Number eleven was blank. As expected, Orac was far too private to have her name on the door. At the bottom of the keypad was a button marked "Manager." He pressed it.

'Can I help you?' said an echoey voice.

'Police. Can you let us in, please?'

There was a buzzing sound, and the voice said, 'Push the door and wait in the foyer, please.'

The Victorian foyer boasted a busy tiled floor and an unexpectedly beautiful sweeping staircase going up three floors.

A small, rotund man emerged from a downstairs room and stared at them suspiciously. He wore a name badge that declared him to be "Edward Beale, House Manager." 'Can I see your identification, please? Can't be too careful with the residents' privacy, you know.'

Jackman and Marie both offered their warrant cards. Beale examined them closely and then nodded. 'How can I help you?'

'Flat eleven C. We need to know that the occupant is safe and has not had an accident. I assume you have a pass key, should she not answer the door?' Jackman had the sudden urge to hurry this procedure up. He was getting a familiar feeling of unease, and he didn't like it.

'Well . . .' Beale looked uncomfortable. 'I'm not sure that I can do that, not without permission from my head office, because—'

'Stop right there.' Jackman glowered at him. 'We go and ring the doorbell, right? You come with us. If there is no answer, I'll ask you that question again, and if there is any delay, I'll have that door broken down, understand?'

Beale swallowed audibly. 'I'll go and get the emergency pass cards. It's the third floor. There is a lift.'

Jackman and Marie were already up the first flight of stairs by the time he'd finished speaking.

'Bad vibes, boss? You too?' Marie spoke as they ran.

'Oh yes.' *Very bad.*

On the third floor, they hurried down a high ceilinged, thickly carpeted corridor and finally located 11C. Jackman pressed the buzzer and held his finger on it, but as he had expected, there was no answer.

'Shit!' muttered Marie. 'Mr Beale? Key, please!'

Beale puffed his way along the hallway and produced a key card. He pushed it into the electronic lock, and they heard a faint click. The door opened inwards.

'Thank you, Mr Beale. Please wait outside now.'

Jackman's voice gave no room for argument, but still the little man expressed his displeasure. 'My company will take a very dim view of this, Inspector. Our residents' privacy is paramount.'

'And their safety supersedes that. Feel free to complain. You know where the police station is.' He pushed the door to, leaving Beale chuntering outside.

The flat was spotlessly clean and minimalist — spartan, to put it bluntly. Clean, empty surfaces. No photographs, no plants, no ornaments, the furniture steel and black, industrial. In the otherwise sterile room, a series of massive pictures were all the more arresting. From the sheer remote beauty and drama of the land and seascapes, Jackman suspected they depicted Ireland. All he could think of to say was, 'Wow!'

'Looks like some of that art you can have produced onto huge canvases from a photograph, doesn't it? It's pictures of where she grew up, wouldn't you say?' Marie looked around. 'But where is Orac?'

The flat was empty. There was no food in the fridge, but Jackman had an idea this was nothing new. Other than that, there was no disturbance, no damage. And no Orac.

The bed was neatly made, and when he and Marie looked in the wardrobes, they found empty hangers.

'I can't find a suitcase or any kind of rucksack anywhere. Most people own something like that, so it looks like she's gone away.' Marie sounded confused. 'But she was at work until really late last night, Leon confirmed that. He said she contacted him around nine thirty about getting in at eight, and she was still at work then, so did she go home, pack a case and bugger off? Does that sound like Orac to you?'

11

It didn't. 'Something happened, didn't it? Probably after she got home.'

Marie nodded slowly. 'I'd say so. I wonder.' She nodded to a single desktop computer with a printer and a few other add-ons on a desk in one corner of the bedroom. 'I wonder if something on that caused her sudden departure. A message, or a threat?'

Jackman grunted. 'Well, if there was anything, we'll never find it, will we? Orac has the most advanced IT knowledge I've ever come across. We'd never crack her personal computer, not in a month of Sundays.' He pulled a face. 'Something strikes me as odd, though. With Orac's insistence on hi-tech security and her apparent need for privacy . . . have you seen any CCTV cameras in this building?'

Marie shook her head. 'First thing I noticed as we came in.'

Jackman walked to the door. 'Mr Beale? Any CCTV coverage in the foyer?'

'We wanted to install one, but the residents were against it. And as we've never had the slightest bit of bother here . . .' He shrugged.

Jackman closed the door again. 'No CCTV.' He looked around. 'But I'm willing to bet she has something in this room, something covert that you and I are not seeing. If Ruth will allow, and if we don't hear something from Orac very soon, I'm going to suggest that Leon sweeps this flat.' He took a last look around. 'Come on, Marie. Let's allow Grumpy Beale to lock up again. Time to go and break the news to Ruth Crooke.'

CHAPTER TWO

Even though Robbie was five minutes early, Stella was already waiting.

He hugged her. 'It's great to see you again, Stella. You look fantastic. Married life must be suiting you.'

'More than I ever dreamed it would, Robbie.' She held him at arm's length and gazed at him searchingly. 'And look at you! You look happier than I can remember. It was a wise move coming to Saltern-le-Fen, wasn't it?'

'Best thing ever, and all thanks to you. If you hadn't contacted your friend Marie Evans and got me the interview, heaven knows where I'd be now.'

They linked arms and walked towards the pub.

The Cargo Hold was a small inn with a big reputation for its bar food, and today it was busy but not overcrowded. 'Grab that table over by the fireplace, Stella. I'll get the food in. Still like the seafood platter? Or something different?'

Stella smiled. 'You don't forget, do you? Seafood is perfect.'

As soon as they were settled, Stella said, 'I appreciate this, Rob, though I'm not sure what you can do.' Her smile had vanished. Suddenly she looked concerned.

He laid down his knife and fork. 'Tell me, and we'll see if I can help.'

'You remember my earlier passion — before I went into the police force that is?'

He grinned broadly. 'How could I forget?'

Stella North had been an adrenalin junkie, into rock climbing, bungee jumping, the more dangerous, the better. She still held the women's record for scaling Excalibur, the world's tallest freestanding climbing wall. But she was talking about her real obsession — urban exploration. She had spent years going out with a team of fellow enthusiasts, getting into abandoned buildings and photographing them. She was a brilliant photographer and using her own work and a whole library of similar photos that she had been left in a legacy, she was planning a book and possibly an exhibition. Now her injuries excluded her from the extreme sports and dangerous pursuits that she had loved, but she still had a strong interest in those abandoned places and the unearthly beauty of decay photography.

'The thing is, my Tom still keeps in contact with several young urbexers. He doesn't go out himself much any more, too busy with the farm and helping me catalogue my photographs, but we do meet up with Razor and Butterwitch sometimes.'

'I met them, didn't I? Ray Zachara and Emily someone or other. I can't remember her last name. Really nice bright university students. Well off, too, as I remember. And you all had those tags, didn't you?'

She nodded. 'Butterwitch is Emily Butters. And, yes, we did, mainly for the stuff we posted on the various websites, but also because it was part of the unwritten urbex code. Sometimes anonymity helped if we got caught or stopped, not that that happened very often. I was Starburst,' she said wistfully.

Robbie remembered. The name had amused him because that was the expression the police used when a gang of joyriders jumped out of their stolen vehicle and ran off in different directions.

'Ray rang Tom four nights ago. He sounded really upset. He and Emily had been due to go on a trip with three other urbexers. They intended to infiltrate some old disused airfield buildings, but Emily was unwell, and then Ray's father pulled some posh function out of the bag and insisted that he attend. So, the other three went without them.' She gazed intently at Robbie and lowered her voice. 'Three kids went into that building, but only two came out.'

Robbie stiffened. 'How do you mean?'

'Exactly what I said. One young man, I don't know his name, just his tag, which is Rainman, went in with the other two. They split up at one point because he wanted to take some photos of a particular part of an old hangar, and the others continued on through the buildings. When he didn't rejoin them, they went back, but he'd disappeared. They found his camera and the rest of his equipment on the floor. They searched the whole place, but there was no sign of him. Neither was there was any sign of a struggle. He just disappeared.'

'Where was this?' asked Robbie.

'A place called Randleby. It's off the beaten track, further up the county. It's not one of the listed Second World War RAF stations — it's one I've never heard of.'

Stella ate in silence for a while. Robbie thought over what she'd said. Randleby meant nothing to him either and he wondered whose patch it was on. Probably well out of theirs, but he could certainly make some enquiries. 'I'm assuming they reported it?' he asked.

'Not until the following day.' Stella wiped her lips with her napkin. 'They were scared of what might happen to them. They aren't experienced explorers, Robbie, not like Tom and I were. My clan were shit hot on safety, and we knew and respected all the rules. We also knew exactly what we could and couldn't get away with. So do Ray and Emily, and those kids should never have gone out without the more experienced guys.'

'When was this?'

'It happened on Tuesday night. They reported it Wednesday when they realised he hadn't gone home. He flat shares with another guy, and the flatmate just thought he was doing an all-nighter, so didn't worry about him . . . until he got a call from his anxious friends.'

'Well, I can give a few people a ring, Stella, as soon as I find out where this airfield is located.' Robbie looked dubious. 'But I'm not sure they'll tell me too much.'

'That isn't all, Robbie.' Stella laid her knife and fork across her empty plate. 'This is the second disappearance of an urban explorer this month.'

'Really? You mean locally?'

'Well, within a twenty-mile radius. The first time it was an old cinema in Greenborough that was infiltrated, and it was seasoned urbexers — two women and two guys. I knew one of the women from way back. She was no rookie, she knew the ropes. Once again, all his stuff was still there — camera, torches, rucksack, food, everything. It was as if he'd simply vanished into thin air. One minute he was with them, the next he was gone.'

'And no one has heard from him since?'

Stella shook her head. 'Not a word, but because he's not classed as vulnerable, and he's an adult, the police aren't interested. He has been registered as missing, and his friends and relatives have been referred to the Missing Persons Bureau and to Missing People.' She leaned towards him across the table. 'I think these disappearances are connected, Robbie.'

It did seem odd. 'Can you get me their full names, Stel?'

'The first one, the cinema incident, his name is Anthony Hood, aka Cruiser. He lives in one of the Saltern villages, but I can get his address easily enough. As to the other lad, I've already asked Tom to contact Ray and Emily to get his details for me.' She pulled a wry face. 'Tom's worried I'll start sleuthing again, but I promised him I won't,' she smiled at him hopefully, 'because I have a friend who is much better placed than I am to do that for me.' She paused. 'Haven't I?'

He returned her smile. 'Of course you have. Can't promise I'll be able to get you answers, but I'll do what I can.'

'Bless you, Robbie.'

They chatted on for another twenty minutes or so, until Robbie said he needed to get back to the station.

'And I have to get home. My lovely Tom still frets when I go out without him.' She glanced rather shyly at Robbie.

'And he has even more cause to now. It's not the aftermath of my head injury this time — we're expecting a baby.'

Robbie beamed at her. 'Oh wow! That's fantastic! I can see why Tom is anxious!' He gave her another hug. 'I couldn't be more pleased for you both.'

After all they had been through, it really was the best news. It felt as if a line had been drawn underneath all the bad stuff, and that Stella was finally living a new, happier life.

Robbie strolled back to the station, his mind a mix of pleasure that his old friend was in such a good place at last, and a niggling worry about the two missing urban explorers. He had a feeling she was right, and that the disappearances were connected. He just hoped that it wasn't the beginning of something more sinister.

* * *

The IT department felt huge and empty without Orac sitting silently in front of her bank of computer screens.

Leon hurried up to greet Marie and Jackman. 'The super says you've asked for a sweep on Orac's home, sir?'

Jackman nodded. 'That's why we're here. You'll need someone with you, and Marie has volunteered.'

She had. At once. With every moment that passed, she was more and more concerned about where Orac had gone. She wanted to make sure she was up to speed on every single piece of information that came in regarding the IT boss's mysterious disappearance.

'I suggest I take Philip with us, he's ace with surveillance stuff, and I'll leave David here holding the fort,' said Leon.

Orac's team of three had been carefully chosen for their particular talents, but what a motley crew they were. Leon Barras, her second in command, was Anglo-French — a man with a brain the size of Wales. David Serlin was Jewish, a small, stocky man with unruly black hair and thick horn-rimmed glasses who seemed to understand complex computer systems with the same ease that Marie brought to the rules of Snap. Philip Adisa, their surveillance and security expert, was an African American with a love of brightly coloured silk ties. Today, Marie noted, he was wearing a vivid purple creation covered with flame-orange hot-air balloons.

Jackman nodded to Leon. 'Go as soon as you're free.' He turned to Marie. 'As soon as you have anything, report back, okay?'

'Of course, boss.'

As Jackman made for the door, Leon and Philip were already organising what they needed. 'Two minutes, Sergeant, and we'll be ready.'

Marie wandered around the big room. Although there were other techies still working, the whole place seemed unusually hushed and subdued. Their boss's absence had affected them all. Probably most of them simply saw her as an elite computer expert who lived for her work, but Marie knew there was much more to Orla Cracken. For a start, she was buried in the bowels of the police station not from choice but because she was exiled here. It was a safe place, where she could work unthreatened. Marie exhaled. Well, it *had* been.

'Ready, Sergeant,' Leon called over. 'Where are we heading?'

She smiled wryly. 'You'll be surprised. And no need for those car keys.'

Marie saw from the expressions on their faces when they arrived outside Heron Court, that they too had been completely unaware that Orac lived practically in the police station's back yard.

Leon shook his head. 'We had no idea! She's always in before us and still there when we leave, and as you know, she gives nothing away about herself.' He looked around. 'Are there garages for this place? Only now I'm wondering if she owns a car.'

Marie had already asked. 'No, each flat has a numbered parking spot along the far side of the building. The manager said she does have a vehicle, although she rarely uses it. It's not in its space. It's a Kia, but he didn't know the model. Right. Let's go get this done, shall we?' She rang the manager's bell and had him take them up to flat 11C.

While Leon and Philip worked, Marie took a slow walk around, searching for anything that might help her understand why Orac would have gone off without a word to anyone. The first thing she checked was a wall calendar. There were a couple of entries on it, reminders to carry out computer checks of one kind or another. She scanned back over the previous months and apart from one name — Theo — that cropped up a couple of times, it appeared that Orac had no private life at all. When she saw a small business card attached to the side of the calendar her hopes rose, only to find the name, Theodore Marks, Dental Surgeon, emblazoned across it. Theo, the dentist. Great! And from the address, his surgery was only a few streets away, hardly a clue as to her whereabouts.

'Sarge?' Philip called over to her. 'We've found a spy camera, very cleverly hidden but I'd expect no less of Orac. It covers most of the flat but particularly the door area. I'm assuming we aren't touching it, are we?'

'Well, originally, we just needed to know whether one exists, and if so, could you access the data from it if the need arose, but maybe we should try?' Marie had visions of trying to explain to an irate Orac why her personal cameras had been tampered with.

The two men looked at each other.

Leon raised an eyebrow. 'We'll give it a try, but chances of accessing the footage are slim — after all, we are talking about the best pro in the world here. It's a clever device with unlimited recording time, as she's connected it to the mains electricity. Plus, it's got a PIR motion sensor chip, which gives extended time anyway.'

'PIR?' Marie asked.

'Sorry, passive infrared sensor. It detects motion, and only turns the camera on when it senses movement,' Philip said.

'And it's not using a memory card to store the footage either and we have no idea where she's specified it to record to.' Leon frowned. 'I'm thinking she has a laptop with her, and the device is sending footage to a remote server which she can access.'

Marie hoped that she didn't look too confused, even though she was. 'Upshot is, she can access activity here, as in the three of us stomping round her pristine home, but we can't use it to find out what happened here last night?'

'Got it in one, Sarge.'

'Okay. Not what I wanted to hear, so back to the drawing board. Time to go, lads.'

'Although,' added Philip slowly, 'if, as you say, it became critical, maybe I could intercept transmissions from the camera. It's actually possible to "hijack" the security sensor, install spyware and remotely watch the occupant of a home through their own camera.'

Leon joined in enthusiastically. 'Yes, it's quite possible to use a compromised device to attack other devices on the netwo—'

'Stop! Guys! Not only have you lost me, just remember what you said a few moments ago. We are dealing with Orac. I bet you a tenner you'll get nowhere. And even if you did manage to intercept the transmissions, that's shutting the stable door after the horse has well and truly bolted. It's last night I'm interested in, not what happens in here after we've locked the door and gone.'

'Good point.' Leon sighed dejectedly. 'Better get back then.'

After making sure everything was as they had found it, and the door securely locked, they left the building. A few steps down the road, Marie stopped. 'Philip? Our own CCTV cameras, the ones that cover the exterior of the police station, do any of them cover the back of the car park? Specifically, the wall that separates the car park from this walkway, and Heron Court?'

He answered immediately. 'Yes, they do.' He paused. 'Of course! As soon as we get back, we'll check the footage. Do we have a time frame?'

'She rang me from IT at around 9.30 p.m.,' said Leon, 'so any time after that, I suppose.'

'Do you think there's a chance that camera will actually cover Heron Court, Philip?' asked Marie.

'I'm pretty sure it covers the whole of that wall, and Heron Court is immediately behind it, and there are lights up the whole staircase. With windows like that,' Philip pointed back to the old building, 'we might get lucky.'

Marie quickened her step. If Philip was right, they could discover if Orac had left her home alone, or with company.

* * *

Ten minutes later, Philip was at his desk and accessing the CCTV footage of the rear car park for the night before. He had been correct in assuming that Heron Court would be seen behind the wall of the nick. It was quite clear, and as it was a three-storey building, it practically towered over their parked vehicles. The whole staircase had beautiful big arch-topped windows on every floor, and as Philip had noted, all the floors were lit up.

They watched in silence as the minutes ticked away. A few people came and went, but it was well after midnight, according to the digital display, and there had been no sight-ing of Orac. Then Marie had a rather depressing thought. 'She took the lift, didn't she? The windows only show the staircase and people using the stairs.'

After a few muttered curses from Leon, Philip said, 'Don't be too sure. I think,' he stared closer, 'if we zoom in on a particular shot on Orac's floor, you can just make out the end of the corridor where the lift shaft is situated. It means a lot more work, like going frame by frame and mag-nifying it every time, but I'm game.' He looked up at Marie. 'Give me a while. I'll ring you if I find anything.'

'Good man, and if you can find a sighting of Orac, I'll treat you to a new tie for your collection.'

His eyes lit up. 'Deal! I have over fifty, but there's always room for originality.'

'Oh, it'll be original, never fear. Now, go to it.'

Marie took the lift back up to the CID room, sought out Jackman and told him what they'd found. 'I'm afraid all we can do now is wait on the techies, boss.' She looked around the busy room, and whispered, 'Can I have a word in private?'

In silence, he led the way to his office and held the door open for her.

Once inside, she said, 'You are probably thinking that all this fuss is ridiculous, that it's total overkill to worry about someone who hasn't turned up for work, even someone with a record for punctuality like Orac's, but there are things you don't know. There are a lot of things I don't know either, but I'm starting to think it's time to go back to the super. She must already know the details of Orac's past. To have the kind of high-level clearance that Orac has, she must have been vetted minutely.'

'Absolutely. The powers that be would never let her occupy her position if she wasn't squeaky clean and completely trustworthy.' Jackman pointed to a chair. 'Okay, Marie. Sit down and tell me what you know. Please?'

Hoping Orac would forgive her, Marie began. 'She's here because she's too valuable to lose.' She thought carefully about what part of it was fact and what her own imagination might have added. 'She worked for the government, Jackman. She was brought in from the field after an attempt on her life left her partially blinded. I believe she was part of a covert team that infiltrated dangerous situations that were a threat to national security. Orac was their "official" hacker.'

Jackman let out a long breath. 'Oh my! Now I understand why we have such a genius in a humble cop shop basement.'

'And why Ruth is as worried as she obviously is,' Marie added. 'She knows far more than I do, I'm sure. I'm fearful for Orac's life, Jackman.'

Jackman stood up abruptly. 'Then you're right, Marie. We should go back to Ruth Crooke.'

CHAPTER THREE

'Sorry, mate, but we reckon he just did a runner,' DS Holiday said.

Robbie waited impatiently. There must be more info than that, surely, although he suspected Holiday, from the neighbouring division, had made his mind up about the missing urban explorer. 'Why do you think that, sir?' asked Robbie. 'I understood that he just left everything, including his camera.'

'Spooked, wasn't he? Stands to reason. Randleby's a creepy spot at the best of times. Loads of ghost stories about dead airmen and that kind of crap. He got frightened and legged it. Big old deserted building like that, found himself alone, heard something, probably just shit himself and took off.'

'But where did he go? He never went back to his flat.'

'No, we talked to the flatmate. Then we had a word with his family, and they've admitted that this isn't the first time he's scarpered.' DS Holiday grunted. 'Broken home. Doesn't get on with his dad's new bit of stuff. Chip on his shoulder because his mum didn't take him when she left, and so on. That's why he's flat-sharing some little bug-hutch with his mate.'

Getting nowhere fast, Robbie nonetheless doggedly pressed on. 'I would have thought he might have contacted his friends, don't you think?'

'Nah. Too embarrassed. Scaredy-cat ran away, didn't he? Chickened out like a baby. No, DC Melton, he's keeping his head down somewhere. He'll turn up before long with his tail between his legs. You'll see.'

Through clenched teeth, Robbie thanked the detective for his time, replaced the receiver and stared at it. That man knew nothing about urban exploration, or the people who were drawn like magnets to abandoned places. He kept seeing a camera, lying discarded on a dusty, grimy floor. That would never happen. Without Stella, he would probably never have known about those explorers either, but he had to admit, it was a fascinating, albeit dangerous activity. These people thirsted to know what lay behind the walls of abandoned buildings. They wanted to research, document and photograph them. They made sure to do no damage, found ways in that didn't involve even breaking locks. They didn't do tags or graffiti and left the places they had infiltrated exactly as they found them. As Stella had said, they abided by the adage, "take only pictures, leave only footprints." And what was the most valuable thing an urbexer carried, besides a phone and an EpiPen? A camera.

'Oh dear! Deep in thought again, sunshine?' Max grinned at him. 'You could be starting to worry me.'

'Ever heard of urban explorers, Max?'

'Yeah,' Max said. 'I had some mates back in the East End who had a thing about getting underground. You know, into all those old tube stations that've been closed down, and tunnels, and sewers and even rivers. Not my bag, you get too dirty, but they were well into it. Why?'

'Right, well, what do you think of this little story?' Robbie recounted what Stella had told him, and then the response he'd had from DS Holiday.

'I'd think one of two things, mate. Your DS is too lazy to get off his arse and do some proper detective work, or,' he sniffed, flopping down into a chair next to Robbie, 'don't you think he was a bit too eager to make you believe the kid had cleared off and was lying low somewhere?'

Robbie hadn't considered this before, but now that he thought about it, Max might be right. 'Yeah. He was pretty quick to dismiss my enquiry. Had an answer for everything, too.' The more he thought about it, the more he distrusted the other detective's opinion. 'Come to think of it, he didn't show the slightest interest in my concerns, neither did he ask why I was enquiring.'

'Then ten-to-one, he doesn't want you sticking your beak in, chum.' Max tapped the side of his nose. 'And that, my dear Watson, tells us something is amiss.'

'Doesn't it just.' Robbie scratched his chin. 'Stella texted me the details about the kid from the airfield, name of Aaron Smith, tag Rainman, but I'm still waiting for her to get me more details about Anthony Hood, aka Cruiser, who disappeared from a disused cinema in Greenborough. I can't see CID in Greenborough being so dismissive, can you? They've always been really helpful.'

'I've seen the name Anthony Hood come up in the last few weeks, so they've obviously put out an *attention drawn* to him as a misper.' Max leaned forward. 'If I was you, I'd talk to DC Cat Cullen. Not much goes on in Greenborough that she doesn't know about, and she's a really cool detective.' His eyes sparkled.

'Careful, Max, I'll tell Rosie!'

Max laughed. 'Funnily enough, before I got together with my girl, I thought Cat was the best thing ever. Smart, trendy and sharp as a tack, and no one could better her undercover work. Her boss calls her a chameleon.'

Robbie considered the name. 'Didn't she get badly injured when that young copper got killed in a hit-and-run?'

'That's her. But she's as good as ever, or so I'm told.'

'Respect,' murmured Robbie. 'I'll certainly contact her when I've heard from Stella. Fingers crossed she doesn't clam up on me too.'

'Can't see it, unless there's some national conspiracy going on.' Max grinned. 'Joking. Can't see a couple of urbexers causing a major security cover-up, can you?'

'Not exactly. They're pretty harmless, just curious.' He turned to his computer. 'Look at these, Max. They're photographs taken by Stella, back in her UE days. Awesome, aren't they?' He scrolled through a series of dramatic pictures of abandoned buildings — old houses, chapels, factories, sanatoriums, chateaux and graveyards. The light was extraordinary, as was the way she captured nature slowly taking back what man had abandoned. Max scrolled from picture to picture, gasping in awe.

'My God! That's the town at the centre of the Chernobyl disaster, isn't it? Your friend went to Ukraine?'

'Pripyat. Yes, into the exclusion zone. Stella travelled all over, as you can see from some of these photos. She tells me that the book she is preparing has some photos of a chateau in Belgium that was always considered an urbex myth, a previously undiscovered place that she said was her most exciting find ever.'

'Does she still explore?' Max asked.

Robbie was suddenly overcome with sadness. 'When Stella was shot, she sustained a brain injury — apart from all her other injuries. She's made a remarkable recovery, but she has moments of weakness. It would have been foolish to continue with such a dangerous pastime. It will always be her one true passion, though, and that's why she's sharing her photographs, along with those of another explorer who passed away. She hopes one day to put them in a gallery.'

'She's certainly got one hell of a talent,' Max said.

'She was just as good as a copper, my friend. She would have gone right to the top. She was a detective sergeant before she was thirty, then . . .' His words trailed away. He felt a hand on his shoulder.

'It sucks, doesn't it, mate?'

'It sucks.' A slight tremor in Robbie's voice betrayed what he felt. 'Anyway . . .' His mobile buzzed. 'A text from

Stella. Ah. I've got the info I need, now I'll see if I can get hold of your Cat Cullen. I wonder how she's going to react to my questions.'

* * *

Ruth Crooke sat behind her desk, her back ramrod-straight. 'Once again, I've been expecting you,' she said quietly. 'Sit down, both of you.'

Jackman wasn't used to this rather subdued version of their caustic superintendent, and he couldn't help taking a swift glance in Marie's direction to see if she was feeling the same. Her expression told him all he needed to know.

'First — and this has nothing to do with Orac — I have some news that I wanted you to hear.' Her eyes were slits, narrowed even more than usual. 'I have just received a message from the court. Alistair Ashcroft has been given a life sentence, without parole, and has been taken to HMP Belmarsh.'

Jackman let out a long low whistle. Marie gave a sharp intake of breath.

'The jury deemed your nemesis to be sane, so a secure psychiatric hospital unit will not be having the pleasure of his company. He is going to jail, along with the other monsters who place so little value on human life.' Ruth's face broke into a sad smile. 'Finally, it really is over for you both.'

Jackman could have cried. Even though they were recovering from the reign of terror that they had so narrowly survived, they had still felt on edge while they waited to hear the fate of the man who had threatened to destroy all their lives. Now they knew, and it really was over.

Without thinking, he reached for Marie's hand and gave it a squeeze.

'So there is a God!' she breathed and returned the pressure.

'And He's on our side,' he replied softly.

'I never doubted that,' added Ruth. 'But I wasn't so sure about whether the jury would see beyond his defence's

27

award-winning performance and listen to his emotional pleas for leniency due to the psychological damage he received as a child. Luckily, they did.'

After a few minutes spent discussing the trial, Ruth brought them back to the present — and Orac.

'We think you should bring us in from the cold now, Ruth. We know a little, and in order to move on, we have to have some facts, and we have to know just how serious Orac's disappearance is.'

Ruth steepled her fingers and gazed steadily from Marie to Jackman. 'I don't know as much as you obviously think I do. However, I am prepared to tell you all I do know. Moreover,' she intensified her gaze, 'I will be insisting that those who *are* in the know communicate with me as soon as possible.'

Thoughts of what would follow the news about Ashcroft still swum around in Jackman's head. The knowledge that Ashcroft would be incarcerated until the day he died was almost too much to get his head around. It wasn't easy to concentrate on what Ruth was saying.

'You're thinking about Ashcroft, aren't you?' Ruth's voice harpooned into his thoughts.

'Sorry. It's just . . .'

'Don't apologise, Rowan. I'd like to put everything else on hold for a while, and let you assimilate what I've just told you, but sadly, I can't.' Ruth was being oddly sympathetic.

He straightened up. 'No, I'm fine.' He looked across at Marie. '*We* are fine.'

Marie nodded. 'Ashcroft is history. Orac is our main concern now. So, what can you tell us, Super?'

Ruth pursed her thin lips. 'Well, one day I was called to headquarters. When I got there, I found the room crowded with more brass than in a foundry. I was told — *told*, mind you, not asked — that I would be taking on a new chief of IT. The lab was going to be extended and new, updated technology installed. I started to call attention to my budget forecast for the year and was informed that this was a separate initiative, having nothing to do with the station finances.' She pulled a face. 'I smelt a rat immediately. They don't give you something for nothing these days. Hell, I have to fight for printer ink, let alone a new state-of-the-art IT department!'

Jackman and Marie glanced at each other and smiled.

'Anyway, it appeared that I had no say in any of it. Clearly, I was the last to know about this brave new initiative because I was soon being introduced to this strange woman with a tragic haircut and eyes like polished ball bearings!'

Marie stifled a laugh at Ruth's description.

'Oddly, I took to her straightaway. She was a woman with nothing to prove. Her professional abilities were above and beyond, and she seemed more than grateful to be allowed the run of our basement. Anyway, most of the gold braid melted away and I was left with the ACC and Orac, in a small locked office. I was told that the room was secure and used only for high-level, top-secret meetings. I can tell you I was bursting with questions, but I managed to keep my mouth shut. This was very far from the normal routine for introducing new personnel, and I heard warning bells ringing all over the place.' She exhaled loudly. 'The ACC began by saying that there were certain sensitive issues surrounding Ms Cracken's posting to Saltern-le-Fen. He handed me a dossier — for my eyes only.'

She unlocked a drawer and removed a large Manila envelope. 'Take it to your office, Rowan. Read it through carefully, both of you, in private, and then return it immediately to me. Understood? And this file never left this room. In fact, you never even saw it.'

'What dossier?' muttered Jackman, taking it from her and laying it flat on the desk in front of him.

'Exactly. This will explain it all much more clearly than if I tried to relay what I was told. Although I believe that this is a very diluted version of the original and was adapted for me at my particular level of clearance.' She paused. 'In accordance with what is outlined here,' she pointed at the file, 'I have notified the ACC that there has been a deviation from

Orla Cracken's usual routine, and I am awaiting instructions. This was one of the stipulations — the slightest departure from the norm must be reported. I even have a dedicated pathway of emergency contacts should a crisis occur.'

'All very cloak and dagger, isn't it?' Marie said. 'It sounds like a James Bond script. Maybe Orac is really Q? You know, inventing ways to turn a traffic car into a gyrocopter at the flick of a switch.'

The thin lips flickered momentarily. 'If it wasn't so damned serious, I'd agree with you. At the time of that meeting I thought the same. It was too bizarre to be true. But it is no film, and as soon as you've digested what's in the file, we'll talk again.' She stood up. 'Right now, I have a conference room full of very boring people who want some motivational words from yours truly on ways to maximise the efficient use of resources, God help me!'

'You know you love it.' Jackman grinned at her and picked up the envelope. 'Go knock 'em dead, Ruth.'

'Believe me, I'd love to!'

* * *

Back in Jackman's office, with the door firmly shut, and the whole CID room warned on no account to disturb them, he and Marie fortified themselves with coffee and chocolate bars, and began.

'Ready?' he asked, undoing the envelope.

'Can't wait,' she replied wryly, unwrapping her chocolate.

'I'll read each page and hand it over, okay?'

It took them around twenty minutes to go through the file. Some of it he had to read twice in order to fully understand the doublespeak obfuscating the salient facts. Considering that, until Marie had revealed to him the few snippets of information that she was aware of, he had known nothing at all about their IT boss, the stuff was riveting.

When they had both finished, they sat back and took a moment to digest what they had read.

Marie broke the silence. 'So, after dispensing with all the jargon and official speak, we find that Orac was an espionage agent for the British government. She actually infiltrated and set up monitoring devices for intelligence gathering.'

'And possibly employed other more illegal and aggressive methods of obtaining secret information. She was a highly trained field agent with unrivalled computer skills,' Jackman added thoughtfully. 'A valuable commodity indeed.'

'Until something went terribly wrong, and she almost lost her life.' Marie bit her lip.

'Now they've hidden her away here in the misty fens,' Jackman said quietly. 'And where better? In the back of beyond, the last place you'd think to find a retired spy.'

'But has she retired, Jackman?' Marie asked pointedly. 'All that state-of-the-art equipment they gave her. Do you think it's really for tracking the licence plates of nicked cars, or homing in on some scrote's mobile phone? I very much doubt it!'

'Valid point. Oh dear, and here I was believing what they said about making Saltern a central technology hub for the whole area, hence the new hardware, even though Greenborough already has one.'

'Well, I'm only surmising, but it makes sense, doesn't it?' Marie screwed up the foil from her chocolate bar and lobbed it into the bin.

'Perfect sense.' The police were not famous for spending their dwindling resources recklessly. 'And if Ruth has been given an emergency pathway to follow should a crisis occur, well, that's a bit extreme for a glitch in a police IT boss's daily routine, isn't it?'

'All adds up.' Marie stared at the file. 'Thinking about it, this tells me little more than I already knew. It just confirms it, makes it real, instead of being a kind of whispered rumour.'

Jackman said, 'And I think Ruth was correct — this is just a brief outline. The most important stuff has been omitted. I'd like to see the official documentation on Orla Cracken.'

'That will never happen,' said Marie grimly, 'if she's the hot property I think she is.' She looked down at her phone. 'Message. Mind if I check it?'

He nodded.

'It's Philip. He says he's pinpointed the time Orac left Heron Court.'

'Does he say if she was alone?' he asked urgently.

'I think we'd better head downstairs, boss. He's not sure, says he'll show us.'

As they hurried through the CID room, Kevin Stoner stood up. 'Sarge, I've traced the licence number and make of Orac's car. Would you like me to start checking the traffic cameras to see if we can find it?'

'No, Kevin,' Marie said. 'That's good work, but I'll give it to IT. They can track it quicker than us. Thank you.' She took the memo from him and caught up with Jackman. 'If Philip is half as good as Orac at accessing cameras, he should get some more answers very quickly.'

In the IT lab the sense that something was wrong persisted. Seeing Orac's station empty, the computers silent and the monitors as blank as her eyes, caused Jackman a jolt. The absence of that startling hairstyle and the lenses that gave nothing away caused him to feel acutely apprehensive. He'd have given anything to feel uncomfortable again, as he always did when he got close to Orac, and that vacant chair made him anxious that he might never see her again.

Did Marie have similar thoughts? It seemed so, or maybe she'd just spent so much time with him that she could read his mind. Whichever it was, she touched his arm lightly and said, 'We'll find her, boss.'

'I hope you're right.'

Philip and Leon appeared. 'Come and look at this, Detectives.'

Philip led the way to his workstation and pointed to one of the several screens. 'Watch this.'

Jackman and Marie stared as he moved, frame by frame, through a sequence of film timed at 2.33 a.m. It was much enlarged and blurry, and the camera only caught a small percentage of the area occupied by the lift doors, but they could make out part of a figure that was undoubtedly Orac. They looked closer. Was that a movement at the lift doors behind her?

'I can't make my mind up about that,' said Philip. 'And if there is someone there, he or she had to already be in the lift when she got in.'

Marie squinted at the screen. 'Could just be shadow caused by the lights inside the lift . . . although,' she looked at Philip, 'you could be right. Someone came up from the ground floor to collect her, or meet her, or . . .' She left the rest unsaid.

'So, next step, Philip, as we now have a licence number and model for her car, is to try and spot her on the road and get the time and the direction she was heading in,' Jackman said.

'And if she's alone, or with someone,' added Marie.

Philip took the piece of paper from Marie. 'You got it, guys. I'm on it. If I find her, I'll text you again.'

'Correction. *When* you find her, Philip. We are relying on you.'

The young man nodded. He understood.

CHAPTER FOUR

As darkness fell, a tall, lithe young woman began her well-practised ritual. Everything she needed was laid out on the bed. All exactly as usual. That way she could see if anything was missing. It didn't do to be sloppy when your life was at stake.

When everything had been checked and double-checked, she began to place the items in her rucksack or in the deep pockets of her cargo pants or her gilet. Her clothes were black, as were her light boots. She examined herself in the full-length mirror on the front of her wardrobe. Her clothes were a kind of uniform, and it felt comfortable. She pulled her long dark hair back into a ponytail and secured it tightly. She looked at her watch. Almost time to go.

Cally Prothero was a seasoned urban explorer, one of the few women who preferred to go out alone. Though she occasionally linked up with a small clan of local explorers, all experienced lads who were great to share a bimble with, she was happiest flying solo. There were times when she didn't want to share the strange beauty of the decaying and abandoned buildings that she found.

Her boyfriend, Joel — ex-boyfriend as of a month ago — had never got it, none of it. This had eaten into their relationship until one day Cally finally had enough of being lectured to on her "totally irresponsible" hobby. *Hobby?* It wasn't watercolour painting. After two years together they went their separate ways, and she was now happier than ever. She missed the sex, which had been good, but very little else.

Like most urbexers, she had a contact in case of accident or emergency. Cally's was an old friend from work who had volunteered to be on call in a crisis. She'd never had to use his services, but she could rest assured that whenever she notified him that she was going out, and told him her destination, there would be a car ready if it was needed. Henry Arnott was a bachelor who looked after his elderly father and was almost always available to be her back-up. She'd rung him earlier, giving him her rough itinerary for the evening and promising to text him when she got back so that he could stand down. As always, he told her to stay safe and enjoy herself, and to ring if she needed him. She finished the call, musing about Joel. That was all she'd ever asked of him, just a few words to tell her he was there for her, but it had never happened.

Dismissing Joel with a shrug, she gathered up her bag, her precious camera and her car keys. Tonight, she was revisiting a derelict hotel, half devastated by a fire. It was only a half-hour drive away, but miles off the beaten track. She had first infiltrated it in daylight and known immediately that she had to go back at night for some dramatic shots. They could be among her best, if there was moonlight.

She stepped out of her flat and looked to the sky. Perfect! A clear, gleaming moon was rising. It was going to be a good evening.

* * *

DC Cat Cullen was no DS Holiday. As soon as Robbie spoke to her, she said she was happy to help.

'It's a kind of personal thing really, DC Cullen. A great friend of mine has an interest in urban exploration and having two people go missing within a month is worrying, to say the least.'

'Skip the formal bit, Robbie, it's Cat. I see your point. What can I tell you that you don't know already?'

'I'm not sure. All I really know is that a guy called Anthony Hood, tag name Cruiser, went missing while exploring an old cinema in Greenborough. All his things were left behind. He comes from Fleet Seas End village, I understand. Other than that, I know nothing.'

'Well, for a start, he's an adult, aged thirty, in good health and we've never had any trouble from him. So, you can see where this is going, can't you, Robbie?'

He could. If they started an investigation for every person who went missing, there would be no time left for catching criminals. People walked out of their homes, and sometimes their lives, every day of the week. Broken relationships, abuse, stress . . . people had a hundred valid reasons to pack up and move on. But not Anthony Hood, Robbie was certain.

'However,' continued Cat, 'we've registered him as missing and put out an attention drawn, and I think you're right, Robbie, there's something fishy about his sudden departure from that cinema.'

Robbie brightened. This was good news. 'The explorer community have said that he's very responsible, someone who'd never leave his friends like that. It's simply not done. They look out for one another — it can be pretty dangerous in these decrepit old buildings.'

'Yeah, I spoke to one of his friends, a woman called Lisa. She said they'd been infiltrating these places together for nigh on five years.' Cat lowered her voice. 'You know when someone is truly concerned, don't you, Rob? Well, Lisa was practically a basket case. She's worried sick.'

'Do you know much about the other young man who disappeared?' asked Robbie.

'Very little. I know he's just a kid, and his name is Aaron Smith. I talked to some tosser who didn't give a monkey's about the boy. More or less told me he was a lost cause and to forget it.'

'Ah. I had the same reaction. Nice bloke, wasn't he?' Robbie said.

'Refer back to my earlier description of him. Got right up my nose!'

Robbie warmed to this plain-spoken detective, who clearly had no time for men like Holiday.

'Listen, Rob, if I get anything, I'll pass it on, and maybe you'd do the same if you hear anything from the UE community? You seem to have a foot in the door, and they aren't really comfortable coming into the police station.' She laughed. 'I think they'd be keener if it had been empty for twenty years and falling to bits.'

'The way the force is going, they might get their wish! But, yes, of course I'll pass anything I get your way. And thanks, Cat. Much appreciated.'

He put the phone down. That was how neighbouring divisions should relate to each other. Friend Holiday should take a leaf out of Cat's book.

'How did it go?' called Max from his workstation.

'Liked her. No flannel, offered to help all she could.' Robbie stuck up a thumb. 'Nice one for suggesting her, mate.'

Max returned the sign and grinned. 'Told you.' He stretched and stood up. 'Now, I'm off to see my lovely wife and kids. Oh, Rob, you have no idea how good that sounds! Who'd have thought it? Me, a dad!'

Robbie laughed. 'Suits you! I've never seen you look so happy. Night, mate, and love to Rosie.' He returned to the report he was finishing off, glancing at the clock. It was time he signed off, too, but once this was done, he would be more or less free. Maybe he'd give it another half-hour. He wondered if the boss would allow him to make a few discreet enquiries, even though neither of the disappearances was on their patch. Frankly, he doubted it. It wasn't done. You helped fellow officers out, but you didn't take on investigations of your own. Mind you, Cat Cullen of Greenborough had more or less asked for assistance, hadn't she? He'd play it by ear, get in early, and hope to catch the boss in a good mood.

* * *

Before Jackman and Marie could leave for the night, Ruth Crooke insisted they meet with her to discuss the file on Orac.

Without a word, Jackman laid it on the desk in front of the superintendent, and equally as silently, she put it in a drawer and locked it, removing the key.

'The IT unit have pinpointed the time that Orac left her flat, Super. Now they are trying to track her car,' Jackman told her. 'Philip said he would stay on until he found a sighting.'

'Her department knows nothing about her background — except Leon, who was merely made aware that she was special in some way.' Ruth shrugged. 'He's totally trustworthy, with the highest level of clearance, but it was decided to keep all information about Orac under wraps and released only on a need-to-know basis.' She sat back. 'So, now you know as much as I do, although I have just received one more piece of information. Apparently, a threat was made a short while ago. It was thought to have been eradicated, but now the powers that be are wondering if that is the case.'

'What kind of threat, Super?' asked Marie.

'A death threat. Not to Orac directly, but the implication was clear. It seems that she refused any further protection or to change her routine, and decided to continue exactly as normal.'

'Why threaten her so long after she was retired out of the job?' asked Jackman, thinking about Marie's suggestion that Orac hadn't completely retired.

Ruth nodded, slowly. 'I asked the same question. It seems that although it was never confirmed officially, Orla Cracken had done serious damage to some of the foreign cells that threatened our national security. Once a price is put on your head, it doesn't disappear with time. There could have been people out there looking for Orac ever since she was injured.'

'And do we know that all the work on that bank of computers is done specifically for the police force?' asked Marie pointedly.

'I have never asked that question, Marie. And I very much doubt I'd ever be given a straight answer. I'm a very small cog in a bloody great wheel,' Ruth said. 'Our job now is to find her. There's one thing that gives me hope in all this.' She looked at both of them earnestly. 'Orac was a very skilled field operative and is probably better placed to look after herself than any officer in this station. If she discovered something untoward, she might well have gone even further underground, both for her, and possibly our protection. It is less than twenty-four hours since she went silent on us, so there is still a good chance that if she can, she will make contact.' She directed her gaze at Marie. 'Watch your messages, Marie. It's my belief that if she contacts anyone, it will be you.'

Jackman was inclined to agree. 'You're the only one Orac ever talked to about anything other than the investigations in hand, so I'll go along with that.'

Marie looked dubious. 'Yes, but we were hardly bosom buddies.'

'Even so, be vigilant. Keep your phone switched on at all times, and check your emails and messages regularly, okay?' Ruth said.

'Understood, ma'am. I do anyway, but I'll do it more regularly.'

'Before you go,' Ruth gave them a slightly bemused smile, 'I didn't know this, but apparently all the flats in Heron Court are owned by the government.'

Jackman was confused. 'In what way are they used by them?'

'I have no idea, but it seems that Orla Cracken qualified for one. I don't think we need to dig further, we'd be wasting our time because we'll only meet with a dead end.' She raised an eyebrow quizzically. 'But, it's interesting, isn't it?'

'In the back yard of a cop shop? On purpose, do you think?' Jackman said.

'I'd think most definitely on purpose. And now, you should both get home. We've set all the wheels in motion, and there's little more we can do tonight.' She stood up, signalling that the conversation was at an end. 'Keep me updated at every stage, Rowan, and I'll do the same. Now, goodnight.'

On their way back down the stairs, Marie asked him, 'Do you really think Orac might contact me?'

'Yes, I do,' Jackman said.

'Then I hope she makes it soon. I don't know her well, but I do care about her, and no matter what Ruth says about being field trained and very competent, all I can think about is that she is blind in one eye, and that can affect a lot of things.' Marie sounded anxious.

'I know what you're saying, but I'm willing to bet she has a sixth sense when it comes down to it. She's still a trained operative, she'll retain all the old instincts and intuition.' He squeezed her arm. 'Try not to worry too much. There's still a chance that there's a completely different explanation for her going off like that, something we know nothing about.'

It wasn't much of a suggestion, but nevertheless, until they had something concrete, anything was possible, wasn't it?

* * *

Cally Prothero parked her car well away from the old ruin of the hotel and crossed the last few hundred metres on foot. She could hardly believe her luck with the weather tonight. The full moon was about as bright as it could be, and when she finally approached the wide overgrown drive up to the derelict building, the moonlit vista took her breath away.

The hotel had been designed in a Jacobean style, with high pointed gables and tall chimneys, and in its day had been a major venue for weddings and society balls. But the right-hand side of the building had been ravaged by fire, leaving only pillars of crumbling brickwork, and a series of skeletal chimney stacks with blackened rafters sticking up like accusing fingers. With its left-hand side almost intact, it made Cally think of a representation of good and evil, light and dark. Whatever its symbolism, it could well give her some of her very best photographs.

She was a good photographer, and when she realised it wouldn't be wasted on her, had invested in a great camera. She had chosen a Sony a7R III and some good lenses, and had spent long hours learning how to get the best from them. Tonight, she was hoping to get some images that would make her name in the decay photography world. She looked at the rather sinister silhouette in front of her. The conditions could not be better, the moonlight was amazing — the rest was down to her and her expertise.

She took a deep breath, shivered in excitement, and stepped forward.

She had discovered East Fleet Manor by accident about a month ago, when she took a wrong turning while looking for a different site altogether. It was completely hidden from the road, and as the fire had occurred some twenty years earlier, the grounds had become a jungle of overgrown trees and shrubs. She had done as much research on the place as she could. It seemed that it had been running at a massive loss for a long time. Then, after the fire, there was a lengthy legal battle over its exact ownership. Finally, it had been abandoned, and as far as Cally could ascertain no one knew who or where the owners were. She had taken a look inside and had been astounded at the architecture, the decaying décor, and the possibilities for a proper urbex trip, preferably by night.

After doing her homework, she had been pretty sure it was what they termed a virgin site, one that the urbex community had not yet infiltrated. Then she had come across a coded message on a site used by a number of local urbexers, and although the exact location wasn't divulged, she was pretty sure someone else was aware of the manor's existence.

So, she had hastened to make her trip, and the cold clear sky tonight made her heartily glad that she had.

Cally let herself in through a side door that had a broken lock. It was safer than entering through the fire-damaged front door. Using her flashlight, she wound her way along a maze of corridors into what had been the ballroom. It was a massive room, chilly, dark, a haunting mix of grandeur and destruction. One end still housed a dust-covered and rotting grand piano, some high-backed armchairs, and, high above her, huge ornate candle chandeliers. The far end, in stark contrast, had simply gone. Open to the night sky, it was a tangled mess of rubble, charred timbers and encroaching plants that had made their way through from the once beautifully tended grounds. The shafts of moonlight that penetrated the desolate room gave it an eerie, unreal atmosphere. It was exactly what she was looking for. Some Gothic moviemaker would have given his eyeteeth for such a setting.

Cally removed her rucksack and selected the equipment that she needed, laying her things out on the top of the piano. She unfolded her tripod and took two small tealight candles and a lighter from one of her many pockets. She lit them and placed them with her lenses and filters, so that she could turn off the powerful flashlight and still find the correct item for the job in hand.

It took around half an hour before she was completely satisfied, and then she gathered up her things and decided to move on to the next area. She had pre-selected four spots that she felt would give her the best chance of stunning pictures, and the next was upstairs.

The staircase was still in remarkably good condition, though heaped with fallen masonry and plaster. She picked her way up, step by careful step. The spot she had chosen was a high landing with a balustrade that looked directly into the fire-damaged part of the hotel. Again, it had that sinister contrast of opulence and decay, the ornate carved woodwork of the balcony against the blackened remains of the damage caused by the inferno. In the moonlight, it was truly striking.

Once again, she set up her equipment and began to concentrate on getting the very best that she could from her camera. While she was shooting her third series, from a slightly different angle and using a wide-angle lens, she thought she heard an odd noise.

Cally stopped what she was doing and stood stock still. She was quite used to being joined by an assortment of visitors in an abandoned building. Sometimes it was other clans out on an explore, sometimes it was security guards on a walk-around and often it was rats or birds. Old buildings, damaged ones in particular, made extraordinary noises — groaning, creaking and even singing, should a draught filter its way through a vent or a cavity. But Cally was pretty sure it was none of those.

If there were other explorers around, you made yourself known to them, you certainly didn't creep up on them. There were codes, and anyway, urbexers tended to be just curious souls with a need to photograph and record places that most people never got to see.

Cally heard the sound of stealthy movement. Someone else was in this old building with her, and he, or she, was endeavouring to remain unseen.

Suddenly, that fourth series of shots that she had planned didn't seem quite so vital. Cally quickly and calmly packed her things into her rucksack and pockets, folded the telescopic tripod and clipped that onto the toggles on her bag. She then heaved it onto her shoulders, secured the straps and switched off her torch. She moved into the shadows and waited, trying to get an idea of where her unwanted visitor was hiding. After a while, she heard another noise, the gentle, almost imperceptible, slapping of footsteps.

Cally slipped down a corridor that led to a floor consisting of bedrooms. Her idea was to check if an old fire escape was unlocked, and if it was, whether the outside stairs could still be used. She didn't want to lose the chance of getting some exterior photographs — that moonlight was too good to miss — but she did not want to be inside this building with an intruder whose motives were unclear to her.

When the door opened, she heaved a sigh of relief. The iron staircase was still perfectly usable and in no time, she was outside and putting some distance between her and the hotel.

She found a suitable spot, well hidden but giving a clear view of both side and front doors, and hunkered down on her haunches. She looked at her watch. She only had around thirty minutes before the moon would have moved too far to shed its wonderful light, and there'd be no more photographs. Did she dare set everything up? Whoever it was could have been a dosser looking for somewhere to spend the night. Couldn't they? Cally shivered. There had been a purpose to those steps, something almost furtive.

She knew that common sense should prevail, but she also knew that it would be a long time before the nocturnal conditions were as good as this again. She pulled a chocolate bar from her rucksack and unwrapped it. This was one time when having a fellow explorer along would have been an advantage. She ate the chocolate, pushed the wrapper into her pocket and stood up. She was going to risk it. There were spots with good visibility that would not be seen from the hotel. And she'd not set up the tripod — she'd just shoot off a whole sequence and hope she got the pictures she had come here for.

Thirty minutes later, she was hurrying back towards her car, thankful that she had concealed it so well, unlike whoever had been stalking around East Fleet Manor. As she had made her way silently through the trees, rather than walking directly back down the drive, she had seen an old Vauxhall Astra parked just inside where the old gates would have been. It was tucked around the corner from the gateposts, so not visible from the road, but it was certainly not well hidden.

Without thinking, Cally memorised the registration number. She couldn't wait to get away from the creepy old hotel. As she approached the main road back towards Saltern-le-Fen, she admitted to herself that this was the first time she'd ever felt scared while exploring alone. Not that it would stop her, especially if the new pictures were as good as she hoped. Even so, all the way home she wondered who that mystery person had been, and why they had been in a derelict hotel in the dead of night.

* * *

The full moon was not quite so welcome in Marie Evans's house. She hated drawing curtains at night, so its glaring brilliance was keeping her awake. She decided to get up and make herself a hot drink. Orac's silence was making her deeply anxious, and she found herself wandering aimlessly around the house while she waited for the kettle to boil. She had always known that Orac had once done an incredibly dangerous job. Having a stiletto thrust into your eye with the intention of reaching your brain was not exactly a subtle warning. Even so, Marie had never really appreciated just how much of a key player in covert government operations Orac had been.

She took her drink back upstairs and idly flicked through a few channels on the television, but nothing held her attention. She switched the TV off and as she did so, she heard a faint buzz. In a second, she was out of bed and over to where her phone was charging. She grabbed it, accessed her messages and found one from an unrecognised caller.

Marie . . . I'm okay, although possibly not safe. Had to go, but it's not what you think. Think carefully and you will know what this is about. Orac.

Marie tapped back a swift reply, but there was no connection. She swore and screwed up her brow in puzzlement. What did she mean, "You will know what this is about?" How could she know?

She sat back on the bed. She should notify Jackman, and Ruth Crooke. If Ruth had people breathing down her neck, then no matter the time, she should be told.

Jackman first. 'Sorry for the late hour, sir, but you were right, she's made contact, even though I have no idea what she meant.' She told Jackman about the message and smiled as she imagined him trying to wake himself up enough to make sense of what she was telling him. 'The first thing I thought was to get IT to try to trace the location of the sender, then I remembered that it's Orac who sent it, so it would be a total waste of time.'

'That's true, she probably bounced it halfway round the world to get it to you. I'm going to suggest that you ring Ruth and put her in the picture, then try to get some sleep,' Jackman said blearily. 'It sounds like something we could possibly work out in a brainstorming session, but that can wait until tomorrow. My brain isn't fully functional at two in the morning.'

'Mine neither.' She yawned. 'Okay, sir, just thought you should know.'

'Thanks, Marie, at least we can relax a bit, though I didn't like the sound of "not being safe," did you?'

'Not one bit. But she's alive, that's the main thing. Now I'd better wake the super and give her the news. Night, sir, see you tomorrow.' Marie ended the call and found the super's number.

Ruth sounded wide awake, despite the hour. 'I thought so! I knew it would be you that she'd contact! Thank God for that! Well, Marie, you are going to have to do some serious thinking. Looks like we are going to be relying on you to locate her, doesn't it? But right now, I have a call to make, and thank you for updating me so quickly. We'll talk again in the morning.'

Marie put her phone down next to the bed. She didn't think Orac would message her again, but just in case, she wanted it close at hand.

As the moon moved out of sight, and sleep finally claimed her, Marie began to worry all over again. The super had made it clear that it was all down to her, and she had no idea where to start.

CHAPTER FIVE

It was early morning, but the CID room was buzzing. The fact that Orac had made contact had lifted everyone's spirits.

'Any news from Charlie Button?' called out Jackman from his office doorway.

Max stood up. 'Yes, sir. Doc reckons another week and he should be match fit again.'

DC Charlie Button, who had been the baby of the team until newly appointed DC Kevin Stoner arrived, had injured his shoulder in an altercation with a drug addict and was reluctantly on sick leave. That left the team one down, but luckily there were no big cases running and their new detective, Kevin, filled some of the gaps. PC Gary Pritchard would be back with them the following day, after attending a three-day course.

Marie headed towards Jackman's office, balancing a tray with four coffees on it.

'Morning, boss. I thought we'd bring Robbie and Max in on the brainstorm, if that's okay?'

He nodded. 'Certainly. The more, the merrier. A different perspective always helps.'

Five minutes later, they were all gathered around his desk. Marie showed them a printout of the message she had received from Orac.

'Surely that means she told you something specific? Something that she expects you to remember?' said Robbie.

'That's what I would have thought,' added Max.

'But we had very few conversations,' replied Marie, 'and it was always rather cloak and dagger. I mean, she told me about the fact that she was stabbed in the eye, she even showed me the damage, but nothing about where or how that occurred.'

'So, what about cases we've been working on, ones that she has helped us with?' Jackman added. 'You are usually the person liaising with Orac. Can you recall one that interested her particularly? Maybe one that had something outstanding? An unanswered investigation?'

Marie pulled a face. 'Not that I can think of. Orac has helped with such a lot over the years, and, yes, she does put a great deal of effort into getting us the information we require, but I can't think of anything that really bugged her, or that she might have done a bit of private investigating on.'

'Then it's going to be a throwaway comment, isn't it?' said Max. 'She's mentioned something to you in passing, something that meant more to her than it did to you at the time.'

'That's possible,' said Robbie, staring into his coffee. 'Might have even been something she never meant to say, you know, like when a remark slips out accidentally.'

Jackman saw Marie stiffen. 'Marie? You've thought of something?'

She hesitated. 'Well, I don't know how this would fit, but, yes, she did say something once, and followed it up with, "I've no idea why I told you that. It's ancient history now."' Marie closed her eyes, frowning. 'It was at the time when Ashcroft was threatening your family, sir. I had told her that you were distraught with worry for your young nephews. Orac said, something like, "Ah, it's always the children."'

Trying to keep his tone casual, despite the pain this memory caused him, Jackman said, 'Go on.'

Marie stared into the distance. 'Yes! I can remember it almost word for word, because it shocked me to the core at the time.' She closed her eyes for a moment. 'She told me that her sister had been stolen from her bed while they were sleeping. She was three years old, and Orac never saw her again. She said it devastated their whole village and nothing was ever the same again. Men looked with suspicion at people they had lived and worked with since they were kids. Brothers distrusted brothers. And they never had an answer. I can recall her saying, "A blight entered our home that night and destroyed everything good for miles around."'

'Oh my!' breathed Jackman. 'Then that could be it, couldn't it?'

'Couldn't it just!' exclaimed Max. 'She said, "It's not what you think." Here we are, all thinking it had something to do with her time as a spy, but if we ditch that for the time being, it has to be her sister's abduction.'

'Yes, you're right, it could only be a family matter. What else would make her rush off into the night like that? Especially if it had such traumatic consequences,' Robbie said.

'I can recall the desolation in her voice when she told me about it,' Marie said reflectively. 'You could tell that the pain was still raw.'

Jackman mused, 'This is both good and bad news, isn't it? Good being that she's not been abducted by a gang of men in black hats, and the bad, that she's out in the open and very vulnerable.'

'She's obviously gone to Northern Ireland,' said Marie. 'First, we need to find her parents' little village.'

'Ruth can ask her shadowy higher powers. They must have records,' said Jackman. 'I'll go and ask her to follow this up for us. Meanwhile . . . just how smart is Leon?' he asked Marie.

'Smart as hell,' she said. 'If we didn't have Orac, he'd be "the man" where technology is concerned. He's up there with Spooky from Greenborough, who is shit hot.'

'Just because she did a runner voluntarily, or so we believe, it doesn't mean that she's not in danger. We need to find her and get her back to safety.'

'You're thinking that she received something on her computer that made her take off so suddenly?' asked Max.

'She lives in cyberspace,' Jackman said. 'If you wanted to get her attention, you'd do it through the web. Robbie? Get around to Heron Court with a couple of uniforms and bring me that computer. Marie? Go and tell Leon to put everything else on hold. We have a job for him. I'm going to see Ruth Crooke.'

As everyone left the room, Robbie hung back. 'Could I have a quick word, boss?'

Jackman pointed to a chair. 'Everything okay, Rob?' Robbie sat, and told him about his friend's request, and his off-the-record enquiries about the two missing explorers.

'Not sure if you know much about urban exploration, sir, but quite a few people have taken it up. There's a big community out there, and if Stella North says they are concerned, then I believe her. She's still got all the old detective instincts.'

'I'm sure she has.' Jackman knew all about Stella. Every copper in the land knew about her bravery in overcoming the life-changing injuries she had sustained after being shot. If it weren't for Stella, Robbie Melton wouldn't be part of his team, so he felt he owed her one. 'Okay, Robbie. Orac comes first, but until we know more, there won't be a lot we can do. So long as you don't ruffle feathers in other divisions or butt in where you're not wanted, you're free to go exploring yourself.'

Robbie grinned broadly. 'Thank you, boss. Cat Cullen did ask for my assistance, even if not in so many words, so I'll liaise with her. I promise I'll keep it low key.' He stood up. 'Stella will be relieved.'

'Give her my best when you speak to her next, Rob. She's well, is she?'

Robbie smiled. 'Looks better than I've seen her in years, sir.' He hesitated. 'But I can't help feeling that . . .' He shrugged. 'Oh well. That's life, I guess.'

Jackman knew what he was feeling. Robbie had idolised Stella North, the brilliant detective sergeant whose glittering career had been stolen from her. It had left him in tatters. It was not surprising that he still grieved the loss. 'She's travelling a different path now, Robbie, but Stella will do well wherever she goes. She's special.'

Robbie brightened. 'You're right, sir. And thanks again.'

All of a sudden, Jackman experienced a feeling of déjà vu. During their last awful case a similar thing had happened. One of his detectives had asked if they could follow up a separate, supposedly minor issue, which had turned out to be of major importance. Was Robbie's inquiry going to go the same way?

Jackman told himself to forget it for the time being. Back to Orac, and he had to go and see Ruth Crooke.

* * *

He didn't need much sleep, he never had. Maybe it was the kind of work he'd done when he was younger, maybe it was just the way his body worked. Whatever the reason, it suited him now. Two hours and he was fresh again.

He'd been for his usual early morning run, showered and changed, and now he was having breakfast. He wasn't much interested in food, so he ate to stay fit. And he was. Considering his age, he was pretty athletic. Lean, muscular in an understated way, with a full head of hair and a mind as sharp as a blade. If it had been down to brains and physique alone, his wife would never have left him.

His brow furrowed. How often had she repeated that tired old phrase, "It's not you, it's me," when it was so obviously him. All along, he had been the one to blame. It had only taken him two months to realise that he should never have married, not her, not anyone, yet they had held on for fourteen more years. Why? It wasn't that they didn't love each other. They did. But the day came when she could take no more, and in a very short time the divorce had been under way. He was only surprised that their son had opted to stay with him. He had no idea why — he would hardly have won a father of the year award. But he did genuinely love the lad. Maybe his son had known it.

His mind moved on to other matters. He began to think about the girl, alone in the old hotel with her camera equipment. He couldn't help admiring her courage. He had deliberately allowed her to know that there was someone else in that derelict place. She hadn't panicked, which he respected her for. He smiled to himself. She had even hung about in the gardens long enough to take some photographs of the exterior by moonlight. Now that took balls! She would have made a great war photographer. The only thing that had caused him some slight concern was that he was pretty sure she had taken his car number. Not that it really mattered. It wasn't in his name, and now the old wreck was consigned to the garage. He'd use a different car in future. In any case a 4x4 would be more suited to where he was going. She'd done him a favour, really.

Smiling, he cleared away his breakfast things. She must have been scared, that girl. Alone in a creepy ruin that was partly ravaged by fire, in the dead of night under a full moon. What could be more sinister? It was positively Gothic! And then to become aware that someone or something was in there with you . . . He chuckled to himself. She didn't know it, of course, but she had been in no real danger — well, not from him. He wouldn't have hurt her. The building itself was far more dangerous. He reminded himself that that wasn't always the case. The next curious explorer he met might not be so lucky.

And that should be tonight, if everything went to plan.

* * *

Ruth Crooke's thin face looked even more drawn than usual. 'I've just returned from another meeting with a bunch of solemn-faced, cash-rich men whose names I've never heard before, Rowan. It was no fun, no fun at all.' Her lips tightened, as if pulled by a thread. 'I'm beginning to wonder what on earth in her previous career that woman got up to. The security surrounding her now is unbelievable!'

'I dread to think, Ruth,' said Jackman. 'However, I do have some information that might help ease your worry, at least somewhat.'

'Then please, do tell me. I desperately need something to brighten my day.'

'Okay, we're speculating a bit here, but we are pretty sure we're on the right track . . .' He told Ruth the story of the stolen sister. 'As far as Marie can recall, that's the only other important thing Orac ever told her, so it has to be why she disappeared so suddenly.'

The superintendent nodded slowly. 'It fits with Orac's suggestion that it's not what we think, doesn't it? Yes, I'd say that's a very real possibility.' Her expression darkened. 'But now we have to work out how to take our enquiries further.'

'Surely, we can get Ireland to talk to her parents, gather up old reports on the original abduction, or at least make discreet enquiries around the village the child was taken from?' said Jackman.

'Sadly, no. That was one of the reasons why I was summoned at the crack of dawn this morning. They knew nothing of this, of course, but I was informed in no uncertain terms that we must not under any circumstances talk to her family.'

Jackman frowned at her. 'Why ever not?'

Ruth took a photograph from a slim wallet on her desk and handed it to Jackman. He stared at it. He had no idea who it was. He looked closer. It showed a beautiful — no, handsome — woman with pale skin, long, straight almost black hair and icy blue eyes that reminded him of Laura's, only hers were soft and sympathetic. 'Who is this?' he asked.

'That, Jackman, is Orla Cracken.'

His eyes widened. 'You're kidding me!'

'This was the woman who went into war zones and secret places as a specialised military intelligence field agent, Rowan. The woman we know is the one that returned, half blinded and with a price on her head.'

'So, Orla Cracken's not her real name?'

Ruth shook her head. 'No, it's Ciara O'Dwyer, only I never told you that. And this is the important bit, Rowan. Her parents believe her to be dead, so we *cannot* barge in and start asking them questions, even if we did manage to find them.'

Jackman sighed. 'Ah, that does make it even more difficult, doesn't it?'

'Almost impossible, I'd say.' Ruth rubbed at her eyes. 'And even if she is off on some private mission, those men who are constantly observing her from the shadows will meanwhile be moving heaven and earth to find her. It's not only a matter of her safety, Rowan, but I'm beginning to believe that they cannot allow our Orac to fall into the wrong hands.'

'She's a genius, isn't she? Heaven knows what her brain and her expertise are worth,' Jackman added.

'Or what that brain knows,' Ruth concluded darkly. 'She's more valuable than that damn great computer she's glued to, day and night. She probably has more highly sensitive material stored away in her head than GCHQ or the Pentagon!'

'And she's off the radar.' He was trying to get his head around it. 'As you say, no matter what the reason, she's not where she's supposed to be. Those men must be shitting themselves.'

'Undoubtedly.' Ruth picked up the photograph and stared at it. 'Beautiful, wasn't she?'

Jackman nodded. 'And still is.' Privately, he wondered what it had taken and how much she had suffered for Orac to lead her family to believe that she was dead. She had given up her past and everyone in it and would never see them again. People who chose the witness protection programme had to endure the same loss, but hers would last a lifetime.

'So, the bottom line, Rowan, is back off. We are going to have to allow Orac to come to us. We cannot chase her, we might risk inadvertently bringing even more danger down on her.' Her face softened. 'I don't want that on my conscience, do you?'

'This is all way above us,' he said.

'Out of our league, Rowan. But . . . I still think she will use Marie if she wants to make contact.'

'They do have a rapport,' Jackman said.

'I think Orac sees something of herself in Marie, apart from the obvious similarities in their looks, judging by that photograph.'

Jackman hadn't thought of that, but she was right. Though Marie's eyes were dark brown, there was a resemblance. Even so, he suspected that what Orac saw was a strong, brave woman with good values and unshakeable loyalty. 'I'll tell her to be vigilant, but I suspect that's unnecessary. She's got one eye on her phone all the time, especially since she got that message.'

'Make sure everyone understands the gravity of the situation. No sleuthing, no enquiries, especially about Orac's past.' Ruth took one last look at the photo and put it back in the file. 'Right, Rowan. Off you go and do some ordinary police work.'

He stood up. He knew he could rely on his team. None of them would want to let it drop, but neither would they endanger Orac's life. 'I'll keep you updated if there's any further contact, Ruth.'

She placed the thin file into her drawer and locked it again. 'And I'll do the same.'

CHAPTER SIX

'I understand, boss,' Marie said. 'No way would I want to make things worse for Orac. I just hate to think of her alone out there, probably hunted by two different groups of "interested parties."' She had been reading up on the history of military intelligence and was well aware that people who were considered to be a continued threat were never consigned to the archives. Someone, somewhere, would be waiting for Orac to make one step outside her safe place, and a hornets' nest would be stirred up.

'I feel the same, Marie, but we have to back off, completely. You are the only one who needs to keep Orac at the front of your mind. Just watch for contact, and make a note of anything you remember, no matter how small, any little snippet of information.' He lowered his voice. 'We'll keep a record, just you and me, in case she needs us to help her in any way, okay? Strictly confidential.'

She smiled at him. 'I was planning on doing that anyway.'

'I know.' He grinned back. 'I've met you in my porridge before, Marie Evans.'

How wonderful Jackman was! No one else was so in tune with her. 'So, boss. What next? I've got a clear desk for once in my life. Alistair Ashcroft is finally locked up and,

Orac apart, all is well with the world, so what do you want me to do?'

'Go and talk to Robbie. Your friend Stella North has some missing mates.'

Marie's eyes widened. 'Stella? Really? Has he seen her recently?'

'He certainly has, but I'll let him fill you in. I'm still dragging reports together on the Kirby case, so you can have a bit of down time with Robbie's "unofficial" investigation.'

Marie hurried out of the office. Back in the CID room, Robbie was typing furiously, his eyes fixed on his screen.

'Hey, Rob! Jackman says I can pitch in with you for a while. Something to do with Stella North?'

Robbie looked up and grinned. 'Excellent, Sarge! Let me get us some drinks and I'll give you the lowdown.' He jumped up and hurried out to the machine in the corridor.

Marie sank down on a chair and waited. Orac was still worrying her, but at least she knew she had taken off of her own volition. She thought back over the last two years. She had spent them looking over her shoulder, waiting for Ashcroft's next attack. She had been terrified for herself, but even more so for her friends. Ashcroft had damaged the whole team in one way or another, Jackman more than any of them, but Ashcroft had hurt her badly too. Now that threat had gone, and there was no way he could get to them. This time, he had been the one to get hurt. He was still recovering from some pretty major leg injuries, and she had heard that he was not handling his lack of mobility well. 'Bloody good job too,' muttered Marie to herself. She rubbed the leg that had been broken during an earlier showdown with Ashcroft. 'Couldn't happen to a more deserving bloke.'

'It's generally considered that talking to oneself is a sign of madness.' Robbie placed a beaker of coffee in front of her.

She laughed. 'I was just sending menacing telepathic messages to Alistair Ashcroft.'

'Ah. Well, that's allowed.' He sat down opposite her. 'Guess what? Stella's expecting a baby!'

Marie forgot Ashcroft. 'Oh, that's amazing news! She's come such a long way, hasn't she?'

'She looks incredible, Sarge. Really fantastic.'

He sounded so pleased for Stella, and so fond. Marie recalled how much he had cared for his old crewmate. 'But something's happened, I understand.'

His expression became serious. 'Two urban explorers have gone missing while they were out exploring at night. One was a bit of a novice, but the other guy was an experienced adult. Stella said the urbex community is worried sick about them.' He looked at his screen. 'I've just checked a couple of well-known sites and they are humming with posts about the two missing guys.'

'Where did these two disappearances occur?' she asked.

'One from a disused cinema in Greenborough, and the other an old airfield at a place called Randleby. I don't know it, but it's north of Fenchester. They both vanished and all their gear was left *in situ*, including a couple of pretty expensive cameras.' He frowned. 'I find that a bit odd, don't you?'

Marie considered the two locations. The Greenborough site she knew, but Randleby meant nothing to her. 'I suppose so. Does Stella suspect foul play? I mean, there's nothing to indicate that this isn't just coincidence, is there? As in, things were bad at home and for whatever reason they just ran away?'

'Fenchester CID would like us to think that about the lad at Randleby. In fact, the DS there, a bloke named Holiday, used every excuse in the book to fob me off. He more or less told me to sod off and forget it,' Robbie growled. 'DC Cat Cullen at Greenborough, on the other hand, was totally different — practically asked for my help. I think they are pretty busy at present, and as the urbexer isn't vulnerable or at risk, and he's an adult, her hands are tied. Stella said the older guy, a man named Anthony Hood, aka Cruiser, is one of a clan that she knows well. He's solid, Sarge, a dedicated explorer who has been doing it for years. His urbex partner, Lisa, is climbing the walls.'

'Have you spoken to her, Rob?' Marie asked.

'Not yet, but,' he lifted an enquiring eyebrow, 'I was just about to ring and see if she can see me. Don't suppose you fancy a trip out?'

'Count me in. This sounds rather intriguing, doesn't it?' For some reason, Marie had a strong suspicion that this "unofficial" inquiry was going to turn into something much bigger. 'And on our way, you can give me a crash course in urbexing. I know it was a passion of Stella's, and of her husband Tom's, but apart from seeing one or two mind-blowing photographs of hers, I don't really know what it's all about.'

'You got it, Sarge.' Robbie picked up the phone. 'Lisa Sheringham? I'm DC Robbie Melton from Saltern-le-Fen. I wondered if you would have time to talk to us about Anthony Hood? We could come over.'

He listened, scribbled down an address and promised to be with her in half an hour.

Marie stood up. 'I'll drive. Where does she live?'

'Fleet Seas End, same village as Anthony Hood. Do you know it?'

Marie nodded. She knew it well. 'Nice little pub there called the Mariners. After we got engaged, my Bill and I used to ride out there on the bikes and have a Sunday lunch. I've got happy memories of Fleet Seas End.' She tried not to sound sad as she spoke of her late husband but from the look Robbie gave her, she hadn't managed very well. She cleared her throat. 'I'll be interested to see if the little place has changed over the years.'

Fleet Seas End was one of the few villages in the area that you could honestly call pretty. The fens had a massive farming community whose clusters of dwellings were often remote and utilitarian, but certainly not chocolate box.

Marie turned off the main road to Greenborough into a long lane with a tree-lined river on one side and expensive detached houses on the other.

'Nice,' murmured Robbie appreciatively. 'Bet they cost a bob or two.'

Marie hid her smile. Robbie came from a well-off family and lived in one of the most expensive apartments in Saltern. 'The ones further down are the most upmarket,' she said. 'As the lane curves away from the river there are houses on both sides, and the ones on the right all have moorings and river frontage.'

Lisa Sheringham lived in an attractive old-style house covered with wisteria. What a sight that would be in the spring, with its heavy clusters of lavender-coloured flowers cascading through the lime green leaves.

To their surprise, the door was opened by a good-looking young man in a wheelchair. They showed him their warrant cards and he said, 'Hi, I'm Will. Come in, Lisa's expecting you.' He spun the chair around and led the way into a large open-plan kitchen. 'Honey! Your police officers are here!'

Lisa appeared from what was obviously a utility room just off the kitchen, a pair of cargo pants across her arm. 'Oh, good. Can I get you some tea?'

'That would be great,' said Marie. 'Milk, no sugar for both of us, thanks.'

Lisa put the trousers aside and filled the kettle. 'Have a seat.' She indicated to the kitchen table. 'Everyone always finishes up in here. I swear most of the house is hardly used.'

Marie would have loved to have a kitchen big enough to hold four people, let alone use it for socialising.

A few minutes later, they were all sitting round the table with steaming mugs in front of them.

'I'm so pleased that someone is actually looking into this, Officers. I mean, I fully understand that there's priorities, and you can't check up on everyone who goes missing, but we know Anthony so well, and something isn't right, it really isn't!' Lisa was a tall, lean woman of around twenty-five, with short, boyish, golden-blonde hair and an expressive face. She looked at Robbie curiously. 'Are you Stella's friend?'

He nodded. 'She was my crewmate. We worked together for years. She's really worried about these two disappearances, and that is good enough for me.'

'What can you tell us about Anthony Hood, Lisa?' asked Marie.

'Well, he's been our friend for years, hasn't he, Will? We all used to go exploring together when we were younger.'

'Then I fell through a damaged attic floor,' said Will, with a rueful smile. 'And, ironically, I wasn't even exploring. I was a plumber looking for a frozen water pipe. Broke my back.'

Marie was amazed at how matter-of-fact he sounded.

'Could have been worse. At least I'm still here, no brain damage, and pretty mobile, all things considered.'

'Hats off to you, Will. Respect,' said Robbie. 'Not sure I'd be so stoic.'

'I've had my bad times, Robbie, as my long-suffering wife here will confirm. But life is precious, even if it's a bit different to what you envisaged.' He sipped his tea. 'Now, back to Tony. He is a bit older than us, thirty, unmarried, no serious girlfriend at present. He lives on the other side of the village in Saltpit Lane.'

'He's a really good urbexer,' added Lisa. 'Reliable and very sensible. Industrial sites are his favourite locations for exploration. He's travelled all over Europe checking out deserted factories and he's even been to the USA to photograph industrial ruins in the Rust Belt.' She made a face. 'Not my thing. Too overpowering, too intimidating. I prefer places that ordinary people used. My interest is the social history of old buildings.'

'Tony is also very supportive of new explorers. He shows them the ropes and makes sure they have all the right values,' explained Will. 'He's a good teacher and very well liked.'

'So, he's not the kind of man to do a disappearing act on his fellow urbexers,' said Marie.

'No way!' Lisa exclaimed. 'Something happened to him, DS Evans. We were all there in the same building, four of us. Tony wanted to get some shots of the old projection room, so we went off to take pictures of the rest of the cinema. When he didn't come back to join us, we turned the whole place upside down looking for him, but he'd gone. I swear Tony would never pull a stunt like that on his friends, or anyone else either. He was hot as hell on safety issues — one of the things he always did was count us in and count us out. It was a ritual of his.'

Robbie took out his notebook. 'Was he a big guy? Small and wiry?'

'Tall, fit, muscular. Tony went to the gym regularly and he ran, too,' said Will. 'If someone attacked him, he certainly wouldn't have been a pushover.'

'And in an old deserted echoey building like that, I'd think you would have heard something, wouldn't you?' said Marie.

'We heard nothing at all.' Lisa sounded miserable. 'I feel we let him down. I just hated leaving that cinema, not knowing where he was.'

'Do you have his email address and mobile phone number?' asked Robbie.

'Yes, and he's on Facebook and Instagram, and he contributes photographs and editorials to two websites. I'll write them down for you.' Lisa stood up and went and got a pad and a pen. 'He works for a company that repairs the bigger farm equipment. It's based just outside the village on the main road. They haven't heard from him either.'

'That's another thing he would never do, just not turn up for work without letting them know,' added Will. 'He loves his job and he's very conscientious.'

'All round nice guy,' murmured Marie.

'The best,' confirmed Will. 'We're desperate to know where he is. We're starting to fear the worst.'

Marie nodded. Their concern was real, and from their description of Anthony Hood, she could see that choosing to just take off would be totally out of character.

Marie and Robbie prepared to leave. 'We can't promise anything,' she said, 'but we will be following this up. We'll leave you our phone numbers, and maybe you'd give us a call if you hear from Tony or if you hear of something like this happening to anyone else?'

Lisa and Will nodded. 'I spend a lot of time online, Officers,' said Will. 'I'm at hospital this afternoon and won't be home till late, but I'll put out as many feelers as I can, and keep my eyes peeled across the urbex sites.'

'Thanks, Will, that's appreciated,' said Robbie, handing him his card. 'We'll be in touch.'

'Give my love to Stella,' said Lisa. 'I'm so glad she mentioned this to you.' She sighed. 'She was one of the greatest urbexers. Such a tragedy, what happened.'

Marie noticed the expression on Robbie's face. He still hated to talk about the shooting.

'It certainly was,' said Marie, and glanced at her watch. 'Goodness! We have to get back to Saltern. Thank you for your time.'

Robbie was rather quiet on the drive back. Suspecting that he was reliving past horrors, Marie decided to bring him back to the present. 'So, let's say this man was abducted for some reason. How would you go about immobilising a big strong fellow and removing him from a ruined building?'

Robbie frowned. 'Actually, I have no idea. Sedated, he'd be a dead weight, so that would make getting him out really difficult, and it would be impossible to do it silently. Sound carries in empty buildings.'

'My thoughts as well. I'm no further than you, unless we step into the realms of fantasy—' Just then a car pulled out of a side road right in front of her. She swerved. 'What a tosser! I nearly had him! Where are uniform when you need them?'

'Lucky you weren't on your bike,' said Robbie. 'That could have been nasty.'

'I ride as if I'm invisible to everyone else on the road, that way I expect the unexpected all the time. My Bill used to say pretend every other driver is an arsehole and you are driving in their blind spot, then you'll stay safe.'

'Good motto to have.' Robbie laughed at the wording. 'But you'd never catch me on a motorbike.'

Marie giggled. 'I know! I offered you a lift once, remember? I've never seen such a look of terror. I wish I'd had my phone handy for a picture!'

'Yes, well, one man's meat and all that.'

They kept things light for the rest of the journey, until Marie was swinging into the parking area.

Robbie said, 'Thinking of that couple we just met, I'm pretty convinced something serious happened that night, aren't you?'

She pulled up and switched off. 'I am. We'd better sort out an action programme. Have we got Max with us as well?'

'Yes, unless anything else rears its ugly head or we're needed in the hunt for Orac.'

She pulled a face. 'That's not likely now, Rob. We've been told to tread very carefully, or we could do more harm than good.'

'I wouldn't want that.' He looked at her quizzically. 'She's certainly one mysterious lady, isn't she?'

'That's an understatement.'

They went into the station, Marie checking her messages for the sixth time that morning. As soon as they reached the CID room, they knew that something had happened, and Marie immediately thought of Orac.

'Boss wants to see you, Sarge,' called out Max.

She tapped on the door to his office. Inside, she found Jackman talking earnestly to Ruth Crooke. He pointed to a chair. 'Sit down, Marie.'

'Don't worry, it's not about Orac.' Ruth had noticed her anxious expression.

'It's just material confirmation of that directive to back off,' said Jackman. 'When Leon and the uniforms arrived at Heron Court, they were met by a distraught house manager. Mr Beale was beside himself because a people-carrier with blacked-out windows had arrived a short while before, and a team of men had stripped Orac's flat of every single piece of technology. Leon has lost his chance to shine, I'm afraid.'

Marie wasn't surprised, just a little put out that they hadn't got there first. She had been pretty sure Leon could have found something on that computer. 'I wish we'd taken it on our first trip, but as you said, Super, we'll have to wait for her to come to us. I just pray nothing goes wrong and stops her.'

Ruth stood up. 'There's nothing we can do for the present, Marie. She knows where we are and I'm pretty certain that she also knows we'd move heaven and earth to keep her safe.' She put her hand to the door. 'Be on the lookout for those messages.'

'I am, Super, believe me.'

After Ruth had gone, Jackman asked Marie what she thought about the missing urbexers.

'We're going to pursue it, boss. Having spoken to one of the explorers who was with him when he disappeared, I believe something bad did happen to Anthony Hood.'

'Okay, then go with it, but with extreme care.' He grinned. 'No causing a divisional war, and no stamping on toes, no matter how deserving said toes really are.'

'Softly, softly is our motto, I promise.' Marie tried to look angelic.

Jackman looked at her suspiciously. 'Hmm. Not very convincing, but it'll have to do. Let me know what you discover.'

Marie hurried back to Robbie's workstation. 'Okay, we'll get this action programme mapped out, then start digging,' she called to Max. 'And, Robbie? This one is yours. You are the boss here, so over to you.'

CHAPTER SEVEN

Cally had downloaded her photographs onto her computer and was now going through them one by one. The quality surprised even her. She had hoped for something special, simply because of the extraordinary light and weather conditions that night, but she had not expected the kind of images that she saw now. Strangely, the ones with the most impact were those hastily shot exteriors that she had taken prior to making her speedy exit from the hotel grounds.

She stared at one of them and tried to analyse what made it so striking. There was a clarity about it, the intense unclouded moonlight making it seem almost unreal. Usually it was mist that gave an ethereal quality to a picture, but it was the opposite in this one. The blackened roof spars etched against the pale night sky looked sharp and spiteful, angry even.

She shook her head. The interiors were good too, very good. One, taken from that upstairs gallery, was definitely worthy of wider recognition. It showed the gradual move from elegance to decay in a single image. The foreground, the interior of the ballroom, still bore all the hallmarks of luxury. The far end of the room, which had been eaten away by the fire, looked decimated. It was now being consumed by a different entity. Nature was taking back what belonged to it.

Cally allowed a smile to creep slowly over her face. It had been worth it!

Then the smile faded. It could have been her imagination, but one or two of the shots gave a distinct impression of fear, even dread. They gave the viewer the feeling that something awful was lurking just out of sight. They made you tense, as if you were listening for sounds — soft footfalls, another's breath at your ear. Cally shivered. Who, or what, had been in East Fleet Manor watching while she took these photographs?

She carefully labelled the images, saved them into a new folder and closed the file. She was a lone explorer, and although she followed decay photography sites on the internet, she wasn't very aware of the local urbex scene. She did occasionally check one local site, where she'd read that others might be about to infiltrate the old hotel. Now she became anxious for these nameless, faceless urbexers. What if she had been lucky last night? She had got out safely, but what if the next lot of enthusiastic explorers weren't so fortunate?

What to do? She could post a warning, but telling an urbexer not to go somewhere was like issuing an open invitation! Plus, it would draw attention to her hitherto unexplored site. What would she say, anyway? That being on her own at night in a deserted building had given her the heebie-jeebies? She could just hear the laughter. With a grunt, Cally searched the contacts on her phone. She knew someone who might have a finger on the pulse of the local urbex groups — Will Sheringham. Years ago, before he met and married Lisa, he and Cally had been pretty close, and she still got in touch with him from time to time.

Cally waited, but his number went to voice mail. She couldn't explain her worries in a few words, so she cancelled the call.

Oh, hell. Perhaps she had imagined the whole thing. Old buildings did make strange noises, didn't they? What if it had just been a cat? Oh, and does that same cat drive a Vauxhall Astra? Be sensible, Cally! Then again, the car could have been dumped there. It was possible, it was a bit of a wreck. Maybe some kids had nicked it, gone on a joyride and then abandoned it.

She left her little makeshift office and went downstairs. You could find answers to everything in the cold light of day. Perhaps she should just take a step backwards and let sleeping dogs lie.

Cally spent the rest of the morning doing housework and getting her clothes ready for work the next day. She did shift work that every so often gave her three days off, which she enjoyed. Working shifts suited her. She'd always been adaptable and had a natural ability to sleep at any time, day or night, unlike most of the people she worked with, who were always complaining about their disturbed sleep patterns.

As she cleared away after her lunch, all her former worries began to seep back. Whatever was going on at East Fleet Manor, it made her uneasy. She ought to warn her fellow explorers to either keep well away or go prepared. But for what? Cally wished she knew. Worst of all, she had no idea of how to warn them.

* * *

Max sat at his desk, eating from a Tupperware pot.

'What's the wife given you today, Max?' asked Robbie.

'Don't rightly know, mate, but it's dead tasty.' Max stared into the pot with interest. 'She says I've got to eat more healthily. If I keep living on Maccy D's and Kentucky Fried, I'll probably drop dead at forty.'

'Funny, I seem to recall a hungry Rosie often grabbing the last slice of pizza in the past.' Robbie grinned and took a bite out of his Subway.

'Since having the twins, she's gone all health conscious. To be honest, I can see where she's coming from. Those little 'uns need us both to be there for them, don't they?' He took another mouthful of the unidentified food and chewed. 'And I plan on living to a grand old age, and watching my kids grow and flourish.'

'Good for you. You never know, maybe they'll even look after you in your dotage.' Robbie laughed. Old age seemed a very long way off to guys like Max and himself, but sometimes hearing some of the older coppers talk about time flying by brought him up short. Having kids must make you reconsider your life, your priorities and responsibilities. To him, Max would always be a cheeky cockney sparrow, but he couldn't help noticing how "sensible" his friend had become since his marriage. Was this maturity?

'Don't know about that, I'm not even sure I'd want them to. Their lives should be lived to the max, not spent caring for a couple of old codgers.'

'Don't you mean a couple of old coppers?'

Max grinned. 'They're the worst kind of old codgers!' He put the lid on his food container with a snap. 'Now, what's my itinerary for this afternoon? And please don't tell me I have to hoof it round some smelly old ruin. I'm wearing my Paul Smiths today.' He gazed lovingly down at his shiny leather Chelsea boots. 'I'll never be able to afford another pair now I'm married!'

'Don't worry, mate, your boots are safe.' Robbie looked across to where Marie was finishing her lunch. 'Marie and I will do the legwork today. You can do some computer searches.'

Max brightened up. 'Good. What am I looking for?'

'The life and times of Anthony Hood. We need to know everything we can about this supposedly perfect bloke. Unless he was randomly targeted, somewhere along the way he must have pissed someone off.' Robbie frowned. 'Or done something that resulted in his death. Then move on to the other lad — but be very diplomatic with this one. DS Holiday at Fenchester was not helpful, and I don't want him knowing that we're fishing around in his pond.'

'Got it. Leave it with me. Where are you going, by the way?'

'Marie and I are going to the cinema. Only there won't be a film showing at this one.'

'No popcorn? What a bummer!'

Robbie grinned. 'If we do find any, I reckon it'll be a bit past its sell-by date.'

'Ready when you are,' Marie called across the room.

Robbie finished his sandwich. 'Would you prefer the stalls or the balcony, madam?'

'I don't think I'm going to want to park my bum on anything in that old place, thanks, Robbie. It closed thirty years ago, so most likely the last occupant of any seat I choose was a rat.' She pulled a face. 'Are we going to have to get hold of a keyholder? If we can find one, that is.'

'Nope,' he said. 'We are going urban exploring. Lisa's texted me instructions of how to "infiltrate" the same way they got in.'

'Ooh, I can hardly wait.' She glanced pointedly in Max's direction. 'Good thing I'm not wearing *my* best shoes, isn't it?'

Max smiled benignly. 'Win some, lose some, Sarge. My lucky day today, I guess.'

'Isn't it just? But if I were you, sunshine, I'd wear something a bit more rugged tomorrow, because this is a one-off.' Marie raised her eyebrows at her workmate. Did Max even own a pair of tough shoes? She looked back to Robbie. 'Okay, urbexer, off to our afternoon of wading around in debris. Just lovely!'

As they drove, Robbie, not wanting to barge into Greenborough's patch without warning, phoned DC Cat Cullen to let her know what they were doing.

She sounded really pleased. 'I'm glad you're following it up — I've got a pile of stuff on my desk at the moment. Keep me posted, won't you? And if I can help with anything, information about locals and the like, just ring me, okay?'

He promised he would and ended the call. 'I don't know why Fenchester can't be more like that.'

'Odd, really,' said Marie. 'If you remember, I had to go and liaise with Fenchester over the Alistair Ashcroft case, and they couldn't have been more helpful. In fact, I still have a number for the guys I was working with. I might just give one of them a call and sound them out about this DS Holiday.'

'Good idea. He's really been bugging me.' It was unusual for even-tempered Robbie to be so aggrieved.

'I worked with a DS at Fenchester called Ralph Enderby,' Marie said. 'He's still there, so when we get back, I'll give him a ring. He's a nice bloke and we got on well.'

They spent the rest of the trip speculating about Orac's whereabouts, and in no time, they were pulling into a half-abandoned car park at the back of the old cinema, an overspill area, rarely used by shoppers.

They locked the vehicle, hoping that the wheels would still be there when they returned. Taking two torches with them, they made their way to a narrow, dank alley that ran alongside the old movie theatre. 'I came here with my dad as a kid,' said Marie. 'It was dead cool back then. The Regal, it was called. I loved it. I remember we watched *E.T.* here.'

Marie's mention of her father made him feel rather sad. She obviously had happy memories of the times she spent with him. Robbie, on the other hand, couldn't remember his dad ever taking him to a film. His parents were always too busy "networking," or socialising or, more to the point, getting rat-arsed at posh venues. He knew that Marie's parents had split up when she was young, but even so, they had both showered her with love. He had very few good memories of his family, other than his Aunt Hazel. He still saw her sometimes. She was an artist who lived in Cornwall, and if he'd had the choice, he would much rather have lived with her than his parents.

'So, how do we get into this place?' asked Marie.

'Down here.' Robbie led the way off the alley down an even narrower path. 'This leads to the old fire exit. Lisa said there's a service door just beyond it, and the lock is faulty. It appears to be locked, but with just a little persuasion, we're in.'

A few moments later they were trudging along corridors that reeked of damp and decay. So strong was the smell that it was hard to breathe normally.

'People actually do this for fun?' Marie exclaimed. 'What's the matter with them?'

Robbie laughed. 'Stella thought it was the best thrill ever. Discovering somewhere that others hadn't seen for years, finding the evidence of people's lives from so long ago . . .'

'I'd rather be yomping up a Welsh mountain in crisp fresh air any day. This place stinks like a midden!'

'Not good, is it? But it'll be better in the auditorium. These service corridors are pretty airless.' Lit up in his torch beam, Robbie saw a set of double doors. 'The footprints in the dust go this way.' He pulled the doors open, and they found themselves in the main seating area.

'Oh my!' he whispered.

Some light filtered in from a strip of narrow windows, high up at ceiling level. Most of the glass had gone, letting a watery light filter through. Robbie noticed the huge Art Deco-style chandeliers, in place albeit thick with grime and cobwebs. The tiers of seating were still there in their rows, now littered with plaster that had fallen from the damp ceiling, and the rotting red velour was covered with a fine coating of mildew. Parts of the walls were still ornately plastered and decorated with angular, geometric designs, though some of it had peeled away to reveal the brickwork beneath. The place felt strange, sad, as if it was waiting.

All at once, he understood what Stella had been trying to explain to him. There was a whole unknown world to be found in these forbidden places. He stared around him in wonder, his mind expanding to encompass a different experience of place. Now he understood what his dear friend was on about. The beauty in this silent, brooding, graveyard of a pleasure-house was like an awakening.

From her silence, he first imagined that Marie was feeling it too, until she said, 'Bloody hell, Robbie, why hasn't someone either pulled this dump down, or spent some money and rebuilt it? What a waste!'

He suppressed a sigh, the moment fading. Okay, she had a point. It was a shame that someone hadn't made use of such a striking piece of architecture before it reached this state. 'Well, Lisa said that Anthony Hood was last seen in the projection room, so I guess that's where we should start. Let's hope the stairs are safe.'

They were glad of their flashlights. Luckily, the staircase was still solid. He pushed the door open and they peered in, their torch beams showing a small dark room that still housed all the fittings, down to shelves of big rusty spools of film labelled "Pathé News." The projector itself had long gone. There was one single aperture, where the lens would have pointed through, and the screen, now in tatters, was just visible at the front of the auditorium.

Neither of them went in. Both had a shrewd idea that this could turn out to be a crime scene.

Robbie looked at the floor. 'This area is heavily trodden, isn't it? More than I would have expected from seasoned explorers. They are very careful and tread lightly.'

Marie shone the beam of her torch across the floor. 'There seem to be at least two sets of footprints, though I suppose a couple of other urbexers could have been in here as well.'

'I'd say it looks more like a scuffle,' said Robbie.

'I think you're right.' Marie continued to let her torch beam sweep backwards and forwards across the floor. Then she stopped. 'What's that?'

Robbie looked. Something glinted. 'Broken glass.'

'*Freshly* broken glass,' Marie said.

It was the smallest fragment, perhaps half an inch long and triangular in shape, but she was right. It seemed to be free of dust or dirt.

'A lens from someone's glasses or maybe from a small torch?' suggested Marie.

'Yes, it's convex like one of them. I think you're right.' Robbie exhaled. 'Now what do we do?'

'Is it enough to warrant the cost of a forensics sweep?' Marie gave a little grunt. 'I'd say definitely not.'

'Well, I suggest we pick it up and take it with us and I'll have a quiet word with Ella. Maybe she can get her boss to take a look at it for us? If there's a problem, I'll pay for the test myself,' he offered. 'But if this case goes further, which I suspect it will, it could be vital evidence.'

'Unorthodox, but yes, I agree.' Marie pulled a small phial and some nitrile gloves from her jacket pocket. 'Shall I do the honours?'

'Please do, your feet are a lot smaller than mine.'

Marie picked her way across to the shard of glass.

'You're right about some kind of scuffle, Rob. When you get closer you can see that the dust has been rubbed off several of the shelves and the wall, as if something had been dragged along.' With two fingers, she picked up the glass and dropped it into the evidence container, which she pushed back into her pocket. She looked around. 'Something happened here alright, Rob. I'd stake my reputation on it.'

'Odd that there's no drag marks out here in the corridor though. If someone had been dragged away, I'd have expected to see the lines their heels made.'

'There's a lot we don't know right now,' said Marie thoughtfully. 'The other thing is the absence of any noise. If Anthony did put up a fight, why didn't the others hear something? I'd have thought it would have echoed all around the auditorium.'

'Lisa said he was a big fit guy,' Robbie reflected. 'It's a puzzle, alright.'

Marie went back to where Robbie was standing and closed the door. 'At least no one is likely to enter this place again and trash any remaining evidence in what could be our crime scene. Remember Will Sheringham said the local explorers had already infiltrated this place years ago. Lisa and Anthony were making a short trip that night to show someone who hadn't seen it before.'

'Bet she's regretting it now.' Robbie sighed.

They went downstairs and into the remains of the foyer. Max's kiosk was still there, advertising soft drinks and ice creams that Robbie could barely recall the taste of. No popcorn.

He peered through the ticket office window and saw small items strewn around, as if someone had closed up for the night fully expecting to return the next day. Pens, a packet of tissues, an opened packet of Polo mints and an old forgotten umbrella leaning drunkenly in one corner. Robbie wondered whose it was. Lost property? Maybe the ticket girl had simply left it behind.

'This place is getting to you, isn't it?' said Marie softly.

'Odd, really,' he mused. 'I mean, we go into all sorts of abandoned properties, pulling out drug addicts and winos or looking for stolen goods, but that feels different. This place wouldn't appear on any urbexer's list of highlights but even so, there's something about it, like you've stepped into a dream world.'

'Well, I guess I'm a bit of a philistine. I see the muck and decay rather than echoes from the past, but I do feel sad when I think of all the laughter and fun that the big old hall made possible. The Saturday morning kids' session was a riot. Now all that joy has gone, and it's nothing but a hollow shell.' She shrugged. 'Did you know it was first opened in the 1930s?'

'Doesn't surprise me, looking at the architecture. All that Art Deco.' They pushed through big swing doors into the auditorium. Robbie looked up. 'I'm betting those chandeliers are worth money. I wonder why the owners just abandoned it, leaving valuable things like that.'

'Happens all the time when things get too expensive to keep running,' said Marie. 'I guess everyone watches films at home nowadays. Cinemas had to reinvent themselves, didn't they? Multiplexes and the like.'

'And now they're popular again,' Robbie added, 'all blockbusters full of explosive action and CGI. You really have to watch those on the big screen.'

Marie nudged him gently in the ribs. 'Let's not forget why we're here. Our missing explorer?'

Robbie smiled sheepishly. 'Lost in the days of Art Deco and laughing children. Sorry.'

'Nicer than abducted explorers, I'll give you that.' Marie frowned. 'But why? If he really was abducted, what for? A grown man, someone who was positively adored, by all accounts. It doesn't make sense.'

'I don't think we are going to find the answer to that here,' Robbie said. 'I guess we'd better go back and see what headway Max is making with Anthony's history. Maybe he has some connection with the other lad who went missing out at that airfield.'

'Yes, I've had enough of this place, thank you. Let's hope the car is still in one piece. That was a shady old car park, alright, just perfect for drug deals,' said Marie.

Outside, it had begun to rain, a fine drizzle that threatened to soak them even on the short trip back to the car. Still, it felt good and fresh. Robbie felt he needed the rain to wash away the strange impression that he had taken something that didn't belong to him. He wondered what it would feel like to enter some truly impressive abandoned property — a chateau or an old hospital. He shook himself. As Marie had said, they were investigating a missing person — well, two — and he needed to get back into detective mode.

'Want to go and see Randleby Airfield?' he said suddenly. 'Give Max a bit more time?'

Marie rolled her eyes. 'Oh, why not? Perfect weather for a leisurely stroll around an abandoned aircraft hangar.'

'Sorry, Sarge. I'd like to get an idea of the location. It's somewhere I've never been before, and I need something to visualise.' He looked at her hopefully.

Marie unlocked the vehicle — fortunately just as they'd left it — and climbed in. 'Okay, you're the boss. Point me in the right direction, or set the satnav, because it's new to me too.'

Robbie smiled. 'Thanks. Head towards Fenchester, and I'll check out the exact location.'

CHAPTER EIGHT

Orla Cracken looked out across the remote landscape but she didn't see the crags of the mountain range, or the endless Irish moorland. Her gaze remained focused on a tiny cottage that nestled in a valley where only birds and the wild animals now made their homes. The abandoned cottage was painted white, although the weather had stripped much of it away. The wooden shutters were closed, as if the old building slept, like the others in the neighbouring ghost villages, whose inhabitants had all fled Donegal at the time of the Great Famine.

It wasn't Orac's first visit. On the previous one, she had committed every detail of the place to memory, and so long as the winds off the Atlantic Ocean had done no serious damage, it would suit her purpose perfectly.

Now she was checking its accessibility and making sure that no one else had been using the place recently. She was on foot, having left her car a mile or so away. No good getting stuck somewhere, either on a flooded lane or a dead end. She could bring the car down later. And a car was easily spotted, whereas a lone figure, in camouflage, moving stealthily and close to the grey stone walls, would go unnoticed.

It took her half an hour to reconnoitre the area, and now, satisfied that all was well, she was making her way back to her car. Hopefully, she would only be spending a day or two roughing it before she had an idea as to whether this mission had been worthwhile or not. Through a cleft in the hills she caught the glimmer of the weak winter sun reflecting off the top of the waves some two miles ahead of her. She took it to be a positive sign. She had waited more than half her life for this. She couldn't be wrong, she just couldn't.

* * *

'I'm not sure what I was expecting,' said Marie. 'But it wasn't this.'

Robbie looked around the deserted airfield and was forced to agree. 'Most of it's just rubble, there's not even much of the control tower left.' Across the scrubby field stood the ruined hulk of the tower, three old hangars and a few brick buildings that looked like stores. He could see nothing remarkable there, certainly nothing that might have attracted urban explorers.

'What a depressing spot,' Marie said. 'I've been to several old Second World War airfields, and they all felt as if they had some historical significance. This has nothing, does it?'

'That's another odd thing.' Robbie frowned. 'DS Holiday told me that this was a creepy spot, somewhere that had given rise to stories about ghostly dead airmen and all that. This place isn't spooky at all, is it? Just dreary.'

'Makes me even more anxious to talk to my friend Ralph at Fenchester about that man,' said Marie thoughtfully. She gazed at the old hangars. 'Do we know which of these the boy was taken from?'

'Holiday said it was a big old place, so I'm guessing it has to be that one.' He pointed to the largest hangar. 'Shall we take a look?'

'Might as well, since we're here.' Marie climbed out of the car. 'At least the rain's stopped.'

Randleby was situated in the back of beyond, surrounded by ploughed fields and a stretch of ragged woodland. The high access gates were padlocked, and the perimeter fence was in remarkably good condition considering it was no longer used, so it wasn't easy finding their way in. Finally, they found a small section of damaged wire fencing that must have been missed in the last maintenance check.

'This doesn't look like RAF to me, does it you, Marie?' Robbie asked, as they made their way across the weed-covered runway. 'And not just because of the absence of ghostly airmen.'

'Can't say it does,' she said. 'I did a quick internet search when you first mentioned Randleby, and it's not listed as being a decommissioned site.'

'Stella didn't know of it, and by the sound of it, her two urbex friends who had had to back out the night the lad disappeared didn't know about it either. Considering some of the exciting places they've infiltrated in the past, I reckon this would have been a big disappointment to them.' He thought about Razor and Butterwitch, recalled the stories Stella had told him about them, and wondered why on earth two seasoned explorers would want to come here anyway.

Picking her way between the puddles, Marie muttered that this place certainly wouldn't inspire her to go adventuring.

'I suppose it could have been a trial run, just to show those other kids how to behave and how to conduct themselves.' Robbie stopped outside the biggest of the hangars. 'Well, I reckon this is probably where Aaron Smith went off the radar.'

There was a big heavy chain and padlock across the huge doors. He tugged at it, but it held fast. 'They didn't get in this way. Let's walk around the back, there's bound to be a personnel door.'

Marie found the way in, and it wasn't through a door. A small section of the back wall had buckled inwards as if it had been struck by something heavy, leaving a gap just big enough to wriggle through. 'I hope this is worth it,' she grumbled. 'If I tear my trousers, you pay, got it?'

Robbie chuckled. He liked it when Marie got grumpy, it always brought out her Welsh accent. He often wondered why, when she had lived half of her life here on the fens, the Welsh lilt had remained. Still, it was a big part of what made her what she was.

The interior of the hangar was gloomy but not dark. Big dirty skylights lined the tops of the walls, allowing some natural light to filter in through the filth that encrusted them. The ceiling was a maze of crisscrossed metal girders. Robbie supposed that heavy airplane parts must have been winched up to them with pulleys. One wall was lined with solid workbenches and still bore various unidentifiable parts from many years before.

'This was not just a hangar to park your plane in,' he murmured, and paused as his voice echoed around the big empty space. 'There was maintenance work done in here, wasn't there?'

'Definitely.' Marie was examining a pile of what looked like rusted metalwork beneath the bench. She pulled back a mouldering cover of sacking and gasped. 'Hell-bloody-fire, Rob! Come and look at this!'

He hurried over and found her staring at an ancient motorcycle. 'Well, I'm damned! You had to find a motorbike, didn't you?'

'It's a Norton! A 16H. The British Army used them for dispatch riders. They were solo bikes, unlike the more powerful version, the 633. That had a sidecar and it was the only British bike to provide drive to the sidecar wheel. They used to have a rack for a light machine gun. I know this one is the smaller version, but Jesus, it's bloody brilliant!'

Robbie laughed. 'That's cheered you up! Is there anything you don't know about motorbikes? That old wreck has to be about eighty years old.'

'My Bill loved Nortons,' Marie said, examining it carefully. 'It's not in bad condition, considering how long it's been here. I wonder who owns this place?'

'Please don't tell me you want it!'

'It shouldn't be left here to rot, that's for sure. It belongs in an Army museum, and in the right hands, it's certainly not beyond being a restoration project.'

'Okay, Sarge, we'll make enquiries. I hate to tell you this, but it's almost four o'clock and the daylight's going. It'll be dark in an hour. We need to check this place out for signs of a struggle before it's too late.'

Marie carefully covered up her precious find. 'Good point, Rob. Sorry. Got carried away.'

They searched the hangar until they were no longer able to see properly. Then, having found nothing of importance, they made their way back to the car.

On their drive back to Saltern, Marie said, 'We need to go back there.'

'You aren't thinking of spiriting that bike away, are you?' Robbie asked.

'Relax! I'm not thinking of nicking the bike. We should take a look in the smaller hangars, the storerooms and maybe even that wreck of a control tower. The place doesn't ring true. It's not RAF, or so we are led to believe. And if it was a civil airfield, why did we just find a bike that was not only used by the British Army, but also by the Royal Air Force? And some of that other junk on the benches . . . I'm no expert, but I swear some of that old stuff was military.'

Robbie thought about it. 'I wonder if Stella's urbex friends had discovered something, and that's why they were coming here. I'll ring Stella and get her to contact Razor and Butterwitch.'

'Why not talk to them yourself, Rob?' said Marie. 'It's their young friend that has gone missing. They'll be relieved to know you're following it up seriously.'

'That's true. I'll get their number from Stella.' He called her, and after explaining that they were embarking on a full, if somewhat covert investigation, he asked her for Ray Zachara's phone number.

'Actually, Robbie, he's coming round here tonight, and so is Emily. Why don't you and Ella join us? We are having a Chinese takeaway, so we could discuss it then.'

'Love to. I need to check that Ella isn't on call tonight, but if she's free, we'd love to see you all. I haven't seen Tom for ages.'

'Seven thirty? Just ring if you can't make it, okay? And thanks, Rob, I owe you.'

Robbie ended the call and told Marie about the proposed meeting.

'That's perfect,' said Marie. 'Your Razor might just open up if you are all having a relaxing evening. I really do have the strangest feeling about Randleby.'

It could have been her influence, but Robbie was starting to feel that way too. All was not as it seemed at Randleby Airfield.

* * *

Grant Leach arrived at his friend Ron Morley's flat at five o'clock on the dot. Ron lived on the upper floor of a small maisonette in Saltern town and let Grant store all his equipment there. He still lived with his parents, and they kept an immaculate home that didn't have room for all the things he needed for urban exploration. He was twenty-four years old, with a love for the outdoors and an adventurous nature — he loved his parents and tried to respect their house rules, but it wasn't easy. Ron, on the other hand, was somewhat more relaxed. Muddy boots? No problem. "Come on in, mate! It'll hoover up when it dries." Nothing fazed Ron. He gave "laid-back" a whole new meaning, and Grant always felt comfortable with him.

The door was open when he got there, and Ron was going through a checklist of what they might need. It was just the two of them tonight, which was how Grant preferred it.

'Brought the new batteries,' he called out as he went in, 'a bag of tea lights and some dust masks. I think we are getting low on them.'

'Good stuff, Grant. Want a cuppa, or a beer?' Ron asked.

'Nah, thanks. I'll be wanting to pee all evening.' He looked over the stuff laid out on the lounge floor. 'Looking good. Phone all charged up?'

Ron nodded. 'One hundred per cent. And tonight I'm going to play with an old camera my uncle gave me, if I can fathom out how to use an SLR with no digital help. All I know is, he took some awesome pictures with the old thing.'

'We've got plenty of time, and the weather forecast is good. Rain's cleared away and they've promised a clear night.' Grant began packing things into his rucksack. 'You said you'd done a recce in daylight?'

Ron's eyes lit up. 'It looked pretty remarkable even then. Should be mind-blowing at night.'

'Shall we post our pictures when we've vetted them?' Grant asked. Sometimes they kept special places to themselves.

'Let's play it by ear. This could be special.' Ron pulled on his rambling boots.

'So how come we missed it before?' asked Grant.

'Just one of those things, I guess. The fire happened ages ago, and it looks as though the insurance didn't cover the rebuilding. You can't see it from the road at all. It's just been forgotten — simple.' Ron grinned at him. 'And by going tonight, we beat Cruncher's crew by a day. I intercepted a couple of messages on his site telling his clan to meet up tomorrow.'

'Neat.' Grant checked his pockets, and then did a final check. 'Good to go, my man.'

'Me too.' Ron's grin widened. 'I've got a feeling tonight is going to be quite a night!'

'Then lead on. To East Fleet Manor.'

* * *

When Jackman arrived home, Laura was just locking her car. They kissed and then let themselves into the old mill house.

'Good day?' he asked her. He still kept pinching himself at the thought that they were really a couple at last.

Laura smiled at him. 'Bit stressful, but nothing a hot bath and a glass of something alcoholic won't cure. What about you?'

'Remarkably quiet, although I know I shouldn't use the "Q" word. If we knew that Orac was safe, things would be pretty well perfect.' It was hard to believe that they were no longer living under Alistair Ashcroft's shadow, and even harder to describe the relief that knowledge brought. It was like a deliverance, light restored to a darkened room.

'I rang Sam today. He says he's doing well on his own now, but he does worry me, darling.' Laura's blue eyes clouded for a moment.

Sam Page, a dear friend of Laura's and a man who had been both tutor and father figure to her, had been badly injured — another victim of the evil Ashcroft. He had stayed with them for a few months in order to recuperate. Last week, he had gone home to his cottage down on the marsh at the edge of a bird reserve, and Laura fretted about him.

Much as Jackman loved being alone with Laura — after all they hadn't been living together for long, and things were still pretty intense — he worried too. 'Do you think he should come back for a bit longer?' he asked.

'He's so independent, isn't he? But I'm really not happy about him being all alone out there. It's too remote. It's the nights that bother me. If he had a fall, or an attack of some kind, I'd never forgive myself.'

Jackman hung up his coat, went to one of the kitchen cupboards and took out two wine glasses. A bottle of Malbec waited on the counter. He smiled to himself. He and Hetty Maynard, who cleaned and sometimes cooked for him, had an agreement. If he left a bottle of red wine on the counter when he went to work, she would open it for him just before she left, so it could breathe. The little ritual never failed. He poured them both a glass, pulled out two chairs and smiled at her. 'Sit down and take a nice long sip.' He set down a glass in front of her.

She drank and sighed. 'Ah! I can feel the stress easing already.'

'That's the plan,' said Jackman. 'Now,' he reached across the table and touched her hand, 'I'm going to make this suggestion. Talk to Sam and make him an offer to live here permanently, if he would like to. I'm more than happy to finish off the work on the old mill-tower, and kit it out as a self-contained flat, after all, the floor above your consulting room is already cleared, and plastered and painted. Ask if he'd like to be our "lodger" on a permanent basis.'

Her eyes widened.

'He owns his cottage, doesn't he?' Jackman said. 'He could keep it for the summers and go bird-watching whenever he liked, but this would be his base, a safe place to be, especially in winter. He would be completely independent from us. I can already see him and old Len Maynard working out how to create a wild garden outside his back door.'

'Really?' A smile spread across her face and she exhaled. 'You're an extraordinary man, Rowan Jackman. It's no wonder I love you.'

'Actually, I've been called quite a lot of things in my time as a copper, but I'll settle for that.' He grinned at her. 'And I love you for caring about the old chap so much.'

The rest of the evening passed in a happy blur while they made plans and just enjoyed each other's company. Such contentment was rare for Jackman. He knew from experience that life had a habit of throwing spanners into the works, but right now it didn't get much better than this, and he was grateful.

CHAPTER NINE

Ella Jarvis had been held up on a call, but she insisted that Robbie go and see Stella and her urbex friends. Robbie and Ella had a good relationship — they weren't joined at the hip, nor did they object if the other needed to go somewhere alone. Robbie was very fond of Ella but was it "love?" He was certainly happy, so maybe not everyone had to experience fireworks. He guessed he was just a phlegmatic type of guy.

Stella and Tom Chalk lived in a barn conversion in the grounds of the family farm. Tom had been managing the land since his father died, as none of his three brothers had any particular love of agriculture.

Stella opened the door and invited him in. 'Sorry Ella couldn't make it. Tell her no excuses next time — I'll cook for just the four of us.'

'It's a deal.'

Robbie looked around. Tom had done a brilliant job on the conversion — he'd designed it and also done most of the graft himself. Tom was a quiet, unassuming man. Other than Stella and the farm, his abiding passion was urban exploration, which he'd been doing since his schooldays. Until recently, no matter what the weather, he had managed to go out once a month with Ray and Emily. Now he had different priorities, and his Cheshire cat grin told Robbie that he was going to be just as proud a father as Max.

Robbie handed Tom a bottle. 'This is for you guys. Not for tonight, it's for you to celebrate with together.'

'Hey, champagne!' Tom clapped him on the shoulder. 'Thank you! We'll save it until you and Ella come for dinner. Sound good to you, Stel?'

'Sounds perfect. Thank you, Robbie, that's very sweet of you.' The doorbell rang. 'That will be Ray and Emily. They're bringing the food, so get ready, folks, plates are warming in the oven.'

The next ten minutes were a furore of greetings and the unpacking of enough food to feed a small army. Ray and Emily, or Razor and Butterwitch, as they had first been introduced to him, were as friendly as ever, but obviously anxious. After they had all helped themselves from the various dishes, Emily said, 'We're so grateful for what you are doing for Aaron, Robbie. We both feel terribly responsible for what happened to him.'

'We should have told the others to back off and wait for us,' Ray said, 'but the site seemed so innocuous. We never dreamed anything would happen.'

'Absolutely,' added Emily. 'No climbing, no tunnels, no particularly unsafe buildings, except for the control tower and that was a no-go area because of the damage.'

'If you don't mind me asking, what made you want to explore Randleby Airfield?' Robbie said. 'Marie and I found it a depressingly boring place.' He grinned. 'Oh, apart from Marie discovering an ancient 1930s motorcycle, and then I thought she was going to explode! She's already planning its repatriation to a museum of some kind.'

Robbie noticed Ray glance quickly at Emily.

After a moment's pause, Ray said, 'It puzzled us, Robbie. It didn't add up.'

'Other crews had been there in the past and written it off as a bit of a damp squib,' added Emily, 'a something and a nothing. Well, we went because one of our new kids is into aviation history in a big way, and as he hasn't been exploring for long, we thought Randleby might be of interest to him. It was a pretty simple bimble for them.'

'Including Aaron Smith?' he asked.

'No, Aaron isn't really a novice. He's been going out with us for a couple of years, off and on. He's really into exploration. He's always encouraging others to have a go. Been like it since his schooldays apparently, he just didn't have a group to explore with. It's the other two who are beginners, and I think what happened has scared them off for life.' Emily frowned. 'Shame, because they show all the signs of being good urbexers.'

'You're saying the airfield didn't add up?' Robbie prompted.

'We did some research,' Ray said. 'We always do. You have to gather what information you can before you infiltrate somewhere new.' He laid down his chopsticks. 'The thing is, it's not supposed to be military, but the layout isn't quite right for a small civil airfield either and not only that, there are no records of it anywhere that we can find.'

'We got the same feeling, and we only spent an hour there,' said Robbie. 'And that old bike Marie found was definitely ex-military.'

'As I said, it doesn't make sense.' Ray frowned. 'We believe there is a secret about that place, but we have no idea why or what.'

'Or,' added Emily, 'whether Aaron's disappearance has anything to do with it.'

Robbie thought for a moment. 'I doubt it, Emily. Considering another urbexer had already gone missing — that guy from the Greenborough cinema — I can't believe it's connected to a particular location. Much more likely it's about the explorers themselves.'

'Aaron's no trouble, Robbie,' said Emily. 'He fell out with his family, I believe, but he works hard and he's a nice lad. I cannot imagine him doing anything that would antagonise someone that much, certainly not to the point of abducting or hurting him.'

Stella and Tom had been quiet during this discussion. Now Stella said, 'And Anthony Hood — well, he's a bit of an urbex hero. He's well liked and respected throughout the community.'

'I can't think of a soul who might wish him harm,' added Tom.

'Well, I've got my work cut out, haven't I?' Robbie said.

Stella smiled at him. 'If anyone can get to the bottom of this, Robbie, it's you.'

Robbie felt a surge of affection for his old crewmate. 'I wish you were working this case with me, Stella. I reckon we'd sort it in half the time it'll take me, even with Marie and Max.'

'We have our ears to the ground, Rob, never fear.' Tom grinned at him. 'We're putting out feelers right across the local community — nothing to frighten people, just asking for people to contact us if they hear or see anything untoward while they're exploring.' He looked at Stella. 'Stella has started a closed group on Facebook for some trusted urbex friends.'

'If anything turns up, I'll be on the phone like greased lightning, Rob, don't you worry.' Stella looked just as she had in the old days, when she'd got her teeth into an interesting case, and Robbie felt a pang of nostalgia. They had been so good together . . .

They spent the rest of the evening talking about some of the group's latest adventures, Tom's farm, and Stella's big news about the baby. The only thing marring a perfect evening was the undercurrent of anxiety about the two missing urbexers. Before he left, Robbie asked if they would email him everything they could about Aaron Smith. He wanted to build up a picture of that young man.

'Find out what happened to him, Robbie.' Emily sounded almost desperate. 'I feel so guilty about that kid, and I'm not going to rest easy until we know what happened.'

'I'll find him.' There was no alternative. Robbie had to find him — and Anthony Hood — if he had to march all over every division in the Fenland Constabulary to do it. Fit and healthy young men did not just vanish off the face of the earth.

As he drove home to Saltern, he remembered the piece of glass that Marie had retrieved. Since he hadn't seen Ella tonight, it would be another day before he could get it to her.

Then his thoughts turned to Randleby Airfield. Why was there no mention of the place, anywhere? It was as if it had been wiped off the face of the earth. But why?

* * *

While Robbie was eating Chinese, Marie had been having a very interesting conversation.

Ralph, the Fenchester DS who had been so helpful to her over the Ashcroft inquiry, sounded really pleased to hear from her again. 'The whole station was cheering when we heard the news that Ashcroft had been sent to a Cat A prison. We'd wondered if they'd opt for a secure hospital, but they got it right. He's where he belongs at last. And you, Marie Evans, are a bit of a local hero in this station.'

Marie brushed this aside. 'I don't think your DS Holiday would agree with you.' She told him how he had more or less ordered Robbie to drop his enquiries into the missing lad, Aaron Smith.

'Mick Holiday? That's odd, he's usually a good old boy. Are you sure your DC didn't misunderstand him?' Ralph asked.

'Dead certain, and he was the same with DC Cat Cullen of Greenborough.'

Ralph was silent for a moment. 'Now you come to mention it, he does seem to be acting a bit weird over that case. I offered to pitch in and give him a hand, but my super said it was already "receiving full attention," and I was not required. Didn't think too much of it at the time, but if Mick is trying to dissuade both you and Greenborough from interfering, it makes me wonder what's going on.'

'Do a little digging for me, Ralph, could you?'

'For you, Marie, anything.'

Marie ended the call feeling all the more uneasy about what was going on, but at least they now had an ally.

* * *

Grant Leach and Ron Morley came to a halt in the over-grown driveway and stared up at the fire-ravaged hotel.

'Awesome,' whispered Grant.

'Thought you'd like it,' said Ron.

'And look at that moon! When it's a bit higher in the sky, it will just be above those burnt roof timbers. That could be a fantastic image!' Grant exclaimed.

'Half an hour, I'd say,' said Ron. 'Let's get inside and do a recce, and then come back and get some outside shots.' He pointed to two of the upstairs windows in the undamaged part of the building. 'Listen, I've got a battery lantern and some candles, so why don't I set up a hidden light source, just to give a soft glow coming from those two windows? It would give a contrast to the eeriness of the ruined part.'

'Nice one, Ron. I'll set up my tripod and leave it here, so we know where to shoot from. It's not as if anyone is going to come along and nick it.'

'Good idea. Right, let's find a way in.'

Ron walked ahead while Grant set up the tripod.

He joined Ron beside the building. 'There's a side door that's not secured properly,' said Ron. 'I checked it out the other day, but I only did a quick walk-through. No major hazards in the undamaged side, but the burnt-out area is lethal. I'd not recommend getting anywhere near that lot. It could cave in at any moment.'

'Understood. Well done for getting us here before Cruncher's crew,' Grant said. 'He's going to be well jarred off when he sees our footprints in the dust.'

In seconds they were inside. Tom stopped short and pointed to the floor. 'You mentioned footprints, didn't you? Look.'

Grant grunted. 'Ah. Not quite the virgin site we'd imagined. And they're not yours from your first trip, they're much smaller.'

'A woman's, I'd say.' Ron shrugged. 'Maybe I wasn't the first one to see Cruncher's message and she's beaten us to it. Well, good luck to her, whoever she is.'

'Let's hope she's not a photographer,' Grant said. 'I'd really like to be the first to post photos of this incredible place on the web. It's years since I've seen anywhere so atmospheric.'

'It is, isn't it?' said Ron. 'I suggest we move on and look at the main hall. And you don't want to miss your window of opportunity to get that special exterior shot.'

Grant could already visualise it — one of those once-in-a-lifetime shots.

They wandered around taking picture after picture, and then Ron set up the lights in the windows for Grant's planned outdoor shot. 'You go on ahead,' he said. 'I've just seen a possibility for a great photo using this lighting and looking through to the fire-damaged section. Plus, I'd like to try and get something special with the old camera.'

Grant couldn't wait to get out into the crisp night air. He drew his jacket closer around him and hurried off down the drive. He glanced back at the bright silver moon being chased by dark scudding clouds, forming the perfect backdrop to the brooding remains of the old hotel. 'This'll be epic,' he murmured to himself.

* * *

Ron took a series of shots with his digital camera, all of which pleased him. Then he took up the weighty old SLR camera. It felt good to handle, and he spent longer than he had intended experimenting with it. It must have been thirty minutes before he decided to go and get some exterior shots of his own.

He doused the lights, collected the lantern and candles and made his way back downstairs. He secured the side door, just in case Grant didn't want to go back inside, and headed for the spot his friend had chosen. The tripod was where they had left it, but it stood alone in the driveway.

Ron stopped and looked around. Grant must have moved to another vantage point. But where? There was no sign of him, and no sound of movement. The cloud cover thickened, and for a moment Ron was completely enveloped in darkness.

'Grant?' He called tentatively, then louder. 'Grant? Come on, mate! Where are you?'

This was not how you worked. You didn't deviate from your agreed plans. That was how accidents happened.

'Grant! Where the fuck are you?'

Ron began to grow afraid. It was so still, so silent. Ron had never been a lone explorer — he liked the feeling of camaraderie, the sharing of finds. He never went out alone at night.

He went back to the tripod and stared at it. Why did he have the feeling that Grant had never got as far as setting up his camera?

He tried to think rationally. He knew that Grant had not gone back into the derelict hotel, he would have heard or seen him. So, where was he? Ron took out his phone. They always had them on, set to mute or vibrate.

There was no answer, and his call finally went to voice-mail. He left a message, asking him to ring back at once. Then he texted, repeating the same message. What to do? He supposed he'd better search the grounds, just in case Grant had met with an accident. He could easily have fallen. There could be overgrown debris from the part of the building that had collapsed. There could be all manner of dangers lurking in the undergrowth — twisted metal or rotten wood. Grant could have dropped his phone and been unable to reach it.

Ron set out to hunt for his friend. After half an hour, he gave up. He made his way back to his car, in the faint hope that he'd find Grant waiting for him, but there was no sign of him.

He unlocked the car and climbed into the driver's seat. Then, with a shaking hand, he locked it again. Grant was not a practical joker, this was not some stupid game. Something had happened to him. He recalled the rumours that had been spreading on the urbex sites about a couple of explorers going missing, but he'd dismissed them as attempts to prevent young inexperienced kids taking up the pastime. Now he wished he'd paid them more attention.

What should he do? Should he stay, just in case Grant had been hurt and managed to get himself back to the car? Or should he go for help? But where would he go at this time of night? They were miles from anywhere.

Shivering and frightened, Ron sat for another hour. Then he called 999.

* * *

Cally rang Will Sheringham at half past nine in the evening, sounding almost hysterical. This was not like Cally.

'Slow down, Cally. Take it from the beginning.'

As she told him what had happened to her, his shoulders tightened. This didn't sound good. Cally was accustomed to going out alone at night and didn't spook easily.

'You're sure it was another person in there with you, and not just rats or structural movement?' he asked, well aware of the odd noises a damaged building could make.

'It was footsteps, no question,' said Cally, 'and I'm pretty sure it was a man. It was a firm, heavy tread. Oh, Will, I've gone over and over this, trying to tell myself that I was imagining it, but the fact is, I wasn't alone in that old hotel.'

'You know there have been disappearances lately, don't you Cally?'

'Yes, I've been looking at the sites. One of them is Anthony, isn't it? That's why I'm so worried. I saw a message from another crew saying they were heading there tomorrow. What should I do?'

Will frowned. 'Which crew?'

'Cruncher's clan, I think. I don't know him at all.'

'I do. I think I should warn him, don't you, Cally?'

'Please do, Will. And whoever was in there never followed me out. If they'd wanted to hurt me, they had plenty of opportunity, but they let me walk away.'

'So, if this has any connection with the two previous incidents, there's a good chance he was checking the place out with the intention of taking someone else, not you,' Will suggested.

'That's all I could think,' Cally said miserably. 'I had a close call, but someone else might not be so lucky.'

'Look, Cally, we are working with the police on this. I'm going to pass it on. The detective we are speaking to is a nice bloke, his name is DC Melton. He's not going to make waves about what we do, he just wants to get the person responsible, okay?'

'Give him my mobile number and I'll talk to him too, if it helps.' She paused. 'I've never been so scared, Will, and you know me, I've been exploring for years. I don't do scared.'

Will laughed. 'I know you don't.'

'Sorry, but I didn't know who else to tell.'

'I'm really glad you called, Cally. This could be important. I'll get hold of DC Melton right now. I'll keep you updated.'

As soon as he'd hung up, Will told Lisa what Cally had said. She urged him to call the detective.

'Do it now, Will. He won't mind that it's getting late.'

Robbie Melton answered almost at once, and Will passed on what Cally had said. Robbie took a while to answer. 'Actually, Will, I think this has come a bit late. I've just had a call to go out to a place called East Fleet Manor. Another urbexer has gone missing from a burnt-out hotel.'

'Oh my God!' Will stared at Lisa. 'You don't know who it is, do you, DC Melton?'

'I don't know anything yet, Will, I'm just on my way there now. But I'll need a statement tomorrow, and one from the girl who was in the place last night. I'll be in touch.'

Will ended the call. 'Too late, babe. The police are already on their way to East Fleet Manor. Another explorer has disappeared.'

Lisa closed her eyes. 'Someone really has it in for us, don't they?'

'And until they find him, I'm going to ask you to stay at home, my love. No more trips out until it's safe again.'

For a moment, she seemed about to refuse, then she relented and nodded. 'Okay, sweetheart. I have no wish to get hijacked by some faceless stranger.' She kissed him lightly. 'I'll be good, I promise. Well — for a while, anyway.'

'Good enough.' He took her hand and squeezed it. 'I love you, kid. I'd be worried sick if you went out while this monster was lurking in the shadows.'

'I know, I know, but don't worry, I'm not a fool. This is a nasty situation.' She frowned. 'Should we tell Cally?'

Now there was a question. Cally was already feeling bad about not having mentioned it before, and she would be doubly upset if she thought that her procrastination had meant someone else had been taken. 'Not tonight. She sounded freaked out enough already, without hearing this. I'll ring her tomorrow and warn her that the police will be in touch, and tell her what's happened.'

'And there was me thinking that the police could set a trap tomorrow night when Cruncher went out there, maybe even catch the guy in action.' Lisa sighed. 'But he got there first. I wonder who it was tonight?'

CHAPTER TEN

Robbie saw the blue lights of a patrol car up ahead of him and was glad they had got here first. He didn't know this area and the satnav didn't seem to recognise it. He was pretty sure he would have driven straight past.

He parked just inside the drive and hurried over to where two uniformed officers were talking to a young man.

'This is Ron Morley, DC Melton,' said one of the constables. 'He says that he and his friend were taking photographs of this old ruin by moonlight, and his friend, Grant Leach, has disappeared. We were told that if anything like this occurred, we should get you out to deal with it.' The constable looked at him apologetically. 'No matter what the time.'

'That's right,' Robbie said. 'No problem.' He introduced himself to Ron, who was obviously distraught.

'I didn't believe all that stuff on the web! Oh God, we should never have come out! Where is Grant?'

Robbie tried to sound reassuring. 'Hey, come on. So far there's no indication that anyone has been hurt, so let's take it steady, Ron. I know a fair bit about urban exploring, but I need you to tell me exactly what happened, and how come you two split up, okay?'

Ron took a deep breath. 'I'm sorry, Detective. I just don't understand what's happened to him. When we got here, we realised that the moon rising behind the damaged part of the hotel would make a great photograph. Grant set up his tripod to mark the spot for later, and then we went inside. I was experimenting with an old camera and decided to stay on for a bit, while Grant went out to get his exterior shots.' He bit hard on his bottom lip. 'I got carried away and when I realised that over half an hour had passed, I went outside to see how he was getting on.' He spread his arms wide. 'But he'd gone, just vanished. The tripod was still there, standing where we'd left it.'

Robbie went over the times with him, and then decided to take a look inside the derelict property himself, while uniform searched the grounds.

'I'll show you how we got in, if you like,' said Ron. 'I don't fancy being out here on my own. This has totally spooked me.'

'That would be a help, Ron,' said Robbie. 'And if it's any consolation, I'd feel the same if I were in your shoes.'

Robbie followed the urbexer into the old hotel. He gazed around, and once again felt that thrill of excitement. Stella was going to be pretty surprised when he told her he was beginning to understand the kick she had got from exploring.

He asked Ron about him and Grant. They were really good friends, had been for years. The more Ron talked the more certain Robbie became that something bad had happened to Grant Leach. No way would Grant have pulled a disappearing act on his best mate.

Ron showed him where he had set up his camera for the indoor shots through to the fire-damaged area. 'We never went further than here. Grant took a few shots, then he hurried back out to catch the rising moon.'

'He went back the same way?' asked Robbie.

'Almost certainly. He hadn't been here before, it was me who did the daylight recce, and I'd made him promise not to go through the damaged section. It's far too danger-ous.' Ron gave a short laugh. 'Turns out that's not the only dangerous part.' He stopped and turned to Robbie. 'Has someone abducted him, Officer?'

There was no point in denying it. 'It looks that way, Ron. In truth, we have no idea what has happened, but we'll find out, I promise you.'

'Grant's a good guy.' Ron gasped, and his face took on a look of horror. 'Oh no! What the hell am I going to tell his parents?'

Robbie patted Ron's arm. 'That's our job, mate, not yours. But let's not jump the gun. There's a lot of ground to cover here and it's dark. He didn't know the terrain, did he? There's a chance he's fallen trying to get his shots. If he knocked himself out, he certainly wouldn't be answering his phone.' Robbie didn't believe his words any more than Ron did, but he supposed there was an outside chance that Grant Leach was lying somewhere in the undergrowth. 'Let's get back outside and see if the other officers have found anything.'

They went back to the patrol car. One of the constables, a young copper called Ian, caught up with them. 'There's nothing that we can see, Robbie. But there's a lot of debris when you get closer to the fire-damaged area, and it's far too dangerous to go there in the dark. We've called out and shone our torches into every nook and cranny that we can get near, but neither of us think anyone has been that way for ages. It's too overgrown.'

Robbie thanked him. 'I guess there's little more we can do tonight, but I'm going to get some guys out here at first light. This could be a crime scene.'

'Want us to cordon the entrance off?' asked Ian.

Robbie thought about it. If they taped the area off, someone would have to stay the night, and resources were pretty stretched. He looked back down the drive. The lone tripod stood there in the moonlight, like a sign.

'Yes, go ahead. I'll contact your sergeant and ask him to arrange for you to be relieved in a couple of hours. I don't want anyone going in here before daybreak. If Grant Leach was abducted, there should be signs of a scuffle, and we won't see it with a couple of torches.'

'And me?' asked Ron. 'What should I do?'

'Are you up to coming to the station and making a statement?' Robbie asked. 'I can do it as soon as we get back, so as not to hold you up too much.'

'Sure. I'll follow you.' Ron paused and stared back at the tripod. 'I feel awful walking away, knowing Grant could still be here somewhere.'

'You won't be leaving him alone. These officers will help him if he does make his way back to the entrance, and if he's hurt, they'll have an ambulance out here in no time, okay?' Grant would not be making an appearance that night. The others certainly hadn't. Anthony Hood and Aaron Smith had vanished into thin air, and Robbie was pretty sure that Grant had gone the same way.

He drove back to town, almost relieved. This had happened on their patch and was now Saltern-le-Fen's responsibility. He had a proper investigation to conduct, and any enquiries he made of the other divisions were totally in order. One thing was for sure: he, Robbie Melton, wouldn't be assuming anyone had simply done a runner. He was looking for a very dangerous person who waited in darkened abandoned buildings for urban explorers and took them away.

Robbie shuddered. What for? Why? And were the missing guys even still alive?

* * *

Midnight. Lisa and Will Sheringham were still awake. Will had rung Kelvin Elliot, known as Cruncher, and warned him not to visit East Fleet Manor. Kelvin had been disappointed, but knowing that Will was no scaremonger, accepted his advice.

'And in any case, the place will probably be off limits and have police crawling all over it,' Will had added.

Kelvin had whistled softly. 'This is all getting a bit weird for me, mate. I'm going back to the day job until they find the creep that's doing this.'

'Sounds like a very sensible move, man. If you hear anything on the grapevine, will you let me know? Lisa and I are helping the police as much as we can. We want this to be over.'

Cruncher had agreed wholeheartedly and promised to keep in touch.

Now, after posting warnings on every urbex site they could think of, they sat drinking tea and wondering what more they could do to help.

'I'm a bit worried that some of the crews will go out just to hunt for whoever is stalking urbexers,' said Lisa anxiously.

'Like vigilantes?' Will sipped his tea. 'Yeah, that's possible, though I wouldn't recommend it. We don't even know if it's one person, it could be two or more.'

'My mind keeps going into overdrive, trying to imagine what has happened to our friends. Now there's another one, and we don't even know who it is yet,' Lisa said.

Will felt the same. Other than Cruncher, no one had mentioned going out there. He wondered how it was that Cally had walked away unharmed. Then it struck him. 'Lisa! Whoever it is, they're targeting particular urbexers! That's why Cally was allowed to leave the hotel unharmed. I'm willing to bet that the mystery predator has a list of names, and Cally Prothero wasn't on it!'

Lisa frowned. 'He could have been checking the place out when she went. If he wasn't ready, maybe he just let her go.'

'Lisa, think about it. Cally is slight. She probably weighs less than fifty kilos. She'd be a walk in the park for someone who could spirit away a muscular six-foot male, don't you think?'

'Then you should tell that to DC Robbie Melton.'

'He might well have worked it out for himself, but, yes, first thing tomorrow.' He looked at the clock above the fireplace. 'Right now, we need to get some sleep. We've done all we can tonight, sweetheart. Let's turn in.'

'You're right. I'm drained.'

'Well, at least someone is finally taking us seriously.' Will had liked Robbie Melton. He sensed the policeman understood the urbexers and would give them his support, especially with Stella North behind him. It certainly wasn't always like that. A lot of coppers considered them mindless trespassers with nothing better to do with their lives than make a nuisance. It was refreshing to meet Robbie, and Will had a feeling that if anyone could help them, Robbie could.

* * *

Orac was beginning to realise that all the time spent sitting at a computer had rendered her less fit than she realised. She had always exercised, making sure she went for a run every night, no matter how late it was when she left the lab. She had often sprinted past coppers who saw her every day at work, but in her hooded running top and leggings, she was anonymous. But she hadn't been fully prepared to go into action again, and that was dangerous. 'I need to be better prepared,' she whispered softly to herself. 'My life could depend on it. Suppose I was being hunted down.'

Before settling for the night, she went around the small room and checked that it was as secure as it could be, considering the decrepit state of the place. She had a small battery-powered lantern and a night light and the shutters were tight. She was certain she was on the right track and tomorrow she would know for sure.

Orac unpacked her tiny lightweight gas stove. It was small enough to carry in a pocket and perfect for solo backpackers. She boiled a kettle to make herself some instant soup. In a cold, damp place like this, a hot drink was essential.

Wrapping herself in her thermal sleeping bag, she thought back to the people she had left behind in Saltern-le-Fen. She regretted leaving her small and trusted team without a word, and Marie Evans, though she suspected that clever Marie would have recalled what she had said about her sister and put two and two together. Her "guardians," of course, would go straight to her flat and take her computer — not that they would find anything on it. She hated the thought of faceless officials nosing around in her private space, but it would be a small price to pay if she managed to establish whether her darling little Grainne was still alive. Not that she would be little now. She had been gone for twenty-four years and her sister would be twenty-seven, but the pain of losing her had never abated.

Orac closed her eyes and the image of that cheeky smile and those beautiful dark eyes rose before her. 'I will find you,' she whispered. 'I will.'

CHAPTER ELEVEN

Marie walked into the CID room that morning to be greeted with a chorus of, 'Your phone's ringing!'

She ran to her desk. 'DS Marie Evans. How can I help you?'

'Ralph here, Marie — from Fenchester?'

'Ah, good morning, Ralph. Have you been ferreting around for me?' she asked eagerly.

'Yes, and getting myself a swift reprimand in the process — not your fault.' Ralph lowered his voice. 'Can I have your mobile number, Marie? I'm going to phone you from outside the office.'

She gave him her number. 'This is getting more and more intriguing by the minute.'

'Give me five minutes and I'll ring you back, okay?'

He rang off, leaving Marie staring at the phone. She hadn't meant to get him into trouble, but how come a detective would receive a telling-off for asking about some old disused airfield?

She took off her jacket and sat down. Then there was that old Norton motorbike, the thought of which still haunted her. She had to find out who owned that place and work out a way to rescue that piece of biking history.

'Morning, Sarge.' Robbie and Gary came in together. Gary looked ready for anything after his time out at a refresher course. Robbie looked like shit.

She grinned at him. 'Hot night on the town with the gorgeous Ella, was it?'

'Actually, it was a bloody cold night in a burnt-out hotel looking for another missing urbex warrior.'

Her smile evaporated. 'Another one?'

'Yep. But it's on our patch, Marie. We're official. No more tiptoeing around the other stations, we can tread on whatever feet we like.' Despite the circles under his eyes, Robbie looked elated. 'I managed to see Ella before she left for work this morning. She's taken the glass fragment into the lab for analysis.'

Marie felt much happier knowing they were working in the open at last. Before she could ask who had gone missing, and where, her mobile rang. 'Got to take this, Robbie. Grab yourself a strong coffee and I'll be with you in five.'

'I need one. You?'

She nodded, mouthing, 'Please.'

'Marie, Ralph again. Look, I'm not sure what's going on, but I've been well and truly warned off.'

Marie groaned. 'I'm so sorry. That was definitely not my intention. For heaven's sake, don't get into trouble over this.'

'If someone asks me to drop something and gives me a bloody good reason, all well and good, but to get arsey with me and not tell me why . . . that stinks!' Ralph was evidently well upset. 'I'm not letting this go for one minute. Bugger them!'

'What happened?' she asked.

'Well, I cornered Mick Holiday in the men's toilet. There wasn't anyone else around, so I asked him what the lowdown was on Randleby Airfield. He went all cagey on me, said he'd no idea what I was talking about. I told him that I didn't come down in the last shower, there was something going on. Then he said he'd been told to assure anyone asking questions about that kid's disappearance that he was a runaway, and that no further investigation was necessary.'

'Like he told my colleague, Robbie Melton.'

'Exactly, and DC Cat Cullen.' Ralph paused, drew in a breath. 'Anyway, I'm pretty sure he has no idea what's behind it all. He's a nice bloke most of the time, but he can be a bit of a stickler for the rules. If he's told to do something, he does it, if you get my meaning. Doesn't ask questions. So, he was in the middle of telling me that he did think it had something to do with the airfield itself when the super walks in.'

'And he heard?' asked Marie.

'Just the word "Randleby." Well, he marched me out of that khazi like a dose of salts, straight upstairs.'

'Really? That sounds a bit extreme. All you were doing was asking a mate about an old airfield that a kid had disappeared from.'

'I know. He gave me a long spiel about not stirring up suspicions, and that the family wanted it kept low-key because their son had run away several times before. He also said that there was considerable confusion over the ownership of Randleby Airfield, and that there was some sort of legal battle going on. Frankly, Marie, I didn't believe a word he said!'

Marie frowned. 'Well, you back right off, Ralph. This isn't your problem. I'm really sorry I got you into trouble.'

'Please, it's not a problem, honestly. I've got a good record here, and I think I convinced the super that I was just being curious. I'll keep my head down and my eyes and ears open, and I'll update you as soon as anything else surfaces, okay?'

Marie smiled. Ralph, it seemed, was something of a terrier. 'Just be careful. But there's something you ought to know . . .' She told him there had been another disappearance, but this time on their turf.

'Well, I'm sorry that someone else has gone missing, but glad it's your case. That makes things easier for you, doesn't it? Keep me updated on what you find out, then maybe we can liaise officially?' Ralph said.

'Sure. It helps to know that your senior officers are being so guarded about that airfield. At least we won't wade in and get fobbed off. I'll tread carefully and do as much investigating as I can without involving Fenchester.'

'Better go. Keep in touch, Marie.'

'Will do, Ralph, and keep your head below the parapet!'

Marie dropped her phone back in her pocket. Robbie was approaching, carrying two coffees. 'Gary wants to know what you've got for him to do. The boss is up with the super and he's at a loose end.'

'Until we know different, I suggest we bring him up to speed on our urbex problem — after you've given him the news about Ashcroft, of course.'

'He knows already, Sarge. It was all over HQ while he was on his course. He's as chuffed as we are.' Robbie yawned. 'I'm not quite as good at these back-to-back shifts as I used to be.'

'Did you get any sleep at all?' she asked.

'Catnapped for a couple of hours, if that.'

'Well, I suggest you get off early today and catch up. Jackman will be fine with it. We don't want you nodding off behind the wheel.' Robbie looked far too tired for such a relatively young man. He normally coped pretty easily with weird hours, but today he looked really rough.

'Maybe I'll do just that. Now I'll fill you in on last night's fun and games.' He beckoned to Gary and Max. 'I'll gather the gang, rather than tell it three times.'

When Robbie had finished, Marie asked, 'This Cally Prothero? Have you spoken to her yet?'

'Only to ask her to come in and make a statement.' He glanced at the clock. 'She'll be here soon, sometime around nine. She's very upset, Sarge. She's beating herself up about not reporting it sooner.'

'If she never even saw anyone, and she wasn't supposed to be there in the first place, I don't blame her,' said Max. 'Wasting police time with a ghost story about a creepy old ruin that you were trespassing in, I'd think twice too.'

'Yeah, it's very easy to know what you should have done with hindsight,' added Gary.

'Even so, she sounded pretty shaky. Perhaps you'd lead the interview, Sarge? That gentle Welsh lilt should calm her down.' Robbie grinned. 'Works for me, every time.'

Marie returned the grin. 'What crap, Melton! It scares the pants off some people, I'll have you know! But, yes, I'll lead. If only because you look like you could nod off mid-interview.'

Robbie pulled a face. 'Sorry, I'll brighten up after a couple of coffees.' He turned to Max. 'So, how did you get on with your searches on Anthony Hood and Aaron Smith?'

Max frowned. 'Well, mate, I got a whole load of info, but there doesn't seem to be any connection between the two of them, and both are squeaky clean. Hood, in particular — apart from his love of sneaking into abandoned buildings with a camera — is well liked and comes across as a thoroughly solid bloke.'

'And Smith?' Marie asked, thinking about Ralph's mention of Aaron's parents' past troubles.

'Clean too, Sarge. Not so much as had his collar felt. Looks like he might have played truant from school a few times, but I spoke to one of his teachers and it seems he was just adventurous. Even back then he was always off exploring. He was a bit of a daredevil apparently. The teacher said that on numerous occasions he had to get him out of attic spaces and off the roof.' Max gave a chuckle. 'I reckon the teacher was fond of Aaron. He said there was no malice in him, he was just, as the teacher said, a "venturesome spirit."'

'Which doesn't tally with what Fenchester wants us to believe.' Marie told them about the dressing-down Ralph got when he was heard asking about Aaron and the Randleby Airfield.

'Curiouser and curiouser,' murmured Gary. 'This case is weird, isn't it?'

'Could say that,' grumbled Marie. She looked at Robbie. 'So, what's today's action plan? After the interview, that is?'

'I want to talk to Stella about this latest victim, Grant Leach, and pay another visit to Will and Lisa Sheringham.

Apart from that, I'm going to ask Max to do some covert computer searches on Randleby and get Gary to go out and have a quiet word with the farmers who work the adjacent land. I want that place's story, but I don't want the world to know that we are wandering onto Fenchester's patch.' He looked anxiously at Gary. 'Can you make it a very *casual* enquiry?'

'Maybe I'll start in the local pub, get chatting and see if there's any gossip going round about the missing boy. I'll buy a few drinks and hopefully find a few people to talk to. Leave it with me.'

'Some people have all the luck, Sarge,' said Max. 'Days in a hotel on a cushy course, then he comes back and his first job's in a pub!'

'You're not doing too badly either, our Max,' said Marie. 'Who sat behind a desk in a nice warm office while I was crawling under wire fences and creeping around a stinky old cinema yesterday? Eh?'

'Ah, if you put it like that . . .' Max drew a finger across his lips.

'Sensible lad.' She pointed to the clock. 'Nine o'clock. Shall we go downstairs and see if your urban explorer has arrived, Robbie?'

He drained his cup. 'Ready when you are, Sarge.'

* * *

Robbie was stunned. Cally Prothero was beautiful. She looked as if she should be sashaying down a catwalk rather than picking her way through decaying ruins. He was rather glad that Marie was doing most of the talking, as he'd been rendered speechless.

'Please don't feel bad about what happened last night,' Marie said. 'It wasn't your fault. We're just glad you've chosen to come forward.'

'I don't know,' Cally said. 'If I'd been thinking straight, I would have rung you immediately. I *knew* there was someone else in that hotel, and if I'd taken the rumours of urbexers going missing more seriously, I could have prevented what happened.' She shook her head. 'I'm so sorry. I'm a fool.'

'Just tell us everything you remember, no matter how insignificant it seems. So far, you're the only person who's been able to tell us anything at all,' Marie said gently.

'Well, I did take his car number.'

Robbie found his voice. 'You saw his car?'

'It was an old Vauxhall Astra, DC Melton. I think it was a dark red or maroon colour. It was hard to tell in torchlight.' She handed him a slip of paper with the registration number written on it.

'That is old. Looks like a 1990/91 plate,' said Marie. 'Can't be too many of those knocking around any more. And he'd just left it parked outside?'

'Inside the gates, out of sight of the road. It wasn't there when I arrived, so he must have followed me into the hotel. I'd parked a little way away and walked in, so he probably never saw my vehicle and wasn't expecting me to be there.'

'And you didn't even catch a glimpse of this person, just heard footsteps?' Robbie enquired.

'Just footsteps, and as I told Will Sheringham, I'm certain they were a man's. They were heavy and purposeful.'

'You must have been absolutely terrified,' Marie said.

Cally smiled for the first time. Robbie thought she was probably the most beautiful girl he had ever seen.

'Not really. Well, not initially. As an urban explorer you spend quite a lot of time avoiding other people, like security guards and sometimes, although rarely, police officers.' She grinned. 'Usually it's other urbexers who have infiltrated at the same time, but that's fine. At first, I was more puzzled than anything. I decided to get my shots and then split. After a while, it started to creep me out, so I packed up early and found a fire escape. I did hang around after I got outside, and I took a few exterior shots. That's when I found his car.'

Robbie was amazed at how cool-headed she had been. Most women — men, too — would have freaked out, given the location and the fact that it was night.

'It wasn't until after I'd got home that I started to wonder if I'd had a lucky escape.' Cally opened a document wallet that she had brought in with her. 'Tell me what you think of some of these photographs.' She carefully laid them out on the desk. 'They don't show whoever was in there, but I swear they've caught something of the atmosphere that night.'

Robbie hoped that the ever-pragmatic Marie wouldn't make one of her usual no-nonsense comments, but she laid them all out and looked carefully from one to another.

'*You* took these?' she exclaimed.

Cally nodded. 'Photography is my passion. I'm always looking for that perfect shot.'

'They are amazing. They're so professional, so beautiful . . .' She paused. 'Although . . .'

'You see it too?' said Cally.

'Menace.'

Robbie leaned forward, surprised at Marie's choice of word. Then he saw it for himself.

'You're right,' he said quietly. 'You've captured a sense of fear, haven't you?'

'I'm not sure now whether it came from me, or the situation.' Cally shrugged. 'Then I wondered if I was imagining things.'

'No.' Marie pointed to one. 'That shot has me looking into the shadows, trying to see what might be lurking there. It's quite remarkable, Cally, and as my colleague here will tell you, I'm usually about as down-to-earth as they come.'

This was not completely true. Robbie was aware that Marie's mother, Rhiannon, was meant to have something like second sight, especially regarding her daughter. Even though she denied it, Marie often knew things instinctively. She called it "policeman's nose," and said it came from years of experience, but Robbie wasn't so sure. He believed that she'd been born with it. When he wanted to tease her, he called her the daughter of a Welsh witch.

He picked up the photo that Marie had been referring to. It looked along a corridor and into an open room, which must have been a function room of some sort. What had been the rear wall of the room was a dark, tangled mass of trees and burnt timbers and a sinister night sky. It almost made him shiver. Marie had indeed used the right word. The room oozed menace. Robbie wanted to turn around and run back down that corridor and get as far away from the place as possible.

'Can we copy these, Cally? We'll let you have them back, of course, and they'll only be used for this inquiry, I promise.' Marie was still looking through them.

'Keep these, DS Evans. I printed them for you.' The smile had gone now. 'I feel I need to do whatever I can to help, considering that I should have come forward earlier.'

'Did you know the two lads who went out last night, Cally?' asked Robbie. 'Grant Leach and Ron Morley?'

She shook her head. 'Not well. I met them once. Ron has posted comments and "likes" when I've shared an image on one of our websites, but that's all.'

Marie leaned forward. 'And you always infiltrate and explore on your own? With no company, or back-up in case of emergency?'

'Mostly. I prefer it that way, and I always leave the details of where I'm going with Henry Arnott, a friend who would come out if I needed him.'

'But you didn't phone him the other night?' Marie stated.

Cally sighed. 'I didn't think I needed to. I thought it was just me being spooked. Frankly, DS Evans, I felt stupid. I didn't even tell Henry about what I'd suspected when I sent him a "home safe" text. I told myself I was being foolish.'

'Understandable,' said Robbie. He showed Cally a statement form that he'd been making notes on while they were speaking. 'Now, if you would just read this through, and if you agree with it, sign at the top and bottom.' He looked at her. 'You've been incredibly helpful, and we do appreciate it.'

Cally read the statement carefully. 'That's all correct. Where did you say I should sign?'

Robbie leaned across and pointed. As he did so, he caught a hint of her perfume. He swallowed. He was in a steady relationship — he shouldn't be feeling like this. He sat back, filled with confusion. 'We'll give you our cards, Cally, and please don't hesitate to ring if you remember anything else.'

'Or if you hear something on your network that you think we should know about,' added Marie. 'And, please, assure anyone that we are on your side. We only want to find out what happened to these three missing men, and to keep you all safe. We aren't about to start lecturing you on trespass or anything.' She smiled. 'Well, not this time.' She handed Cally her card. 'Day or night, Cally. I mean it.'

Robbie fished around in his pocket and found one of his own. 'That goes for me too.'

They walked Cally to the front door. As soon as it closed behind her, Marie turned on him. 'Robbie Melton! What was that all about?'

'I . . . I . . . Well . . .' All he found to say was a lame, 'She's very beautiful, isn't she?'

Her eyebrows shot up. 'Should I remind you that you have a perfectly gorgeous girl of your own?'

'Probably not, but—'

'No buts, Detective!' Marie said sternly. 'Jeez! You were practically dribbling!'

Robbie groaned. Marie exploded in peals of laughter. 'Get a grip, Melton! You fall in love far too easily. Now, back to the investigation, if you can recall what it's about?'

She marched off down the corridor. Robbie, trailing in her wake, could hear her chuckling to herself as she went. All he hoped was that Cally Prothero hadn't picked up on it too.

CHAPTER TWELVE

Jackman had just spent over an hour with Ruth Crooke. He'd hurried off to see her, believing that she had more news of Orac. To his surprise, what she wanted to discuss had nothing to do with their missing IT chief.

'The thing is, Rowan, you are not the only one trying to take Kirby off the streets.'

He had frowned. He had been busy drawing together all the loose ends in the case of the money launderer, Bryan Kirby. Another week and he would have enough to pass it to the CPS.

'It appears that your man has been busy, only this time on the streets of London. The Met have been watching him for some time, and they want him for much more serious fraud offences than the ones he's committed here in the fens.' She had looked at him hopefully. 'We have two options, and I'm hoping you'll chose the one I've opted for. We can work with them, giving them complete access to everything we have, and also allowing them to take the lead, or,' she looked at him intently, 'we can hand over everything you have, and give them carte blanche to bring the investigation to a conclusion. They will get the kudos of course, but Kirby will go away for considerably longer.'

Jackman opened his mouth to answer but she hadn't finished. 'Option one will mean having two Met officers temporarily working out of Saltern, with you as their liaison. They are very anxious that our smaller inquiry doesn't jeopardise their chances of getting him for the big stuff. Option two . . . we miss out, shut up shop on the work you've already done, and walk away from it.'

Jackman frowned. 'Bottom line, there's a good chance Kirby goes to prison either way, but if his empire is growing, I'd let the Met have him, Ruth. The more years he gets, the better. I'm not going to be precious about this case. They can have it. Option two is my choice.'

Ruth had nodded. 'Then option two it is. They'll be pleased with that decision, Rowan. As am I. I'll contact them and get the ball rolling.'

They had then begun the process of collating the information Jackman had already accrued, and how he should prepare the reports for handover.

That done, Jackman grinned at her. 'To be honest, Ruth, they're welcome to it. It's been one of the most boring cases I've had in years.'

'Ah, you are getting too used to murder most foul, my friend. Saltern has been home to too many evil souls over the last few years. You should welcome the dull and boring investigations — they're far less dangerous, and equally less vexing to the spirit.'

She was right. 'Probably. And I have to say, not having to look over my shoulder or feel threatened from morning until night has its appeal. The team look positively rejuvenated.'

'I had noticed the lack of haggard expressions, including when I look in the mirror.' Ruth nodded. 'It's like a terrible weight has lifted, and that includes the gold braid. Apart from this concern over Orac, my commanding officers are mightily relieved.' She sighed. 'And that makes my life considerably less stressful.'

'Well, I think a couple of days' work should see me ready to wave goodbye to Mr Bryan Kirby,' Jackman said.

'Will they come here to pick it up, or will everything be sent electronically?'

'You'll get a visit later today I should think, so stay around. They'll tell you what procedure to follow.' She looked across her desk at him. 'Thank you, Rowan. I believe that's the right decision. Now, what have you got lined up next?'

Jackman told her about the young man who'd disappeared from an abandoned building on the outskirts of Saltern. 'I'm going to request complete disclosure, Ruth — from both Greenborough and Fenchester. I want us to have this case.' He looked at her eagerly. 'Sort of a reward, if you like, for giving up Kirby.'

She shrugged. 'Sounds fair enough to me. And since they're little more than missing persons cases to the other two sections, I can't see anyone objecting. Use your usual tact, and I'm sure they'll be glad to hand it over.'

Jackman wasn't quite so certain, but at this point he decided not to mention Fenchester's odd behaviour regarding Randleby Airfield. Clearly, Ruth knew nothing about it. 'Excellent. So, if that's all, Ruth. I'll go and make a start on wrapping up Kirby.'

'Fine. Off you go, and I'll give the Met the good news.'

How nice it was, thought Jackman, to see Ruth Crooke smile again. It hadn't ever happened often, it wasn't her way, but today she must have smiled about four or five times. So, along with losing the Kirby case, things were going well.

* * *

Marie was wondering why a beautiful young woman like Cally Prothero would want to spend her nights alone, exploring dangerous old wrecks of buildings, when she heard a cough — a civilian was standing at her desk. 'DS Evans, a letter has arrived for you.' The young man handed her an envelope with a printed address label.

She stared at the letter, wondering who could be writing to her at work. Though it was a local postmark, she suddenly had a premonition that it had to do with Orac.

116

She tore it open and read the single sheet of paper:

Marie, go to my locker in the IT department. The key is wrapped in a handkerchief in the stationery tray on my workstation. Take what you find there and wait for my call. Orac

She glanced at Jackman's office, but the door was still closed. Okay, she'd tell him later. She folded up the note and pushed it into her pocket. Orac must have posted it just before she left town, so her disappearance had to have been carefully planned, and she hadn't been forced to flee. But why?

The IT department was oddly quiet. A couple of technicians were head down, working in the back office, but there was no sign of Leon, David or Philip, which was fortunate.

Marie went over to Orac's workstation and slid open the top drawer, which was divided into compartments that held pens, staples and other assorted stationery. The small key nestled next to some memory sticks and a pack of AA batteries.

Glancing around to check she wasn't being watched, she took the key, and then made her way to the department rest room.

One wall was lined with six tin lockers. Two were open and empty, so that left four to try. Marie held her breath, hoping no one would come in. She guessed that this was something Orac wanted kept between the two of them.

The second locker opened easily, and she immediately saw exactly what she was supposed to take. The locker was empty save for a cheap mobile phone and a charger. Marie picked it up and pocketed it, hurriedly locked the door again and left the room. No one even looked up as she left the department.

Back in the CID room, she sank down into her chair and let out a sigh of relief. That had gone surprisingly well. Now all she had to do was wait. Easier said than done. She should be concentrating on the missing urbexers, but all she could think about was Orac. Marie glanced up and saw Jackman making his way along the corridor to his office, a smile on his face. She stood up. Apart from needing to tell him about the mobile phone, that smile needed investigating! People rarely emerged from Ruth's office looking so cheerful.

He told her what had been said.

'That's a result, Jackman — the bad guy goes to prison, and you are spared all the paperwork and the court case that would no doubt have dragged on for months.'

'Well, I might have to appear, depending on what they charge him with, but basically, yes, it's a result. The main thing is that Kirby is stopped, and I'm not too worried about who gets to slap the cuffs on him.'

'Generous, sir, very generous.' She grinned at him. 'Although I've an idea your decision might have been swayed by the thought of having two Met detectives camped out in your office for weeks on end. Or am I barking up totally the wrong tree?'

Jackman gave her an angelic smile. 'My decision was entirely altruistic, Marie. How could you possibly think otherwise?'

Marie raised an eyebrow. 'So, I was right. Thought so.' She told him about the more serious matter of Orac and took the mobile phone from her pocket.

'Sit down,' said Jackman. 'This throws a slightly different light on things, doesn't it?'

Marie sat down. 'That's what I thought. We might not have been correct in our assumption that she took off suddenly. To buy a phone and leave it for me to find, then get a letter into the post — it all smacks of forward planning.' She drew in a breath. 'Then again, she could have had some inkling about what was going to happen, and prepared this,' she pointed to the phone, 'just in case she had to move fast.'

'That's possible,' Jackman said. 'Now you're going to be on tenterhooks until the damn thing rings.'

'Too right. I'm already watching it like a hawk! It's not good for the nerves, you know.'

He pushed it across the desk to her. 'Keep it close. She'll contact you when it's safe to do so. Meanwhile, I have Ruth's go-ahead to join in the urbex investigation, so, before I buckle down and start preparing for the Kirby case handover, I'm going to ring both Greenborough and Fenchester and give them the heads-up.'

Marie got to her feet. 'I'm eager to see what our Gary finds out from his pub crawl around the Randleby area. That, and what in Orac's absence our Max has managed to find on the internet about that airfield.'

'That's a point, isn't it?' said Jackman. 'If Orac were here, we'd know every detail in a matter of hours. I'm told her team are now rushed off their feet trying to keep up with everything, so I don't like to ask for their help just yet. As you say, Max is good. Let's hope he can find something.'

An image of that old motorbike rose in her mind like a banner, signalling to her. 'I so need to know who is responsible for that place.'

'And who to ask about a certain old military Norton, or so the grapevine tells me.' The good humour was back.

'Maybe . . .' she said casually.

'I'd say definitely! You get this dreamy look every time you think about it.'

'Well, it's such a waste, sir! I know a bloke who'd give his eyeteeth to have a go at restoring something like that. It belongs somewhere it'll be cherished, not stuck under a bloody bench and rusting into the ground. And that Aviation Centre, the one where they do the Lancaster bomber taxi runs on the runway, I bet they'd bite my hand off for it.'

'Okay, Marie, you win,' said Jackman. 'As soon as I'm through here and have packed Kirby off with the Met boys, I'll do a bit of digging myself and we'll try to salvage your old machine.'

'Oh, there you are then! I'm going to hold you to that, sir!' Even she realised that her Welsh accent had come to the fore, and they both laughed.

As she left the office, it hit her that no one in CID had laughed properly for a very long time. It felt good!

* * *

There were two decent pubs in the Randleby area, but the first had thrown up nothing of interest. In fact, the landlord, who appeared to be having a bad day, was far from helpful. The second, the Golden Compass, was just a mile away from the airfield, and was Gary's best bet.

He went up to the bar and was about to order a drink when a voice called out, 'As I live and breathe! Gary Pritchard!'

He knew the voice immediately, even though he hadn't seen its owner for many years. 'John Beard! Well, I'm blowed! How are you?'

John Beard was tall, with a ruddy face and a mop of curly grey hair. He was dressed for the country, with a wax jacket and sturdy boots. 'It's damned good to see you, Gary. It's been far too long.' He clapped Gary on the shoulder. 'What are you having?'

'Half of best bitter, please, John. Have to take it easy, I'm driving.' And I'm on duty, he added to himself. Still, he needed to look the part and an orange juice wouldn't hack it. 'What are you doing in these parts? Harlan Marsh is your area.'

'It was. Moved here two years back. Nice little village property, half a mile from the pub, what more could you want?'

Better and better, thought Gary. He had met Beard through Gary's late sister. She and John's wife had been good friends and had spent a fair bit of time together, walking their dogs and helping out at the local church. After his sister died and he moved to Saltern-le-Fen, he and John had lost touch.

'Still in the police?' John asked, setting his beer down in front of him.

'For my sins, yes, and I'm really enjoying where I am now.'

'Nowhere could be worse than Harlan Marsh! God, that place was a dump! My wife used to tell me how unhappy you were there. They had a major shake-up, didn't they? And you transferred out?'

Gary nodded. 'I'm with a great team now, the best.'

'Glad to hear it. You're a good copper, you deserve it.' John beamed at him. 'I retired early after my Nancy had a bit of a windfall. She got left an old aunt's place in Surrey. She sold it and we found ourselves quids in, so we decided to move here and live the good life while we can still enjoy it.'

Gary had always liked John Beard and was very happy to meet up with him again, but he did have a job to do. The great thing was, John was totally trustworthy. The man had been a Customs and Excise officer until a car crash had prevented him from doing his job and he'd left and taken a civilian desk job with the police in Fenchester.

Gary sipped his beer and decided to take John into his confidence. There was a chance that this unexpected meeting could turn out to be hugely beneficial to the case, especially given his connection with the Fenchester station.

'Let's sit down,' Gary suggested, pointing to a quiet table in the far corner of the room. He lowered his voice. 'I'm actually on duty, and I think you might be able to help me.'

The glint in John's eyes told Gary that early retirement was already beginning to pall somewhat.

'Okay, mate, spill the beans.'

Gary gave him an abbreviated version of the story. 'We believe that the old airfield has a history that for some reason no one wants the world to know about. We've been warned off by Fenchester station, and so has one of the Fenchester officers.'

'Who would that be?' asked John.

'DS Ralph Enderby. He was trying to assist us and got hauled upstairs.'

'Ralph? Blimey! He's a top bloke, Gary. I can't imagine anyone having to tick him off.'

'And another detective, a chap called Mick Holiday, seems to have been brainwashed into deflecting all enquiries about Randleby Airfield. He's been telling anyone who asks about the missing kid a whole load of bull.' Gary sipped his beer. 'Something isn't right, and I need to find out what that airfield is all about. You live here now, John. Have you heard anything? Any local rumours?'

John was silent for a while. 'Funnily enough, I've been wondering about that place myself. As you know, my work with Customs took me all over, and to all sorts of locations where we suspected smuggling was going on. Randleby wasn't on any of our lists of airstrips, so I was quite shocked to find it a mile from the place I'd just moved to. It seems to be completely unknown.'

Gary leaned closer. 'What do you make of it? Civil or military?'

'Military, without a doubt, but why isn't it on the list of decommissioned sites?' John shook his head. 'I took the dog out there one day, just walked the perimeter, and there were men out there, checking the fences. Now I could be wrong, but they looked "official," if you get my drift. But why be so careful about a place that's not been used for aeons?'

'Why indeed?' said Gary.

'And another thing. I went to a gathering at the parish church over at Scamble — that's a village just a couple of miles away. There was a display in the church of wartime memorabilia and photographs of this area of the fens. Now, I could have been mistaken, but I'd swear I saw the tail of a military plane in one of the old photos. And not only that, there were other pictures of the area where the airfield is, and I'm dead certain the layout has changed.'

'Maybe they sold some of the land off to local farmers after the war?' suggested Gary.

John shook his head. 'No. The thing is, it's not smaller now, it's bigger. What was once an adjacent field is now within the fenced-off perimeter.'

'This is getting odder by the minute,' Gary muttered. 'Do you reckon you could make a few enquiries for me? On the quiet, nothing to get yourself noticed. Maybe a word or two with a few of the older residents who might remember something?'

'Sure, I'll give it a try. I'll start with the historian who put on the photographic display. He's well known for talking the tail off a donkey where local history is concerned.' John laughed. 'It'll cost you a couple of pints, mind you, if I'm to have my ear bent for half an hour.'

'It'll be worth it, mate. I might even throw in some pork scratchings. Now, can I get you another?' Gary asked.

'No thanks, Gary. My Nancy will be expecting me back for lunch. I'll tell her we've met up again, she'll be delighted.' He lowered his voice. 'She was devastated when your sister died, she never really got over it. They were really good friends. Nancy still misses her.'

'She's not alone, believe me. I miss her every day of my life. Give Nancy my best, and here's my number.' He handed John his card.

John Beard took out his mobile and tapped in the number. 'Gotcha. I'll ring you, and then you'll have mine.'

Gary left, feeling that the day had been worthwhile — both for the investigation, and for him. He didn't have a lot of friends outside the team, and John, despite being older, had always been good company, a laugh when you needed one, and a good listener. In Gary's opinion, John would've made a pretty good detective. He had an enquiring mind, a shrewd intelligence and even better, he knew the officers at Fenchester. They might just open up to an old colleague. Yep, it had been a good day.

CHAPTER THIRTEEN

Robbie was just about to call Stella when his desk phone rang.

'It's PC Vanda Rodgers, from East Fleet Manor. PC Ian Little told us that we should contact you directly if we found anything.'

Robbie leaned forward. 'And have you?'

'What appears to be the site of a scuffle. We've cordoned it off, and a SOCO is heading there now. I thought you might like to come over and check it out.'

'Thanks, Vanda, I'm on my way. See you in around fifteen minutes.' Robbie grabbed his jacket from the back of his chair. 'Max! Would you tell the sarge I've had to go over to East Fleet Manor, and would you also ask her to ring Stella and see if we can visit her sometime this afternoon? Oh, and Lisa and Will Sheringham, too.'

'Got it, mate. See you soon.'

* * *

The old hotel no longer seemed so menacing in the bright light of day. As he was locking his car, Robbie saw Vanda waving to him, and he hurried over. Then the SOCO, wearing a blue hooded coverall, looked up too. It was Ella, smiling at him from behind her mask.

For a brief moment he felt guilty, as if he and Cally Prothero had been conducting an affair. Telling himself he was making far too much of a few words with an attractive woman, he smiled at his girlfriend. 'Morning, again! What have we got?'

He stood behind the small square, cordoned off with blue-and-white police tape, while Ella pointed to the ground. 'Two distinct sets of footprints.' She indicated the bushes lining the drive. 'Branches that have been recently broken, and grass that's been trodden underfoot. The frost earlier this morning has left us some nice clear prints.'

Robbie frowned. 'So, the attacker was waiting in the bushes and jumped Grant Leach on his way back to the tripod.'

'Looks that way,' Ella said. 'But I need to know what make of shoes the other explorer was wearing so as to eliminate any footprints he might have left.'

Robbie called Ron Morley. 'Ron? Robbie Melton here. We need the shoes you were wearing last night for forensic examination. Any chance you could drop them at the station today?'

Ron said that he would. 'And I can tell you exactly what shoes Grant was wearing, if it helps. He leaves all his urbex stuff with me, and he always wears one of two identical pairs. They're canvas walking shoes.'

'That's brilliant, Ron. Have you got the other set?'

'Yeah, and they have quite a distinctive tread. I'll bring them with me.'

Robbie repeated what Ron had said to Ella.

'That makes life much easier. If we can identify what the urbexers were wearing, we're left with your abductor.'

'Have you been inside the hotel yet?' Robbie asked.

'Not yet,' she said. 'Creepy old place, isn't it? Is there anything you are looking for in particular?'

Robbie nodded. 'We believe the person who may have taken Grant was in the hotel doing a reconnaissance a few nights ago. Another explorer was here, taking photographs, and she thinks she heard them.' An image of Cally's lithe figure rose into his mind. Robbie dismissed it. 'Er, if you could, we'd like more footprint pictures, so we can eliminate that explorer as well.'

'No problem — as long as there aren't too many different sets.' Ella smiled. 'I'll get onto that as soon as I've finished here.' She looked into his eyes. 'Better get on, Robbie. I'm up to my neck today.'

'And I'd better get back to the station. I need to keep moving on this. This makes three disappearances, and I'm beginning to worry about how many more there'll be.'

'I'll ring you later this afternoon and hopefully get some images to you.'

'We'd really appreciate it, Ella. Oh, and any luck with that piece of glass I gave you earlier?'

'Prof Wilkinson himself is checking it out. He's pretty sure it's a lens from a torch. I'll let you know about that too.' She gave him a smile. 'See you tonight?'

He winked at her. 'For sure.'

What on earth had he been thinking? Ella was gorgeous, and he was lucky to have her. He really should get a grip — even Marie had noticed the way he looked at Cally. If the mess room got a hold of it, they'd have a field day, and then it would get back to Ella. He'd have to get Marie to deal with Cally Prothero in future.

* * *

While Robbie was out, Marie had been liaising with uniform regarding Grant Leach's parents. Though anxious not to alarm them unduly, the team had to be sure that Grant hadn't returned home late the previous night. Like the other missing urbexers, he wasn't answering his phone, and his family were growing more anxious by the hour.

Marie had just rung Stella and arranged to visit her that afternoon, when she saw two men in smart suits being escorted into Jackman's office. The Met obviously hadn't wasted any time in coming to claim the Kirby case. She smiled. Jackman would be delighted, and he wasn't the only one. She looked forward to his input on these strange disappearances. The more she thought about it, the more she believed they had a predator, someone who was targeting urban explorers. Lisa and Will Sheringham were convinced that this was the case. But why?

'Sarge?'

It was Gary Pritchard. 'Hope you can still walk in a straight line,' she said, 'or was it a really good pub crawl?'

'Sober as a judge, and there was only one pub that was any use.' Gary told her about his chance meeting with his old friend John. 'My sister Anne and John's wife Nancy were inseparable, and I trust him. If he can help us, he will.' He frowned. 'That airfield has been bothering him too. He swears it was military. I wonder what's going on there.'

'Maybe Max will be able to tell us more. He's been on the phone for an hour, and I reckon his keyboard is ready to ignite — he's been hammering away on it all morning.'

'Well, I bet he gets nowhere,' said Gary flatly. 'I have a feeling there's some kind of government cover-up to do with that place.'

Marie knew that kind of thing happened, but having visited the place and found it to be a boring, miserable bit of land with a crumbling tower, a few empty and decrepit hangars and stores on it, a cover-up didn't make sense. 'But there's nothing to cover up, Gary. It's just a useless chunk of flat ground.'

'Nevertheless, something about it stinks,' said Gary flatly. 'Why maintain the perimeter fences so carefully if there's nothing there to protect?'

'You're right. All I can think about is that lovely old bike, rotting away under a workbench,' said Marie sadly. 'I need to get it out of there.'

Gary smiled. 'Oh, what it is to have a passion.'

She grinned at him. 'I know, I know. I'm an anorak where bikes are concerned.'

'Like those urban explorers,' said Gary. 'I guess it starts when we're kids. We all have it, don't we, the urge to slip through that hole in the fence, peek through the windows of the local haunted house. I know I was desperately inquisitive as a child. Maybe it never goes away in some people.'

Like Cally Prothero, thought Marie. If you added that childlike curiosity to her determination to capture the perfect photograph, then you had a woman who would happily explore a strange building alone at night. Marie thought of her own love of fast motorcycles. Perhaps they weren't so different after all.

'Blimey! You two look deep in thought,' Max said. 'Where are you both?'

'I'm riding my bike along a moonlit fen lane, thank you,' said Marie.

'And I'm trying to crawl into Mr Watkins's barn without tearing my school trousers,' said Gary wistfully. 'Happy days.'

'Of course.' Max nodded sagely. 'Should I call the men in white coats now or later?'

Marie smiled at him. 'It's alright, Max, we haven't really lost our marbles. Believe it or not, it's loosely related to the case.'

'Very loosely, I'd say.' Max didn't look convinced. 'But if I could drag you back to the real world for a moment, this bloody airfield is a closed book. I've decided I'm wasting precious time on it. If Orac were here it would be different. She has ways and means that aren't available to me.'

'Told you,' said Gary. 'It's a whitewash, a cover-up for some reason, at a very high level.'

'I think you're right,' Max said. 'As soon as Rob gets back, I'll tell him it's a dead end. I need to be working on these people who've gone missing, not chasing rainbows.'

'Agreed,' said Marie. And then the phone rang — the one Orac had left for her.

Marie jumped up, muttering, 'Excuse me, fellas, need to take this,' and hurried out into the corridor.

It was a great relief to hear Orac's voice.

'Are you safe?' asked Marie at once.

'For now, yes, Marie. I'm sorry for all this deception, but I had to go. I hope you understand?'

'Your sister?' chanced Marie.

'My sister, Grainne, yes.'

'Have you found out what happened to her?'

'I have a good idea. Today I met with a woman who remembered everything from back then. She has given me the name of a contact, another woman who could be the key to it all. At least I now know that my dear sister didn't die on that fateful night. She was abducted for a reason.'

She sounded excited, almost elated, which was not like Orac at all. Marie could understand why. 'It's been so long, Orac. I hope you get the news you want but, please, go carefully. Jackman and I know more about you now, and we are terribly concerned for your safety.'

'I knew the risks before I embarked on this, Marie, but thank you for caring.'

'Is there anything we can do? Anything practical?' Marie asked.

'I'll text you if there is, I promise. I have to find my sister, but I will be back,' Orac assured her. 'By the way, does anyone know about the mobile phone?'

'Just Jackman, and I'll need to tell Ruth, but she is behind you on this, all the way.'

'I know. Ruth is a good woman, even if a little terse.' She gave a characteristic dry chuckle.

'That's very true,' Marie said, smiling to herself.

'I have to go, Marie, but I'll be in touch. Feel free to keep Ruth updated, I know it won't go any further. Take care.'

The call ended, leaving Marie almost trembling with relief and desperate to give Jackman the news. She would have to wait until he was free of his Met colleagues before she could do that.

She returned to the CID room and found that Robbie was back, looking pretty cheerful.

'We have clear indications of a scuffle outside the hotel. Ron Morley has just brought in a pair of walking shoes that are identical to the ones Grant was wearing. I've sent them directly to forensics.' He opened the gallery on his phone and showed her the shot of the footprints. The tread had a very distinctive pattern that resembled pointed leaf shapes.

'I've not seen any like that before,' Marie said. 'It will certainly help us to trace Grant's movements.'

'Ella's onto it now, so by this afternoon we'll hopefully have an idea of exactly what occurred.' Robbie flopped down into his chair. 'So, what's been happening while I was out?'

While they were telling him, a civilian brought in a memo.

'DC Melton, uniform traced the vehicle that was seen out at East Fleet Manor. It's registered to a Mr Edward Carter at an address in Hull. The problem is, he died a month ago, apparently, and since he was something of a loner, no one realised that his old car wasn't at his property. Footage from traffic cameras is being checked to try and spot it on the local roads, but the sergeant isn't hopeful.'

Robbie took the memo and thanked the bearer. 'Another dead end.'

'You can bet your bottom dollar that car has already gone through a crusher,' said Gary, 'or it'll be found burnt out somewhere on the fens.'

'I'd still get Humberside Police to check it further,' advised Marie. 'Our stalker might have a connection to this Mr Carter, or to Hull. It's a long shot, but it needs following up. Shall I give them a call?'

Robbie nodded. 'Please, Sarge, if you would.'

'Then it will be time to go and see Stella. I said we'd be there around half two.'

'I'll grab a sandwich and a coffee then.' Robbie looked at the other two. 'Would you both do a search for everything you can find out about Grant Leach?'

'You got it,' said Max. 'It'll make a change from looking for non-existent airfields.'

* * *

He lay back on his bed and concentrated on his breathing. He had been meditating since his late teens as a way to escape the world and calm his thoughts.

He wouldn't be going out tonight. He'd given himself a free day to recoup and get some well-earned rest and relaxation. He had worked out for an hour, taken a shower and was now clearing his mind. Besides physical strength, his task required a cool head. He had known it wouldn't be easy, that the psychological side of it would trouble him most, but he was utterly committed to it.

Finally, his head clear of troublesome thoughts, he sat up slowly. Today, he would set aside all plans, eat well, sleep well and go for a long walk along the sea-bank. Today was his day. Time enough to resume his mission tomorrow. Everything was in place, and God willing, the next operation would go as smoothly as the ones before.

He allowed himself a moment to think of them. He was now over halfway there. Three debts had been settled, and those three irresponsible explorers were safely ensconced in one of the places they had spent their lives trying to infiltrate. Only this time, they weren't getting out.

CHAPTER FOURTEEN

Professor Rory Wilkinson, Home Office pathologist, wore a satisfied smile. 'Result!' he said to himself as he replaced the receiver. 'And I don't feel the slightest bit guilty about pulling strings to get it.'

For some time now, his chief technician, Spike, had been carving a niche for himself as a specialist in forensic ballistics. Trouble was, this threatened to take him away from his beloved fens. Spike had been what Rory called a "slow burner," in other words, he had shown little promise. However, over the last two years, he had turned a corner, making himself practically indispensable to Rory. In the process, he had developed a keen interest in the area of ballistic trauma and gunshot wound trajectory analysis. Rory encouraged him on his chosen path, but at the same time he was reluctant to lose him. The perfect foil for Rory's offbeat sense of humour, Spike had had become a trusted and well-liked colleague.

However, the lab and the morgue needed to function smoothly, and they couldn't do that while his number two was being constantly called away to conferences or seminars. So Rory had requested help, which had arrived in the form of "Cardiff" Erin. Erin Rees had embarked on a career in archaeology, but then changed tack and decided to give forensics a go. This exacting science had soon become her life's work and true passion. Erin was proudly Cardiff-born, prone to expressing herself in Wenglish, a hybrid of English and Welsh, along with Welshisms, phrases only ever heard in Wales. He had taken to her immediately and, more remarkably, she quickly developed an understanding with her unconventional boss.

Now he had the best of both worlds. Spike was to remain in Greenborough, still working at his side when available, and his new protégée, whom he had dubbed "Cardiff," was to be his permanent number two.

Perfect.

'Some boxes have arrived for you, Prof.' One of the lab technicians had his head around the door. 'They're labelled "Personal."'

Rory rarely had anything personal delivered to the morgue so, curious, he went to check them out.

Two sturdy brown cardboard boxes stood on the reception desk. They had been posted in Peterborough and bore no return address. All their lab supplies were delivered by courier or directly from the supply companies. He hadn't ordered anything online. Rory eyed them suspiciously.

Reminding himself that all incoming packages were screened, he lifted one up. It wasn't particularly heavy. With a muttered, 'Here goes,' he opened it up, to find a neatly packed brown paper parcel tied with string. He laid it on the reception desk and untied it.

He found himself staring down at a carefully folded pile of clothes, most definitely a man's, including jacket and shoes — and a bulky Manila envelope. Leaving them on the desk, he called his lab.

'Cardiff? Can you come up to reception immediately, please, and bring a camera, a couple of large paper evidence sheets and some gloves.'

While he waited, he tried to recall what this reminded him of. Then it came to him. It looked like the official return of personal possessions after a death, especially a military one.

Erin Rees appeared and handed him a pair of sterile gloves. 'Prof? What's occurring?'

'I'm not sure, Cardiff, dear. But I have an idea we should proceed with caution. Photos, please. Take the box itself, and this parcel, and then get pictures of every item as I lift it onto the evidence sheets.'

He laid the sheets down on the floor. Then, very carefully, he took each item of clothing and placed it on a sheet. He opened the envelope. It contained a leather belt, a wristwatch, a mobile phone, a small transparent packet containing a single gold ear stud, and a wallet. The last item was a folded sheet of paper. After Cardiff had photographed it, Rory read it out:

'Name: Aaron Smith.
Date of birth: 03/04/2001.
Status: Single.
Address: Little Grebe Cottage, Salt Acre Lane, Fenchester Eaudyke.
Occupation: Trainee engineer with Seymour and Sons of Fenchester.'

Cardiff shook her head. 'Oh dear, that sounds like—'

'I know exactly what it sounds like, Cardiff.' He took his phone from his pocket. 'That's why I'm calling DI Jackman.'

* * *

In just over half an hour, Marie and Gary were at the lab.

'Jackman apologises, Rory, but he's tied up with an investigation handover,' said Marie, staring at the clothes and belongings spread out on the evidence sheets. 'You haven't opened the second box yet?'

Rory tilted his head. 'Left that for you, dear heart. Because I suspect you know exactly what you're going to find, don't you?'

'Anthony Hood,' she said solemnly.

'I thought you'd know. We've already photographed this lot.' Rory indicated the objects on the floor. 'Now I'll get some of my team to start going through them. However, from the scent of lavender that assailed my nostrils when I opened the box, I surmise they've all been laundered and treated to a hefty dose of fabric conditioner.'

'Handy having them delivered directly to the forensic lab, isn't it? I mean, a bit too handy, if you ask me,' said Gary, with a puzzled expression on his face.

Marie had thought the same. Not only that, how did this person know who to send it to, even down to his name?

'If he keeps this up, you'll be getting another one soon, Professor. Effects belonging to Grant Leach.'

'While we get the other box down to the lab,' Rory said, 'you can tell me about this mysterious purveyor of freshly laundered clothes.'

'Actually, Rory, we know nothing at all about this man,' Marie said, 'assuming it is a man, that is. Those clothes indicate a very bleak outlook for the men who went missing. Until now, we had no idea what had happened to them, there was always an outside chance that they had run away or something. But now . . .' Her voice trailed off.

'As you say, the outlook is pretty depressing, but you never know.' Rory patted her shoulder. 'Once, many years ago, a similar thing happened, though I wasn't involved. In that case, the parents of four missing teenagers were sent their children's clothes and other sundry items, and we all feared the worst. However . . .' he paused for effect, 'in fact, they had been kidnapped and recruited into a cult, which forbade everything modern, they were forced to wear simple uniform tunics and pants. All their possessions were returned to their parents, along with a note asking them not to try to find them, that they were happy and were now part of a new "family." All crap, of course — they had been abducted and brainwashed — but luckily we managed to lift enough forensic evidence from their clothes to be able to locate the place where they were being held.'

'I heard about that case, Professor,' said Gary. 'It was over Market Deeping way, wasn't it?'

'That's right. Around fifteen youngsters were finally returned to their families, all thanks to developments in forensic science.' He pulled a face. 'Although I get the feeling that this man won't have left too many traces in his little present.' He set down the unopened box on an examining table. 'Right, let's see what we've got this time. Cardiff! Over here with that camera, please.'

They made their way to the lab, where Rory took his time, cutting through the tape with a scalpel and leaving the rest intact in case any residue had been left on the adhesive. 'Oh, we do love sticky tape,' he crooned. 'It attracts all kinds of remnants, especially skin cells and hairs.' He raised the lid to reveal another brown paper package.

Rory lifted it out and laid it on the table. Denim jeans, a black T-shirt, a hooded sweatshirt with a logo on it, underwear, socks and a many-pocketed gilet. A pair of walking shoes and a bulky Manila envelope rested on top.

The clothes matched those Lisa Sheringham had said Tony Hood was wearing on the night he went missing. 'Would you open the envelope, please?' Marie asked. 'Only I've been told Anthony Hood had a wristwatch of a very particular design — a black skeleton with scarlet hands and a black link strap.'

Rory took out a mobile phone, a signet ring, and an unusual-looking black industrial watch with red hands. He looked at it closely. 'Goes by the name of Weird Ape. A Yorkshire company, I believe — inventive original designs.'

'That's it. That's Anthony's watch.' Marie sighed, despondent. No longer were they investigating a slightly oddball mystery, they were after a killer.

Rory opened the note.

'Name: Anthony Francis Hood.
DOB: 11/07/1993.
Status: Single.

Address: 14 Culpepper Avenue, Fleet Seas End, near Greenborough.
Occupation: Transport manager for the Anglo Plant Company, Greenborough.'

He sniffed the air. 'Lavender again. And all the clothes neat and clean. Ironed as well, by the look of them.' He peered closer. 'Ironed very well, actually. Even I'd be proud of that job. Look at that T-shirt! Not a crease anywhere, other than the folds. If he wasn't clearly deranged, I'd ask him if he was looking for a job. My David's a stickler for immaculate clothes. He'd pay good money for a home help with these skills.'

Marie giggled. Rory was good at lightening the mood. 'I'll ask him when we catch him, shall I?'

'Maybe let's wait and see what he's actually done first. On second thoughts, I'm not sure I'll want him in my utility room wielding my steam iron.'

'Best that way,' added Gary dryly. 'He's probably very strong.'

'Why's that?' asked Rory.

Marie spent the next ten minutes giving Rory the whole story.

'Ah! So that's the glass fragment Ella Jarvis gave me. I see now. And it's all to do with this case that's sending her trotting around taking pictures of decrepit old ruins. She was at some burnt-out hotel this morning, I believe.'

'That's the place young Grant Leach disappeared from last night, Rory. I expect you'll be getting a box of his things in a day or so.' Marie sighed again.

'I'll let you know immediately they arrive. And I'll try and fast-track it for you. I've had a spate of rather sad natural deaths recently that have kept me busy, but hopefully we've seen the last of those for a while, so I'll be able to get back to these more interesting cases.'

As Marie and Gary prepared to leave, Rory said, 'Before you go, I received a message via the ever-efficient grapevine regarding your nemesis, Alistair Ashcroft. My dear one, I cannot tell you how thrilled I am about his new home! For once, justice really did prevail. The culture shock he's probably suffering couldn't happen to a more deserving fellow.' He squeezed her arm. 'You must be feeling so relieved, Marie.'

'Beyond words, Rory. We're all feeling the same way. It's like a massive weight has lifted from our shoulders and we can breathe again.'

'I know what you mean. And after you find Laundry Man, life will be complete.'

On their way back to the station, Gary rang and told Robbie what they had found.

'I've already got a list of what Grant was wearing from Ron Morley,' said Robbie. 'And if Rory gets another delivery, we have a pair of identical shoes, so there will be no difficulty confirming whose clothes they are. Oh, and can you tell Marie I've postponed our visit to Stella until later this afternoon, and Lisa and Will until tomorrow?'

'It's okay, I put the call on speaker. We're only ten minutes away, so we'll fill you in when we get back.' Gary ended the call and sat in silence. Finally, he said, 'Why do that? Why return all their things? And why send them to the forensic laboratory? It doesn't make sense.'

Marie had no answer. It was all so organised. Everything about these disappearances seemed to have been planned in meticulous detail — the men so quickly and silently taken from the abandoned buildings, and culminating in those neatly pressed clothes arriving in tidy bundles. 'You're right, Gary. It doesn't make sense, but it obviously makes perfect sense to whoever is orchestrating these disappearances. This whole thing is being carried out like a military operation.' But what was his motive? 'As soon as Jackman is free of the Kirby case, we need to have a serious brainstorming session.'

'The sooner the better, Sarge. I'm starting to get a bad feeling.'

'You're not the only one, Gary.'

He smiled at her. 'Would one of Gary Pritchard's famous steak and ale pies be of any help? I've got one ready for tonight's dinner, and there's far too much for one.'

Marie returned his smile. 'My hero. There's nothing I'd like more, Gary.'

* * *

Marie had been to Stella and Tom Chalk's converted barn before. It was the perfect setting for the two former urban explorers. They had spent years inside magnificent unusual buildings and now they lived in one, although this one wasn't decaying.

'We are having sleepless nights over this,' Tom said, handing round mugs of tea.

'That's right,' added Stella with a sigh. 'Who on earth would go after urbexers? I mean, they're just inquisitive young people with a taste for history who want to record it before it disappears. They do no harm.'

'Not everyone thinks that way though,' said Marie. 'A whole lot of people, and that includes a lot of police officers, would view them as trespassers and people with no respect for other people's property. They equate them with vandals and graffiti artists, unless they are shown to the contrary. I mean, before I saw all the amazing photos and talked to you guys, it seemed madness to me to go crawling around filthy, dangerous, abandoned buildings.'

Tom laughed. 'Very true, it's a popular misconception. But thinking about reasons, we wondered if it was someone who has chosen urban explorers for no other reason than that they are vulnerable,' suggested Tom. 'They frequent places where few other people go. There is little chance of being caught in a dark uninhabited building, is there?'

'Possibly,' said Robbie, with a glance at Marie.

'It's a thought, alright,' she said, 'but it seems to me that it's too deliberate, plus there was always someone else there when he took his victims.'

'Yes,' said Stella. 'On reflection, we thought the same. It was much more likely that those men were specifically targeted. Have you found any connection at all between them — other than their shared hobby, that is?' Stella obviously had her old copper's hat on.

'Not yet, Stella,' Marie said. 'So far, we haven't had time to delve into Grant Leach's life, but Anthony and Aaron are very different, and we can't find any links between them.'

'We asked Ray Zachara and Emily Butters, and they can't shed any light on it either. They don't think Aaron ever even knew Tony Hood, other than by reputation. They are still talking to other explorers, but nothing has emerged so far.' Stella took a sip of her tea. 'They're still feeling responsible for young Aaron's disappearance. Emily in particular is on a crusade. She's determined to get this guy, whoever he is.'

Marie didn't like the sound of that. 'Try to dissuade her, Stella. She should leave it to us. She could get herself into trouble.'

'Believe me,' Stella said, 'we've both warned her off, but she's not listening.'

'Well, if she tries anything that worries you, tell us, and I'll have a quiet word.' The last thing they needed was a young woman charging in and finding herself in mortal danger.

'Hang on. What if he has a list?' said Tom suddenly. 'It's been bothering me ever since you told Stella that Cally Prothero was in that hotel alone with the stalker and he let her go. Why? Because she wasn't on his list.' He looked from Robbie to Marie.

This was exactly what Marie had been wondering. 'I'm inclined to agree. That's why we are desperately trying to find a link between these guys.'

'But what could they have done to get on his list? There has to be a reason,' said Robbie.

'If it's not connected to who they are, it has to be where — a particular abandoned building that they've all explored, and maybe inadvertently damaged in some way. Some kind of shrine? Somewhere that means something to the stalker, and that they violated in some way?' Stella volunteered.

'Hey, good thinking!' said Robbie enthusiastically. 'That's a new avenue for us to take, isn't it, Marie?'

'It is.' Marie's mind was going into overdrive. 'Just their presence could be enough to send a deranged mind into killing mode.' She paused. 'Do you guys keep diaries of your expeditions?'

'Most do, though often in the form of photo albums. Some we share, others we keep to ourselves. Stella has a massive photo library of her explorations, don't you, sweetheart?'

'Written records too,' she added. 'I'd say it's definitely worth checking their computers and their homes for both of those. That's one of the reasons we do what we do, to record and share, or at least record before those places are destroyed, either by man or nature.'

'So, if we can pinpoint a particular place they have all been to — maybe somewhere not well known — we might just have a lead,' Robbie said excitedly.

'Slow down, Tiger,' said Stella with a grin. 'There are very few lesser-known places left these days. You'll need help from people in the know. We've been out of the loop for a while now, so I'd suggest either Will and Lisa Sheringham or Ray and Emily.'

'But it is a real possibility,' said Robbie, undeterred. 'We'll definitely get some of your urbex friends in on this line of enquiry.'

'I think Lisa and Will are your best bet, Robbie,' said Marie. 'Will lives on the internet, so he probably picks up all the chat about who's going out and where, and Lisa explores all the time.' *And she's not as emotionally involved as Emily,* she thought to herself.

'I agree,' added Stella. 'Talk to Lisa and Will.'

'We'll be seeing them tomorrow. We got held up and it's too late to go today.' Marie checked the time. 'Speaking of which, we should get back. And, Stella? Do your best to warn Emily off, won't you?'

'Of course,' said Stella. 'Although I can't promise it'll do any good. She can be a headstrong little mare.'

* * *

'Stella looks good, doesn't she?' Marie said on the drive back.

'I can't remember when I've seen her so happy — well, not since she was still at work and nicking the bad guys,' Robbie said. 'And Tom's a great bloke. I like him a lot. He's good for Stella, keeps her feet on the ground but doesn't hold her back. Not easy with a vibrant, enthusiastic woman like her.'

'Her injuries are hardly noticeable now,' Marie said. Besides her other injuries, Stella had suffered brain damage. Two bullets had torn into her, one in the head and one in her side. The physical wounds had healed well, but she had been left mentally impaired. Over time, and with the help of her adoring grandmother, Beth, and Beth's partner, Michael, she had got her life back. All that was noticeable now was a slight tremor in her hand, the occasional loss of balance and sometimes of concentration. Her life as she had known it had been blown apart that day. The journey back had been rough but she had pulled through, and now she was both happy *and* pregnant.

Marie dragged her mind back to Tom's suggestion. 'I've been thinking.'

Robbie looked at her expectantly. 'And?'

'If Tom's right about the urbexers finding his special place and him taking revenge on them, that "special place" must have enormous significance for him. So, what could turn an abandoned building into somewhere sacred?'

'Could be anything, I guess,' said Robbie. 'Where he met the love of his life? A place that once belonged to his family? Where he lost his virginity?'

Marie laughed. 'I know that last thing is pretty significant, but even so, I'm not sure it's worth murdering people for!'

'Okay, I'm clutching at straws. What do you think?'

'Something a little darker. What if he wanted to make sure they never went back because he had hidden a body there?'

'Oh right, as dark as that!' Robbie exhaled. 'If it was the final resting place of someone he loved, maybe someone he'd even killed accidentally, then he would be sincerely pissed off if groups of kids started trampling all over it.'

'Or he simply didn't want the body to be discovered and killed the urbexers to save his own skin.' Marie turned this idea over in her mind, and by the time they were parking the car at the station, she had convinced herself that she was right.

CHAPTER FIFTEEN

Orac had expected Summerhayes Court to be an old rambling place, but for a retirement village with a nursing home attached, it was very modern. She found a large single-storey complex, comprising a main block surrounded by neat bungalows and chalets.

She reported to reception and was told that Mrs O'Leary was in one of the smaller chalet homes, number twelve in Cedar Grove.

As she walked across the car park and headed in the direction the receptionist had indicated, she grew increasingly and uncharacteristically nervous. This was the closest she had come to finding out what had happened to her sister after she was taken. There was no guarantee that this woman would be able, or willing, to talk to her, but she was the only lead Orac had. According to her informant, Clodagh O'Leary knew more than anyone about little Grainne's abduction. She had then added, rather enigmatically, that sufficient time had passed for Clodagh to let go of her secrets.

Orla Cracken looked nothing like young Ciara O'Dwyer, as she had been then, but as she stood with her hand on the doorbell, she looked nothing like Orla Cracken either. This woman, wearing denim jeans, a roll-neck sweater and an old

well-worn wax jacket, had dark shoulder-length hair and —
thanks to a new pair of lenses — brown eyes.

Clodagh O'Leary opened the door and stared at her. For
a moment neither woman spoke. Orac had the odd feeling
that Clodagh knew exactly who she was and why she was
there.

'I wonder if you would have the time to talk to me?'
Orac asked without introducing herself.

Clodagh hesitated. Then she held the door open and led
the way into a small, comfortable living area.

This was bizarre. For all Mrs O'Leary knew she could be
selling something — insurance or religion.

She sat in an armchair, one of a matching pair. Clodagh
O'Leary lowered her thin body into the other, exhaled loudly
and said, 'I've always wondered if one day . . .' she paused, 'if
one day someone would come.'

Orac closed her eyes briefly. So she did know! 'Can you
help me find my sister? I've been looking for over twenty
years.' Her voice faltered.

'I don't know if I can, my dear. I have no idea where
she is, but I can tell you what happened. It's time this was
finally shared.'

Orac looked at her, both desperate and full of hope. She
saw a woman who was far too thin, whose hair was red and
wispy and had a flat look to it, as if every drop of moisture
had been leached away. Her clothes were clean but old-fashioned and starting to wear.

The woman crossed herself. 'I didn't want to meet my
God without speaking out. What happened has been weighing heavily on me for some time, and I believe that your coming was ordained.' A faint smile ghosted across her narrow
lips. 'I'll make some tea, shall I?'

'That would be nice.' Orac watched her make it, her
slow deliberate movements, and wondered if she was playing
for time and what she was thinking. Would she feel absolved,
or would she feel all the more guilty for keeping it to herself
for so many years?

Having placed tea, in a china cup and saucer, on a small table in front of her guest, Clodagh sat down again. She winced with pain and Orac realised that she was ill. Maybe that was why she had spoken about meeting her maker.

'First, you have to understand that no malice was intended when that child — your sister — was taken. It was done at a time of terrible confusion and madness, and for a long time no one knew about it.'

Orac leaned forward. 'I want to know everything, all of it, but first, please tell me — is she still alive?'

'Until two years ago when I last saw her, she was very much alive, Miss O'Dwyer. It is Miss O'Dwyer, isn't it?'

'Yes, I'm Ciara.'

'I thought so. There is something about you, although I have no idea what.' She picked up her cup in two shaky hands. 'She looks a little like you.'

Orac wanted to laugh and cry. Grainne was alive! She had Dara to thank for this, the man who had sent her that first lead. As soon as she got back to England, she would contact him. Maybe they could meet up again. They hadn't seen each other for many years but he had never stopped helping her in her search for her sister. *Dara, I'm for ever in your debt. I'll pay you back somehow.*

'It was my sister-in-law who stole your sister from her bed. We believed she was in the psychiatric hospital at Ballydonal, but she had run away. She took the child and passed her off as her own. It seemed she had been planning it for months.'

Orac tried to recall the family, but she had been too young. 'Why was your sister-in-law in a psychiatric hospital, Clodagh?'

The old lady looked down at her hands. 'Her own child died in tragic circumstances, and it sent her over the edge. She refused to believe that the baby was dead.' She shuddered. 'I remember it as if it were yesterday. She was mad with grief. She acted as if the child was still there, making food for her, washing her clean clothes over and over again.

And the conversations she had with the dead girl . . . oh, it turned your stomach and broke your heart.'

Orac tried to take this in. Everyone had assumed it was a man that had taken the child, and subsequently killed her. Orac suspected that even her parents had believed the worst. Only she had refused to give up on Grainne.

'We never knew. You have to believe that, Ciara. We searched for three days, along with every other family in the village. We were truly devastated.' Clodagh's voice trembled. 'Then we got the news that Mairead had disappeared from the hospital and she became the focus of our attention.'

'They didn't notify you immediately?' asked Orac. 'Why not?'

Clodagh gave a sad laugh. 'Things weren't like they are now. Our family was poor, we didn't even have a telephone, Ballydonal Hospital was forty miles away . . . and there was something else too.' She drew in a deep breath. 'My brother had lost his only child. His wife was insane with grief. After she attacked him when he insisted that their beloved little girl was gone for ever, he could take no more. She had been in and out of psychiatric clinics, and the local hospital, but nothing was working. Eventually the doctors sectioned her, and she was taken away. Brendan was advised not to see her for at least a week, maybe longer. He agreed, going so far as to tell them that he didn't want to know anything about Mairead until he chose to visit. He needed time to grieve for his dead daughter.'

'Surely, if she'd run away, they would have told him?'

Clodagh's lips tightened. 'The hospital was under scrutiny. They were terrified that if it became known that one of their patients had escaped, they would be closed down. The notes from the local doctors said that she'd run away before but had always returned after a day or two, so they decided to wait, and cover it up. In their favour, they were aware that Brendan was also in a fragile state. But when three days had passed, they relented and sent a messenger to us with the news.'

'How soon was she found?' asked Orac.

'She wasn't, my dear. My brother never saw her again. My lovely Brendan died a year later, by his own hand.' Now her tears fell freely.

How had none of this become common knowledge? Orac wondered. Or had it, and no one had told the O'Dwyers? She remembered from her childhood, times when people came together and took a vow of silence. On one occasion, a man was shot dead over some issue connected to the Troubles. Everyone in the village knew who the perpetrator was but not a soul spoke out.

Orac let Clodagh cry for a while, and then she gently asked, 'How did you find out what had happened?'

Dabbing her eyes with a tissue, Clodagh went over to a battered old writing desk. 'I received this.'

She retrieved an envelope and handed it to Orac.

'Read it. You may keep it. I'm passing on to you everything I know. The story belongs to you now, Ciara O'Dwyer. Should you ever meet your sister, it will be your decision as to what to do. You see, she has no memory of her early days. She knows nothing of what happened.'

The well-thumbed letter had obviously been read many times, but Orac doubted its full contents had ever been shared with anyone else.

Dearest Clodagh, it began. *Please don't hate me for this. Try to find it in your heart to forgive me.*

Orac struggled to read it. The account was written in graphic detail, as precise as some of the police reports that had come her way. Finally, she folded the letter and said to Clodagh, 'She overcame her mental distress enough to look after Grainne and care for her?'

'The child wanted for nothing. Mairead had an old friend in Dublin, a wealthy man who was in love with her. She went to him for help, and he saw your sister through school and university.'

'And asked no questions?' Orac said.

'He believed she was Mairead's daughter, and that Mairead had fled an abusive marriage. He looked no further.'

Clodagh paused. 'Or maybe he didn't wish to. He had what he'd always wanted, the woman he loved.'

'And meanwhile our family suffered. I'm still suffering to this day. It changed my parents for ever. They resented me and my brothers to such an extent that we left home as soon as we could. Has she no idea what she's done? How many lives she's ruined?'

'*Had* no idea. Mairead is dead, Ciara. We met, just the once. The letter doesn't mention how she changed Grainne's name by deed poll because she wanted to free her daughter from her past. But that is something I must leave with you. As I said, it's your decision.'

'You saw her? Grainne?'

Orac hadn't noticed that Clodagh was holding something besides the letter. She handed it to her.

Orac found herself looking at the photo of a young woman with dark hair and deep blue eyes beneath perfectly arched eyebrows. 'Grainne,' she whispered.

'She's called Louisa now. Louisa Kennedy.'

Orac swallowed hard.

'I saw her three times in all. Once at Mairead's funeral, then twice after that, on the anniversary of her death.' Clodagh sighed. 'It wasn't easy, lying to her, swallowing my words whenever she called Mairead her loving mother. That's why I lost touch with her after she moved on.'

'Mairead died quite young, didn't she? Another suicide?'

'No, cancer.' Clodagh sat back into her chair and shook her head. 'You'll have some soul-searching to do, Ciara. Your sister has forged a life for herself, she is happy, content in the belief that her mother and her benefactor did their very best for her.' She looked at Orac intently. 'I hope you won't make a decision that will hurt your sister.'

Clodagh was right. She did need to examine her conscience. Orac exhaled. 'Nevertheless, I have to find her. After that, I don't know. I don't want to hurt her, but I do believe that some things should not be kept hidden. Secrets and lies fester, and the poison always finds its way to the surface eventually.'

'I'm proof of that,' said the old lady bitterly.

Orac saw that she was growing tired. 'I should go, but there's one last thing, if it's not too much to ask . . .'

Clodagh smiled wearily. 'You want the address in Dublin, don't you? The place where she grew up.'

'Please. Did Mairead tell you anything else that might help me to find Grainne?'

'I will give you the address but I can't help you further. If nothing else, you know she isn't dead.'

Orac wondered how many times she had relived that moment. Waking and finding an empty bed. Searching, calling her name, running to their parents. Mairead had ripped the heart out of her family, destroyed it and left it broken. One of her brothers had taken to drugs. The other went to America and never came back. And Ciara? There was no Ciara after that.

She shook herself and mustered a smile for the old woman. 'Thank you for telling me all this. I can't tell you how relieved I am that my sister is alive and happy.'

They both stood up. Clodagh O'Leary wrote down the Dublin address and handed it to her. 'The man's name is Wilson Flaherty. He's a good man, Ciara.'

'I don't doubt it.' Orac paused at the door. 'Clodagh, if anyone should ask, I was never here. You aren't the only one with secrets. None of this will go any further, and I don't exist. Okay?'

CHAPTER SIXTEEN

By the time Marie got back to the station, she had convinced herself that the young explorers had been killed because of a place they had visited, rather than something they had done. She was very interested to hear what Lisa and Will Sheringham would have to say when she and Robbie met them the following day. It was practically time to go home, and as far as she knew, Jackman had been ensconced in his office the entire day. Then she saw his door open and hands being shook. The two Met detectives were finally taking their leave.

Jackman looked exhausted.

'Done and dusted?' she asked him.

He ran a hand through his hair. 'Plenty of loose ends to tie up, but with the help of Berry, our new office manager, we've pretty well nailed it. I should think there's smoke coming from the photocopier! Bit of a baptism of fire for poor Berry, but she's been a star.' He smiled at her. 'From what they've told me, our friend Kirby could be looking at a very long stretch indeed.'

'Music to my ears,' said Marie. 'Then you can help us with our urbex problem.' She told him about the parcels of clothes that had been delivered to Rory.

'Why on earth do that?' he asked.

'It had a kind of finality to it, rather like what you said about tying up loose ends.'

'It certainly indicates that he has killed them,' said Jackman soberly.

'I said that too,' said Marie, 'but the Prof suggested that they might have been made to ditch all their own things in favour of some kind of uniform, like in a cult.'

'Sadly, I think my idea is going to prove to be the right one,' Jackman said, yawning. 'I'm telling you, I get more tired sitting in an office dealing with paperwork than I ever do racing around chasing villains. I wouldn't want the super's job however much they paid me.'

'Me neither,' said Marie with feeling. 'You look done in. Can I get you a coffee? Then I suggest you go home.'

'Yes to both of those. A coffee would be great while I clear my desk, and then I'm going home to soak in a hot bath.'

'Glad to hear it, boss. Start afresh tomorrow. Let's just hope no one goes missing tonight. Apparently, there's a warning been posted on all the local urbex sites telling people to back off for a while. Stella doesn't think they'll take any notice, but it might deter a few.'

'We can only hope.'

Marie got Jackman's coffee and took it to his office. Turning to go, she said, 'Oh God, I wish Orac was here.'

'That sounded heartfelt, Marie.'

She clicked her tongue. 'I keep thinking that if she were here, she'd be able to work out the connection between our mispers.'

'Have you heard from her again?'

'No, and I can't stop thinking about it, wondering if she's safe. She won't be able to stay under the radar for long, Jackman. The people that are after her are far from stupid.'

'And they have serious resources at their disposal.' He stared into his coffee. 'She's worrying me too, Marie. I can't help thinking of how vulnerable she is with her injury.'

'Me too. If only she were here.' Marie leaned against his desk. 'But in her absence, what do you think about asking Leon and the rest of the team to try and run a search on our missing urbexers? Maybe they can come up with something Max can't. I'm not knocking his computer skills, but they're experts. Orac herself chose them, so they have to be the best.'

Jackman nodded. 'Go and see Leon in the morning. It's certainly worth a try.'

She straightened up. 'Good, I'll do that. Now, I'll let you get on. And anyway, I've got a date.'

Jackman's eyes widened. 'Yeah? Really?'

'With one of Gary's steak and ale pies, actually. So don't be jealous.' She grinned broadly at him.

'Actually, I am jealous! I've sampled those before. Oh well, enjoy.'

'I will. Goodnight, sir. See you tomorrow.'

* * *

Nightfall across the fens. Alone in her flat, Cally Prothero glanced at the window and swore. Normally on a night like this she would be preparing to go out on an exploration. As it was, she was lying on her sofa flicking listlessly through the TV channels and finding nothing to interest her.

She stood up, went to the kitchen and opened the fridge. She had already eaten her supper but boredom always gave her the munchies. She took out a cold quiche and bit into it, hating herself for giving in to temptation. She closed the fridge door quickly.

Her near miss at the hotel had shaken her badly, and young Grant Leach's abduction from the very same place had only compounded it. Now she was angry, as well as scared. Apart from anything else, this maniac had stopped her from doing what she most loved. To make it worse, she had a gem of a place lined up to investigate, and instead, here she was, channel-hopping and fridge-raiding!

153

Cally paced the room. Maybe she should just go out. This strange vendetta against urban explorers had nothing to do with her, did it? It couldn't have, or he would have taken her when he had the chance. No, this was something personal between him and the particular men he'd abducted.

Then she remembered the serious faces of those two detectives. Supposing she ignored their warnings and something happened to her?

What to do?

Her phone rang.

'Jimmy! I'm so glad you called. I'm going quietly nuts here. I feel like I'm under curfew.'

Jimmy Cooke, a Scot, was one of two fellow urbexers who she did occasionally go out with. He was an experienced explorer and a very good photographer. His expeditions usually had her climbing towers or shinning up onto high roofs.

'Well, you probably won't be surprised to hear that Hughie and I have decided not to comply.' He gave a throaty laugh. 'Let's face it, what are the odds of running into this fruitcake? He can't be everywhere at once, can he? And that brings me to the purpose of this call.'

Cally's stomach tightened in anticipation.

'After hearing about your close call, we reckon lightning doesn't strike twice, so you'd be a pretty safe bet to go out with. We've been listening to some interesting stuff on the grapevine—'

'Ah, so this is entirely for your own benefit. You want to take me along as your lucky talisman!'

'Of course!' He laughed again. 'Actually, Cally, we know you pretty well, and Hughie reckoned you might be going stir-crazy but don't fancy going solo until this lunatic has been caught. Is he right?'

Hughie was Jimmy's younger brother, a gentle, quiet lad with an encyclopaedic knowledge of church architecture. Visiting an abandoned or deconsecrated church or chapel with Hughie was an education. 'Shall I get my boots out then?'

'Perfect! Now, we have a couple of suggestions, unless you have somewhere in particular that you're itching to infiltrate?'

For a moment, she hesitated. The place she had been thinking about earlier was supposed to be something really special that she had planned on keeping to herself. On the other hand, it could be ages before she felt like going out alone again. 'Well, as it happens . . .'

'Tell us more!' Jimmy said excitedly.

Cally hoped she wouldn't regret sharing it, but she really wanted to see this place. Plus, she liked and trusted the Cooke brothers, and was grateful to them for asking her.

'I think this could be right up your brother's street,' said Cally. 'But we need to get out to Hallows Fen.'

'What on earth could there be out there, Cal?' Jimmy sounded puzzled.

'Ah. It's one of those droves that wanders off into acres of fields with a scattering of cottages and barns and nothing but long stretches of road between each.'

'So? What's out there to interest us?' Jimmy asked.

'Our final destination appears to be a cluster of old trees.' She paused. 'Until you look closer. You drive across a rickety bridge over a deep water-filled drain and on the other side is an old driveway.'

'And? Stop teasing! Tell us!' Jimmy exclaimed.

'An old church,' she said smugly. 'Part ruined, part intact, and as far as I know, unexplored.' She heard Hughie, listening on speaker, give a whoop of delight. 'The thing is, apart from a few old locals, no one knows it's there. The trees obscure it on one side, and then there's nothing. Even walkers don't use that section of the sea-bank. You wouldn't even see it from a boat, as the sea defences are higher than the fields. It's a gem, lads, an unexplored gem.'

Jimmy whistled softly. 'Speaking of gems, Cally Prothero, you're a diamond.' He hesitated. 'But don't we need to scout it out in daylight? It sounds like we'll need a whole lot of lights if we go tonight. There's no moon and there's heavy cloud cover forecast for the night.'

'The lights shouldn't be a problem. I've researched the farmland, and it's leased. No one lives anywhere near the place, and the trees would mask the lights from the road.' She'd done her homework, believing that she would be alone out there. 'And it's remarkably easy to access. The drive is still intact, any graves must have been removed when the church was deconsecrated, and although you'd need to go careful in the ruined part, the body of the old place has been well protected by the trees. It's perfectly possible to go there at night.'

'Well, from the look on little brother's face, I reckon you should get those boots out right now. Shall we pick you up?'

Cally thankfully switched off the TV. 'Give me thirty minutes — and bring as many powerful torches as you can. We are going exploring!'

* * *

At around ten o'clock, Orac called Marie, who had just got home from Gary's. She was putting her Triumph in the garage when she heard her new phone ring.

'I need to talk, Marie. Is it a bad time?'

Marie heaved a sigh of relief. 'It's perfect, Orac. I was just about to chill out for half an hour before turning in, so I have all the time in the world.'

Orac laughed. 'Just as well.' She paused briefly. 'I found her, Marie. Well, not exactly, but after all these years, I know what happened to my sister.'

'My God! That's wonderful!' She added doubtfully, 'I hope.'

'Oh, it's wonderful, alright.'

Marie went into her tiny conservatory and flopped down into a rattan armchair. 'Tell me everything.'

Orac repeated what Clodagh had told her and emitted a loud sigh. 'Now, I have so many questions going around in my head. I mean, how could Mairead's family allow ours to suffer all those years, knowing that little Grainne hadn't been murdered but taken by a woman deranged by grief over the loss of her own child? It was inhuman. If we had been told, maybe we would still be a family, not a disconnected group of lonely, angry misfits.'

Marie said nothing, not knowing how to respond.

'And now I'm torn apart. I don't know what to do next.'

'I suppose you have two choices: track her down, reassure yourself that she's as happy as your Clodagh says she is, then walk away, or find her and tell her the truth about herself.' Marie was far from certain which of those two options she would choose.

'That is difficult enough, but there's another dilemma. My parents believe I went missing on duty. They really need to be told about Grainne, but how on earth do I go about that, when they believe I'm dead?'

'Good point. And of course, if they think she's still alive, they'll be desperate to see her, talk to her, have her back . . .' Marie sighed. 'And God knows what that would do to your sister's mental health!'

'As I said, so many questions.' Orac sounded on the verge of tears.

'Can I make a suggestion?'

'Oh, please do, Marie.'

'Why not go to Dublin, speak to this man who was her benefactor, tell him you're a friend who has lost touch, and see if you can find her? See your sister in the flesh, but don't attempt to speak with her. Then come home, give yourself time to make a considered decision, and then do whatever you decide to be right.' Marie paused. 'You are far too close to it out there to make a rational decision. And . . . if you don't want to speak to that man, you have your sister's new name, so you can track her electronically. If anyone can find her, you can. But first, come home to Saltern-le-Fen.'

'Wise words, Marie. I'll sleep on them and ring you again tomorrow. I have to move away from here in any case. I'm not certain, but there might be someone watching me. I'm safe for tonight — I wasn't followed here — but I need to get well away by morning.'

Marie grew frightened again. 'Come home, Orac, please?'

'Don't worry, my dear, we'll talk tomorrow, I promise. And thank you for listening. I appreciate it.'

'I'm always here, anytime, day or night. Just stay safe, and for God's sake get yourself back where you belong!'

Marie lay awake for a long time that night, pondering the decision that Orac had to make. On the surface, the most wonderful thing had happened — her sister was alive and well, and to all intents and purposes, a happy, well-balanced woman. But, whatever Orac chose to do, someone would get hurt. Marie believed in speaking the truth, but what if that truth damaged someone? Do you steal someone's faith in the mother who loved and cherished them? Do you destroy their precious memories? Or do you let them live a lie?

Tossing and turning, Marie began to think that there were no perfect answers. It would all boil down to what Orac's conscience determined.

She hadn't asked Orac where she was, because Orac couldn't tell her. It would be too risky. Marie's heart went out to her, alone somewhere, and confused, not knowing the right thing to do. And on top of all that, someone might be watching her.

CHAPTER SEVENTEEN

Hallows Fen was a nowhere place. There was no village, no signpost, no visible boundaries, just fields and ditches and dykes and the occasional cluster of windblown trees, weathered barn or rundown cottage. It gave new meaning to the word "bleak."

'Not quite a tourist attraction, is it?' commented Hughie, as they drove across the endless dark fields.

'You may not believe it, but it's even worse in daylight,' said Cally. 'At night you can imagine that there're other things out here that you just can't see. In the daytime, it's all out in the open, a big expanse of nothing.'

'Except a possibly virgin exploration site,' said Jimmy. 'How long ago did you find this place?'

Cally thought about it. 'Probably around four weeks ago. I'd already found the hotel at Fleet Seas End and decided that it was more likely to be discovered by other explorers, so I researched that first.'

'How come you find all these fresh sites?' asked Jimmy. 'I thought we'd well exhausted this area and then you turn up two, one after the other!'

'I'm just nosey, I guess.' She smiled. 'And I have a knack for finding things by accident. Both these sites were the result of either getting lost or ending up somewhere by mistake.' She stared ahead into the darkness. 'Slow down a bit, Jimmy, we're almost there.'

In minutes, they were crunching their way slowly down the overgrown drive to the church.

'I see what you mean about being well concealed from the road.' Hughie looked at the surrounding trees illuminated in the headlights. 'Although I'd have noticed these old trees — they have always featured in churchyards. Still are. Look — that beautiful old yew must be really old. And as the draining of the fens was begun back in the 1500s but only really implemented in 1631, the church would have been built when the first habitable village emerged around that time.'

'Oh Lord! He's off!' grumbled Jimmy. 'Professor Hughie takes the floor.'

'Piss off,' said his brother amiably. 'This is exciting.'

'Right, let's get organised.' Cally stepped out of the car into the cold night air. A wind was blowing in off the Wash and she shivered. Now it came to it, she was very relieved not to have attempted this bimble alone. Having the lads with her made it so much more enjoyable. Even so, she had adhered to her normal routine and had rung Henry Arnott to let him know where she was going. He surprised her by saying that he knew the place. He had been there many years ago while he was working for the local council as a surveyor. If anything went wrong, Henry would know where they were.

They took all their gear from the car boot and headed off towards a set of rusted wrought-iron gates and a dilapidated lych-gate. The place looked eerie in torchlight, like somewhere from *Tales from the Crypt*.

Jimmy started making soft 'woo-woo' noises, trying to be either a ghost or an owl. Not very convincing.

Then they saw the church.

'Oh my!' breathed Hughie. 'I was wrong! This is much, much, older!'

'How come, when this is supposed to be reclaimed land?' asked Cally.

'Oh, there are hundreds of really old churches right across the county. There were settlements on slightly higher "islands" that remained dry when the lower marshy areas of the fenlands flooded. The church at Algarkirk, close to the Wash, is twelfth century. Lincolnshire has the finest collection of medieval churches in the country. Travellers used to navigate the flat landscape by the different church spires and towers.' He stared up at the old church. 'This would have been a lovely old church. I wonder what happened to it.'

Part of it, mostly one end of the nave and the chancel, was in ruins, but the tower, a two-tier construction, was intact. 'It wasn't very clear,' said Cally, 'but I think this area took several hits during the Second World War.'

'That's quite possible. They did target the docks and the port on this part of the east coast,' said Jimmy. 'Which is not far along the Wash from here, and they used to dump their remaining bombs if a mission didn't go to plan, or if they'd taken a hit and had to limp home.'

'This place is a bit like that hotel, East Fleet Manor. It's in two halves. There it was fire damage, here it looks like a bomb, but in both cases, some of the structure still stands.' The similarity between the two brought back some of the fear she had experienced in the old hotel.

'I can't wait to see inside,' said Hughie eagerly.

'Then let's go.' Jimmy started forward, then stopped. 'You lead the way, Cally. It's your place.'

He squeezed her arm. Hughie was right, this was exciting. She wasn't going to let one bad experience ruin all her other explores.

'Okay, follow me. There's a door at the back that has rotted, and the lock and latch have fallen off. We turn right inside, or we finish up in the ruin, and that's too dangerous. We want to see the two remaining side chapels and the tower.' Cally stepped forward. 'There is remarkably little overgrowth on the pathway so it's pretty easy to navigate, but the trees around the tower are massive and there are one or two of the branches down, so watch your step.'

Soon they were inside.

Hughie directed the beam of his powerful torch around the ceiling and sighed with delight. 'Beautiful, just beautiful.'

'What's left of it,' said Jimmy, down to earth as ever.

Some lovely plasterwork remained, some decorative ribs and bosses, but sadly much had been lost. 'The chapels are intact,' Cally said, 'and it looks like the tower has survived remarkably well.'

Jimmy looked first at the part that was in ruins, and then back. 'The font looks as if it's waiting for the next baby. Now that's really nice.'

'Let's get some pictures,' said Hughie. 'There are some glorious shots just waiting to be taken. I mean, look at that statue of Christ! It's perfect, silhouetted against all that bomb damage. It's really evocative. Could be a winner of an image.'

Cally had already seen it. She'd got her camera out and was wondering how best to set up some lighting. 'What if we up-lit it? Put a light source below it, shining upwards but out of the picture?'

They all had a variety of torches with them, along with battery-powered searchlights and LED construction lamps for floodlighting.

'Yeah, good idea, Cally, and maybe do a really low-lit one with just candles all around the base. That would empha- sise the religious feel of it.' Hughie grinned at her. 'Let's play!'

Cally pulled a lamp from her rucksack. It was great to have these two with her. For a while, especially after her ses- sion in that interview room with the two detectives, she had wondered if she would ever go out again. Thank heavens Jimmy had called her.

They got several shots that they both had high hopes for. Cally was itching to see them on the computer screen. One in particular had amazing contrast of light and shadow, and could be Hughie's predicted "winner of an image."

'I'm just going to see if the tower is accessible,' called out Jimmy from the font area. 'The stairs probably go up from behind this door.'

'Wait for us,' called Cally. 'Best not to go alone, it could be dangerous. I didn't check that out when I came before. I think the door was either locked or jammed.'

She picked up her torches and the LED lamp and went down to where Jimmy was trying the heavy old wooden door.

'It's just stiff, I think. There's no key in the lock, and . . .' He stopped. 'Well, if you didn't open it, someone else certainly has. Look.' He pointed to a curved mark in the dirt on the floor where the door had swung back and scraped across the stone slabs.

Cally thought back to when she had come here in the daylight. There had been no footprints and certainly no scuff marks on the floor. This was recent.

'No matter,' said Hughie optimistically. 'Even if another clan have been here, I bet our pictures will knock spots off theirs, eh, Cally? I swear we've got a couple of gems with that statue.'

Cally began to feel apprehensive. She told herself that Hughie was probably right about it being another group of urbexers, but what if it wasn't?

'Happens all the time, doesn't it?' said Jimmy. 'The main thing is that we've never seen this place before, and it's pretty awesome. If I can get up the tower, I'll be as happy as a pig in shit, believe me!'

She laughed. 'Pig in *chiffon*.'

'Please yourself, but I know which one the pig would prefer!' He lifted and pulled, and the door swung back.

In front of them was a flight of spiral stone steps, their surface indented and worn away by the countless feet that had trudged up there over hundreds of years.

She wasn't a great fan of heights, in fact she preferred underground spaces, but she wasn't going to let a fellow urbexer go off alone when they hadn't done a recce in daylight. She followed him up the stairs.

Jimmy was light on his feet and took the steps rapidly. Cally was more cautious. She could hear Hughie behind her, which was slightly reassuring, but she couldn't help wondering if the previous visitor had been the man who had abducted the other urbexers.

As she climbed, she started to make unpleasant connections in her mind.

He had been at East Fleet Manor the night she had gone there. He returned the next night and took one of the other explorers. What if he had been here in Hallows Fen Church last night? Did that mean he was planning on taking one of *them* tonight? Her mouth went dry.

'Jimmy! Hughie! I'm not sure we should go up there! This doesn't feel right!' She tried to keep the panic out of her voice, but she wasn't being very successful.

'It's okay, Cally,' called back Jimmy. 'I'm just about to go into the bell-ringers' loft. I'm sure there's no one in there, so relax.'

'And I'm right behind,' called up Hughie. 'No one's following me. And for future reference, bro, it's called a ringing chamber, not a bloody loft.'

His banter calmed Cally somewhat. She was starting to understand that she had been more deeply disturbed by her encounter with the stalker than she'd realised.

She reached the top step and went into the stone chamber, with Hughie a few steps behind her.

'Can't wait to see the chamber,' Hughie panted. 'Those rooms are so cool. You often find fascinating memorabilia left by ringers of long ago. They used to have rhymes, or sometimes you find lists of the captains, the head bell-ringers, from centuries gone by.'

'Jesus! This place stinks!' called out Jimmy. 'Must be dead rats or something. Hold your noses when you come in.'

Cally and Hughie went in together.

'Agh! That's terrible!' gasped Hughie. He shone his torch across the floor. 'And what's all that muck where the ringers would have stood?'

Trying not to gag, Cally looked and saw a mess of dark liquid and some sort of glutinous substance covering the central area of the small tower room.

'Maybe some big bird of prey got trapped in here and died,' said Jimmy. 'I wanted to get to the top of the tower, but I'm sure not walking across that lot.'

Cally began to retch. 'I have to go down again. Sorry, boys, but this is gross.'

'Let's just see if the bells are still *in situ*,' said Hughie, 'then we'll all get out of here.'

They all shone their torches up into the tower where the bell-frames were housed.

Cally screamed.

The shock of what she saw kept her riveted to the spot, and although all she wanted to do was run, she could not drag her eyes from the scene above.

Three bell ropes still dangled loosely into the chamber, but high above them on the remaining ones swung three decaying bodies.

'Oh my God!' Jimmy took charge, shepherding Cally and Hughie back through the door to the spiral staircase. 'Out of here! Now! But don't panic, or you might fall. Just get back down the stairs as carefully as possible.'

They needed no second telling. Hughie went first, making sure that Cally was close behind him, then Jimmy closed the door on the nightmare scene and followed them.

At the bottom of the staircase, they paused to get their breath back and take a lungful of cleaner air. Then they grabbed their things and ran from the church.

'We get away from here,' called out Jimmy, fumbling with the car keys, 'as fast as possible, then we call the police.'

They threw their equipment into the car and clambered in.

'Just go!' said Hughie, his voice shaking.

Cally was silent, certain that the picture burnt into her memory would never go away. Three bodies, all suspended upside down, secured to the bell rope by one leg. In the torchlight it had seemed as if they were swaying grotesquely, arms hanging down, dead hands reaching out towards her.

'You okay, Cally?' Hughie put an arm around her.

She wasn't. But she couldn't tell him. She couldn't say anything.

'Jim, she's in shock! I'm calling an ambulance.'

She heard him clearly enough but was unable to respond. It felt as if she were trapped back in that room, in the darkness and the stench and the silence. She felt the car pull to a halt and heard Hughie talking to the emergency services, asking for both police and an ambulance, and as quickly as possible.

Mmm, she thought vaguely. *Probably a good idea.*

CHAPTER EIGHTEEN

Navigating the hazardous fen lanes towards little-known Hallows Fen, Jackman saw a single rear light some way ahead of him and smiled. *Marie.* She would be in her element. She loved night riding, the more difficult the better. Lanes like these were bad enough in daylight, but Marie, on her Triumph Tiger, took every bend and curve with all the skill of an accomplished rider. It frightened the hell out of him, but she revelled in it.

The call had come in at around midnight, and they had little idea of what they'd find at the scene. The only solid fact was that three urbexers had defied the warning to stay away from abandoned buildings and had been badly frightened. Apparently one of them was in a bad way, so whatever had happened must have been traumatic. The young man who phoned it in had been almost sobbing. He kept talking about bodies, hung up somewhere. "Bodies," he had said, not "a body."

Jackman slowed to negotiate a sudden double bend, then pulled away onto the long straight stretch of road that led to Hallows Fen. He had been here only once before — it was that kind of place. He had been on traffic duty, during his days in uniform, and had been chasing a joyrider in a stolen car. The young driver had made the mistake of swinging off the main road thinking he could lose the police on the back doubles, unaware that the road to Hallows Fen led to a dead end. It nearly had been a dead end too, as the kid had lost control of the car and spun off the lane into a deep drainage ditch. Jackman had pulled him out, unconscious, while the stolen car slowly filled with muddy water.

Ahead he saw a small collection of flashing blue lights, the single brake light came on and the motorcycle pulled off the road.

Jackman frowned. He didn't recall having seen any buildings on his one and only visit to this desolate spot. He pulled in behind a police car and an ambulance and got out.

He saw Marie, wearing full leathers, carrying her helmet under her arm and toting a small backpack over her shoulder. Behind her were two uniformed officers and a paramedic, all talking to two young men. From the way they were dressed, Jackman knew that these were the urban explorers. So where was the third?

'Evening, sir. Or should I say morning?'

Marie sounded remarkably bright. He gave her a wry smile. 'Another rude awakening, eh? So, what have we got?'

'Three urbexers, or whatever you call them, were exploring an old church, just up ahead. According to them, they've made a rather unpleasant discovery, but uniform have waited for us before going in.'

'Thoughtful of them,' muttered Jackman.

'If what these kids say is true, we have a major crime scene, sir,' Marie said. 'Possibly three dead.' She raised an eyebrow.

His heart sank. 'Ah, and we have three missing explorers, don't we?'

'Exactly. That's why our presence was requested, and why they waited for us.'

In the harsh lights of the vehicles, the two young men looked like pale ghosts. 'Where's the third?'

Marie pulled a face. 'The third one, sir, is Cally Prothero. I don't know if you remember, but she was the woman who came forward after being followed at that ruined hotel — East Fleet Manor.'

'The third abduction site?' asked Jackman, who was out of the loop, having been occupied with the Kirby case.

'That's right, boss. She's in deep shock. Whatever they saw, it scared the shit out of her! She's not speaking, hasn't spoken since they found the bodies apparently, and the medics are getting ready to take her to Greenborough General.'

'Not Saltern?'

'They are really worried about her, sir. Greenborough has better facilities for psychiatric care — including an excellent on-call psychologist, as I recall?'

'Laura.'

'Laura. I suspect you won't be the only occupant of Mill Corner whose sleep is disturbed tonight. Well, I guess we shouldn't hang around. Ready?'

He hoped so. After everything he'd seen of late, he had been looking forward to slightly less traumatic times. But it seemed that wasn't to be.

Soon they were making their way down an old weed-covered gravel drive. They found themselves staring into a thick cluster of giant trees, lit up in the beam of their torches. A single police vehicle was parked in front of a dilapidated lych-gate. Jackman frowned. 'So, where's the bloody church?'

One of the constables, carrying a powerful flashlight, came towards them. 'Let me go ahead, sir, I've got a better torch. Lizzie's just fetching a couple of halogen lamps from the car. We've taken a brief look at the entry point, but not having coveralls, we didn't want to compromise the scene.'

'It could be nothing, even some sort of scam, but looking at the faces of those two urbexers, I fear the worst. What do you think, Marie?'

'Me too,' she said. She reached inside her backpack and produced two plastic bags. 'I brought these, just in case.' She handed him a protective coverall. 'Or we can wait for a SOCO?'

He took a package and tore it open. 'No time like the present and, frankly, this is our responsibility.'

They followed the constable further along the drive and around the dark brooding church to the back door. Then, in their "zoot suits" and shoe-covers and two powerful lamps, they went in.

'You'd think we'd be used to this by now, wouldn't you?' whispered Marie.

'Not me,' Jackman said grimly. 'Every time, I try to prepare myself. And then we walk into something totally unimaginable.'

'Maybe that won't be the case this time.'

This was said without much conviction. Both were thinking of Cally Prothero, a seasoned explorer who wasn't afraid to enter abandoned buildings alone at night, now crouched in the back of an ambulance, unable to utter a word.

Jackman went first. He was only halfway up when the smell hit him. It was unmistakable. He stepped inside the bell-ringers' chamber and steeled himself. He switched on the powerful light, gazed up into the illuminated area, and froze. His initial reaction was to stop Marie from entering, but he was too late. She was already at his shoulder. He felt her stiffen, then step back. Now he knew why Cally Prothero was in the state she was.

Marie laid a hand on his arm.

Jackman cleared his throat. 'I suppose we should try to make some kind of sense of what we're looking at.'

'The work of a bloody maniac is all that comes to mind right now,' Marie said through gritted teeth. 'Hard to see past that, isn't it? God, that stench!' She coughed, and said in a monotone, 'Three bodies, each suspended by their left ankle from bell ropes. One, er, one appears to have been here considerably longer than the others, one not quite as long, and one very recent.'

'Little doubt we are looking at our missing explorers, is there?' Jackman said. 'Hard to tell from down here, but they all appear to be male.'

'And all dressed in the same outfit.' Marie squinted. 'I wonder why, what that means?'

Jackman had noticed it too, but what it meant could be dealt with later. 'We've seen enough, Marie. It's time to ring it in. We need everything we can get with this one — forensics, the fire service to get them down and a truckful of coppers to secure the site.'

'I just hope everyone involved has a bloody strong stomach!' Marie added. 'This is beyond madness.'

Jackman swung the halogen beam away from the three dead men, committing them back to the dark. 'Let's go. We need to get those poor sods out of this hellhole as soon as possible.'

Making his way back down the spiral staircase, Jackman mused on the awful sights the police confronted almost daily in the course of their working lives: horrific road traffic accidents, drownings, drug overdoses, burnt bodies . . . the list was endless. You could cope with those — life was tough and such things happened. But cruelty, torture deliberately inflicted on another human being, that was horror of a different order. How did you cope then?

The relief at being out of there, breathing in cold, fresh night air, was incredible. The two constables waiting outside looked into their faces and made no comment. They didn't need to.

Finally, the constable called Lizzie said quietly, 'We'll organise setting up a crime-scene log, sir. You'll be arranging everything else?'

Jackman nodded. 'And, Lizzie, no one at all is to set foot in there until I say so. Is that understood?'

'Completely, sir. We'll get our side under way immediately.'

He was glad she hadn't asked any questions. He glanced at Marie. 'You okay?'

She rolled her eyes. 'Just when I thought Saltern-le-Fen had finally got back to normal, this happens! I'm beginning to wonder what "normal" is.'

He sighed. 'Wouldn't it be nice to get a simple crime of passion — husband finds wife in arms of other man and flips — or a drug dealer that gets taken out by someone he short-changed. Something straightforward, you know.'

'And something that doesn't tattoo your brain with horrifying images.' She echoed his sigh. 'I'm thinking of those kids who walked in on this, totally unprepared. They're going to need professional help — all of them, not just Cally. I know what I feel like, and I'm an experienced copper.'

Glad to be putting that ruined tower behind them for a while, they walked quickly back towards the vehicles. 'I'll set the wheels in motion for this circus, Marie. Would you go and talk to the two lads? Maybe try to gauge how they're reacting?'

'Of course,' said Marie. 'And I'll make sure they understand the importance of accepting as much help as they can get at this early stage. I know what macho young men can be like, but I'll get the point across.'

In her boots and motorcycle leathers, Marie certainly looked persuasive. If this Amazon told you black was white, you'd seriously consider the possibility!

Jackman watched Marie settle the two young men in the back of the patrol car, and then returned to his own vehicle to set the official wheels in motion. He must inform the super but would get all the basic practical stuff out of the way first, which would take a while. The least he could do was let Ruth have another hour's rest before he dropped this one in her lap.

* * *

Stella had not been sleeping well. It might have been something to do with her pregnancy, but she guessed it was more likely to be worry over the missing urbexers. At two in the morning, she got up and went down to the kitchen to make tea. As she waited for the kettle to boil, she tried to fathom why on earth anyone would bear a grudge against urban exploration. It didn't make sense. They weren't vandals, it was they who cared! They cared about the fading past, the beautiful buildings left to rot, their history and all the things they had meant to people in their day. All they did was take photographs to preserve what would soon be lost. Where was the harm in that?

'Can't sleep again, sweetheart?' Tom was standing in the doorway, pulling his dressing gown around him and yawning.

'Oh, I'm so sorry, Tom. I didn't mean to wake you — you have to get up so early. Go back to bed.'

'And miss the chance of a brew? No way.' He sat down opposite her. 'To be honest, I'm not sleeping well either. I keep thinking about the disappearances. I feel so helpless, knowing that I can't come up with some valid explanation for them.'

'Me too, babe. And maybe because of all my years in the police, and some of the things I saw, I have a terrible feeling this is going to end badly.' Stella took two mugs from the cupboard. 'I feel helpless too.'

Tom sighed. 'What worries me is how many more kids are going to go missing before the police find this maniac? That's not meant to be disrespectful to your mate, Robbie, or the police. But where do you start when you have no known motive and no clue as to where he'll strike next?'

'Oh, they'll get him, sweetheart. I have no doubt about that. The killer will either make a mistake, or they'll find some piece of evidence, or maybe a witness will come forward. And Robbie won't let this one drop, believe me. He's a damned good detective, and the team he is with now are the best.' She placed a mug of tea in front of her husband. 'But you're right. How many more will he attack before he's taken down?'

'I keep wanting to ring all our friends, just to make sure they're safe, but I can't keep bothering them. They've been warned off, so hopefully they'll have the sense to stay away from exploring for a while — or go way out of the area.' He held his hands around his mug. 'Razor was telling me that a couple of groups have gone to Belgium for a few days to explore some of the old chateaux there, just to be completely on the safe side.'

173

'Don't blame them.' Stella sat down again. 'I doubt he'll follow them that far.'

Tom frowned. 'Unless he's targeting particular individuals.'

Stella frowned. 'I still think it's unlikely he'll stray too far away from where he's comfortable. After all, he has to have a plan of how to get his targets away from the abduction site, and as they are possibly unconscious, they'd be a dead weight. And he will most certainly have a destination in mind for where he's taking them. So, no, babe, he won't be chasing urbexers to foreign shores. He'll stay on his own patch, I'm certain of it.'

'Once a copper, always a copper! You sound just like you used to.' Tom smiled at her, reached out and took her hand. 'I hope being a farmer's wife isn't too boring for you, Stel?'

She shook her head. 'I couldn't be happier! That was another life. I'll help Robbie all I can, simply because it's our friends that are being targeted, but from the comfort of our own home, okay? No wild escapades. And anyway,' she patted her belly, 'we have something very special to concentrate on, don't we?'

'We certainly do! Now, my beautiful woman, you need your rest. Let's go back to bed and take the tea with us.'

But an hour later, while Tom snored peacefully, Stella still lay awake. There had to be more she could do. Urban exploration was something she understood better than the police, and it was her community that was being terrorised. Surely, she was better placed than they to find that missing motive?

She closed her eyes and started drawing up a mental list of people to talk to. Okay, there would be no wild escapades, but a bit of undercover sleuthing was a different matter, wasn't it?

CHAPTER NINETEEN

Orac huddled in her sleeping bag. The wind was blowing in off the sea, hammering at the deserted cottage on the edge of the ghost village. In the distance, she could hear the waves crashing onto the shore.

In her early days as an active agent, she had been fearless out in the field. This was what she was born to do. Now, however, some years older and suffering a serious disability, she felt vulnerable. She had done things that the other side would never forgive, intercepting and stealing crucial information that had proved vital to British security. She would never be truly safe, but especially out here, alone, and in a very remote spot, the odds were piled high against her.

Over the years she had managed to compensate for her monocular vision. She had found ways to adjust to the change in depth perception and the more restricted field of vision. But it was still a disability, and apart from the frustration and the anger it caused her, it had made her aware of her more limited capabilities.

It was telling her now that this must be her last night in the cottage.

During the previous day, she had noticed several small incidents that had given her cause for concern, minor occurrences, but nonetheless they were things she couldn't dismiss. For one, she had noticed the same car in two different locations. That alone was enough to worry her. She would leave at first light, possibly earlier.

She shifted uncomfortably in her thermal sleeping bag. She needed to sleep but her mind was too active. Being in Ireland again had stirred up old memories and her solitary state had brought flashbacks to her time as an agent.

From an early age, Orac had been aware of her natural ability to understand the workings of technology. She wasn't the only one to recognise it. A perceptive teacher had spotted her potential and had brought it to the attention of the school headmistress. Soon, she found herself separated from her schoolmates and given one-on-one tutoring. She was often sent on IT "courses," and the results of tests set her, and at which she excelled, were subjected to close scrutiny. Without realising it, she had been selected and was being groomed by a shadowy department within the government, destined for a very particular role in national security.

Then she met her nemesis, a man who finally ended her stellar career when he plunged a stiletto into her eye. Her fellow agent, Dara Quinn, had overpowered him and gone on to save her life, and part of her sight, by getting her medical attention in the nick of time. It was Dara, too, who had given her the lead to Grainne, so she was doubly indebted to him.

Dara and she had been close, they worked perfectly together as a team, and Orac was certain that even if they never met again, they would always remain close. You don't put your life in someone's hands and then forget them.

It had been Dara's job to get her, the "brains" who did the clever stuff, in and out of some very dangerous situations and keep her safe. Until they met the "Evil One," as people called him, and found themselves betrayed.

Dara had been devastated when she stood down, and for a while she had worried that he too would give up, but he had continued to serve for another five years.

If only Dara could be here now, thought Orac. Her resolve was failing, and she wanted to go home. "Home," she realised, was no longer Northern Ireland, but Saltern-le-Fen of all places, somewhere she felt safe, among the few remaining people that she liked and trusted.

* * *

Rory arrived at the old church with a rather weary-looking Spike at his side. 'I tossed a coin,' he told Jackman. 'You can guess who won from the look on his face.'

'He'll be even more unhappy when he sees what we've got for you tonight,' said Jackman dourly. He took Rory aside. 'In all my years on the force, I've never seen anything like this. It's horrible.'

'We had the brief before we left. I must say, you seem to have excelled yourself this time. A triple tragedy?'

'But why hang them all by one foot?' said Jackman. 'It's bizarre.'

Rory shrugged. 'Dear Jackman, you should know by now that a deranged mind is capable of all manner of monstrous acts. Good Lord, you've seen one or two right blinders yourself in the past.'

True, but it didn't make this one any easier.

'Okay, we'll go and take a look for ourselves,' said Rory. 'Come, Spike, gird your loins and we'll sally forth.'

As he passed, Spike muttered, 'He doesn't get any better, Detective Inspector.'

Jackman smiled. 'You'd have it no other way, none of us would.' He decided that they could deal with this one by themselves. After all, he told himself, a narrow spiral staircase and a chamber full of decomposing human material didn't offer too much space to manoeuvre. He'd just be in the way, wouldn't he?

Fortunately, Marie didn't notice his sheepish expression. 'Nice lads. Brothers — Jimmy and Hughie Cooke. They are happy to accept any help on offer. That ghastly sight in the bell-ringers' chamber has shaken them rigid, and I think that seeing the effect it had on Cally has upset them even more. The older one, Jimmy, says it's his fault for talking her into coming out. He says he should have known it was too soon after her scare at that old hotel and then hearing about what happened there the following night.'

'Well, I doubt he dragged her out kicking and screaming. They're a feisty bunch, these urbexers. She'd probably have gone out anyway.' Jackman knew all about guilt trips. 'Hindsight is a wonderful thing, Marie. Shame we don't have it when we make the decisions in the first place.'

Marie leaned back against the car. 'When Cally came to the station, I really believed she intended to back off for a while. Frankly, I'm very surprised that she came out again so soon. She seemed too sensible.'

'I think this exploring game is addictive,' said Jackman. 'I googled some of the sites yesterday evening. Some of the photography is stunning. Something like that can get into your blood.'

'The lads were saying much the same,' said Marie. 'When you find what you suspect is a new, untouched site, you just have to go and look, and you want to be first. There's quite a bit of kudos attached to the finding of somewhere hitherto unexplored.' She yawned. 'Stella North is the person to talk to about urban exploration, boss. She's about to release a comprehensive catalogue of amazing photographs of abandoned buildings. If there's such a thing as an expert, she's it.'

'I'd like to talk to her anyway, Marie. I'm hoping she might be able to shed some light on the motive for this.' Jackman extended a hand to the church. 'But first thing tomorrow, I'm going to need you to bring me up to speed on it all.'

'I'll let Robbie give you the sit rep, boss. I gave him the lead on this, so he'd probably appreciate it if I let him present you with a full report.' She looked at her watch. 'Nearly three thirty. I'll ring him at six. He needs to know about this before he gets to the station. It is his baby, after all.'

Jackman agreed, full of affection for Marie and the team. There was no rivalry amongst them, which was rare. This job could be shitty enough without internal bickering and point-scoring. 'You can get away if you want, Marie, and grab a couple of hours' shut-eye. I'll stay here until everything is in place, then I'll try to do the same.'

'Sounds like a plan, if you're okay with it? I've done all I can with the Cooke brothers. They'll be coming into the station around lunchtime to give their statements.'

'Just drive carefully on these roads, Marie. I know how good you are on that bloody great bike, but even so, if a mist comes down out of nowhere some of our best traffic cops can be caught out.'

'Jackman! Relax, I'm totally aware of the dangers. And in future I'd appreciate it if you didn't call my beautiful Tiger a "bloody great bike." Okay?'

He held up his hands, laughing. 'Please convey my apologies to Tiger.'

'I should think so too.' She grinned back. 'I'm going home for a boiling hot bath, with some of the sweetest-smelling bath oils I can find. I can still smell that loft. I just feel for Rory and Spike, having to deal with all that. Even they must be struggling with this one.'

'They wouldn't be human if they weren't. Now, get on your beautiful Tiger and go.'

A few minutes later, he heard the low growl of Tiger's engine. All he needed now was a report from Rory and he could go home himself. Once the whole place had been secured, and fire and rescue knew what was expected of them, it would be over to forensics and uniform. Surely, somewhere within this disaster zone, they would find some trace of the killer?

Jackman went back towards the tower.

* * *

'I would have thought that, after all this time, I'd be used to seeing death in whatever form it took.' Spike seemed to be talking to himself.

Gazing up at the three suspended bodies, Rory said, 'You'll never get used to it, dear boy. And the day you do is the day we part company, because then you will have lost your humanity. It takes a very special person to do this job,' he mused. 'You need the ability to look objectively at a person who, until just recently, was no different to yourself, someone with the same hopes and dreams. You must be able to cope with terrible damage to what was once a living, breathing human being and be detached enough to use your skills to understand what has happened to them. Yet you must still be able to feel compassion for both them and their loved ones. It's no easy task, dear Spike.'

'Then I'm not being weak when I say that this,' he pointed upwards, 'is almost too much to cope with?'

'Not in the slightest, my young friend. But consider this. They aren't objects of disgust or horror, they're three victims who've been treated terribly by an insane mind, and we are all they have right now.' He looked earnestly at Spike. 'Only we can help both them and those who will grieve for them. We bear a big responsibility on our shoulders, but we're also in a privileged position. We have it in our power to provide the police with answers that will lead to whoever did this being locked away, hopefully for ever.' He smiled gently at Spike. 'It might not feel like it right now, lad, but you're special. You will perform this unpleasant task like the professional that you are.'

'Put like that, maybe we should pull our fingers out and get them down? And, please, no more sermons, Reverend Wilkinson, or I'll be shouting "Hallelujah!" and falling on my knees.'

Rory cast a dubious glance at the stinking mess beneath the suspended bodies. 'Not something I'd recommend, considering the state of this floor.' He grimaced behind his mask. 'But now we've got that over with, I'll go and tell the unusually absent Detective Inspector Jackman that we are ready for some ladders and some muscle to get these poor souls back on terra firma.'

Rory went back down the stairs, relieved that he had chosen Spike and not his other assistant, Cardiff Erin, for this job. He had cheated when flipping that coin. He wasn't being sexist — after all, Erin was as professional as they come, and he had no doubt that she would have coped equally as well as Spike, but even so, Rory had wanted to spare her this one. She had not been working in forensics as long as Spike, she'd already had a lot of bad cases to deal with, and he didn't want to overload her too soon. She was worth holding on to. Once they were back in the mortuary, she would be working with him on the bodies, which would be fine, but at least he'd spared her the sight of them *in situ*. He would have done the same for Spike if his and Cardiff's roles had been reversed.

He stepped outside, pulled off his mask, took a lungful of night air and saw Jackman walking purposefully towards him. The poor detective looked almost anguished. Time to lighten things up a little.

'Another one like this, DI Jackman, and I'm asking for a transfer to Midsomer. It's quieter there!'

'I can't argue with you there, Prof. Sorry.'

'Apology accepted but do try to keep your deaths to one at a time. Sending them in bulk does rather overload the mortuary tables.' He exhaled. 'But on a serious note, that was not the nicest of crime scenes, was it? Our dear Spike needed one of my famous calls to arms in order to get him back into work mode.'

'Oh, you bored him into getting back to work, did you?' Jackman was looking more relaxed.

'It was inspirational, I'll have you know. I stirred his inner pathologist.'

'Of course.' Jackman looked at him hopefully. 'Any thoughts on the hanging by one foot thing, Rory?'

'Not really. Not yet.' Rory puffed out his cheeks. 'Although . . . I can see you're not the sort of man who regularly enjoys having his fortune told, but have you ever looked at a pack of Tarot cards?'

181

'Er, no.' Jackman looked puzzled.

'Then do. Check them out on Google and take a look at the one in the major arcana entitled the "Hanged Man," and tell me what you think.'

'Arcana? What's that?'

Rory shook his head. 'Don't worry about it. When you have a moment, just look at the picture. Right now, however, we'd like to request some help to release our three victims from that tower.'

'I'll get that sorted straightaway, Rory,' Jackman said. 'The fire crew are already awaiting instruction, and then I'm getting away. Uniform will assist you in any way you need. And I really am sorry about this one. It's affected everyone badly.'

'You don't need one of my inspirational homilies, do you, because I'd be very happy—'

Jackman held up his hand, grinning. 'No, no. I'm fine, really.'

'Ah well, your loss, Detective.'

Rory watched in amusement as Jackman almost ran to where the fire chief and his crews were waiting. It was encouraging but also worrying that Jackman and Marie still felt so deeply about the horrors they had to confront. He supposed they all became hardened to a certain extent, but sometimes he did wonder how much people could take before something snapped.

Rory shook himself. Now was not the time to indulge in introspection. The fire chief was already shouting orders, and men and women were bringing equipment from the appliances. Getting the bodies down would be no easy task, and he wanted his new charges to be treated with as much respect and care as possible.

* * *

Hearing the blare of sirens, he looked out of his window. This was no minor incident. From his vantage point close to the station, he saw vehicle after vehicle leave the car park and head out of town.

He grabbed his car keys and ran to his car. Making sure to keep well within the speed limit, he followed the blue lights out into the fens. He had to know where they were heading.

His fears were soon realised. As soon as they turned into the familiar back road, he stopped and turned back towards town.

This was only a setback, he told himself, unfortunate but there it was. Life threw you curve balls. After all, that was what this whole thing was about, wasn't it? He'd been thrown the biggest curve ball ever, and he was dealing with it.

He practised his deep breathing: In. Hold. Breathe out.

He wondered how they'd found the place so quickly — another damned explorer most likely. Places like that attracted the idiots like a magnet. No matter. His second storage facility was equally as suitable, so nothing had been lost.

Breathe in. Breathe out.

Tomorrow, he'd write to his wife. She deserved to know the truth.

He rehearsed what he might say in his head . . . *Dearest Helen, it is with great sadness* . . . No, too formal. *Dear Helen, do hope you are keeping well.* Oh, please! *Helen, you need to know the truth, no matter how painful.* Ah, that was more like it.

He opened his eyes. He'd write it now, and then it was done. He'd post it when the whole thing was over.

'All over,' he whispered.

God, he was tired. Initially, he had been galvanised, pumped full of adrenalin. Now he was just looking forward to bringing down the final curtain.

All over.

CHAPTER TWENTY

Jackman listened to Robbie's detailed report on the urbex case. 'It's our belief that the urban explorers were taken, and we now know, killed, because they managed to find their way into a place that was very important to the killer. Somewhere he needed to protect, to the extent of killing whoever intruded on it.'

'That makes sense,' Jackman said.

'Stella and Tom agree, and so do the Sheringhams,' Robbie added. 'Will Sheringham said that years ago, when they first got into exploring, they discovered an old disused chapel in the middle of some town somewhere. They were keen to infiltrate it, but the more experienced urbexers told them to steer clear because of an old tramp who used to attack anyone who got inside. Turned out the poor old guy had buried his beloved dog there and couldn't bear anyone going near its grave.'

'So maybe our man has also buried something,' suggested Marie, 'something more important than a pet.'

'Like a body?' Jackman nodded slowly. 'Yes, the killer could be protecting a burial ground, or maybe punishing anyone who desecrated somewhere he considers to be a shrine. It's a distinct possibility.'

Kevin Stoner raised a hand. 'Boss? Do you think we could give this man a name? You know, like we often do with some unknown suspect.'

'Agreed,' said Jackman. 'Any suggestions?'

'Gollum?' ventured Gary. 'He was a nasty slimy creature who lived in a very dark place.'

'Uh yes, although people might start whispering, "My precious!" at every available opportunity.' Jackman smiled at the thought. 'Anything else?'

'The Bell Ringer? After all, he made bleedin' good use of those bell ropes,' suggested Max.

Jackman shuddered. 'Too close to home, thanks, Max.'

'How about the Magician?' Marie proposed. 'He does make people disappear.'

'Now you're talking!' said Robbie. 'The Magician is good, don't you think, boss?'

'The Magician it is,' Jackman said.

Robbie's phone rang. 'Can I take this? It's Stella.'

'Go ahead. And stick it on speaker.' Jackman smiled. 'As long as it's not personal?'

Stella sounded excited. 'I've been awake half the night, Robbie, and I've had a thought. What if the abductor knows where people are at given times because he's following the urbex websites and the chat rooms the clans use? I can get onto a few I know about, and Will Sheringham is compiling a list for you, but if you guys get IT on it, you might be able to find the subscribers' email addresses.'

'Good point, Stella.' Robbie looked at Jackman and mouthed, 'Can I tell her about last night?'

Jackman nodded. It would soon be all over the press in any case. Stella and the other urban explorers needed to know.

'Listen, Stella, I have to tell you that, last night, we found three bodies.'

'Oh my God! They're our missing friends?'

'We believe so,' Robbie said. 'They were only discovered a few hours ago, so they haven't been identified yet, but it looks that way. I'm so sorry.'

Stella was silent for a while. 'Robbie, you have to get him before he kills again. Next time it could be Ray, or Emily, or someone really close to us. Until you know who is on his list and why he's doing this, we're all living in fear.'

'I know, Stel, and we are doing everything we can, I promise you. Jackman is working with us now, and we are pulling out all the stops. Just keep your ears and eyes wide open and tell the others to do the same, but if anyone hears or sees anything, anything at all, tell them to come directly to us — no turning detective. He's far too dangerous.'

'Don't worry, I've been on the phone to Will and Lisa this morning, and we've decided to form a kind of online watch group, warning everyone we can to be vigilant and to back off all infiltration for the time being.' She gave a grunt of frustration. 'Bit like shutting the stable door after the horse has bolted, but we have to assume he's not finished yet, don't we?'

'Absolutely,' said Robbie. 'Just keep us informed of anything that comes your way. And, Stella, don't forget — you are not a police officer any more, so no heroics! You have previous, my friend, so just stay safe.'

Robbie ended the call. 'I'm really worried about her, boss.'

'She's no fool, Rob,' Marie said. 'And she's not going to jeopardise her baby, is she?'

'I guess not, Sarge, but I've never known a more driven detective. Some of the old Stella must still be there.'

'She'll be fine,' Jackman said. They were wandering off course. 'Let's consider her suggestion, shall we, that we use IT to track anyone watching those chat room sites.'

'Oh, where's Orac?' muttered Marie.

'In her absence,' Jackman said firmly, 'you'll have to use Leon and the others. Get the list from Will Sheringham and take it down to them. You said yourself that Leon is hot as mustard, so give it to him, and tell him it's a priority.'

'I'll call Will now.' Marie left the room.

Jackman turned to the others. 'In the absence of anything more concrete, our prime concern for now is to try and isolate one particular place that each of our explorers visited, meaning the Magician's "shrine." Then we need to know who was with them, because they could be next on his list. It's just a theory, but it makes sense.'

'Will and Lisa were compiling a list of local explorers for us to go out and talk to,' said Robbie. 'I guess that's the direction we need to go, boss?'

Jackman nodded.

'He was going to email it to me this morning,' Robbie said. 'As soon as I get it, can I take Max and Kevin and hit the streets?'

'As fast as you can.' Jackman had the distinct feeling that even if they shut the Magician out of his lair, he wouldn't stop until he had put a line through every name on his list. 'And, Gary? Would you man the phones this morning? I want every bit of information that comes in carefully collated. We can't afford to let up the pace on this. Every kid that sticks his nose inside an abandoned building could be the Magician's next target.'

Gary nodded. 'I'll liaise with Berry. We'll keep it all under control, never fear.'

'Right. I'm off to see Ruth Crooke, and after that, I'll pitch in with whoever needs me most. Let's reconvene in my office after lunch, okay?'

The team dispersed in a murmur of quiet conversation. Jackman stood up. He wasn't looking forward to describing what they'd found at the ruined church. Nor having to look at the sickening images adorning his murder room whiteboards every time he entered the CID room.

* * *

Orac had said goodbye to her not so desirable "holiday" cottage long before daybreak and in the dark had hiked the mile or so to where she had concealed her car. One unfortunate effect of having monocular vision was the difficulty of seeing in the dark, so the walk across the rough terrain had been pretty treacherous.

Luckily her sight was fine for driving and as soon as she set off away from the ghost village, she began to relax. Dawn was staining the grey sky with pale strips of apricot and cream as she approached the nearest town. She wasn't totally sure where she was heading. Her head still wasn't clear, and she couldn't decide. Her heart cried out that she must go and seek out Grainne, but her head told her to let it lie.

After driving for almost two hours, she saw a welcome sight, the neon lights of a Supermac restaurant. All at once, she was starving. She ordered a burger with regular fries and a coffee to go and took them back to the car.

Having devoured the food, Orac sat back with her coffee in one hand and her phone in the other. A habitual loner, she was surprised at her sudden need to talk to someone.

She sipped the scalding hot drink and tapped one of the only two numbers in the phone's contact list.

'Dara? Sorry it's so early.'

'Ciara! How good to hear your voice. How's it going?'

Hearing his deep voice, she pictured Dara as he used to be — tall, muscular, with a head of wild black hair and dark, dark eyes. Dara Quinn, or whatever his name was now, would for ever remain young in her memory.

'Once again, I have a lot to thank you for, dear friend.'

'You've found her? Already?' He sounded surprised.

'Oh no, not yet, but she's alive, Dara, she's alive.'

'I always believed it, and I'm so glad my contacts were of use. I wasn't totally sure, but they sounded okay.' He lowered his voice. 'Are you safe, Ciara?'

'I hope so, but I'm in a quandary, and I need some advice.'

Words tumbling out in a rush, she explained her dilemma and then waited for his response.

'You have to see her! You can't give up now, having come this far. Listen, I'm in Dublin for a couple of days. Come and see me. We can talk, and if you like, I'll help you track down this mysterious benefactor and discover where Grainne has gone. You have to at least lay eyes on her. You might never get back here again and if you leave without seeing her, you'll regret it for the rest of your life. Say yes, Ciara. It'll be like old times.'

'I hope not,' she replied drily. 'I don't have the best memories of our last sortie.'

He gave a laugh. 'I didn't mean that one! Think of the successes. We were unstoppable back then.'

He was right, but she was a different woman now, and she wasn't sure that he would like the uncertain shadow his comrade in arms had become. 'I'll ring you later this morning, Dara. Thank you for listening and for offering to help, but maybe this is one journey I should make on my own. I'll have to think.'

After she ended the call, Orac rang Marie.

Her friend's obvious relief at hearing she was safe was heart-warming. Orac smiled to herself. They hadn't been close, but Marie had been a rock throughout this whole escapade. Once again, she explained her predicament.

'I can only say what I think, Orac. You must not only follow your gut instinct, but also consider what is safest for you in the long run. I've been thinking about what you told me, and I may have an alternative solution,' Marie said.

Orac straightened up. 'I'd be grateful for anything that would give me an alternative to this rock and hard place I'm wedged in at the moment. So, what is it?'

'First, you sensed you were in danger, so don't ignore that. Your own safety must be your priority. Come back here. You're probably thinking that this is the only chance you'll get to your sister, but it isn't. When you've had time to consider and still want to go and see her, a safe passage can be arranged for you, Ruth has assured me of that. Or Grainne could be brought here.'

Orac listened intently.

Marie continued. 'But, if you don't want to cause massive upheaval in your sister's new life, this is what I suggest. I'm sure there are ways that we can locate Grainne's family solicitor. You write a letter to Grainne, along the lines of "you have a sister who loves you dearly," then explain what occurred all those years ago. We lodge it with her solicitor, to be given to her only if she ever decides to ask about her early years, or if the solicitor deems it to be in her best interests. It will give you time to make a decision that you won't regret later. Acting without prior reflection can be disastrous in the long run. End of sermon.'

Orac considered her words. 'You're right, Marie Evans. It's true, I'm not feeling safe here. Maybe I should get myself home, probably on the ferry to Liverpool. I could be a sitting target at the airport. Right now I'm heading south towards Dublin, but your advice is so persuasive, I'll reroute across to Belfast. I do need time to consider the effect it will have on Grainne, but I can do that just as easily from the safety of Saltern-le-Fen.'

'And you don't have to do it alone. I promise I'll help.' Marie laughed. 'On a purely selfish level, we need you back, believe me! We have a triple murder that we need your help with.' She lowered her voice, serious. 'We're struggling, Orac. You have no idea what an impact your going has had on us.'

'A triple murder, you said?'

'And more looming ahead.'

Orac experienced a pang of guilt. She hadn't considered her colleagues and what her sudden departure would mean for them.

'I know how this will sound, and I don't mean it to, but there is something about this case that makes me loath to share too much information, even with Leon.' Marie sounded perplexed. 'It's not a ploy to get you back, Orac, and I can't explain why I feel like I do, but there it is.'

Taken aback, Orac didn't know what to say. 'Leon is brilliant, you really can trust him, Marie. Use him until I return, then I'll do all I can to assist you.'

Call ended, Orac sat toying with her cold coffee. Two people she cared about and two different pieces of advice. She seemed to be back where she started.

But wait. Dara had been speaking to Ciara, someone who no longer existed, but Marie had appealed to Orla

Cracken, and not only that, she was thinking solely of Orac's safety.

She drained her coffee and started the engine. It was time to go home.

As she pulled out onto the road, she saw another car slowly leave its parking spot — the one from a few days ago. Her heart sank. Then she shook herself and gripped the steering wheel. *Okay, pal, think you're going to stop me going home, do you? Well, let's see how good a driver you are!*

CHAPTER TWENTY-ONE

'An update, Jackman, while I still have the energy to speak.' Rory sounded exhausted.

'You've been up all night?' asked Jackman.

'Well, if you will present me with these challenges, what do you expect? I just dread looking in a mirror. I must look positively haggard! God knows what it's done to my complexion.' Rory sighed loudly. 'However, although we haven't completed our examinations, and we won't have anything major for you until tomorrow, I can tell you right now that these are undoubtedly your three missing men.'

He knew that already, of course, but it was a relief to hear it from the horse's mouth. 'Thank you for that. I appreciate it, but before you go, do you have any ideas on the clothes they were wearing?'

'Ah, strange that. Bit of a mystery actually. Oh, and we've just received the third box of lavender-scented and beautifully laundered clothes, courtesy of your killer. The note enclosed is in the same format as the other two and refers to a Grant Leach.'

Again, this was no surprise. 'So, back to the clothes they were wearing when you found them?'

Rory paused. 'Well, they were all wearing identical garments. Naturally we'll run tests on the material used, but it's a sort of tunic, roughly fashioned out of hessian. I'll tell you more, but right now I need my beauty sleep. Cardiff and a small team of technicians will continue to work on them, while I and dear Spike, who is as hollow-eyed and fatigued as I am, get away for a long, hot shower and some rest.'

'Thanks again, Rory. Sleep well.' Jackman hung up. The victims' next of kin would have to be informed, but only after official confirmation of their IDs. Meanwhile, it was imperative that they find a connection between these three men. Only then would they know if there were others who might be a target of the Magician. He had a feeling that there were, but what worried him even more was the possibility that the killer simply hated male urbexers. Cally Prothero might have been spared simply for being female. Jackman idly spun the globe on his desk, watching the countries spin past in a blur of different colours. The latter wasn't high on his list of probable motives, but he had to consider everything.

He stood up. He needed to get the whiteboard organised. A whiteboard focused the mind and ensured the case remained in the forefront of their minds, even if some of the pictures were hard to look at. He picked up the three recent photographs of the victims — three healthy, smiling young men. And what had they become? Three grotesque marionettes dangling from ropes in an obscure ruined church.

Stepping out into the CID room, he saw Marie hurrying towards him. 'Orac is coming home, sir! Well, I'm pretty sure she is. She's in danger out there, and she knows it.'

'Oh, that's good news, Marie. Not being in danger, of course, but coming home. Do we know when?'

'She said she'll keep in touch with me.' Marie looked happier than she had for some time.

'All no doubt down to your powers of persuasion?'

'I could only tell her what I believed, boss. It was her decision. I just hope·she doesn't change her mind and try to see her sister after all. I'm certain it would be a terrible mistake at this point in time.'

'Well, fingers crossed she listens to you.' He held up the three pictures. 'Rory has given us a preliminary ID. They are our urbexers. And the third box of clothing has arrived at the morgue, same presentation as before.'

Marie puffed out her cheeks. 'Leon is working on the list of websites and chat rooms and hunting for what he calls "peeping toms." You know, someone who is listening in on other people's conversations but not participating. He'll get the IP address of anyone he finds, and we'll check them out.'

'Good.' Jackman went over to the whiteboard and wiped it clean. 'We'll start afresh now this is a confirmed murder case.' He wrote the words "Hallows Fen Church" across the top and stuck the three pictures beneath it. Then he wrote down the locations they had been abducted from.

'I'm still wondering about that old airfield,' said Marie softly.

'Correction — still wondering about that old bike,' said Jackman, with a smile.

'Well, yes,' she admitted. 'But the location as well. It's very odd that there's so little information about it, and why on earth not sell it off for farming? Instead of that, they seem to have extended the place. Doesn't make sense.'

Jackman had been mulling that one over ever since it was brought to his attention. 'I've got a theory about that.'

Marie pulled up a chair and flopped down. 'Do tell, because I'm totally stumped.'

'It stinks of MOD, doesn't it, even though they swear it wasn't an RAF field. So,' he sat down beside her and leaned forward, lowering his voice. 'What if that land got contaminated in some way, a spillage of something very nasty? Supposing a plane got into difficulties while carrying some hazardous material? Something top secret?'

'Oh my!' whispered Marie. 'Now there's a thought!'

'It would explain a lot, wouldn't it?'

'It certainly would,' she said. 'Just like that area near Woodhall Spa back in 2017. They found more than one hundred and fifty canisters of First World War mustard gas in the woods and in a nearby lake.'

'Exactly. That's what made me think of it. The papers were full of it and I have a relative who lives right by there. He told me that they had to move three tonnes of contaminated soil from a popular woodland area in order to clean it up. Luckily the lake remained uncontaminated, as those canisters never leaked,' Jackman said. 'It was banned in 1925. Heaven knows what might have been around at the time of the Second World War.'

'I bet you're right, Jackman.' Marie's face fell. 'Oh no. That means I might never manage to get hold of that old bike. I'd make a fair offer for it if I knew who to buy it from.'

'Well,' Jackman said, 'whatever is in that soil can't be of grave danger any more, or it would have been properly dealt with and we'd see some form of heavy security around the perimeter. I reckon they just don't want it disturbed or planted on.'

Marie nodded slowly. 'Good point.' She smiled at him. 'I won't give up on it, you know.'

'Oh, I know that! One way or another, Marie Evans will get that little rust bucket of a motorbike out of Randleby Airfield. I have no doubt of it.'

'My mum, who by the way is coming to stay next week, has this theory that precious things always find their way to a home that loves them, one way or another.'

'What a delightful idea. Be nice if it were true.'

Marie shrugged. 'I remember her searching through our attic once, hunting for a little cream jug that had belonged to her mother. Made a right crusade out of it, she did. When she found it, she had me marching it round to the vicar's wife. When I handed it over you would have thought I'd given her the crown jewels! Turned out she collected this particular type of old china and she'd been searching for that very cream jug for donkey's years! So, there you are.'

Jackman laughed. 'No arguing with that. It'll be good to see Rhiannon again.' He sighed. 'Let's hope we aren't still knee-deep in this investigation or you won't have a lot of time with her.'

'In that case, boss, we better get a wriggle on. Just for once, I want a bit of quality time with my mother — oh, and her new dog.'

'You are having a dog to stay? I thought you were a cat person.'

'I am, but only because of the hours we work. I like cats *and* dogs. Mind you, if Mum is bringing a German Shepherd with her, it's probably a good thing my lovely Rover is no longer with us. She would never have let Lloyd cross her doorstep.'

Marie's cat had made it to a stately nineteen and had died not long before. Jackman coughed. 'Right, well, as you say, let's crack on, shall we?'

'Absolutely. Oh, have we heard about how Cally Prothero is?'

'Ah, yes, I had a call from Laura,' said Jackman. 'She has managed to get the girl talking again, but she had to be quite heavily medicated and will require a great deal of therapy.'

'That's not surprising. Doesn't she live on her own? Not good in her current state.'

'Her parents live abroad, and it appears there's little love lost between them, so Laura contacted a friend of hers, a man called Henry Arnott. Apparently, he went immediately to the hospital and has offered Cally his guest room and volunteered to look after her. Seems he also looks after his father, but the old man has gone into a nursing home for a week or two for some specialist care. Laura said he seemed really upset by what had happened to Cally and told her he was glad to be able to help. He was an urbexer for a while too, and he understands what drives Cally and her friends.'

'Well, that's a satisfactory short-term outcome, I guess, but I do worry about her future,' Marie said. 'She's a cracking photographer, but this could ruin her chances of getting any more shots like the ones she took at East Fleet Manor. They were remarkable. Such a shame.'

'Don't write her off, Marie! Think of some of the unholy crap you've seen and had to deal with but you're still out there and fighting, aren't you?' Jackman looked at her. 'She might well surprise you once the shock has worn off. It certainly didn't take her long to get back to exploring again after her fright at that old hotel. Something like that would have frightened a lesser mortal off.'

'Let's hope so.'

Marie didn't sound convinced, but in Jackman's opinion, someone who habitually wandered dangerous places, alone and at night, was very likely to bounce back. 'Now, I've just remembered something. Come to my office. We need to do a bit of research on Google.'

They sat down at his computer, and after searching for a few moments, he clicked on an image.

'Tarot cards? Good Lord! We aren't that desperate, are we, sir?' Marie exclaimed.

'Don't panic, it's something Rory asked me to check out, that's all.' He looked at the deck of cards and chose the one called "The Hanged Man."

'Rory? He didn't! You must be joking.' Marie looked at him in amused surprise.

In silence, he pointed to the image that had just appeared on the screen.

'Oh, right . . . I get it,' Marie said.

So did Jackman. The card depicted a man wearing a brown tunic and tights suspended upside down by a rope tied to one ankle.

Jackman scrolled through numerous variations of the same card. They differed in what the man was wearing and the position of his arms, but he was always tied by one ankle to a wooden branch wedged across two growing trees.

'Well, I see the point Rory was making,' Jackman said, 'but I have no idea what the killer is getting at.'

'These cards have meanings, don't they, sir? Could he be sending us a cryptic message?' asked Marie, her eyes still on the image.

He skimmed down the text. 'Not much use to us. It says it's one of the more controversial of the cards. Even readers' feelings about it differ, depending on what deck they use. It says it contains symbols of Nordic paganism, Christianity, depression, drug addiction, sacrifices and enlightenment. Take your pick.'

Marie pulled a face. 'And by the look of it, those are just some of a whole lot of different interpretations.' She looked up. 'Even so, maybe someone should do a bit of research on it and see if anything amidst all that gobbledegook might relate to our dead men.'

'Yes, but not us. I'll farm that one out. Actually, I'll give it to Kevin. If Rory thinks it's a relevant line of enquiry, it can't be ignored.'

'Never advisable,' said Marie wryly. 'So, what next?'

'I think I'd like to take a trip out to see Stella North,' said Jackman suddenly.

'Stella *Chalk*, boss. She's married now, don't forget,' said Marie.

'Well, she'll always be Stella North to me, I'm afraid. That's the name on the Roll of Honours board at HQ, and that's how she'll stay in most coppers' memories. The thing is, I don't think I'm totally *au fait* with this whole urban exploration game, and to understand what links the victims, I need more of an insight into what drives them.'

'I'll ring and see if she's in, shall I?' offered Marie.

'Please, and if it's okay, we'll go straightaway, while the boys are out talking to other urbexers.'

While Marie called Stella, Jackman noticed Gary walking towards the office door and beckoned to him.

'Sir, my contact John Beard out at Randleby has asked to see me. Would it be okay if I slip out for an hour? He says it's about something to do with that old airfield, and he'd rather not speak on the phone. He sounded quite excited.'

'Okay, but don't get too side-tracked, Gary. As soon as the forensic reports start to come in, we'll be pretty busy dealing with our three dead urbexers.'

'No problem, sir. We're meeting halfway, so I shouldn't be too long. I'll report to you the minute I get back.' He turned to go, then stopped. 'It was a bit odd, actually. He said he'd rather not come to the station to see me but asked if I could meet him at the big garden centre just off the Fenchester Road.'

'What? He doesn't like police stations?' asked Jackman. 'Why is that odd?'

Gary laughed. 'He worked in one for years, sir! He's as used to them as you or me. But he sounded quite cagey. I'm really interested to hear what he has to say.'

'So am I, now you've told me that. That airfield has had us all thinking.'

'Well, let's hope John can throw some light on the mystery. See you later, sir.' Gary hurried out.

'Stella's in all morning, boss,' said Marie. 'Shall we go now?'

Jackman stood up.

* * *

Will Sheringham exercised religiously every morning. He needed good upper body strength to compensate for his paralysed legs, and he was determined to put as little strain on Lisa as possible. If he could find a way to do something, he'd do it without help. One thing he did have was determination. He placed the weights back in their rack, took a long drink of water, and returned immediately to his computer.

Sometimes the days dragged, so he was pleased to have a purpose, and was giving it his all. He and Stella had set up several closed groups online, keeping their fellow explorers in the loop, dispensing warnings and advice. Now, they were asking for help. Stella had called him earlier and told him that the three missing men had been found dead. He had already guessed that must be the case, but it had been a shock to have it confirmed. Now he was determined to redouble his efforts and ensure that no other kid with an adventurous spirit finished up the same way.

He had already emailed DC Robbie Melton a list of names and the contact numbers of explorers who were prepared to assist the police. Now he was taking that a step further. He had taken three sheets of white card and written one heavily underlined name on top of each sheet: Anthony Hood, Aaron Smith and Grant Leach. Next, he had added the names and numbers of the other members of their clans. Now he was adding other explorers they were known to have explored with in the past, close friends, and people they chatted with on social media.

He was in quite a unique position to do this. Because of his injuries and his limited mobility, he had been following others on their expeditions. Becoming an armchair explorer had been a means of keeping his old passion alive and his brain active, even if his body wasn't able. Hence, he probably knew more about the urbex community than anyone, apart, maybe, from Stella. She too had limited mobility nowadays but was not nearly as restricted in her movements. And, because of her plans for her massive gallery of decay photography, she had kept right up to date with the urbex scene.

Will examined the three cards. There had to be a link among all these names. And if there was, it would be connected to a particular place that they had all explored, somewhere they had infiltrated and badly upset someone dangerous by doing so.

He sat back in his wheelchair. But where? He tried to recall any messages posted on their sites warning explorers to be wary or to steer clear of a certain location, but nothing came to mind.

Over the next hour, he set up three mailshots, one for each of the dead explorers. This way he could contact every name on each list in a single hit, and if he sent it as a BCC, they would be unaware of the others' email addresses. He knew he would be inundated with answers, but, hey, what else did he do with his days? Go for a jog? Pop down to the pool for a few lengths and a sauna? Jump in the car and take his lovely wife out to lunch?

Will cursed himself. Shut the fuck up, Sheringham! Do something constructive and use your talents to help catch a killer. That's more important than going out for a jog.

He returned to his keyboard. *Hi there, I badly need your help, if you can assist me, we might find justice for our murdered friends. Please, can you recall ever going anywhere that . . .*

He pressed Send.

* * *

When Gary arrived at the garden centre, John Beard was already waiting. 'Sorry for the cloak and dagger stuff, mate, but I have a feeling that if we take our enquiries into that old airfield any further, we might be opening a can of worms.' He appeared to be both amused and concerned by the prospect.

They strolled over to the evergreen plants and John pretended to pay close attention to some conifers. 'I've been warned off, mate.'

Gary frowned. 'By whom?'

'Oh, not in any official sense. Just a word from two separate sources.' John picked up a plant and examined the label. 'Then I saw something that appeared to confirm what my contacts had told me.'

Wandering up and down the aisles, John relayed what he had discovered.

'The main thing — and I got this from the farmer who owns the land adjoining the airfield — is that the original farmer was paid a very large sum of money to sell off a parcel of his land. The sum far exceeded its worth. Then, well, he sold up completely and moved away from the area.'

'Do you think we could take that further?' asked Gary.

'No way. For one thing, we are going back to the forties, and another, the chap I talked to said that he only found out because the farmer had been a close friend of his grandfather, who has since passed away. His grandfather apparently told him to forget about what he'd told him. It was old history and he should let sleeping dogs lie.' John shrugged. 'My new farmer friend said he'd made a few enquiries, simply out of interest, but soon realised that no one was prepared to talk about the airfield. In the end, he gave up and strongly advised me to do the same.'

As far as Gary could see, this just seemed to deepen the mystery. 'And the other person you spoke to?'

'That local history buff I told you about, the one with the photographs.' John stopped at a display of terracotta pots. 'He didn't like my questions at all, Gary. He told me in no uncertain terms to back off, stop asking questions about the place. He said there's nothing to know, other than that it had once been an airfield, and there had been a long-running legal battle over the ownership of the ground. End of story. He wasn't friendly, or as verbose as he usually is about local history. It was weird.'

'You say you saw something?' prompted Gary.

'I decided to go out there again. I took my old neighbour's dog with me, so my presence wouldn't look suspicious. There was an unmarked van and a 4x4 parked at the gates. There were three men inside the fence. One of them seemed to be taking soil samples, and I'm damned sure that the one sitting in the car was watching me through binoculars. I didn't hang around, I can tell you.' His brow furrowed. 'Now I have a strange feeling that I'm being watched — hence all the cloak and dagger. Frankly, I'm expecting a visit at any time.'

Gary drew in a long breath. He was beginning to regret asking his old friend to watch the airfield. 'John, I'm sorry I got you involved. I think you'd better forget all about it.'

John laughed. 'Come on, mate, you don't dangle a carrot in front of my nose then whip it away again! I'll keep my head down, never fear, but this has really got me interested. Know what? I haven't felt so alive since I was chasing smugglers.' He chuckled. 'Now I'm going to have to buy something to justify our presence here. You really will owe me a pint and a packet of scratchings by the time we're done.'

But Gary wasn't laughing. 'I'm just not happy about it.'

'Oh, cheer up! No one is going to do anything drastic, are they? With any luck I'll get a backhander to keep my mouth shut. And I'll pass on to you everything I find, even if I have to redesign my garden to do it.' Smiling happily, John picked up a bushy choisya plant. 'This'll do for starters.'

There would be no dissuading him, Gary saw. All he could do was insist that John contact him immediately if anything concerned him.

Gary drove back to the police station. Maybe John was getting carried away and had imagined all this clandestine activity. Why would such a dreary tract of land be of such interest? And to whom? Why subject someone like John to surveillance? It made no sense.

CHAPTER TWENTY-TWO

Still wary, Orac was nonetheless pretty sure she had lost her pursuer several miles back. Now she had to work out how to get back to England without being spotted. Whoever was following her would now be concentrating on her destination, in the hopes of cutting her off.

She had headed towards Dublin, even though she had no intention of actually going there, but if these people were professionals, that wouldn't fool them for long. They would calculate that she had three possible objectives. One, she really was going to Dublin to continue the hunt. Two, she would try to fly out of the country. Or, three, she would get a ferry. Her shadowy followers could be part of a big organisation with the capacity to place people at all three locations, or . . . ? Maybe the car she kept seeing was something far less sinister. Surely, a big organisation wouldn't keep using the same easily identifiable vehicle?

Orac pulled off the main road and drove into a quiet little village. She stopped in a small car park at the back of a post office-cum-village store and regrouped. So, how to get home? She was just over an hour away from Belfast now, and she knew that the ferries there ran a couple of times a day. The trouble was that the crossing time was eight hours.

Dublin to Holyhead was much quicker, but then there'd be a long drive at the other end.

Orac made her decision. She already had an emergency passport and driving licence. She might not need the passport — Northern Ireland to England didn't require one — but it was good to have it with her. She would drive to Belfast port and leave her hire car at the ferry terminal, then get a taxi to the city airport, only a nine-minute drive from there. With luck, she'd be able to get a last-minute flight to East Midlands airport. She could get a police vehicle to collect her from the airport and take her to Saltern-le-Fen. It was risky, but doable.

Orac turned on the ignition.

* * *

Robbie and Max were suffering from information overload. They had spoken to four urban explorers during the morning, and each one had given them a shedload of information about the places they had infiltrated and the people they had explored with. It was almost too much to deal with and, as Robbie knew, was only the tip of the iceberg.

As they drove back to the station, he said to Max, 'One thing that worries me is the distances these guys are prepared to travel to get to these abandoned places.' He stared at his notebook, which was crammed with names, dates and locations. 'There's a very good chance that the Magician's sacred place is, or was, miles from here. Our victims could have gone anywhere — in or out of the country.'

'I was thinking the same thing,' murmured Max, straightening out of a sharp bend. 'I was gobsmacked by how far they travel for one of those "bimbos," or whatever they call them. Anyway, one thing we have learnt is that Hood, Smith and Leach never went out together. They each had their own clans that they explored with.'

'So, if we are right about them trespassing on the Magician's turf, they all went there at different times.' Robbie groaned.

'And you never know, we could be totally wrong about the killer. He could just be some fruitcake who hates urbexers.'

'Too true, mate,' said Max. 'Maybe we should just concentrate on the victims. What do you reckon? Forget trying to interview the whole bloody brotherhood of urbexers — we don't have the time. While we're out taking notes, the next kid on his list could already be swinging from a roof somewhere.'

Robbie tended to agree. They had looked at each of the victims, talked to their families and people who knew them and got as much as they could, but they needed to go deeper. Somewhere in their relatively short lives, these three had committed a crime in the Magician's eyes, a hanging offence — literally. 'And what's that all about? Hanging them upside down by one foot?'

'Search me, but it has to be significant,' said Max. 'In fact, I have a suspicion that the way the killer "hangs" the bodies will be crucial to finding him.'

'The linchpin,' Robbie breathed. 'The one vital component.'

'Yup. That tiny little pin that stops the bloody wheels falling off.'

They drove the rest of the way back in silence.

* * *

Jackman and Marie drove away from Stella and Tom's farm with much the same thought on their minds.

'What astounding photographs!' said Jackman. 'And our Stella travelled so far to get them. I had no idea.'

'It makes you realise what a mammoth task we have on our plates. These urban explorers travel all over the world, so there is a very good chance the Magician's special place isn't local at all, just somewhere they all happen to have visited.' Marie shook her head. 'It's mind-boggling.'

Jackman exhaled. 'We need a new action plan, Marie. We have to look at this from a different perspective. But where to start?'

Marie shrugged. All she knew was that with every passing hour nightfall drew closer, and the Magician might be out hunting urbexers. She just hoped that whoever was next on his list had taken heed of Will and Stella's warnings to stay away from abandoned buildings and remote places — if the killer even *had* a list. What if he was just choosing his victims at random? What chance did they have of tracking him then? She said as much to Jackman.

After a while he said, 'I think we'll solve this case with a mix of forensic evidence, maybe from those three clothing parcels, or the strange clothes that the victims were wearing, and technology. We have to hope that Leon can find some connection between the three victims.'

Marie wasn't so sure. She was still convinced that only Orac could find that missing link. She chided herself for her lack of faith in Leon, but there it was.

'Let's hope Rory doesn't oversleep. We need everything his forensic team and his big brain can get for us,' she said anxiously. 'I have a nasty feeling we haven't seen the last of the Magician.'

'Knowing Rory, he'll be back pretty quickly. He won't rest until he's dragged every ounce of information from his three silent witnesses.' Jackman was silent for a while. 'Who is killing these young men, Marie? And why defile their bodies by dressing them that way and hanging them up, for heaven's sake? It's obscene.'

'It's not as if they'd committed any terrible crime. All their friends are full of praise for them. They certainly aren't low-lifes, and from what we've dug up on them already, not one of them did drugs, not even marijuana.' She recalled some of the descriptions of the oldest explorer, thirty-year-old Anthony Hood: reliable, sensible, supportive, well liked, a good mentor. A good person. 'I keep coming back to your initial theory that they accidentally infiltrated somewhere that the killer held sacrosanct.' She gave a soft groan. 'Which brings us full circle, and looking for a needle in a haystack.'

They drove into the station car park. 'I don't think we should get too fixated on that — after all, I was only hypothesising,' Jackman said. 'Let's see if the others are back, and then we'll get together and do a little critical thinking on what we do know, not my wild imaginings.'

In Marie's opinion, his idea was far from being either wild or too imaginative. 'Let's pray that Rory's team hurry up and send us something concrete to work with.'

* * *

'We have *no* suspects.' Jackman's words hung in the air like a bad odour. 'Not one.'

After a long silence, Gary said, 'This is certainly not an attention-seeking killer, is it? Not like some of the others we've come across who all seemed to need to crow over their ghastly achievements.'

'No, this is someone who's sorting out a very personal matter,' Rob stated. 'I shouldn't think he has the slightest interest in us. He has a vendetta to complete, and he has no intention of broadcasting what that is.'

'Yet he sent those parcels of clothes,' said Marie thoughtfully. 'But even that seemed more, well, like he was following a procedure rather than sending a message.'

'Yes,' Max said, 'those notes he included were very formal, weren't they?'

'Which tells us he's an organised killer.' Jackman frowned. 'I hesitate to use the term serial killer, because I believe that once he has eliminated everyone who has "transgressed," he'll stop. He's not killing for fun, or for the sake of it, I'm certain.' He pulled a face. 'Even though he has killed three people, he doesn't quite fit the definition. I'm with Rob on this one, he's settling a score.' He glanced at the clock. 'And until we get some forensic evidence to follow up on, which won't be today, it seems we are at an impasse.'

For a while no one spoke, then Robbie said, 'Do you think it could be another urban explorer? Could some urbexer have become fixated on one special abandoned building and be killing any other explorer who dares infiltrate it?'

Jackman frowned. 'Possible, I suppose. I know we've been told how tolerant they all are of others who get to a special location before them, but it must be galling. It could just tip a deranged mind into chaos, I guess.'

'Shall I ask Stella and the others if they've ever had reservations about one of their fellow explorers? Someone a little overzealous, or whose behaviour struck them as worrying?' asked Robbie.

'Why not?' Jackman stood up. 'Meanwhile, I suggest we all try to get away on time at the end of the shift. When the forensic reports start to come in, I'll be asking you to work late, so take advantage of this lull, because it ain't gonna last, believe me.'

Jackman hadn't said that the second reason for getting away was to compensate for the fact that there might well be a call after midnight — the duty sergeant reporting yet another missing young man.

* * *

Orac was in the taxi from the port car park to the airport when she heard her phone ring. It had to be either Dara or Marie. But when she looked at the display, she found it was neither. But who could possibly have this number? Then it came to her. 'Clodagh? Are you alright?'

'I am. I just thought I might be able to save you a journey, depending on your plans.'

Orac frowned, wondering what she was about to hear.

'I'm not sure that this is good news exactly, but I had an unexpected letter from your sister this morning. It was one of those round-robin things that you send out to all and sundry if you have some special news. I have no idea how long it's been in the post, but it says that she is thrilled that she has been offered a place at Berkeley, California, and she's accepted. As far as I can gather, she should already be on her way. I'm afraid you are too late to see her.'

Orac felt a rush of despondency. She had been so close! Now her sister would be travelling thousands of miles away from her. But, on the other hand, it meant that her decision had been the right one. She thanked Clodagh and ended the call.

She sank back in her seat with a sigh. For now at least, her quest really was over. Who cared if they had invaded her flat, taken her computer and changed her locks? All she wanted was to go home.

* * *

Kenny Asquith was a privileged young man. His mother having walked out on them when Kenny was a boy, his father tried to compensate for the loss by giving him anything he wanted. His father was one of the richest men in the county, and money was no object.

That was why Kenny was eagerly unpacking one of the smartest cameras on the market and itching to get out there to use it. Urban exploration was his one true passion, and he was determined to try out this new marvel, despite the warnings posted all over the urbex websites.

His route into the urbex world had been rather unusual. He was a bright kid, and had little trouble getting into university. His problem was that he had no direction. After his father's overpowering cossetting, his time in student accommodation at Teesside University had been a revelation. He became close to Norman Keating, who was studying photography. Before long, Kenny switched from graphic design to photography where he discovered his forte, and because Norman was deeply into decay photography, Kenny was also drawn into urban exploration. They had both graduated with honours and found good jobs freelancing for a top agency. Eventually, Kenny decided it was time to move back home. Norman also moved to the fens and bought a studio flat in Peterborough. They remained close friends and continued to explore together.

His father, thrilled to have his son back, still lavished gifts upon the twenty-eight-year-old man. Hence the new camera equipment. Kenny had to show it to Norman.

For some time now, they had been considering getting inside an old deserted hospital, located on the outskirts of a small village five miles from Saltern-le-Fen. They had been there once before but had failed to get the shots they had been hoping for. It was not a virgin site and numerous other urban explorers had infiltrated the place, but he and Norman had seen its potential for some extraordinary images. With the right lighting and his new camera, they could be onto a winner.

Norman answered the phone almost immediately. 'Getting a little stir-crazy, are we?' he asked sardonically. 'Or desperate to show off the latest offering from your sainted father?'

Kenny laughed. 'Both, actually. Are you up for a bimble?'

For once, Norman didn't jump at the offer. 'I'm not sure that's wise, you know. Have you seen the news? The police have found three bodies near Saltern-le-Fen. No names, no location, but ten-to-one it's our missing urbex brothers.'

Kenny's heart sank.

'So, much as I'm desperate to get back out there, I value my life. Waiting a little longer won't kill us.' He paused. 'Whereas acting irresponsibly might.'

This was not like Norman. Norman was always up for anything.

'Think about it, Norm. What are the chances of meeting up with this weirdo? We don't post on any site. We haven't planned this ahead of time, or told anyone else. We've sent no texts, no emails regarding our plans, how could he possibly know where we're going? There must be a hundred abandoned places within travelling distance from here. He could never watch them all, could he?'

'True, but Butterwitch is desperate to prevent any more disappearances. I had her on the phone earlier, begging me to warn off anyone who was stupid enough to ignore the risk involved. Sorry, Kenny, I hate to call you stupid but you didn't hear her. If I didn't know her better, I'd say she's heading for a breakdown.'

Butterwitch, or Emily Butters, had been one of the first explorers they had gone out with when they came to the fens. She was intelligent and fearless, and Norman had been captivated. Discovering that she was gay made no difference to their friendship, and whereas Kenny preferred to go out with Norman alone, Norman himself was happy to crew up with Emily and her clan brother, Razor.

But Kenny wasn't to be deterred. 'I'm sorry she's so flaky, but it's natural — it was on one of her bimbles where a kid went missing, wasn't it? Of *course*, she's anxious — but we're not her.' He sighed. 'Heavens, we are both adults, we can look after ourselves. Remember all those security guards we outfoxed in that old power plant we infiltrated? I'm still not sure how we managed that one!'

'Kenny. Just stop there. I care about you, man, okay? I don't want either you or me to end up as another unidentified body out on the fen. The police will get him, or he'll move on because it's just too hot for him here, so cool it, kid, okay? No bimbles just yet. Play with your camera by all means, but not in abandoned places in the dead of night.'

First deflated, then angry, Kenny kept a lid on it. The odds that they'd be anywhere near this nutter were pretty low. Norman had only been put off because of Butters. Gay or not, Norman clearly fancied her and wouldn't want to antagonise her. 'Okay, Norm, you win. I still don't agree, but I'll back off if you say so.'

They chatted for a while about the merits of the new camera, and then he hung up.

He spent the next hour studying the camera's manual, until the light began to fade. That familiar, exhilarating feeling crept over him. He wanted to go out. He needed to.

Kenny picked up his phone. He struck lucky with the third call. At last, someone who felt as he did.

Kenny went to his wardrobe, quickly changed his clothes and grabbed his rucksack, which was already packed. His father was out, so he left him a scribbled note, picked up his new camera and left.

Crazy Hazy, as Kenny knew him, was waiting outside his house, the boot of his 4x4 open, ready for Kenny's gear.

'All set, Kenzo?' Hazy grinned at him, revealing his crooked teeth in the glow of a streetlamp. 'No last-minute reservations about the bogeyman?'

Kenny grinned back, his own perfect teeth the work of an expensive orthodontist. 'Like hell. Let's go.'

They climbed in and headed for the main road out of town, chatting excitedly.

Neither of them noticed another dark-coloured 4x4 following at a discreet distance behind them.

CHAPTER TWENTY-THREE

After supper, Stella and Tom drove over to Will and Lisa Sheringham's place. Robbie's request to consider explorers who had given them cause for concern had set them all thinking, and they had decided to discuss it together.

It still saddened Stella to see the once athletic Will in a wheelchair. She too had battled disability, but with time had regained an almost normal life. Will, on the other hand, had no hope of ever walking again. She, more than any of them, was able to appreciate his courage in dealing with the battles of everyday life.

They sat around the kitchen table. Here, at least, they were all equal.

'Anyone fancy a glass of wine?' asked Lisa. 'Or maybe a non-alcoholic beer if you're driving, Tom?'

'Sounds good,' said Tom.

'Wine, please, Lisa. Just a small one, I've seen your measures before.' Stella smiled.

'Wine for me, babe. I'm definitely not driving tonight,' said Will dryly.

Stella detected an unusually bitter note in his voice and wondered as to the cause. He caught her gaze and lifted his hands in a gesture of surrender.

'Sorry! Moment of ridiculous self-pity. All over now.' He shook his head. 'It's these deaths. I want to get out there and help, do something positive, instead of sitting here vegetating.'

Tom laughed. 'I'd hardly call setting up all those mail-shots and contacting practically every urbexer within a hundred-mile radius vegetating. I couldn't do that, not in a month of Sundays.'

'Stella's helped, especially with the closed group updates and social media posts. I can't take all the credit.'

Lisa set down their drinks and a bowl of crisps. 'Okay, rogue explorers. Where are we?'

Stella noted the rapid change of subject. Nice one. She proceeded to elaborate on Robbie's theories, especially the idea that the killer was protecting some "special place."

'There was that bloke who used to hang around with Crusher's crew for a while. Big fellow, very intense.' Will pulled a face. 'Crusher finished up disbanding his group for a while, until he moved on. What was his name, Lisa? Can you remember?'

'Roy, I think. Yes, that's it, Roy Ferris! Tag name, Helter Skelter. I only met him once, but that was enough. Scared the life out of me!'

Stella frowned. 'Not a name I know.' She opened a note-book that she had brought with her, conscious of being back in police mode — well, it would always be in her blood. 'What else do you know about him? Description?'

'Tall. Muscular. Dark, wavy hair. Very strange eyes, kind of staring. Really made you feel uncomfortable.' Lisa actually shifted on her seat at the memory.

'Local?' asked Stella.

'One of the Saltern villages, I think. That's how he tied up with Crusher, but he moved further up the county a while back,' said Will. 'That was when Crusher restarted his group.'

'And how exactly did this intensity manifest itself?' asked Stella.

Everyone laughed, and she looked at them in confusion.

'Detective Sergeant North, has no one told you that this is not an interrogation room?' Tom chuckled.

She put a hand to her mouth. 'Sorry! I just can't help it.'

Will swirled the wine around in its glass. 'Actually, it *is* an investigation. It came to me earlier that we have the edge on the police, because this is our world. Starburst,' he looked at Stella, then to Tom, 'Cave Bunny.' His gaze travelled to Lisa. 'My Spider Girl, and me, Free Will. We understand this game, and we have inside knowledge. It could well be down to us to discover who the killer is.'

Stella was not going to argue with him. 'So, let's sort out the oddballs, shall we?'

For the next hour they debated various characters that had never fitted into the community. These were few — in general, urbexers were all of the same mind and inclination.

Finally, Stella said, 'Okay, we are down to three who have big question marks next to their names. Do we think that's it?'

'Can't think of anyone else, can you, darling?' said Lisa, looking at Will.

He shook his head. 'No, I can't.'

Stella read out the short list of names. 'Roy Ferris, aka Helter Skelter. Intense. Disregard for others while exploring. Always wanted to be first inside anywhere, and not a team player.'

'You can add: pretty well universally disliked,' said Lisa with a shudder.

'Jeff Saville, aka Road Runner. Daredevil, irresponsible, moody. Put others in jeopardy by his actions and hated it when someone beat him to a newly discovered site.'

'Add volatile temper,' muttered Will. 'I saw him flare up a couple of times, and it wasn't pretty.'

'And finally, a man we knew as Pickwick, first name Henry. Can't recall his surname, and he hasn't been on the scene for years. Older man, very obsessive about particular types of buildings. Wasn't particularly generous of spirit if another clan got into somewhere first. He loved factories and old workplaces like granaries, mills and wharves, anything industrial.' Stella looked at the others enquiringly.

'He was almost fanatical about them,' Tom recalled. 'We never wanted him along, but he was very knowledgeable, and sometimes what he knew about how old industry worked was very useful. Even so, he was a bit scary.' He paused, looking slightly puzzled. 'Then he just disappeared off the scene, and I can't recall hearing why.'

There was a silence, broken by Lisa. 'Thinking about it, there is one more person who unsettled me, although I don't know his name at all. Will? Remember that guy who came along when we went to that old manor house in Yorkshire?'

Will frowned, then it dawned on him, and he nodded. 'Yes, I do, and you're right, he was no urbexer. I'm not sure how he came to join us on that trip, or why, for that matter. He was a miserable sod, wasn't he?'

'He complained about everything,' said Lisa. 'He had none of the right equipment, not even a camera, just used his phone for a few shots.'

'Odd thing was, he knew more about that old house than any of us. Now I think of it, Lisa, didn't we think at the time that maybe he had an ulterior motive for tagging along?'

'We did. Although we never fathomed out what it could have been. Wish I could recall his name. Maybe one of the others would remember.' She turned to Stella. 'Six of us went, we hired a minibus. We'd heard about an abandoned Elizabethan manor house, miles from anywhere, that had recently been found. It was discovered when a girl went missing and the area was searched by police, mountain rescue and a whole load of volunteers.'

'It was a gem of a property,' added Will. 'We got some great shots. I'll download a couple for you if you like, Stella. It was a real find.'

This looked promising. A missing girl, a police search, coupled with a stranger tagging along on a bimble, someone who obviously wasn't who he said he was. 'When was this?' Stella asked.

'The year before I had my accident. I have the actual date on the photograph file,' said Will. 'I'll sort it out for you before you go.'

'If you do come up with his name, I'd appreciate it.' The warning lights were flashing in Stella's mind. She told herself to calm down as there was very little chance of there being the slightest connection to what was happening in Saltern. She closed her book and glanced up at the kitchen clock. Time was getting on and Tom started work early in the morning. 'I do hope no one has ignored our messages and gone out tonight,' she said softly.

'If they do, they are fools,' grumbled Will. 'We couldn't do more than we have, could we?'

'You've done more than anyone could, Will,' Tom said, 'and you too, Stella. As Will says, if anyone goes out before this man is apprehended, they need their heads examined.'

Will pushed his chair back from the table. 'I'll get those pictures and the date for you now, Stella, before I forget.'

He was back shortly with some printouts on his lap, his face registering concern. 'Just had a message.' He coughed. 'And it's worrying. I don't know if you've met Norman Keating yet?'

Stella vaguely recalled the name.

'No matter. He's flagged up an urbex kid that's possibly gone out on a bimble tonight. I set up a special post where if anyone hears of kids putting themselves in danger, they notify me.'

Stella shook her head resignedly. 'Well, someone's bound to, aren't they?'

'No, but Norman's particularly bothered about this lad because he's asthmatic. It's his regular urbexing partner, they explore together, have done since university. He refused to go out tonight when the kid asked him to go along. The kid swore he'd stay in and wait until the killer was apprehended, but Norman's pretty sure he's gone out. His phone isn't answering, and he's ignored a text.'

Tom groaned. 'Oh hell. I just hope he's not been stupid enough to go out alone.'

'Does this Norman know where he's heading?' asked Stella.

'No. He knows where they would have gone together, but he doesn't think he'll go there without him. He knows that Norman is particularly interested in getting some special photographs of the place. It's not an unexplored site but it's somewhere that isn't too well documented — an old cottage hospital outside Saltern, on the way to Fenchester.'

'He could have gone there without his mate,' said Lisa. 'If he's happy to go off without him anyway, I can't see him being thoughtful enough to consider Norman's feelings, can you?'

'Where is this hospital exactly?' asked Tom. 'Stella and I could drive past it on our way home, just to check it out.'

Stella nodded. As fellow urbexers they knew exactly the kind of places where he would conceal his vehicle, and they knew all the signs to look for. 'If he wasn't asthmatic, I'd say forget it, but under the circumstances, I think we should.'

'Saltmere End. It's just off Church Lane, lies right back in some overgrown grounds. The entrance is down a narrow farm lane on the left-hand side.' Lisa had been there herself and knew it. 'Shall I come with you?'

Tom shook his head. 'It's okay, Lisa. We'll find it. We'll check it out, ring you guys and go straight home from there. I've got an early start, as usual.'

Stella stood up. 'Then we better be off. Okay, what's this kid's name?'

'Kenny Asquith.'

Stella's eyes widened. 'Asquith? Not Matthew Asquith's son?'

Will nodded. 'Yep, the millionaire businessman.'

Stella pulled her phone from her pocket. The image of a newspaper headline flashed through her mind. That would be all the police needed! 'Sorry, girls and boys, I'm ringing DC Robbie Melton. It's probably a blind alley, but this is one he can't afford not to check out. If this kid does go missing, the repercussions will be huge. He needs to know.'

* * *

219

Marie became aware of her special mobile ringing.

'Orac? Are you okay?'

'Never better now I'm on English soil again, but I'm still keen to be back safe in my basement.'

'Where are you? I'm coming to get you.'

'Ruth could get a car here, I'm sure,' Orac said. 'You've got enough on your plate.'

'Shut up and tell me where you are.'

'East Midlands Airport. I'm staying inside while it's still busy. I got in earlier but laid low until there were no more flights in from Ireland, just to be on the safe side,' Orac said.

'It will take me around one and three-quarter hours to get there from here, Orac. It would be quicker on the bike, but—'

'Then bring a spare helmet. I've no luggage other than a rucksack,' Orac said. 'And I don't look quite as you remember me, so I'll watch out for you, okay?'

'On my way.'

Like some courier transporting urgent medical supplies, Marie rode as fast as she dared. And with a speed camera warning app activated through her helmet earpiece, she managed the trip a whole lot faster than a car.

* * *

A stranger approached Marie on the airport concourse. Marie only recognised Orac when she spoke.

'Well, the disguise clearly works, although I just can't wait to be myself again.'

Marie wanted to throw her arms around her friend, but something held her back. Orac just wasn't someone you hugged. Marie made do with handing her a crash helmet. 'Let's get you back where you belong.'

For a moment she thought Orac was going to cry. No, it had to be her imagination. Orac didn't do tears either.

'Can't wait. How fast does that bike of yours go?'

'Fast enough,' Marie assured her. 'And tonight, you're coming back to my place. Now I've finally found you, I'm not letting you out of my sight again. It's a comfy bed, which I guess will be welcome. Then, after breakfast, I'll deliver you into the arms of Superintendent Ruth Crooke. No arguments now.'

'Even if I wanted to, Marie, I'm too exhausted to object. It sounds good.'

* * *

Orac proved to be a perfect pillion rider. Marie was amazed when, after the journey, she told her she'd never ridden pillion before. But then Orac never ceased to amaze her.

Marie put together a meal, poured them both a brandy and they sat in her lounge before turning in. There was so much she wanted to ask, but Orac needed to sleep. The questions would have to wait.

'Now I'm back home, I'm beginning to wonder exactly what happened out there.' Orac sounded unsettled.

Marie tilted her head and waited.

Orac took a mouthful of brandy and exhaled. Now she was no longer wearing the dark wig, she looked a little more like the old Orac. 'I'll be for ever grateful to my old friend for finding the contacts that led to my sister, even though I never saw her. I was being watched, and I'm pretty certain it wasn't anyone "official." It was too, well, too amateur. It doesn't make sense.'

Marie knew that if a government agency had been keeping tabs on Orac, she probably wouldn't have known. There was no way they could be called amateur. 'Do you think your friend was watching out for you? If he knows you well, he would have been aware of the risk you were taking in going back to Ireland.'

Orac gave a rare laugh. 'Oh, Marie, if Dara had been following me, I would have had more chance of spotting a white rhino in a service station than seeing him! He was my bodyguard, for want of a better word. It was Dara who spirited me in and out of some very dangerous places indeed.'

'You worked together? He was an agent too?' Marie was surprised that Orac still kept in touch with anyone from her old life.

'Indeed he was, one of the best. I owe him my life.' She smiled again. 'No, it wasn't Dara following me, that's for sure.'

'Maybe the local police were alerted by someone over here and asked to keep an eye on you,' Marie suggested. 'I can't see too many rural police being very skilled at under-cover surveillance.'

Orac shrugged. 'Maybe I'll never know.' She stretched and yawned. 'Or maybe I was imagining it.'

And maybe not, thought Marie. *I don't believe that for one moment.* 'I think you should get some sleep. Let me show you the guest room and the shower, then I'll let you rest. There's everything you need in the bathroom, just help yourself.'

Orac finished her drink and stood up. 'I appreciate this, Marie. You're a good friend.'

Marie laughed. 'You probably won't think so tomorrow, because after the powers that be have given you the third degree, we'll be needing you to catch a triple murderer.'

'I will, don't worry. If there's any way he can be traced using IT, I'll find it.'

Marie led the way up the stairs, more hopeful than she had been for some time. There was just one last thing she had to do before she turned in — give Jackman and Ruth the good news. She took out her phone.

CHAPTER TWENTY-FOUR

Robbie decided against ringing Jackman until he was certain this wasn't a false alarm.

He drove to the site, grateful to Stella for alerting him. They had agreed to meet in Saltmere End village, from where she and Tom would take him to the abandoned hospital.

A few minutes later, he was pulling in behind Tom's vehicle. Stella told him what they suspected, and it didn't sound good.

'We'll get as close as we can, Robbie. If he is there, I have a good idea where he'll leave his car. After that, we go on foot. It's not a big place. Lisa said there's a window with a broken catch that allows easy access.' They set off at once.

'Here?' Tom asked her, pulling into a narrow lane.

'Yes. About a hundred yards on, you'll see the old entrance. Go past it towards the trees over there. That's where he'll park his vehicle.'

But the clearing was empty.

Robbie wasn't sure whether to be relieved or annoyed. 'Could he have parked elsewhere and walked in?'

'Possibly, but there aren't many other places where you can hide a car.' Stella hesitated. 'Well, maybe I over-reacted . . . I'm sorry.'

'Forget it, Stella. What if you'd been right? Since we're here, I think I'll just check that window. You never know.'

'Tom can go with you. I'll wait here and call Will.'

Tom, carrying a powerful torch, led the way. It didn't take long to find Lisa's window, but it was covered in dust and cobwebs. No one had been through that for some time.

'Any other ways in, do you think?' Robbie whispered.

Tom smiled grimly. 'There are always ways in.'

Robbie recalled that Tom was renowned for his ability to get into absolutely anywhere.

'I'm pretty sure there's no one here tonight, though. You get a feel for places when you've been playing this game as long as I have.' Tom looked up at the dark ruin rising above them. 'And this feels empty.'

Robbie understood what he meant. That feeling you got when you were after some villain. You instinctively knew when to tread warily and when the bird had flown.

They looked briefly around, and then returned to the car. As they drew near, they heard Stella calling.

'Tom! Rob! I've just heard from Will. Butterwitch — Emily — has been following Kenny. He met up with another urbexer and they headed out into the fen. She was about to follow him when she saw another vehicle behind them, so she tailed both cars. She knows the area well, and she thinks they are heading towards an old abandoned control tower out on the fen. It's just beyond an old pumping station out on the Catchwater Drain. Both buildings have been shut down for years. Head for Saltern, Tom, then turn off for Hartley Fen.'

As they drove, Stella explained that earlier that evening, Emily had called Norman Keating. She was still eaten up with guilt about Aaron Smith dying on her watch and was desperately contacting all and sundry to try to stop anyone going out at night. Norman called her back later and told her about his fears that Kenny Asquith might be stupid enough to do just that, so Emily had driven to his home to try and talk him out of it. She arrived just as he was driving off, so she followed him. Then she realised she wasn't the only one.' Stella sounded frightened. 'I was afraid she'd do something like this. Now she's in as much danger as Kenny and his friend.'

Tom sped up. 'I know the spot. There's a bit of woodland — some small copses around the back of the pumping station — and there's a car park of sorts — that part of the drain attracts birdwatchers. You could easily walk to the control tower from there.'

Robbie said nothing, wondering what to do. Did this warrant a call for assistance?

'I know what you're thinking,' said Stella quietly.

Robbie sighed. It had always been that way between them. 'So, what do you think I should do?'

'Check it out first. Assess the situation, then make a judgement call.'

'My thoughts exactly.'

Emily had said that she would stop a short distance from the pumping station, where there was a disused barn. She would wait for them there.

Stella's phone rang again. 'Crisis averted — well, part of it anyway. That was Will. Emily has contacted him again and apparently the car she thought was following Kenny didn't turn off to Hartley Fen but went straight on down the main road.'

'But that still leaves Kenny out here with another explorer who possibly doesn't even know about his asthma,' Tom said. 'I suggest we find Emily, then we go and check him out anyway. We can give him a bollocking, if nothing else.'

Soon Tom was slowing down. 'This is the lane to Hartley Fen. I think the barn is about five hundred yards further down.'

Robbie spotted a 4x4 parked in front of the old farm building. The beam of their headlights caught a slim figure standing next to the vehicle.

Emily whispered her thanks. 'I'm sorry if this turns out to be a fruitless exercise and I've wasted your time. I was certain that second car was following them, but when Kenny turned off at the pumping station, he just went straight on towards Fenchester.' She looked thoroughly miserable. 'This whole horrible thing has me so hyped up I'm seeing danger everywhere.'

Understandably so, thought Robbie. 'There's a murderer on the loose, so don't beat yourself up. Tom and I will try to find them and give them an ear-bashing about being so irresponsible.' He noticed she was almost haggard with worry. 'You stay here, Emily, and you too, Stella.' He nodded slightly towards the former. 'Our Emily looks wrung out. Tom and I will do a quick recce and report back, okay?' He hoped Stella wouldn't object to being left out, but she seemed to understand.

For the second time, he and Tom moved off together, making their way stealthily along the lane towards the old buildings.

'The trees have grown since I was last here,' whispered Tom. 'You can barely see the old control tower. I wonder which of the two abandoned buildings they were heading for?'

'Which one is more interesting?' asked Robbie.

'Depends what you're looking for. Neither is exactly awesome, but each has its merits. I'd choose the control tower myself.' Tom slowed down. 'So, what's the plan, Robbie?'

'I reckon we start by checking out where they left their car, then try to see where they've gone. And I suggest we be as silent as we can, Tom. It's a real long shot, but the Magician could be here somewhere.'

'Oh great. Thanks. You do know I'm about to become a dad?' Tom muttered.

Robbie stopped. 'Er, maybe . . .'

'Come on, I was only kidding you.'

Tom strode ahead. Robbie had to hurry to catch him up. 'You don't have to do this, Tom. I mean it. I'm beginning to think I should have called DI Jackman.'

'Let's just have a swift nose around, then you can decide what to do. As you said, there's only a remote chance that anyone else is out here.'

'Okay, but please be careful. Stella will kill me if anything happens to you.'

'Well, I didn't hear her trying to stop me, did you? Let's get this over, now we're here.'

Several stretches of the pathway down to the pumping station had very little cover. Fortunately, they were both wearing dark clothing. Finally, they emerged from one of the copses and saw the indistinct shape of a car backed in close to one of the crumbling brick walls of the station. There was no sign of a second vehicle. Robbie moved closer and it revealed itself as an old, battered 4x4. A glance at the empty packets and crushed Styrofoam cups inside made it plain that the owner was a young male.

Tom was now displaying his skill as an expert urbexer, slipping silently in and out of the shadows, occasionally — and rather disconcertingly — disappearing entirely.

He appeared at Robbie's shoulder, whispering, 'There are no other cars on this stretch of the track. I'd say they're alone in there.'

Robbie chuckled. 'You're good at this, aren't you?'

'I've slipped past more security guards than you've had hot dinners, pal. It's all part of the fun.'

The moon, though not full, was still bright, which both helped and hindered their passage. Robbie had decided to act as if danger still lurked within — just in case — so they kept their torches switched off.

'From now on, we take special care,' he said to Tom. 'If there is anyone else in here, he could easily be watching them from a distance.' Robbie was wishing that he had rung Marie or the boss.

'Look!' Tom laid a hand on his shoulder.

Robbie followed the direction of his pointing finger. There, at the end of the track, he saw a shadow moving quickly beneath the trees. Was it Kenny? His friend? Or someone else?

They stood stock still for a few moments, hardly daring to breathe. Then Robbie pulled on Tom's sleeve and they slowly retreated down the path. As they went, he checked his mobile. The signal was very weak, and he couldn't risk raising his voice.

When they were far enough away, Robbie told Tom to go back to the car and tell Stella to ring DI Jackman. 'Explain the situation and tell her to ask him to make a silent approach.' He paused. 'And tell them to stay in the vehicle, doors locked, and not to move. We can't be too careful.'

Tom nodded and started forward. Then he stopped. 'What are you going to do?'

Good question. 'Try to get closer for a better look. I could be over-reacting, but at least if Jackman's here, I'll feel a whole lot better. I'm still afraid that those two kids could be in terrible danger.'

'And if that's the case, you could be too, so don't do anything heroic. I'll be back in a moment.'

And he was gone. Robbie steeled himself and moved forward again.

* * *

Knowing that Marie was looking after Orac, Jackman decided not to call her but to go to Hartley Fen on his own. He knew the area fairly well from the times he took his two young nephews bird-watching at the Catchwater Drain. Back then, he'd never even considered that the old control tower could be of interest to anyone. He had vaguely registered the wire perimeter fence, the big "Keep Out" and MOD warning signs and thought no more about it. As he recalled, the place had been rather well boarded up as well, although he now knew that such measures wouldn't deter any enthusiastic urbexer.

The hurried message from Stella had told him everything he needed to know, and he was dressed and on the road in minutes. It might all be a false alarm but nevertheless, Robbie could be in big trouble if there was someone else out there. Jackman had a bad feeling about this, but not enough to bring in the heavy mob. He had heard on his radio that there had been a serious RTC on the A17 and uniform were in attendance. He floored the accelerator and just hoped nothing unexpected happened before he got there.

Jackman swung into the lane that led to the pumping station and as he approached an old barn, he saw Stella and another woman waving him down.

'DI Jackman! So glad you're here! My Tom and Robbie are somewhere in that copse that surrounds the control tower. We haven't heard from them for over fifteen minutes and we're worried sick.' Stella looked gaunt in the pale moonlight.

'You two get back in your vehicle.' He squeezed her arm. 'They'll be fine, Stella, they won't do anything stupid.' He wasn't totally sure about that, but he tried to sound convincing.

'You're talking to a retired copper, DI Jackman,' said Stella dryly. 'We *all* do stupid things when we believe someone's life is in danger.'

He made no comment. She was right, of course. 'Sit tight. I'll go see what's occurring.'

'DI Jackman?' Emily's voice was shaky. 'I'm sure it's nothing. I panicked when I saw that car following Kenny and his friend. Then, when he drove on towards Fenchester, I realised I'd been foolish. I'm so sorry.'

'Relax. We get call-outs all the time that turn out to be nothing, but we can't afford to ignore them, can we?'

He didn't know about her, but he certainly hadn't convinced himself. This wasn't exactly the ideal situation. Traipsing off into an area he didn't know, at night, struck him as foolhardy in the extreme. He liked to be prepared, to know the terrain and the possible pitfalls. Above all, he liked to know what he was up against, and now he had no clue.

Luckily, the moonlight, although intermittent, was bright enough to light up the path, but the silence was still unnerving. A strong wind was blowing off the Wash and up the river, which at least carried sound away from the control tower. No one would hear him approach. Step by careful step, he made his way past the old pumping station. Stella had said Tom believed that Kenny and his friend would have made for the old control tower. Jackman glanced around. This place had seemed very different when he'd come with his nephews — peaceful and interesting, a great place to watch waterfowl. Tonight, it was menacing. He strained his ears for the slightest sound or movement, his mouth dry.

He was almost at the tiny track that led to the control tower, and he had had seen nothing of Robbie or Tom Chalk. All he could do was pick his way around the old building and see if they were on the other side. Surely they wouldn't have gone in without him? He had passed a car, half concealed in some bushes, so he knew Kenny and his mate were in there somewhere, but where was Robbie?

A figure suddenly materialised beside him.

'For fuck's sake!' he hissed, his heart pounding.

'Sorry', the man said softly. 'Robbie is still watching, he asked me to liaise with you.'

He gathered himself. 'I guess you must be Tom. So, what's the situation?'

Tom whispered, 'Robbie's concerned that there's someone else in there. He says he has no evidence to back that up, but he's really edgy.'

If Robbie was right, thought Jackman, it would be two against one. Pretty good odds, so long as the other man wasn't armed. 'Take me to Robbie, Tom.'

They made their way closer to the old RAF tower, a decaying relic of the Second World War, where Robbie was waiting. He sighed with relief at the sight of Jackman.

'I'm really sorry if I've called you out for nothing, sir.'

'Actually, Rob, as I made my way through here, I remembered that there's another route into this place. It's a bit hazardous, but it is accessible — you get to it from a drove further down the road to Fenchester. It takes you to the far side of the control tower. If the car that Emily saw was following them, it could well have clocked her and made a detour to throw her off the scent.'

Robbie exhaled. 'So he really could be in there, with those kids?'

'I hate to say it but, yes, there is that possibility.'

For a while they stayed where they were, assessing the situation. Visibility was poor, with fast-moving clouds now obscuring the moon. The wind had gathered speed, but luckily the direction was still in their favour. They needed to act fast.

'Okay,' Jackman began. 'Somehow, we have to get in. I don't know much about this kind of building, but it's not too big. I suggest we get inside and go and look for Kenny and his friend. If there is anyone else in there, he'll see he's well outnumbered and probably make a run for it. If that does happen, you stay with the explorers, Tom, and Rob and I will go after him and try to take him down.'

'I'll get you in,' Tom said. 'It's a standard "fort type" watchtower, so I can help you with the layout as well.'

'How many entrances?' asked Jackman, suddenly pleased they had Tom with them.

'At least two on the ground floor, and one fire escape up to the tower and observation platform. Of course, there's also internal stairs from the watch office up to the tower.' Tom spoke from years of experience. 'I think this one has two big offices downstairs, plus a couple of smaller ones along with storerooms, and a control and operations room upstairs, with the exterior platform above.'

Not too good, thought Jackman, but it would depend on where the two explorers were. He hoped Robbie had got it wrong, and the young men were alone, under no threat other than a dressing-down from him.

'Okay, Robbie, you and I will check the back of this place, to see if there is another car here. Tom, you can find a way to get us inside.'

They moved off.

As soon as he and Robbie got to the back of the control tower, they knew they were wasting their time. It was overgrown, impossible to negotiate in the dark without powerful torches. They made out old ramshackle buildings that had all but collapsed, a jungle of nettles, brambles and saplings.

'If anyone did come in this way,' muttered Robbie, 'he'd checked it out beforehand, that's for sure.'

Jackman agreed. 'We just have to assume he is in there and be prepared for the worst. Let's go and find Tom.'

Tom did one of his unsettling appearances right beside him. 'I wish you wouldn't do that,' Jackman said.

'There's a ground-floor window missing. We can get in there easy.'

Jackman would have preferred a door, somewhere from which you could make a hasty exit if you needed to. But a window would do. 'Lead on. And let's stick together, just in case.'

They crept as silently as they could around the perimeter of the building until Tom came to a halt before the empty window frame.

Jackman went in first, closely followed by Robbie and Tom. He used his phone to light the way. Inside, the place had been trashed. All the main fittings had gone, and plaster, broken glass and rubble lay strewn across the floor. A switchboard covered most of one wall, its wires and fuses dangling haphazardly.

Looking at the floor, Jackman realised it would be hard to walk across it without making a noise. He could hear nothing at the moment, but they might be up in the tower itself. As he considered this possibility, he recalled the three dead bodies hanging from the bell tower. This killer certainly liked towers.

As quietly as he could, he made for a door at the far end of the big room and went through into a wide corridor that had several other doors leading off it. He held up his phone. One was marked "Stores," another "MOD Police." He pushed this one open and saw an area containing a curved reception desk and some broken chairs scattered about.

A flight of stairs at the end of the corridor obviously went up to the tower, and double doors into what he assumed would be another big room. He turned off his phone torch and listened carefully. Behind him, he could hear Robbie's rhythmic breathing. It should have reassured him, but it didn't. He was used to having Marie with him, and wished she was here now. Robbie was a good detective, but he wasn't Marie, and he and Jackman didn't have the same unspoken trust.

He hesitated before opening the door. The silence was ominous. Earlier, they had heard noises drifting towards them on the wind. Now there was nothing.

Taking a deep breath, he opened the door and switched on his phone light.

At first it looked like the rest of the place — dirt, peeling paintwork, old plaster and broken glass — but this room also contained shelving and numerous rusting filing cabinets strewn about. It seemed to be another dead end, so that left upstairs to check and, other than the observation platform at the top, there was nowhere else the urbexers could be. He shone the small light around, just to make sure he'd missed nothing. Then he heard a faint groan and froze.

At the far end of the room, partially obscured by the old office furniture, he saw a figure lying on the floor. Robbie saw it at the same moment and they both dashed forward.

'Police! Stay where you are!'

He shouldn't have worried. The figure on the floor wasn't going anywhere. Jackman dropped to his knees beside him, using his proper torch to see more clearly.

Robbie stared down at the prone figure. 'I think this is Kenny Asquith, sir,' he said shakily. 'Is he . . . ?'

'Phone this in, Robbie, and quickly. We need an ambulance, fast!' Jackman was checking the young man's pulse. It was erratic, and he was barely conscious, but at least he was breathing. 'This isn't just an asthma attack. Something's happened to him.'

Robbie wrestled his phone from his pocket. 'Weak signal, but still stronger than it was in the woods. I'll try. If not, I'll have to run back to the road.'

Jackman heard him bark out his request for assistance, relieved that he'd got through. Then he stopped. 'Where's Tom?'

'He's right behi— Oh, God!' They ran to the door and Robbie flung it open.

Tom Chalk was lying on his side on the filthy, glass-covered floor.

233

'Oh, sweet Jesus! No, not Tom!' Robbie fell to his knees and placed his finger on the side of his neck. 'He's alive! But he's out cold. I didn't hear a thing, did you?'

Jackman had heard nothing either. 'Ring again, Robbie, we need two ambulances. You stay with these two. Don't move away from them.' He dashed upstairs, taking the grimy steps two at a time.

He burst into the control room and looked around. The room was empty. He turned and slithered back down the stairs.

'Damn! Damn! He must have slipped out after disabling Tom. But we can't leave these men, so there's nothing we can bloody well do.'

'We can't blunder around out there in the dark in any case, sir. Far too dangerous. I'll tell uniform. Maybe they'll be able to cut him off?' Robbie called the station and told them what they suspected. 'They have a car close by, sir. They've rerouted it to the Fenchester Road.'

It was the best they could do. 'I'm going back to Kenny,' Jackman said. 'You stay with Tom.'

Jackman cursed himself. He had really messed up. He should have rung it in the moment they suspected that the Magician was close by. He grunted. They'd certainly given him the right name. The Magician. How the hell did he get the other young man out of this building so fast? If he'd knocked the explorer out and bolted, attacking Tom as he exited the building, Jackman could have understood, but to spirit his victim away at the same time? It was damn near impossible.

He sat on the floor beside Kenny Asquith and tried to fathom what had happened to the lad. He didn't seem to be in a critical state — in fact his breathing had regulated and his pulse was settling. He was just not fully conscious. Drugs? He didn't think that was the case, not this time. 'Hey, Kenny! Can you hear me? Can you wake up for me? It's the police, Kenny. You're safe now.'

The young man stirred and tried to raise himself up, then sank back down again without a word.

'It's okay, kid, the ambulance is on its way. They'll get you sorted in no time.' He hoped so, but he wasn't at all sure what was going on with Kenny Asquith. 'How's Tom?' he called out to Robbie.

'Coming round, I think, but he seems to be in pain. Thing is, I can't find any injuries on him. There's none on his head, there's no blood anywhere that I can see, and no bruising. What the hell happened here?'

'I've no idea. I just hope those medics arrive soon.' Then he thought of Stella. 'Oh shit, Rob! We need to phone Stella and Emily! If the blues and twos and a couple of blood wagons show up, they'll have a coronary!'

Robbie groaned. 'I'll call them, sir, but I won't mention her husband, not yet. Especially in her condition.'

Jackman closed his eyes. Oh yes, there was that as well. Jesus. Why on earth had he not sent Tom back to his pregnant wife and let them take the risks alone? He had been some kind of fool tonight, hadn't he?

As he waited beside the inert figure of the young man, Jackman wondered if he'd have acted any differently had Marie been with him. She had the ability to see a situation from a different perspective, and their combined decisions were often the right ones. Well, there was no going back now. The Magician had taken another victim, this time from right under his nose, and he'd have to live with that. He just hoped that uniform had got to the other end of the fen lanes before the killer. It was highly unlikely, but if they had really been in the area, it wasn't beyond the bounds of possibility.

'Stella's aware, sir!' Robbie called out. 'She says she can see blue lights heading across the fen lanes. She'll direct them in.'

Not a moment too soon, thought Jackman, wishing bitterly that he could go back and begin tonight's episode all over again . . . and damned well do it differently.

CHAPTER TWENTY-FIVE

When Marie woke, she heard her shower running. Orac was already up and around. Early as it was, she decided to go and prepare some breakfast. Since having Gary for a lodger, she had come to appreciate a cooked breakfast, even if it had added a few extra pounds.

She was just dishing up slices of grilled bacon when Orac appeared, and this time it was the Orac Marie knew. The wig had gone. Her hair was white-blonde again, back in its Mohican style, and once again those disconcerting metallic eyes flashed.

'Sleep well?' asked Marie, adding tomatoes and scrambled egg to the plates.

'Like the dead,' Orac said. 'I haven't slept like that for ages. For days I've been catnapping, listening out for the sound of approaching danger.'

'Take a seat, breakfast's ready.' She set a plate down in front of Orac. 'Toast coming up. Tea or coffee?'

'Tea, please, Marie. You really shouldn't have gone to all this trouble, you know.' Orac picked up her knife and fork. 'But I'm mighty glad you did.'

They had almost finished when Marie's phone rang. It was Jackman, sounding as if he was out on his feet. Marie listened and then gasped. 'Hospital? Where? Why? What happened, sir? Are you alright?' She put the phone on speaker so that Orac could hear.

'I'm okay, Marie. Last night Robbie and I had a run in with the Magician. We have two injured explorers, Tom Chalk and Kenny Asquith, knocked out, and another young man abducted.' He expelled a long sigh. 'I made a real cock-up of the whole thing, Marie!'

'I doubt that very much, sir. I know you better than that. You will have done what you thought was right at the time. You don't have a crystal ball to get things right every time.'

'Maybe not, but last night was a car-crash.'

He hadn't sounded so negative in a long while. 'Look, give me the whole story later. Right now, I'd like to know how Tom is, and then what I can do to help you.'

'Tom's obs are all good, but he's pretty woozy. I'm hoping to have a proper talk with him soon. Meanwhile, when you take Orac in, would you tell Ruth where I am and then get everyone organised for the day?'

'Of course. Then I'll get straight down to the hospital and you can fill me in.'

'We hoped that uniform would be able to set up a roadblock at the bottom of the fen lane, but the killer beat them to it and got away. The missing explorer's tag name is Crazy Hazy, proper name Keith Hazell, and I have no idea how the Magician got him out.'

'Tell me all this when I see you, Jackman. We'll set up an action plan, and then you can go home and get some sleep.'

After she'd hung up, Orac said, 'I picked a bad time to go away, didn't I? But the moment I've had my wrist slapped and got clearance to start work again, I'll help you, okay? I promise.'

'Well, I could certainly do with it,' said Marie grimly.

'Oh, you will have it. You'll be my number-one priority.' Orac drained her cup and got to her feet. 'Let me help you clear up.'

'Dishwasher. Best invention ever. I throw everything in, and it's all done.' She grinned at Orac. 'It's good to have you back.'

Orac produced a rare smile. 'I didn't realise how much I love it here until I'd left.' Her face darkened and her brow wrinkled in puzzlement. 'I'm still trying to fathom out why I was being watched, and by whom.'

'Have you spoken to your friend, the one who found you the leads to your sister?' asked Marie.

'Yes, he's still in Dublin. We spoke last night, and he's as confused as I am. One good thing, he's off to California on business in a month's time, and he said he'll try to make some covert enquiries as to how Grainne is faring over there. That will be a comfort of sorts.'

Marie felt sorry for her. After years of not knowing what had happened to her beloved sister, she'd found that she was alive and well but couldn't see or talk to her. It must be heart-breaking. 'One day you'll see her, Orac, but you were right to come home when you did. I'm totally sure about that.'

'I'll be eternally grateful I listened to you. Now, I must get myself together and decide what I'm going to say to Ruth Crooke.'

'I'll just grab a shower, then we'll go, if that's okay with you? If we have another young man missing, possibly murdered, I'm going to have my work cut out today.'

'Ready when you are,' Orac said. 'And as soon as I've finished with Ruth, I'll get straight down to work.'

'Leon will be pleased to see you back. He, along with David and Philip, have been really helpful but, frankly, they're like fish out of water without you there.'

* * *

'Sarge?' Gary called out. 'The Prof's been asking for you. Can you ring him, please?'

Marie had just left Ruth's office, and all hell was breaking loose around her. She wanted to get to the hospital, but it was vital to hear the news from forensics. 'I'm on it, Gary, thank you.'

Rory sounded oddly subdued. 'I hear DI Jackman is here at the hospital?'

'He is, and I'm just heading that way myself,' said Marie. 'I haven't a clue as to what happened to the two young men who were with him.'

'Right, then maybe you'd like to call in at my morgue while you're here? Jackman too, if he's finished in A&E. I've got a preliminary report on your three urban warriors, and it would be good to talk to you in person. There are a few anomalies.'

Marie's heart sank. No more anomalies, please. How about something straightforward for a change? 'Of course, Rory. Around eleven, if that's alright?'

'I'll be here, dear heart, and if you are good, I'll even provide coffee and doughnuts.'

'Doughnuts?' said Marie.

'Well, you see, my two stalwart colleagues, Spike and Cardiff Erin, have been taking bets on who makes the best doughnut in southern Lincolnshire. They've been conducting in-depth research into the various attributes of the different products, resulting in a veritable plethora of said delicacies. We are thus prepared to share, in exchange for an honest opinion.'

Despite these light-hearted words, he still sounded rather dispirited. Marie said she'd be happy to partake — purely in the interests of science, naturally. She ended the call, wondering what was worrying him. Those "anomalies," or something else?

At the hospital, she found Jackman in conversation with a distinguished-looking silver-haired man in a smart if somewhat old-fashioned suit and bow tie. He looked out of place in this setting.

'Marie, glad you're here. Please meet Mr Hugh Gillespie, he's a trauma specialist and a good friend of my father.'

Marie smiled to herself. How many times had she heard that by now? And how many good friends did Jackman's father have? 'Pleased to meet you, sir.'

'Hugh has been taking a look at Tom and Kenny Asquith. He has made a rather surprising suggestion regarding what might have occurred last night.' Jackman seemed a lot brighter than when they spoke on the phone.

The man placed a hand on Jackman's arm. 'Look, apologies, but I have to go now — some ghastly board meeting to attend — but do contact me, Rowan. I'm pretty sure my analysis is correct, so if I can be of any more help . . .' He turned to Marie and bent forward in a kind of half bow. 'So sorry not to able to talk more, must dash. Oh, and regards to Lawrence.'

'Strange little man,' Marie said as they watched him hurry away, an incongruous figure amid the chaotic bustle of A&E.

'Maybe, but he has an absolutely brilliant mind.'

Marie looked enquiringly at Jackman. 'Okay, so do you want to tell me what he was talking about? Or is it best to start at the beginning?'

'The whole story would be best.' He yawned. 'But let's get a coffee and go somewhere quiet. I've spoken to Tom, so I think I'm through here now.'

'I've got the very place, extremely quiet, in fact deathly so, *and* there are doughnuts on offer.'

He stared at her blankly.

'Rory wants to see us, and it sounds like he's practically got a bakery going over there.'

A few minutes later, they were sitting in Rory's office with mugs of coffee, in front of a large white box containing a variety of sugary doughnuts. Declaring that he had had quite enough of decaying flesh for the time being, Rory sounded keen to hear what had happened.

Jackman described the events of the previous night. 'Hugh Gillespie is quite certain that both men were incapacitated by expert use of force exerted on pressure points.'

Marie looked dubious. 'As in some sort of martial arts technique?'

'Exactly. He says it takes a master to know at exactly which angle to strike the right nerve point.'

'The touch of death,' Rory said. '*Dim mak* in Cantonese, *kyusho jitsu* in Japanese. It's a very controversial technique, and there are doubts as to whether it's even possible.'

'When we did our training, there were certain places on the body that we were told never to hit, even in self-defence. Is that the kind of thing we are talking about?' Marie asked.

'There are parts of the anatomy that, if struck, can cause intense pain in the victim. So intense, in fact, that they may black out. Something like the old "Vulcan nerve pinch" so beloved of Star Trek fans — except that doesn't exist of course, but still, a blow or a squeeze applied to certain points can damage an artery, which in turn can lead to a blockage in the supply of blood to the brain.'

Jackman nodded slowly. 'I've heard about people receiving a blow to the chest that has resulted in their death. Is that really possible?'

Rory nodded. 'Cardiac concussion. It messes up the heart's electrical current and leads to sudden heart failure. And the thing is, you never know what underlying medical problems a person may have, so a blow that in one man would cause excruciating pain for a short while could possibly be fatal in another.'

'Kenny Asquith has asthma,' Jackman said. 'What if he received one of these stunning blows?'

'It could have a particularly bad effect on him,' Rory said. 'There are two pressure points in the neck so close together that if you strike one, you usually get the other too. A blow on those can cause an instant drop in blood pressure and a resulting vassal faint. Those are the ones that can cause terrible problems if the person has a heart issue. It can even cause plaque in the arteries to dislodge and bring on a stroke.'

Marie was staring at him. 'Er, Rory . . . you seem to know an awful lot about these lethal forms of martial arts. I'm beginning to get rather worried.'

'Oh, heaven forbid!' Rory waved his hands. 'I'm more into Ikebana — you know, the Japanese art of flower arranging.' He sighed. 'The reason I'm so erudite on the subject is that last night I spent several hours researching it.'

'Our three urban explorers?' Marie said.

'Exactly. That's why I wanted to see you, and these latest attacks have confirmed my suspicions.'

Jackman sat forward. 'What did you find, Rory?'

'Small areas of localised bruising in very specific places on their bodies. My nocturnal studies revealed dozens of these sites, and all follow the body's meridian points according to traditional Chinese medicine. They've been assigned code numbers according to medical standards. For instance, there is one called TW-17, standing for Triple Warmer 17, located behind the ear in the depression between the mandible and mastoid process. Striking someone there can be devastating, possibly even causing the skull and the spinal column to separate, it's that dangerous.'

'And that's how the Magician felled those men?' Jackman looked horrified.

'Not using that particular blow but I'm sure from the bruising that they experienced such intense pain that they blacked out. He could then tie them up and transport them away from the attack site.'

As he described this, Rory was far from being his usual verbose self. He simply stated the facts, with no embellishments. It was completely unlike him.

'So, what has you so down, Professor?' Marie said. 'That isn't all, is it?'

'Very astute, Marie. I'm afraid you know me too well!' He pulled a face. 'Okay, you won't want to hear this, but when your young men were raised up on those bell ropes, they were still alive.'

Marie let out a groan. 'Oh no! Surely not.'

''Fraid so. The tests will be conclusive, but I know it already.' He gave a sad smile. 'Hence my rather depressed mood, Marie. Some things actually do penetrate my armour-plated exterior. And this was one of them.'

Jackman closed his eyes. 'Then we have to find this other missing explorer before the Magician carts him off to his place of execution. If he's still alive, there's a chance we can save him.'

Marie didn't hold out much hope. They were no closer to knowing who the Magician was than when they'd started. Okay, they now had something to go on — their man practised some form of the Japanese martial art of pressure-point fighting. But how far would that get them? They had no hope of drawing up a list of people with that particular skill.

She turned to Jackman. 'Boss, you need to recharge. You're no good to anyone on no sleep. I've got this, okay? I'll get Max chasing up the martial arts clubs immediately. Go home and rest. If you'll forgive me for saying, sir, you look like shit.'

'I second that wholeheartedly,' added Rory. 'You need to be right on the ball to catch this killer. Do as the dear woman suggests. And the sooner the better.'

Jackman reluctantly gave in. 'A few hours, then I'll be back. And ring me if there are any developments.'

'Of course,' lied Marie.

CHAPTER TWENTY-SIX

It all felt unreal to Orac. She was back in Ruth's small office, Ruth next to her at the desk, and opposite them a tall officer, chisel-faced, whose vast array of insignia impressed even her.

'You are aware of the considerable anxiety that your disappearance caused, not to mention the exorbitant sum of money the search for you drained from our budget?' he began.

Orac tried to look suitably contrite. She had decided that the best thing she could do was be honest with them. She admitted that she had been aware of the furore her departure would cause, but this was something that had haunted her and her family since her childhood. She had weighed it up and felt she had no choice but to risk her life and cause chaos into the bargain.

'I can only apologise, sir, and tell you that now I have some measure of closure on the matter, it will never happen again.' She looked down. 'I do honestly appreciate everything that has been done to keep me safe. My sudden departure from my usual routine was unforgivable.'

There was a lengthy silence. Then the officer, who seemed to have either forgotten or possibly chosen not to introduce himself said, 'A terrible family tragedy such as this must have had far-reaching effects. I appreciate your reasons but I still feel that you could have taken a far less hazardous route.'

Orac chose not to answer. If there had been, she would have taken it, obviously, but she couldn't argue the point.

'Well, you are back now, and voluntarily, so we need to make plans to move on. Superintendent? You seemed to have been a staunch defender of Ms Cracken. Are you happy for her to remain and resume her duties?'

'Of course, sir,' Ruth said. 'Ms Cracken is a key part of this constabulary, and we are very lucky to have her based with us.' She paused. 'In fact, sir, we have a serious case running at the moment and her input is desperately needed.'

'All in good time.'

Orac groaned inwardly. Just how much grovelling would she need to do before she could get back to her basement? 'I'm anxious to return to work as quickly as possible, sir. I've caused enough trouble already.'

The officer looked at her as if she was a small and irritating child. 'You seem to be forgetting all the fail-safes that were put in place after your unannounced departure, Ms Cracken. Your computer systems were isolated and quarantined. They will all have to be reinstated. Even the locks at your apartment were changed, and other surveillance devices were set up that need to be removed. We didn't take your disappearance lightly, you know. We feared for your life.'

Feared for the threat I posed to national security more like, thought Orac cynically. She wondered if this officer was aware of exactly what IT skills she possessed. Didn't he know what she was capable of? Did he not realise that she had set the system up in the first place? There wasn't a single technician anywhere that could successfully disable her computer.

The officer opened a drawer and took out a key card. He handed it to her. 'Your new access key for 11C Heron Court. I apologise if your home is somewhat in disarray. Naturally, it was searched thoroughly for any indication as to where you might have gone or been taken.'

Mea culpa. 'Easily cleaned up, sir. It's of no consequence.' It was, but now wasn't the time to complain. Then she had a thought. 'Sir? Might I ask if you managed to track me to Ireland?'

'Our people only established your whereabouts on your return to England. You were picked up by airport security while you were waiting for DS Marie Evans to collect you. You left before an official could approach you.'

So, whoever had followed her as she prepared to get home certainly wasn't from here, not that she thought they had been.

Orac sat up straighter. She'd done her apologising, now it was about time this faceless bureaucrat realised just how important an asset she was, to the police and anyone else in the government that needed her services.

Finally, the man stood up. 'I'll put the wheels in motion, Ms Cracken. Take the rest of the day off to sort out your flat and report for work tomorrow.' He narrowed his eyes. 'I'm sure I don't need to remind you that if anything like this happens again . . .'

'It won't, sir. It's over.' Orac held his gaze. He was the first to look away.

When he'd gone, Ruth let out a sigh of relief. 'Could have been worse.'

'Sure, but he's still a supercilious git.'

'Agreed. So, what are you up to now? Off to do a spot of housework?'

'I'm going to assess the damage, and then come right back and get my computers up and running again. Without the help of whoever tried to shut them down.'

'Thought so.' Ruth stood up. 'In which case, Jackman and Marie need you, Orac.'

'I know, and I'm all theirs, for as long as it takes.' She smiled at the super.

Ruth smiled back. 'Welcome home. I'm glad you're safe, and don't you ever, ever scare me like that again.'

For a supposedly cold, emotionless woman, there was genuine warmth in those words. This was Orac's family now.

* * *

With Jackman and Robbie absent, they were thin on the ground, and Max and Gary were working flat out. Marie had intended to get Max ringing round the martial arts clubs but decided to do it herself. He seemed to be juggling enough already.

She stepped into another world. She had been surprised to find so many clubs in the fenland area, but soon found that a lot of them were mainly devoted to kickboxing, and only one or two offered a different type of training. After a few calls, she decided to start with a centre in Saltern-le-Fen's business park, and soon she was driving across town to meet one of the instructors.

The building was impressive, vast and divided into various halls whose purpose was unclear.

She was greeted by a rotund, smiling woman of around forty — not the kind of person Marie would have taken for a martial arts instructor. She introduced herself as Anna and took Marie into a plush office with comfortable leather chairs. Pictures of some of their junior black belts lined the walls, mainly school children.

Anna briefly introduced herself and told Marie a little about their particular martial art. 'How can I help?'

'It's to do with an ongoing inquiry, Anna. I can't give you the details, but the forensic evidence suggests that the victims were immobilised using their pressure points.'

The woman raised an eyebrow. 'Victims?'

Marie nodded. 'As I said, I can't elaborate at this time.'

'If someone was deliberately injured using pressure-point techniques, I would look outside the martial arts world, Detective Sergeant.' Anna handed Marie a beautifully scripted laminated card. 'Our pledge. Everyone who studies here must adhere to this, from the youngest child to the Grandmaster himself.'

The pledge stated that the practitioner would give equal regard to all persons, irrespective of class, creed, race or religion. It was a declaration of peace and goodwill, loyalty, learning and personal development. Marie set it aside. 'This is very admirable, but how do you prevent anyone disregarding the principles set down here?'

'I would be very, very doubtful that you would find a martial arts expert who failed to act according to the pledge. It would be impossible to practise correctly.' She pointed to a picture on the far wall. 'This man is our founder. He started his training at five years old, and he is now seventy. He is a master in pressure-point techniques, and in order to reach that level, he has lived and breathed the pledge. He would never have got where he was if he hadn't.'

Maybe it was the work she did, but Marie wasn't convinced. 'I appreciate what you're saying but sadly, a personal crisis can change a man or woman.'

'This technique is all about physical, mental and spiritual development, DS Evans. Even though it is also a form of combat, it is mostly about self-discipline and self-defence, not killing people.' She looked at Marie. 'I assume someone has been killed?'

There was little point in denying it. The media would soon be all over it anyway. 'A death has occurred,' she said noncommittally, and looked through the office window at the rest of the dojang. 'I had no idea this place existed. It's massive, isn't it?'

'It's a state-of-the-art training facility for *Kuk Sool Won*, a Korean martial arts system. We've built it up over ten years.' She smiled at Marie. 'You should try it. We run two free classes so people can see if it's something that might benefit them. After all, your job is so stressful.'

'It's a thought,' said Marie, knowing that certainly wouldn't happen. 'You must love it.'

'I'm a third degree black belt instructor, and it's the best part of my life, especially helping the young colour-belt students.'

'It must be very rewarding, and I'm sure it directs a lot of young people along a better path than some I see down at the station. But, Anna, can I ask you if you've ever come across someone who may have wanted to train here for the wrong reasons?'

Anna shook her head. 'It would become apparent very early on. This is not a fast-track route to learning how to hurt people, and if anyone displays the wrong signs, they are asked to leave.' She looked earnestly at Marie. 'I believe there are people on the web who offer to teach various martial arts techniques for exorbitant sums of money using home courses. Of course, they aren't accredited, and I would warn anyone not to go near them, but,' she shrugged, 'you might find someone a little more unscrupulous through those sites, don't you think?'

Marie agreed and thanked her for her time. Anna walked her back to the foyer. 'Don't forget, come and give us a try. Or just watch a class in action. We have a comfortable viewing lounge, and everyone is very welcoming.' She held the door open for Marie. 'For stress relief, it's quite amazing.'

Marie returned to her car and examined her reflection in the rear-view mirror. She must be looking very stressed indeed since Anna had mentioned it twice, both times with a slightly anxious look. 'I reckon it would take more than dressing in pyjamas and kicking people to calm me down,' she muttered to herself. Right now, catching the Magician was the only thing that would lower Marie Evans's stress levels.

* * *

The CID room was unusually quiet when she returned. Of her team, only Gary remained at his desk. 'Max has gone to have a word with an urbexer who has flagged up concern about another member of his crew, or whatever they call their exploring groups. He said he won't be long.' He looked at her hopefully. 'Any luck with what you're looking at, Sarge?'

She sank down on a chair next to him. 'Not really. Although I've been given another possibility regarding this martial arts thing — online courses.'

'Definitely worth a check, I'd say,' said Gary. 'After all, there's no controls over that sort of thing. Anyone could set one up.'

'Any news on Tom and the other lad, Kenny, while I was out?' she asked.

'Yes. Stella North, sorry, Chalk, left a message for you. I put it on your desk.'

Marie hurried over and picked up the memo.

Tom coming home this afternoon, no lasting effects, or so the docs hope. Call me when you are free. Stella.

Marie called at once. 'Stella? It's Marie.'

'Oh, bless you for getting back to me. It's just that Tom told me he spoke to DI Jackman but he was still a bit woozy at the time. He's much more his old self now, though, and wanted to talk to you. Can I pass you over?'

'Of course,' said Marie. 'Hey, Tom! I hear you got taken out by Spock's Vulcan nerve pinch.'

'I'd never have had you down as a Trekkie. But yes, it appears that's exactly what happened.' He gave a nervous laugh. 'Hell, Marie, I've never felt pain like it! All my nerves just shrieked out and hit my brain like a lightning strike! I went down like a ton of bricks.'

'Lucky punch? Or a deliberate move, would you say?'

'Oh, he knew exactly what he was doing. One sharp jab into the side of my ribcage and my world exploded.' He paused. 'But I did catch a glimpse of him just before he hit me.'

Marie blinked. 'Really? That's brilliant.'

'Not particularly.' He sighed. 'I only had a small torch and he came down the stairs like the wind, just as I stepped out into the hall. All I can tell you is that he was white, tallish, very muscular, was wearing camo trousers and some kind of bomber jacket. I only caught a glimpse, but it was a bit like those flight jackets that you see in American films, and I think it had a logo or a badge on it, but it was just a blur.'

'Well, that's certainly the best we've had so far,' said Marie, trying to hide her disappointment.

'One last thing, Marie. As I lost consciousness, I saw him go back up the staircase, not make a run for it towards the entrance. I don't know if that's relevant, but I only thought of it after DI Jackman had left.'

That was odd. She had rather imagined him heading out immediately. He only had a very short time in which to make his exit, so why go back up the stairs? 'Thanks for that, Tom. I'll tell Jackman the moment he arrives. Now, you get some rest, and thank you so much for giving us that description. Could I have Stella back for a moment?'

Stella took the phone. 'Hi, Marie, he's done well to remember anything after a knockout blow like that, hasn't he?'

'Yes, he has. He's the first person to see the Magician up close and live to tell the tale. Look, Stella, please ring me when you're both back home again. I'll try to get over to see you when we finish, unless it's very late.'

'Don't worry about us, Marie. Once we're home and he's rested, he'll be right as ninepence again, I'm sure.'

'And you, Stella? How are you coping?' Although she never mentioned her disabilities, Marie knew that Stella did suffer.

'It was a fright, I was so worried about Tom.'

Marie was suddenly transported back to the motorcycle race circuit — the crash, then realising that the emergency crews were tending her own husband, and then seeing their faces and knowing they were too late. For a moment she couldn't speak. 'I'm so sorry, Stella, it must have been simply awful for you.'

'Lucky he's as strong as an ox. That other lad, Kenny, is still struggling. They're keeping him in for observation and treatment for his breathing problems.' Stella paused. 'No news about the young man who was abducted, I suppose?'

'Nothing, and I fear for him. Until we get a handle on this killer, we're stuffed. You know how it is.'

Stella exhaled loudly. 'Don't I just! Will Sheringham and I are still chasing up every suspicious posting on the internet. It's all we can do.'

'You guys are probably our best hope, my friend. Just try to keep a tight rein on Emily. Tell her to leave it to the pros, and not to dash off like bloody Angelina Jolie. This is Saltern-le-Fen, not an out-take from *Tomb Raider!*'

Stella laughed. 'Well, if it wasn't for her, no one would have known about that control tower, so I can't yell at her too much. Anyway, she's learned her lesson. Last night's fiasco scared the shit out of her.'

'Glad to hear it.' Marie finished the call, then tried to fathom why the Magician had not run immediately. After a moment she groaned. 'I really am over-stressed! What an idiot! He went back for Crazy Hazy!' He'd most likely immobilised him and left him on the staircase. And if the guy was as strong as Tom seemed to think, he must have used a fireman's lift to carry the Hazell lad out of the building. That would account for what Tom saw.

Marie stood up and went back to Gary's desk. 'Have either you or Max had a look at Keith Hazell's background yet?'

'I have, Sarge, and I sent a heads-up over to Will Sheringham. I decided their exploration community would be faster at finding out about him than me.' He fished around the piles of notes and printouts on his desk and pulled out an email. 'This is his initial reply, but he knows someone who can give us more. He's getting back to me later.'

Marie read it.

DC Pritchard,
Hazy has a reputation of being a bit of a loose cannon.
He's not dangerous, but he does take low-grade risks, and he

encourages others to perhaps step outside their comfort zones.
He's still quite popular, though, because he's funny and never
opts out of a challenge. He does love exploring and has since
he was a kid, just doesn't know when to put the brakes on!
I'll speak to an old clan member who knew him better than
me and get back to you.
Will.

She pulled a face. 'No wonder he went out with Kenny when he'd been warned not to. Kenny hit on the right one when he rang him.'

'Or the wrong one, depending how things go at the hospital,' added Gary. 'I would have thought crawling around old buildings was the last thing an asthmatic ought to be doing. Think of the amount of asbestos that was used in days gone by. He could kill himself if he chose a bad explore. Silly sod!'

'If urbexers are happy to enter the exclusion zone after Chernobyl, I reckon they won't be put off by a lungful of asbestos. It's a kind of obsession, Gary, they can't help themselves.' She'd seen some of Stella's breath-taking photographs and although she preferred looking at action shots of Barry Sheene on one of his record-breaking bikes, she understood the attraction. The intensity pouring from Stella's images was almost palpable.

'You're right, of course.' Gary pulled out another report. 'But from our point of view, this Keith Hazell has never been in any trouble. Not a whisper, or a mention anywhere on the PNC. He lives with three other students, they rent a house in Calder Street and again no trouble from any of them.' He sat back. 'So, he's a bit reckless, but there's nothing sinister in his background.'

'How about his parents? Have we contacted them yet, Gary?'

He nodded. 'Uniform went to their home out Randleby way, but they are apparently off on a jolly in a motor home. Destination unknown at this time. Uniform're using the vehicle's licencing details to try to pick it up. Otherwise, it will be over to the super to put out a request on TV and the radio for them to come forward.'

It wasn't what Ruth would want, but they couldn't afford to hang about, considering what had happened to the other explorers so soon after their abduction. Marie bit on her bottom lip, not even wanting to consider that right now. Plus, the mention of Randleby had immediately conjured up a vision of that old Norton. 'Anything more from that old friend of yours, Gary? The one who was doing a bit of sleuthing for you out at the old airfield?'

'Oh, you mean John Beard. No, I thought I'd give him a ring tonight. I might even go over there and have a pint with him. I don't want to lose touch. We were good mates and I'd hate to drift apart again. It's so easy when you're busy not to make time for old muckers.'

Marie knew what he meant. She was hardly an "old mucker," but her mum was due here in four days' time, and she hadn't even spoken to her since the week before. Life got in the way, especially with a job like they had. 'Too true,' she murmured. 'Keep me posted about that old place out at Randleby, Gary.'

'Naturally. I'll pass on anything John tells me.' He looked up at her. 'In fact, while I was over there the other day, I noticed that the pub, the Golden Compass, had a pretty good bar menu. Fancy a meal, and meeting John? He worked at Fenchester nick for years as a civilian. I think you'd like him.'

Marie brightened. 'I'd love to, as long as we don't get caught up here.'

'Excellent. I'll give him a bell and see how he's fixed.'

Marie was about to speak when she heard her desk phone ringing. She hurried over and snatched it up.

'Marie, it's Ralph at Fenchester.'

'Goodness. I was just talking to a colleague about that airfield, and now you've called! You haven't been getting into hot water again, I hope?' She hated to think of him getting his wrist slapped again because of her.

'I've been as good as gold, Marie — well, that's what my boss thinks.' He laughed. 'But I have been doing a little "off-duty" detecting, and although I've nothing conclusive, I think I might have hit on a bit of a lead.' Ralph was obviously not going to let this drop.

'Tell me more, Secret Squirrel,' said Marie with a smile.

'I've met someone else who is interested in the place, Marie. He used to work here but he's retired now, nice bloke. Anyway, we decided to pool resources. Thing is, are you free for a chat this evening? I'd rather tell you in person than talk on the phone.'

Marie frowned. 'You aren't talking about a guy called John Beard, are you?'

'The very same! But how did you know?'

'This is weird, but he's a friend of my colleague, Gary Pritchard, and we were hoping to meet him tonight in the Golden Compass at Randleby.'

'Well I'm damned! Room for a little one? We can all talk then,' Ralph said.

'Perfect! I'll tell Gary and hope he's been able to get hold of John. How does seven thirty sound?'

'I'll be there. And even if John can't make it, we'll meet anyway. I think you might be interested in my news.' Before he rang off, Ralph said, 'I meant to ring you anyway, Marie, when I heard about you and Jackman finding those kids' bodies. I'm really sorry. It must have been pretty tough on you. Any leads?'

'Not really. We have one witness who actually saw the Magician, but the description could fit pretty well any athletic, white man of fortyish. Not enough to try to get an e-fit.'

'That's a bummer.'

'Yeah, isn't it? But one thing, he wore a bomber jacket, a bit like a US flier's jacket with a logo of some kind on it.'

'Mmm, that's interesting. Sounds like it could be something he wears all the time. We blokes get attached to items of clothing that we feel comfortable in, especially jeans and jackets.'

Very true. Her Bill had owned an old leather biker's jacket that he adored. He had plenty of other smart leather riding gear, but what did he always choose? The old, scuffed and well-worn favourite. It was still in the wardrobe. She had never had the heart to throw it away, and on occasions, she had worn it herself, perhaps hoping to find a hint of his scent still clinging to it.

Marie dragged herself back to the present. 'Yes, Ralph, that's a good point.'

Ralph rang off, and after the flood of her memories had abated, Marie was left feeling quite excited. She might just be a step closer to retrieving that precious bike from the mouldering aircraft hangar.

She looked across to Gary's desk. He was giving her a thumbs-up. 'We're on,' he called.

'Plus one,' she called back. 'Ralph Enderby is joining us.'

Gary looked mildly surprised but nodded. She'd explain later. Right now, she had to get her head back into the murder inquiry. She scribbled a note reminding herself to ring her mother that evening, no matter what, and rubbed her temples. Concentrate, Marie! What's next with this case?

Before she could answer herself, she noticed someone approaching her desk. 'Orac! Great to see you back in the fold.'

'Good to be here, believe me!'

'How was the fourth degree? Painful?'

Orac took a deep breath. 'Could have been worse, but I got tired of it pretty quickly. I'm grounded until tomorrow, or so I'm told, but I've chosen to ignore that, and Ruth is on my side, so . . .' She looked down at Marie. 'I need everything you have on this murder case. I said it would be my number-one priority, and I meant it. My systems will be fully functioning by morning, and in the meantime, I want to read up on the situation so far.'

'Music to my ears, and Jackman will be ecstatic when he gets in. Give me an hour or so, Orac, and I'll bring you everything we have to date. I'd already started getting it together, so it won't take too long.' She puffed out her cheeks. 'Doesn't make pleasant reading.'

'I never thought it would. But it's time I started making amends for all the trouble I caused you, Marie.' She lowered her voice. 'I've decided to put all my personal stuff on the back burner until this case is closed. Then I'll decide what I'm going to do, but,' she flashed those odd eyes, 'your idea of placing a letter with her solicitor is by far the most sensible. We'll see when a little more water has flowed under the bridge.'

It was good to hear Orac sounding like her old self and seeing things more clearly. Though heaven only knew what she might have done in the same circumstances. 'Sensible move, and you wouldn't believe how relieved I am that we have you back. I bet your lads downstairs are partying, aren't they?'

Orac gave a rare laugh. 'I've never seen a bunch of anoraks so animated! I thought Leon was actually going to hug me!' She shuddered. 'See you in an hour.'

'You will.' With renewed energy, Marie began putting together the reports, statements and notes from various pocketbooks. It suddenly felt like progress, as if they were firing on all cylinders again. This time, she was certain, things would move forward.

Crazy Hazy. It was as if he had called out to her, reminding her that time was running out for him. 'Okay, Keith, you just hold on,' she whispered to herself. 'We're doing our best for you.'

CHAPTER TWENTY-SEVEN

Robbie and Jackman arrived back in the CID room at the same time. Jackman was looking a lot more rested than the last time Marie had seen him. He had slept solidly for four hours, followed by a hot shower, a change of clothes and a quick lunch, and now he was feeling human again.

'Okay, Marie, where are we now?'

Marie let out a long sigh. 'I'm trying to prepare something for Orac to work on, and it's getting complicated as we've all been looking at different areas of the investigation.'

Robbie joined them. 'Stella's just emailed me with a list of urbexers, possibly rogue ones, that she, Will and Lisa got together for us last night. She'd understandably forgotten all about it when she heard about Emily chasing after Kenny Asquith, then Tom having been rushed to hospital.'

'Any names that register with you, Robbie? Anyone known to us?' asked Jackman.

'Not at first glance, sir, but I'll run them through the PNC.' Robbie looked at the email. 'There is one that flagged up concern for Stella, but no one can remember his name. It wasn't him so much as the sequence of events and the man's sudden appearance on a trip to Yorkshire that worried her.' He read from the paper. 'She says they were looking at an old manor house from where a girl once went missing without trace. She's chasing that up on her UE website for us.'

'Good. What are the other names, by the way?' Jackman asked.

'Roy Ferris, Jeff Saville, a chap called Henry, and the man with no name.' Robbie skimmed to a postscript. 'Ah, she's added that she's since discovered that the guy called Henry's surname is Arnott.'

Jackman and Marie looked at each other.

'That's who rushed to the hospital to see Cally Prothero after she had that terrible fright the night before last!' exclaimed Marie.

'And she's gone to stay with him,' Jackman breathed, feeling suddenly nauseous.

Robbie pulled a face. 'Stella said he's not a serious contender for being a person of interest. His main problem was being over-intense about industrial buildings and locations. He was very knowledgeable by all accounts, just not well liked.'

That didn't make Jackman feel any easier. 'Marie, have we got his number?'

'Yes, I noticed it as I was sorting this info for Orac. I'll get it.' She hurried across to her workstation.

'Ring him and talk to Cally. I need to know she's safe,' called out Jackman.

'I'm on it, boss.'

A few moments later, he heard her speaking. 'Henry Arnott? Sorry to bother you, sir, I'm DS Marie Evans at Saltern Police station. I'm phoning to see how Cally Prothero is now.'

Jackman and Robbie came and stood beside her, so she put the conversation on speaker.

Henry Arnott had a well-spoken, educated voice. 'Oh, thank you for enquiring, Sergeant Evans.' He sighed. 'She's some way from being recovered, as you would expect after a shock on that scale, but she is much better than when she was in hospital.'

'That's good to know,' said Marie cautiously.

'She sleeps a lot, but I guess that's the medication — she said she never takes drugs, prescription or otherwise, so I think they've affected her a little more than someone who is used to taking medicines regularly.'

The man sounded reasonable and apparently very caring.

'I wondered if I could have a quick word with her, Mr Arnott? Just to assure her that we're doing all we can to find the person responsible. I don't want her to feel that we're treating her situation lightly. We are very worried for her.'

'She'll appreciate that, I'm sure. I don't have to tell you to be diplomatic though. You'll understand that she's still very shaky. She just wants things back to normal, but I fear that will take time. Hold on, Sergeant, I'll take the phone up to her room.'

They heard the sound of his footsteps on the stairs, and Jackman began to relax a little. The man seemed quite happy to let them talk to her. He heard the sound of a gentle tap on a door, then Arnott calling her name.

They all waited, then heard the door opening.

'Damn it!' Arnott exclaimed, and groaned. 'She's not here, Sergeant! Her joggers and sweatshirt have gone, and her running shoes. She said she wanted to start getting back to her usual routine, but I told her it was too soon to go running.' He groaned again. 'I'm so sorry. I should have watched her more closely, but I thought she was sleeping. I haven't seen her for a couple of hours.'

With a grimace, Marie said calmly, 'Try not to worry, sir. Have you any idea of the route she would take?'

'None at all. She isn't familiar with this area, so she could have gone in any direction. Oh hell!'

'Has she got her phone with her, sir?' demanded Marie, more forcibly now.

There was a short pause, then he said, 'No, it's still beside her bed.'

Jackman closed his eyes, all the old anxiety flooding back. A seasoned and expert lone urbexer like Cally would never leave their phone behind when going jogging in a strange area.

'Stay put, sir. We're on our way.' Marie ended the call and stared at her notes. 'He lives in Leasholm village, on the main road out of Saltern in the Fenchester direction. House named Heathersett, in Coldharbour Lane. Shall we attend, sir?'

He turned to Robbie. 'You hold the fort and get to work finding all you can about Henry-bloody-Pickwick Arnott! And get Gary, and Max, when he returns, onto the other two on Stella's list. We need backgrounds on them all.'

Robbie nodded. 'Got it.'

'Right, Marie, let's get moving. Do you know where this Coldharbour Lane is?'

Marie pulled on her jacket. 'More or less, boss, I know the village, and I'm sure that lane leads out onto open farm-land. I'll drive, if you would put the location into the satnav, just to make sure?'

Ten minutes later, they were on their way out of town and heading for Leasholm.

'More bad vibes, boss. I'm getting pretty sick of them,' Marie said.

'Me too. That kid has suffered enough. I'll never for-give myself if we've let her walk into a trap.' Had Henry Arnott been properly vetted? Maybe not. After all, according to Cally, he was a close friend, so why check him at all?

'Knowing how vulnerable she is, we should have looked more closely at that man,' he muttered.

'We can't check everyone, sir, you know that. It was her choice to call him, he didn't march in and insist on taking her out.' Marie was being perfectly reasonable but he couldn't help worrying about Cally Prothero. After what she had wit-nessed, her mental state was bound to be precarious.

'She trusted him, Jackman. Let's hold onto that, shall we?' Marie said softly.

'Not everyone deserves the trust that others place in them,' he said. 'We've seen that demonstrated countless times. I'll only feel better once I've seen her for myself.'

'Okay, I agree. What did you make of him when you spoke?' she asked.

Jackman thought back to the phone call. 'Initially, I was reassured, especially when he offered to take the phone up to her. He sounded like an academic, didn't he? Someone used to sitting in libraries, rather than exploring old buildings.'

'Strikes me, sir, that these urbexers come from every possible background. Take Kenny Asquith, a millionaire's son, and then Aaron Smith, a schoolboy daredevil who fell out with his parents and lived in a tiny flat with another kid. This exploring game clearly attracts all sorts.' Marie negotiated a roundabout and swung off down a leafy lane towards Leasholm village.

A few roads later, the satnav told her to take the next left and in five hundred metres she would have reached her destination.

'Heathersett,' said Jackman, pointing to a rather pleasant detached house set back off the lane. 'And will you look at that!'

Seated on a garden bench outside the front of the property was a tall, well-built man of around forty-five. He had his arm around Cally Prothero's slender waist.

'I just rang your office. I'm so sorry, I'm afraid I've brought you out on a wild goose chase.' Henry Arnott held out his hand to them. 'Come in, I'll make a drink.'

Jackman was supremely relieved.

Inside, Henry ushered them into a comfortable lounge. Somewhat dated and dominated by a recliner and walking frame, it was clearly arranged to suit an elderly person.

Cally sank into an armchair and looked at them apologetically. 'I'm so sorry, Officers. I know I should never have gone off alone like that. I just felt — well, trapped, I guess. I'm used to doing things whenever I feel like it, and being active, not crashed out in bed for hours at a time. I never meant to scare anyone, especially Henry. I thought I'd be back before he noticed I'd gone. It was just that the walls were coming in on me.'

Jackman noted that she had a kind of hollow look about her, but he guessed that was to be expected after what she had seen. It had been bad enough for them, and they were hardened to such sights.

'As long as you're safe, Cally, that's all that matters,' said Marie.

'Oh yes, and Henry's been so kind. When he's not visiting his father, who's in respite care for a week or so, he's been looking after me like a mother hen, bless him.' She sank back in the chair as if she lacked the energy to even sit up. 'I don't understand why this has affected me like this. I'm usually so strong and independent. I feel like a weak child. I only ran a little way, and then I had to walk back. I was so exhausted I didn't think I'd make it back to the house.' She looked near to tears. 'And I forgot my phone. I never do that.'

'Don't underestimate what shock can do, Cally,' said Jackman. 'And Henry's right to let you sleep as much as possible. It will help.'

'I've never slept so much in my life.' Cally looked thoroughly miserable. 'I went to bed at nine last night and didn't wake up until after seven this morning. That's unheard of for me.'

Jackman wished he had the chance to sleep like that. 'I expect the doctors gave you something to help you relax, didn't they? I'm betting it's making you sleepy, so don't fight it.'

Henry had brought a tray of drinks. He set it down on the coffee table in front of them. 'Help yourself. Hope you all like tea. I don't drink coffee, so there's none in the house, I'm afraid.'

They thanked him, and then Jackman said, 'Did you explore too, Henry?'

Henry sat down in the recliner. 'Many moons ago. I gave up when my father began to need more care. When I moved in with him and became his full-time carer, it put an end to my urbex days.' He gave a little laugh. 'And to be honest, I wasn't very popular with the others. I was a bit too intense for some of them. I have a real passion for Victorian industry, and like nothing better than getting into an old mill or a factory, but I do get a bit carried away.' He glanced across to Cally. 'We became friends through work, and then discovered that we shared an interest in urban exploration.'

Jackman decided to chance his arm. 'This is a long shot, but did either of you ever hear of an expedition to some Elizabethan manor house up in Yorkshire? Apparently, it attracted a bit of an oddball, someone the urbexers decided had an ulterior motive for going out with them.'

On hearing this, Cally, who'd been looking half asleep, roused herself. 'Was that Will and Lisa Sheringham's clan?'

Jackman nodded. 'It was a while back — before Will got hurt.'

'They put a warning up on one of the websites after that incident,' Cally said. 'They were quite unnerved, as I recall, but to my knowledge he never reappeared. He must have only been interested in that particular old house.'

'Oh well, it was worth a try.' Jackman swallowed a mouthful of tea. 'We should let you rest, Cally. We'll let you know how the inquiry goes, I promise. But no going off alone and scaring Henry again, alright?'

She looked thoroughly contrite. 'I promise. And thank you for coming out. I'm sorry I wasted your time.'

As they drove back to Saltern, Marie said, 'So, what's your opinion of Henry Arnott now?'

Jackman was forced to admit he had been wrong. 'Not what I thought. He genuinely cares about her, doesn't he?'

Marie laughed. 'He does more than that! Didn't you notice the way he was looking at her?'

'Oh.' Jackman looked blank. 'No.'

Marie rolled her eyes. 'Men! He's head over heels in love with her!'

'He is?'

'Oh yes. I'm not sure if she's aware of it yet, but I'm guessing he won't be able to conceal it from her for too much longer.' She laughed again. 'Well, that's cheered me up. That look of total bemusement on your face, Jackman. It's priceless!'

* * *

Marie spent the next hour collating info for Orac, and then she took it down to the basement.

As soon as she walked into the IT department, she sensed a totally different atmosphere. As always, everyone was busy, but there was a buzz about the place. The best thing was seeing Orac seated once again in front of her massive array of screens as if on a throne.

From across the basement, Leon beamed at her, and David and Philip gave her friendly waves, like zombies who had suddenly been raised from the dead.

Orac accepted the armful of reports and notes Marie handed to her and licked her lips. 'I can't wait to get to grips with the work I love. *My* kind of detective work.'

'Neither can I!' said Marie with feeling. 'All I can think about is that young man, Crazy Hazy, and wondering if he's alive or dead. We know what the Magician has in store for him, so it's whether we can find him in time to prevent it happening.'

'Philip has just located his parents' mobile home, DS Evans, so we know where they are,' called Leon. 'Would you like the details, or should we tell uniform?'

'Both. Notify uniform immediately, but I'll make a note of it as well. Good work, Philip. You're definitely getting closer to that new tie.'

Philip ran a hand down his chosen tie for the day, a scarlet blaze of flames leaping into an indigo sky.

'Wow,' said Marie. 'Must be unique.'

'Probably because no other silly bugger would be seen dead in it,' said David with a grin.

'Jealousy,' muttered Philip, 'pure jealousy.'

Marie turned back to Orac. 'I'll let you have anything else that comes in.'

But Orac was already head down and reading.

* * *

As soon as Marie was back, Jackman held a serious case emergency meeting. Uniform — represented by the duty officer, Sergeant Terry Curtis — several PCs, and as many detectives as could be mustered. They all needed to be able to see the whole picture, not just the aspect of it that they were dealing with.

'In brief, we have an unknown white male, who we are referring to as the Magician, seemingly cherry-picking certain young men who practise urban exploration. He isolates his victim, immobilises them with the use of an extremely painful pressure-point technique, and takes them to another abandoned building where, while they are still alive, he suspends them by one ankle, until death occurs.' The image of what he and Marie had seen in that bell-tower rose before him and he paused briefly. He pointed to three of the photographs on the whiteboard. 'These are the deceased — Anthony Hood, Aaron Smith and Grant Leach.' He then indicated to a fourth picture. 'And this is Keith Hazell, known to his compatriots as Crazy Hazy. Last night, he was abducted from an abandoned control tower on the Catchwater Drain at Hartley Fen.' He looked around the room. 'The Magician achieved this despite the presence of myself, DC Robbie Melton and another man, Tom Chalk, an expert urban explorer. We fear that he intends, or maybe already has, murdered this young man in the same way as he did the others.'

Jackman drew in a breath. 'We can find no connection whatsoever between the victims, or the locations he chose. The Magician has only been seen once, indistinctly, by Tom Chalk just before he was attacked. He describes a white male of around forty, well built, and wearing camouflage trousers and a distinctive bomber jacket with a logo on or above the breast pocket. Even though a roadblock was set up to stop him getting off Hartley Fen, the Magician got away. Traffic cameras have failed to pick up a vehicle leaving on the main road, so we suspect he used the back lanes to get as far as possible from the site.'

'Slippery bugger, isn't he?' murmured someone.

'And very dangerous,' added Jackman. 'I've seen first-hand what he's capable of.'

Sergeant Terry Curtis stood up. 'We have had officers watching as many abandoned buildings as we can, sir, but there are just too many, and too scattered to watch them all. It's an impossible task.'

'And probably a waste of time and resources,' agreed Jackman. 'We have no idea what his agenda is or where he will strike next. In short, we know sod all.' He began to pace. 'Our hopes now lie with forensics, that maybe he's left a trace, some DNA on one of the victims, and we can track him that way. We also have IT doing a comprehensive computer search, hunting for anomalies and possible connections. The solution to this case might come down to technology and science, rather than manpower and the human element.'

He was giving them so little to go on. He smiled rue-fully. 'I know, I know. This is not what you wanted to hear, but there are one or two peculiarities about his MO that are worth considering.' He pointed to a gruesome post-mortem shot of Aaron Smith. 'The Magician removes the victims' clothes and dresses them in a kind of sacking tunic. Their own clothes and belongings are then carefully washed, packed, and sent to Professor Rory Wilkinson at the morgue. The packages include a list, plus the name, age, and occupation of the victim. So, what is that all about?' He paused. 'Then there is the way he hangs them by their left ankle. It has been noted that this position is reminiscent of the Hanged Man in a set of Tarot cards.' He pinned a printout of an enlarged picture of the card on the board next to the forensic ones. 'DC Stoner? Anything show up on that?'

Kevin stood up. 'Nothing that I can find, apart from the resemblance to the image. Like a lot of cards in the deck the meanings vary, some are negative, some positive, but I can find no connection to any other aspect of the case. Sorry, sir.' He sat down again.

Jackman spread his hands. 'So, we disregard that line of enquiry for the time being. Thank you, Kevin. Which means, bottom line, the Magician has a list, and he is working his way through it. We have no way of knowing whether Crazy Hazy is the last, or indeed how long the list might be.' He looked at Robbie and Max. 'Were either of you able to check out those possible "rogue" urban explorers that we were given?'

Max raised his hand. 'No luck with Roy Ferris. Seems to have disappeared from the area.'

Robbie glanced at his notebook. 'And it can't be Jeff Saville, because his volatile temper caused him to deck a police officer a week back, broke his jaw, so he's in custody in Hull.'

'And Marie and I saw Henry Arnott ourselves. He is looking after his friend, the urbexer Cally Prothero, and he doesn't give us cause for concern.' He caught a glimpse of Marie grinning at the word "friend."

'The last one, the anonymous male who joined the trip to the Yorkshire manor house, was possibly a journalist,' added Max. 'No proof yet, but from his description, we think that might have been the case.'

Jackman ended the meeting. 'Okay, people! It's now your job to find me something, *anything*, no matter how small, that indicates who the Magician might be, or why he's doing what he is.'

Back in his office, he phoned Rory Wilkinson. 'I hate to push you, Prof, but I'm struggling here. Do you have anything for me on those three victims?'

'I wish I could say I did, but you are not alone in struggling, dear Inspector. We have identified the type of material used to make those tunic things, but I fear it won't do you much good. It is indeed hessian, but it's a very common sort used for all kinds of different purposes, from building, to protect brickwork from frost, to gardening where they root ball large plants and use it for weed control. Oh, and the manufacture of sandbags.'

Jackman sighed. He had feared as much.

'However, I have yet another little conundrum to add to the growing list. We found ash in the hair and on the faces of all three bodies. It was easier to see on the last to die, young Grant Leach, and it appeared to have been smeared over his face and head. The ash came from burnt wood, kindling to be exact, and newspaper. So, we have sackcloth and ashes. Now what does that tell you?'

'Penitence,' Jackman said immediately. 'This supports the theory that they violated a sacred space and have been made to pay, doesn't it?'

'That would be my take on it,' Rory said. 'And they paid dearly.'

'Nothing else?'

'Your man wore gloves all the time. We could find nothing in those boxes of clothing and possessions, not even on the sealing tape he used, and no trace evidence on the bodies either. He was extraordinarily careful.' Rory sounded slightly puzzled. 'It was all so clinical. As you well know, whatever we do, we leave traces of ourselves, but in this case . . .'

'Don't stop looking,' said Jackman. It was almost a plea.

'As if! What a suggestion!' Rory exclaimed. 'We still have to collate all the crap, sorry, evidence, that we collected last night and early this morning from that old control tower and the surrounding scrubland. He made three attacks there, so let's just hope that at some point he either got sloppy, or simply overlooked something. It's possible. After all, he couldn't have been expecting such eminent company to turn up.'

'Don't remind me about that fiasco, Rory. If only I'd done things differently.'

'Rubbish! Get a grip, Inspector! That young lad, the millionaire's son, would have died if you hadn't got the paramedics out so quickly. That sort of attack on a boy with his condition could very easily be fatal, so forget the guilt trip and give yourself a pat on the back!'

Jackman had to smile at this.

'And, finally, he used a car. We found where he parked it, and there were some juicy tyre prints, so we might well get you a make of vehicle. Have faith, dear man, we are still on the case!'

After he'd hung up, Jackman pulled a memo sheet towards him and drew a line through Jeff Saville and put a question mark next to Roy Ferris. He was about to do the same with Henry Arnott when, for some reason, he hesitated. Recalling their meeting, he was forced to admit that Henry's gaze did rather linger on Cally. Jackman had put it down to simple concern. Marie had interpreted it differently. What if they were both right? What if that look had been one of obsession? Arnott had admitted that he was obsessive about things. What if that extended to Cally Prothero? And another thing bothered him. The hospital had given the girl a prescription for a mild sedative, but she had exhibited all the signs of near sedation along with moments of full alertness. That seemed rather strange to him.

He stood up and went to his door. 'Marie! Got a minute?'

Marie heard him out with a look he knew well. It said that she was not convinced but possibly prepared to consider it.

'But are you saying he's drugging her?' she added. 'That's a bit extreme, isn't it?'

Jackman scratched his head thoughtfully. 'I don't really know what I think, Marie, but somehow the whole scenario doesn't sit well with me, especially since you pointed out that he appears to have feelings for her.'

'Then I suggest we keep in close touch with Cally, just to be sure she's safe. We can't let anything else happen to her after all she's been through.' Marie drew in a long breath. 'And keep Henry on the list of possible suspects. I've just remembered that Cally said she slept right through, from nine at night until seven in the morning, so Henry Arnott doesn't have an alibi, does he?'

Jackman considered Arnott. He had been an urban explorer, so he knew his way around deserted buildings. He was the right height, the right age, more or less, and quite well built too, but did he have the strength to lift a grown man and get him away from the control tower and across to his car? It was possible, because at some point in the conversation Henry had admitted that he occasionally had to lift his father into bed. 'Rory has tyre prints from out at the Catchwater Drain, Marie. We need to know what car Arnott drives, and also if he has more than one vehicle. As you say, just to be on the safe side.'

Marie nodded. 'I'll get Kevin to do the honours, shall I?'

'Please, Marie.'

As he watched her leave his office, Jackman had an idea. He picked up the phone and rang Laura.

'Hello, darling. Are you okay?'

Her voice immediately lifted his sprits. 'I'm fine. A few hours' sleep has done wonders. Listen, Laura, when do you have a follow-up appointment with Cally Prothero?'

'Er, tomorrow afternoon, I think. I'll check the diary if you like.'

'No, it's okay. I was going to ask if you could ring her later this afternoon. Just to check on her progress, and make sure she attends that next appointment.'

'What's wrong?' Laura said. 'Are you worried about her state of health?'

'I'll tell you when we get home. I just need to know someone is keeping a close eye on her. Are you okay with that?'

'Of course,' she said. 'But it would help to know why.'

'Later, I promise.'

'Okay, Mister Mystery Man, I'll do what you ask, but you'd better fill me in as soon as possible, just so I know what to look for.'

Somewhat relieved, Jackman hung up. Laura had a perfectly valid reason for calling Cally, and she would report back to him should anything concern her. So, he could set that aside for the time being and press on with other problems. He sighed. His one big worry now was the whereabouts of Crazy Hazy. Was the lad still alive?

CHAPTER TWENTY-EIGHT

It was twenty to seven when Marie and Gary finally got away, just enough time to get to the Golden Compass for their meeting with Ralph Enderby and John Beard. Reluctantly, Marie agreed to go in Gary's car, leaving her bike at the station with strict instructions to the night shift to keep a close eye on it.

Marie was looking forward to seeing Ralph again. He was the kind of detective she liked. He had been enormously helpful during the Ashcroft investigation, and even though there was usually considerable competition between Fenchester and Saltern-le-Fen, he had never had the slightest problem with sharing information.

'How long have you known John Beard?' she asked Gary.

'Oh hell! Must be well over twenty years, I suppose. We lost touch when I relocated to Saltern-le-Fen, and then he and his wife, Nancy, moved to Randleby, and frankly I didn't expect to see him again. I'm delighted we've met up, he's a really good bloke.'

'And he and Ralph know each other?' Marie smiled. 'That's handy, since we're all looking into the same mystery.'

Gary nodded. 'John worked at Fenchester station as a civilian for several years. His experience with Customs and Excise made him quite a useful fellow to know.'

He pulled into the car park of the Golden Compass and managed to slot into the last remaining space.

'Busy tonight,' commented Marie.

'Busy every night, according to John. The food is good, so I guess that explains it.' They got out. 'Bang on seven. At least we aren't late.'

John and Ralph were already at the bar waiting for them. After the introductions, Ralph said, 'I wondered if you'd manage to get away, what with all the commotion in your neck of the woods at present.' He smiled warmly at her. 'But I'm glad you did. What are you both having?'

Marie decided to try the local best bitter and Gary opted for a half of lager.

'We've got a table,' said John. 'There's a little alcove just off the main bar, so we can talk without being overheard.' He led the way, threading between groups of exuberant people, all waving glasses.

'First on the agenda,' said Ralph, 'is food. Let's order.'

While the others all had steak, Ralph, to Marie's surprise, chose the vegetarian option. Marie didn't know too many vegetarian coppers and she wondered what he ate out on obbo, when the only place to grab a snack was a greasy spoon. She asked him, and he grinned at her. 'Careful planning, Marie. I never leave home without a snack box.'

'Now I feel guilty about the steak,' she said.

Ralph laughed. 'You go ahead. If I got all sanctimonious about meat eaters, I wouldn't last long in a police station, would I?'

'So, who's first?' she asked, looking from John to Ralph.

'After you, John,' said Ralph, taking a gulp of his beer.

John leaned forward and lowered his voice. 'Well, I do have a lead. It means a short trip out of the county, but I'm happy to do that. Nancy is planning a shopping trip with her cousin tomorrow, so I thought I'd have an away-day of my own.'

Marie asked where he was going.

'Overstrand in Norfolk, close to Cromer.'

'Okay,' said Gary. 'Tell us what you've got.'

'Well, about five years ago, the great-grandfather of the lad that helps me with the garden moved from Randleby to a little seaside chalet at Overstrand. Young Josh reckons that if anyone can tell me about that airfield, it's this old man. His name is Sidney Packer. Josh says that one of old Sidney's favourite stories is about a "big wartime secret" involving the old airfield. Josh had never heard the story himself. In fact, he wondered who his great-granddad actually did tell, because everyone in the family knew there was a secret, but no one seemed to know what it was.' John shrugged. 'Maybe it's just a myth, an old man's joke on his family, but I don't think so. And since I could do with a breath of sea air, I'm off to Overstrand tomorrow morning.'

'It does sound promising,' said Marie. 'Although once again it's leading us to believe it's an old RAF field, which could pose problems should we delve deeper.'

'Big problems,' added Ralph solemnly, all the laughter gone from his voice. 'And my news adds more support to the military theory. I ran it past a mate of mine that works in IT and we did a bit of online ferreting on his personal computer. He loves rooting around in old archive stuff and he knew where to look, but we couldn't find a thing.' He stared into his beer. 'Well, this well and truly pissed off my friend, so I left it with him. He rang me this afternoon and said he'd got hold of every available list of decommissioned and former RAF stations and airfields, and there was no mention of Randleby anywhere. He then went the local history route and found just one reference — a record of a foreign Second World War military aircraft making an emergency forced landing at an RAF airfield in Lincolnshire. The name had been blacked out, but from other info in the document, including where the plane had been heading, he worked out that it had to be in this area. And that was all he could find. Every single bit of information on it has been erased. According to all official records, it doesn't exist.'

'Yet there are old airfields all over this county,' John said. 'During the Second World War there were thought to be a hundred military airfields, including dummy ones and emergency landing strips. You can look up the history of almost all of them with no trouble at all.'

'They destroyed a lot of paperwork after the war,' said Gary. 'I watched a programme about it on the History Channel. So, I suppose it's possible that all the records on our airfield went up in smoke.'

'That would be perfectly understandable, but why are the higher powers deliberately obstructing all enquiries about the place? Why did I get a bollocking just for asking a few casual questions? Why are people lying?'

'Forget my last comment,' said Gary glumly.

Marie was intrigued. She knew Lincolnshire was known as "Bomber County" because at the outset of the Second World War the bulk of all the bombers took off from the county. But there was so much more that she didn't know. She determined to find out more as soon as the urbex investigation was over.

'You mentioned old bases that were just abandoned, John,' said Ralph. 'Well, while I was surfing the net, I came across a site that showed a massive one in Shropshire that one of Marie's urban explorers got inside of and found everything practically intact, even down to an RAF fire truck still in a garage.'

'Bit like RAF Manby Hall here, with all its equipment just left to rot,' said John. 'That's quite eerie. They reckon it's haunted too. Like a lot of places, they have all these regeneration projects lined up for them, and nine times out of ten they fall through and they are left to become derelict.'

So I'm no closer to retrieving my old Norton, thought Marie. That sad little motorcycle, discarded underneath a workbench, still haunted her. 'I have a question,' she said. 'What will happen if I decide that, as Aaron Smith was a murder victim, I want to cordon off the place as a crime scene? After all, that was where he was most likely taken from, unless he wandered off and was picked up somewhere else, which we all know is rubbish. Especially as he had no vehicle of his own and those three kids travelled there in the same car.'

'Now, won't that be interesting,' murmured Ralph with a grin. 'Is that your plan?'

She returned his smile. 'We have to, don't we? The other places that victims disappeared from are already shut off while forensics go over them, so why not this one? Okay, Rob and I did an "unofficial" visit that showed up nothing,' *except for a very tasty motorcycle,* she thought to herself, 'but there was no forensic sweep. I reckon we should go straight out there in the morning.'

'Well, I can't wait to hear how *that* goes,' said Ralph. He glanced up. 'Ah, here comes our food.'

Ralph turned out to be not just a friendly and helpful detective, but great company too. He hit it off immediately with Gary, which pleased Marie. She and Gary had become close friends and had shared some pretty rough times during the hunt for Alistair Ashcroft, and it was nice to see him relaxed and enjoying himself with like-minded people.

After the waitress had cleared the table, Marie said, 'I know your friend is obviously brilliant at IT or he wouldn't be doing that particular job, but we have a genius tucked away in our basement at Saltern.'

'Ah, the legendary Orac,' said Ralph with reverence. 'Part human, part cyborg.' He laughed. 'So, she really exists?'

'She does, and she's absolutely incredible. I was wondering if she could do a little research into our non-existent airfield. What do you think?'

'Good idea,' said Gary. 'She does have access to sites that others don't.'

Gary went off to the Gents and John said he needed to ring his wife, so Marie and Ralph were left alone.

'We'd better make a move soon — early start and all that,' Marie said, rather regretfully. 'It's been a really nice evening.'

'We could do it again,' offered Ralph softly. 'Just you and me?'

Marie stiffened. It had become an automatic reaction whenever she caught the slightest hint of a prospective date. Then she heard herself say, 'I'd love to, as soon as we have this case wrapped up.' Now where had that come from?

'Great! And meantime, I'll be dying to hear what happens when you take a load of coppers and SOCOs out to the airfield.'

'I'll keep you posted, Ralph, I promise.'

John Beard lightly touched her shoulder. 'I'm off now. I'll let Gary know how I get on in Overstrand.'

'Good luck, John, it's been nice to meet you.' She shook his proffered hand. 'Take care.'

Soon she and Gary were driving back towards Saltern, Gary singing along with the radio as he drove.

'That was a really nice night,' she said. 'I like John, he's a solid bloke, isn't he? And Ralph's great fun too.'

Gary smiled at her. 'I think Ralph is quite smitten with you.'

'Gary Pritchard! What are you suggesting?'

'I bet you anything you like that he asks you out before the end of tomorrow!' Gary laughed.

'Well, you're too late. He has already.'

'I knew it! So? What did you say?' Gary was almost bouncing in his seat.

'Hold up! We have a big case running, remember? No time for any of that until we have the Magician locked up.'

'And then?'

'Maybe . . .' She dug him in the ribs. 'Anyway, I don't do dates, Gary. You know that. I'll probably say no in the end.'

'Well, maybe it's time for a change. A good-looking detective who's also a nice man could be just what you need.'

He glanced at her, suddenly serious. 'Have some fun, Marie. We're a long time dead.'

She knew that he was thinking of his lovely sister, who had died far too young. 'And what about you, Gary? You're a fine one to talk. You never date anyone, either.'

He sighed. 'True. The fact of it is, many years ago I got hurt, really hurt, and, well, I've never met anyone since who I feel I could share my life with. Since that one affair, all the women I've come into contact with have been just good friends, or colleagues, like you. Buddies, comrades in arms and, in your case, a dear and trusted friend.'

She squeezed his arm. 'I'm sorry, Gary. It must have been bad.'

'It was a long time ago, Marie. I should have moved on, but after I lost my sister I couldn't cope for a while. Work became the be all and end all, and I just stopped looking at women. I think I was scared of losing someone else — after all, I didn't have a very good track record of hanging on to them, did I?'

Marie suddenly recalled a saying she'd heard about grief. It never ends, but it changes. It's a passage, not a place to stay. 'Grief is the price of love,' she said softly.

'And maybe we've both been paying the price for too long,' added Gary.

'There have been an awful lot of maybes talked about this evening, haven't there?'

'Then *maybe* it's time to turn some of them into positive actions.' Gary slapped the steering wheel. 'Okay, Marie Evans. After you. I'll see how you get on first, and then I might just give it a try.'

Marie recalled Ralph's infectious laugh and good looks. A drink together, maybe even a meal, certainly wouldn't do any harm, would it? 'Okay, Pritchard, you're on — well, maybe.'

* * *

At exactly 23.45, the man pushed open the heavy door into the abandoned warehouse. The building was in a very poor state and due for demolition within a month or two. But it was perfect for what he needed.

This unremarkable three-storey redbrick building had once been a pea-sorting warehouse. Locally grown peas had been brought here, transported by horse and cart, and were cleaned, sorted and packed for export. On one floor, the skeletal remains of one of the old pea-cleaning machines still sat, a rusting hulk of twisted metal.

It wasn't easy getting the boy up the treacherous stairs. The man wore a helmet light and carried a powerful torch, but he was hampered by the struggling kid. He couldn't afford to immobilise him again, he wanted him awake and fully conscious, so he could appreciate exactly why he was here. That was vital.

Finally, he reached the top of the stairs and manhandled the terrified explorer into the vast open area at the top of the building. He had already prepared for this, so it was just a matter of getting the timing right and winching Mr Crazy Hazy into position.

He flung the boy to the floor and stared down at him. Lying there, trussed like a chicken, he looked much younger than his twenty-odd years, especially since he was snivelling like a baby.

'Please, please, don't hurt me! Let me go! I won't tell anyone anything, I swear! Just let me go!'

The man sank down onto his heels and shook his head. 'It's too late. I've told you that, haven't I?' He sounded patient and calm, as if explaining something to a child. He looked at his watch. Five minutes to go. He'd better get him into position.

Closing his ears to the screams, he dragged Keith Hazell, aka Crazy Hazy, along the filthy floor towards the end of a rope that was dangling from one of the old rafters.

It took only moments to loop the climbing rope around the left ankle and secure it tightly. It was expensive sports line, lightweight, flexible and very strong. Once he had him secured, he stepped back and calmly assessed the situation. The rope would slide easily over the rafter. He had sanded the area carefully until it was smooth and free from splinters.

'Time to go,' he said softly.

With gloved hands, he pulled the loose end of the rope and slowly took the weight of Crazy Hazy's body. Once his victim was clear of the floor and some four feet in the air, he secured the rope to a temporary hook he had screwed into the floor, took a sharp knife to the nylon twine that bound him and allowed his limbs to fall free. He then took a sealed plastic bag from his pocket and scooped out a handful of ashes, which he rubbed over the young man's head. He stood back.

The shouting and coughing gradually subsided to a painful sobbing. 'What are you doing to me? What have I done? Why me?'

He didn't reply. He needed all his strength to pull the body up and under the rafters.

This took him exactly one minute. Then, breathing deeply, he tied the rope off and stared up at the figure in the sackcloth tunic. The alarm on his watch beeped. It was done.

He sat on the floor. 'How does it feel?'

There was a croaking, sobbing sound. 'Please! Please! Get me down! I'm scared.'

'I know, I know, and that's as it should be. You have to understand, Keith, actions are followed by reactions. It's how the world works.'

'But I haven't done anything!' The voice rose into a wail.

'But you have, Keith — or should I say Crazy? I know you, Crazy Hazy, and I know exactly what you've done. And now you're finally paying for it. The simple law of cause and effect.'

He stood up, took one last look at the young man suspended above him, and walked towards the door. The screams grew more and more hysterical, but he shut them out. Screaming would do young Crazy Hazy no good. This strange old place was remote, the spot attracted no one. And the building itself was pretty sound-proof. Maybe it had been built that way on purpose.

He smiled in satisfaction, closed the door, negotiated the staircase and finally stepped outside into the night chill. He took a lungful of the crisp, clean air and exhaled loudly.

* * *

Orac sat on in the half dark of the basement. She desperately wanted to talk to someone, but she didn't have the heart to disturb either Dara or Marie at two in the morning.

Her table was scattered with reports, interviews, statements. Her gaze was drawn to the photographs, and the image of a man's left foot, tightly secured with the cord rope that rock climbers used. The knot ensured that the attached weight would not slip or come loose. Why did that seem so significant?

She stood up and paced the big area, which was silent other than the hum of the air conditioner and the occasional chirrup from one of her computers as it made yet another update or download.

This was not how she had envisaged her homecoming.

Thoughts swarmed in her mind, not all to do with this nightmare of a case. Her beautiful sister, and the sorrow of knowing that she had been so close yet turned away. Would she make another attempt? Possibly not.

Orac went through to the locker room. There was no point in staring any longer at those reports. She would go home and sleep for a few hours and then come back and try again to make sense of what was worrying her.

She took her jacket from the locker and pulled it on. It would be good to sleep in her own bed again, even if her apartment had been trashed by the agents trying to discover where she had gone. There had been no real damage, however, just objects out of place and furniture moved. She could live with that. And she mustn't forget to go and pick up her car. She had taken it to a lock-up garage that she had

281

rented in case she ever needed it. She had left her car there as a decoy, to make people think she had gone off in it and so waste time hunting for her in the traffic cameras. From there, she had rung a twenty-four-hour taxi firm and paid an extortionate fee to be taken to the airport. She booked a flight for the next day, stayed over in the airport hotel and the following morning left the country.

Now she was home, worrying over the case that had broken in her absence. Jackman and Marie needed her help badly, and she was determined to help them. She could, she knew, she had the skill, but if she had never gone away, would those young men have died?

What if . . . ? Orac shook herself. She must be very over-tired, she *never* thought like that. No one could rewrite the past. She ought to know that more than most.

She slammed the door shut and went up to reception. As she passed, the night-duty sergeant lifted a hand to her and called out, 'Goodnight, Ms Cracken. Good to have you back.'

She didn't recall him ever speaking before. It felt good. 'Thank you, Sergeant, and goodnight to you too.' Yes, it was good to be back.

CHAPTER TWENTY-NINE

Still a little jaded but better than he had been, Jackman got in early. The previous night, he and Laura had sat up late, discussing their old friend Sam Page. Laura had rung Sam and put the suggestion to him. How would he like to come and live with them at Mill Corner, but in a separate self-contained flat? Overwhelmed by their generosity, Sam's voice had broken. Weeping, he had turned down their offer. He was settling in again, happy in his solitude. Laura said they would leave the offer open, and that if he should ever change his mind, there was a home for him at the mill. Jackman was partly relieved but sorry too. He knew how Laura worried about her old mentor and his safety, out there on the edge of a bird reserve.

'Sir?' Kevin tapped on Jackman's half-open door. 'Can I come in?'

'Sure, Kevin. What's the problem?'

'No problem, sir. The sarge asked me to find out the make of Henry Arnott's car. It's a Kia Sportage SUV, sir, a 2018 model in what Kia describes as "Mineral Silver" — grey, to you and me.' He handed him a memo with the registration number written on it. 'The tyres are Hankook, in case we need to compare the tracks.'

'Nice one, Kevin. Thank you.' Jackman looked up at the new member of the team. 'Sit for a moment.'

Kevin sat, looking a trifle nervous. He was smartly dressed, wearing what was obviously a brand-new suit. Jackman was pleased — it showed he took a pride in his work.

'I'm sorry you've been dumped in at the deep end, Kevin. It was my intention to take the time to show you the ropes, but that's the nature of detective work — you can't always do what you'd like. You will get more attention, I promise, but you can see how difficult it is at the moment.'

'I'm very aware of the circumstances, sir. Please don't give it another thought. I'm happy to help in any way I can.'

'And how are you getting on, Kevin? Has the transition from uniform been a shock to the system?' What Jackman really wanted to ask was whether Kevin had recovered from the horrors of the Alistair Ashcroft case, but that wasn't possible. Kevin Stoner was lucky to be with them still, and to have retained his sanity after some of the things he had witnessed.

'As you say, sir, takes a bit of getting used to. I knew my old job backwards, but there's a lot I have to learn here.' He hesitated, suddenly anxious. 'I just hope I can make the grade.'

Jackman smiled at him. 'Don't worry, Kevin, it's early days. You'll settle in no time at all. You're a good copper, and I'm glad you've joined us.'

'I appreciate that, DI Jackman. I won't let you down.'

'I know you won't. Now, what are you working on at present?' Jackman asked.

'I'm waiting for the sarge to come in and find me something to do, sir.'

'Right, well, unless she's got something special for you, perhaps you would find out which abandoned properties were checked and cleared last night in the hunt for Keith Hazell. I need to know which ones we can cross off our list, and which still have to be visited. Liaise with uniform. That young man can't have been taken far.'

Kevin stood up. 'Straight away, boss.'

Jackman watched him go. He seemed to be holding up really well, but only a few months ago, the lad had been in a terrible state. He had to have been damaged by Ashcroft. At least Kevin hadn't been present at the finding of the three hanged bodies in the church tower. That might well have pushed him over the edge. The forensic photos up on the whiteboard were like the news on the TV — they couldn't convey the horror of witnessing sights first-hand. And what of Keith Hazell? Was he already hanging somewhere, suspended by one ankle? And if he was, how long did he have to live?

He wondered if it was too early for Rory to be in. He picked up the phone.

Rory answered almost immediately. 'Oh my! Before breakfast, too. Thank you, dear Inspector, and a very good morning to you as well!' He paused, listening to Jackman's question, then asked, 'Is he young?'

'Early twenties, Rory.'

'Overweight?'

'Far from it. Wiry, and quite skinny. Probably one of the reasons he was carried off so quickly.'

'Well, that goes in his favour. The younger you are, the more likely you are to survive.'

'But how long for, Rory? How long do we have before . . . ?'

Rory sighed. 'I can't tell you, Jackman. Our bodies aren't designed to hang head down. The lungs can't take in enough oxygen if they are being crushed by the heavier liver and intestines. Blood can pool in the brain and cause ruptured vessels or even a brain haemorrhage. The heart struggles, it slows down because it's receiving more blood than it can cope with, and it can't maintain blood pressure. And all that is without simple dehydration, the pressure building in your eyes, and finally asphyxiation.'

'Please, Prof, just a ball-park guesstimate.'

'I read about a man who lasted twenty-eight hours once, after a rappelling accident. He too was suspended by one foot, but he died because they couldn't free him from the

285

crevice he'd fallen into.' Rory took a breath. 'I'm assuming your killer will use the same method as before, so at a wild guess, I'd say somewhere around twelve hours from the time he was suspended. And that is assuming he is fit and healthy with no underlying medical conditions.'

Jackman groaned. It wasn't long enough. It was already almost eight in the morning, and Keith could have been hung up at any time during the previous evening.

'Listen, don't hold me to that, Jackman. It's very much an unknown area. And there are so many variables. He could last much longer if he finds some way to reach the rope and get his head up again. Don't give up on him. He's young, he could surprise you.'

'*If* I can find him.'

'Well, I'm in so early because I want to try and find some forensic evidence to help you identify your killer, and I've dragged poor Spike and Cardiff from their respective beds to help me. So, *nil desperandum*, as they say.'

Jackman thanked Rory and hung up.

He looked up to see Marie standing in the doorway balancing two cups of coffee and a brown bag on top of a pile of reports. She was smiling broadly.

'You look ridiculously bright. Did the Postcode Lottery knock on your door this morning?' Last night Marie had looked anxious and tired, now she positively glowed.

She laughed. 'Amazing what a good night's sleep can do. By the way, I have a favour to ask.'

He stared at the brown bag. 'Is this a bribe?'

'Consider it more of a goodwill gesture.'

He opened it. Inside was a filled breakfast croissant, the local coffee shop's ham and cheese speciality. It was still warm. 'Okay, ask away.'

'I want to go out to Randleby Airfield. It was the last place Aaron Smith was seen alive, and I want a forensic sweep done.' She stared at him hopefully. 'I know Fenchester is insisting he ran away because he was frightened and that it's not a crime scene at all, but I think differently.'

Jackman thought about this. The fact of the other young men, all dead, seemed to point to Marie being right and Fenchester wrong, but he wondered if there was any point. Would anything show up there, when the other two scenes had thrown up zilch? He said as much to Marie, adding, 'The budget is pretty strung out already, Marie, and didn't you say your mole inside Fenchester nick had been warned off rather conclusively? Most importantly, we have that missing kid, Keith Hazell, to find and time is running out for him.'

She nodded. 'I know that, sir, but what exactly can the two of us do? Uniform are searching every available abandoned building in the area, and Max, Robbie, and Gary — Kevin too — are tracing any and every lead we have. From this morning, we also have Orac on the case, which is massive. So, couldn't you spare me for a few hours so I can take a couple of uniforms and a SOCO out there? Just to do an official walk-through in daylight and see if there's anything that doesn't look right.'

Marie wouldn't have asked if this wasn't important to her. She didn't often beg him for favours. 'Okay,' he sighed. 'Let's say I agree, but we need permission to carry out a search if we don't have a warrant.'

'Not if we hear cries for help or distress,' said Marie angelically. 'Or are there to sort out a reported disturbance of some kind.'

'Or,' he said soberly, 'we could obtain a warrant, Marie, because we believe there is material on the premises which is likely to be of substantial value to our investigation. It would cover our backs.'

'And take precious time, boss. I don't want to be away from here for any longer than necessary.'

She sounded so reasonable. Finally, he said, 'Be back here by eleven at the latest, and if you see anything worth flagging up, ring me. But don't, I repeat, *don't* bring the wrath of Ruth Crooke down on us by stepping out of line. We both know there is something odd about that place and I can't afford to let anything at all interfere with the search for that missing explorer.'

Marie stood up. 'I'll try and arrange for a crew to accompany me and get a SOCO to meet us there. I promise I'll be back in under three hours.' She stopped at the door. 'Thank you, Jackman.'

'Bugger off, Marie! And hurry back.'

Even Marie wouldn't go this far to rescue a motorbike, so he hadn't mentioned it, but it did cross his mind that she would use the opportunity to check that the old Norton was still under that bench.

And she was right. The place was probably the scene of an abduction that had led to a death, so it should be checked as thoroughly as the other crime scenes. It was just that he had very bad vibes about Randleby Airfield.

* * *

Now that her computers were all up and running, Orac began to feel a little more human again. And the others all seemed happy to see her back at her workstation.

Philip brought her some information she had asked for. She noticed he was wearing a new silk tie — sunshine yellow and covered in bright green Irish four-leaf clovers. This made even Orac smile. Grinning broadly, Philip told her it was a present from Marie Evans.

She stared at the thick file Marie had brought down for her. She was now ready to tackle it. Prior to her trip to Ireland, she would have gone straight into work mode and put everything else aside. Now she found that she had lost that single-minded capacity to concentrate — pictures of her beautiful Grainne kept floating into her head, distracting her. She carried the photo in her bag. Deep within the dark-haired, beautiful young woman — so grown up now, so self-assured — a child lived on. The child she remembered, her dear baby sister.

She took a few deep breaths. *Concentrate, Orac.* In some ways she wished she'd never made that trip to Ireland. It had done little but leave her more disturbed than before. Yes, she now knew that her sister had survived and even prospered, and that was of incalculable value, but now she had new dilemmas to untangle, and some very difficult decisions to make.

She stood up and went through to the locker room. Maybe a few words with Dara would settle her racing mind.

He answered at once.

'My Ciara! Are you alright?'

'I'm fine,' she lied. 'Just a little wobbly after everything Ireland decided to throw at me.'

'I hope I didn't cause you more trouble?'

'Of course not, Dara. You gave me back my sister, how could that be a trouble to me?'

'It's still an almighty shock, so just relax for a day or so, take some time off to assimilate everything.'

His calm voice was so reassuring. 'So, where are you now, my friend?'

'Still in Dublin, just about to pay a visit to Trinity College. I've been promising myself a look at the Book of Kells since I don't know when. I'm looking forward to soaking up a little of our heritage. And then it's back home.' He sighed. 'I wish you'd stayed here. We could have continued your search for your sister together. I know you had to do the first part alone, but as soon as you knew she was alive, I could have gone with you, supported you, like in the old days.'

'I almost did, I was so close, but then I realised I was *too* close. I needed to think, and I couldn't do that there,' she said.

'Well, as long as you believe you did the right thing. Oh, I almost forgot! I think I've solved the mystery of the amateur sleuth who was stalking you. And I'm afraid I'm inadvertently to blame.'

She frowned. 'How so?'

'I confess to being afraid for your safety, Ciara. I persuaded a very capable friend of mine to track you down and then keep a watchful eye on you. He couldn't find you at first.' Another laugh. 'You obviously still have your old skills. But, anyway, when he finally located you, he was taken ill and finished up in hospital, and I thought that was that. What I didn't know was that, not wanting to let me down, he asked his brother to watch over you. Evidently, he wasn't very good at surveillance. I'm so sorry. He must have frightened you. That wasn't how it was meant to be at all. I only found this out last night.'

It was Orac's turn to laugh. 'I wasn't exactly frightened, his ineptitude just puzzled me. But at least that answers one question that was bothering me.'

'Good. Now, when I get back, shall we have a meal together? It's been far too long since we met.'

'I'd like that. Ring me when you're home?'

'Of course. Two days and my business will all be finished. Remember, take some time for yourself, it will do you the world of good. See you soon.'

Orac returned to her computers feeling much less anxious. Marie had been right all along — Dara had been worried about her. Nevertheless, she would ignore his advice. What she needed right now was work. She flexed her fingers and began her research.

CHAPTER THIRTY

Robbie entered Jackman's office. This case, his baby, had rapidly turned into a nightmare. If he was in for a dressing-down, well, he deserved it. Surely, by now he should have found something that tied the victims together. But he'd found nothing.

Jackman pointed to a chair, and Robbie sat, feeling like a rabbit caught in the headlights.

'Any progress, Robbie? Anything at all that might tell us where this killer could have taken young Keith Hazell?'

Robbie shook his head. 'Kevin Stoner has brought back the list of abandoned buildings that were searched, and we've been trying to put the remaining ones into some sort of order. Every available fenland copper is out there searching, but it's like looking for a needle in a haystack, sir. I've even got Will Sheringham and Stella checking my selection since they know most of these old places better than us.'

'Good idea.' Jackman nibbled absentmindedly on his thumbnail. 'And, of course, the Magician could have squirrelled Keith away anywhere. We're only guessing that he wants to do a repeat performance of his weird hanging routine.'

'I think that's his objective though, boss, don't you?' Robbie relaxed now he knew he was not in for a talking-to. 'I can't help looking at that Tarot card of the Hanged Man.'

'Indeed,' said Jackman. 'But on a different subject, were the press outside when you arrived, Robbie?'

'Were they! A whole bunch of reporters and cameras gathered all around the entrance. The duty sergeant said the super will be making another announcement this morning.'

'Then I'd better go and speak to her. Oh, and if my desk phone rings, could you get it for me? Marie's out at Randleby and I don't want to miss her call if she rings on the landline and not my mobile.'

'Sure, boss. I'll listen out.'

Robbie was concerned for her. Everything they'd heard about that place screamed trouble, and he didn't want Marie getting into hot water over it. He would have gone too, or at least sent Gary to accompany her, but she had insisted they were needed on the hunt for Keith Hazell, and he could hardly argue with her. He had been horrified to discover just how many buildings in the area were empty, abandoned or deserted. It was a mammoth task.

Back at his desk, his own phone rang. It was Stella.

'I'm not sure if this is relevant, but our emergency website, *UE SOS*, has coughed up the name of a local lad who says he's afraid that he might be next in line for an abduction. He's well frightened, Robbie. I think he's worth a visit.'

Robbie grabbed a pen and scribbled down the name — Alfie Brown. 'Address?'

'Anvil Cottage, Rustings Lane, Cartoft village.' She gave him Alfie's mobile number.

'Could be useful. I'll check him out straightaway. Stella, did he say why he felt threatened?'

There was a short silence, then she said, 'Because he's the first person we've found that has been out exploring with all four of the killer's victims.'

'Thank you, Stel! This could be the break we need.' Robbie immediately rang the number that Stella had given him.

'I'm at work, Officer, but I have a break in three-quarters of an hour. I'm a porter at Saltern Hospital — if you could come here?'

Robbie said he would and hung up. Even in that short conversation, Alfie Brown had managed to sound strung out. The hospital was only a five-minute drive from the station. He went over to where Max was furiously typing something into his computer.

'Max, I've got a UE to see. He reckons he could be next in line for one of the Magician's disappearing acts.'

Max looked up. 'How come?'

Robbie explained.

'Wow. If he's right, he could be the missing link, couldn't he?' Max opened his eyes wide. 'He might know something or somewhere that connects them all.'

'I'm going to meet him at his workplace, but if he really is a possible link, I'll bring him back to the station and let Jackman talk to him.' He frowned at Max. 'And he might need protection. If the Magician realises Alfie knows he's after him, he could just snatch him off the streets.'

'Well, if I were you, I wouldn't wait. I'd get my arse round there right now. Our killer could have his eye on him already.'

So far, all the urbexers that the Magician had taken had gone out despite the danger. But if someone on his list, Alfie Brown for instance, decided against exploring for a while, then he would have no alternative but to abduct him either from his home, the streets, or from where he worked. 'You're right. Tell the boss what I'm doing, would you? And, Max, can you field any calls to Jackman's office? Marie might ring and he doesn't want to miss her call.'

'You got it, Rob. I'm all ears.'

As Robbie hurried across to one of the CID cars, he saw a squad car pull in. Two uniformed officers and Marie got out. He went over to her. She looked like thunder.

'Warrant or bugger off — at least, that was the gist of it. And how on earth did they know we were going there in the first place? We arrived to find a couple of vans and a 4x4 there, then some bloke said they were surveying the ground in preparation for work being carried out and he couldn't let us in without the owner's permission.'

'So, who is the owner?' Robbie asked.

'He couldn't, or wouldn't, say, just said to come back with a warrant and he'd make sure the owner was present.' She kicked at some loose gravel. 'Frankly, I didn't dare take it further and I couldn't afford to waste time out there. Jackman's right, we have more serious things on our hands right now.' She shrugged. 'It's just galling. And where are you off to?'

'Actually, I need to rush.' He explained quickly and made to hurry away.

'Take care!' called out Marie. 'One hint of concern for him, you bring him straight back here, okay?'

'Wilco,' he called back, and ran.

* * *

When Marie entered the CID room, Jackman was just coming out of his office. His look of relief at seeing her was almost comic.

'You were right, boss. I got sent packing and told to get a warrant. Wish I'd never gone.' She pulled a face. 'But it's bugging me even more now. Clearly, something's going on out there. We didn't tell a soul where we were going.'

'You're right, Marie, it is odd, but I'm afraid it will have to go on the back burner for a while. And to be honest, I don't think we'd find anything by way of interesting forensic evidence there. After all, none of the other abduction sites did.'

He looked distracted. 'Has something happened?' she asked.

'Laura's just called. She phoned Cally Prothero to check her appointment time, and Henry Arnott told her that Cally was sleeping. He said she'd had a bad night, and he was loath to disturb her.' Jackman gave an annoyed grunt. 'It may be absolutely genuine, but oh, I don't know. Am I being paranoid?'

'No, sir, no way. But it's a tough call. Going back again could be construed as harassment.'

'Laura asked Henry to get Cally to ring her as soon as she woke, so I guess we can only wait.' He rolled his eyes. 'And now the press are everywhere.'

Marie sighed. 'I ran the gauntlet coming through the gates.'

'Ruth has already gone down and made one of her famous statements that manage to say just about nothing, but there's a press conference booked for later this afternoon.' Jackman grimaced. 'And she wants me there.'

'Inevitable, I guess. You always hope they'll hold off for as long as possible, don't you? They get in the way, not to mention muddying the waters by stirring up the public.' Marie was no fan of the media, but then, none of them were. 'Mind if I pop down to see Orac, sir? I know she won't have anything yet, but I thought I'd make sure she knows that Henry Arnott could do with a bit of special attention.'

He nodded. 'Certainly. And ask her to add the name Alfie Brown to those with links to the victims.'

'Is that the man Robbie's gone to see?'

'He's our only hope at present. I hate to pin too much on him, but he's all we've got.'

Watching him stride back to his office, Marie could sense his frustration. It was coming off him in waves. A young man's life was in jeopardy but they had no idea where to find him.

She descended the stairs to the basement with a heavy heart.

'Marie! Don't tell me you have more for me?' Orla gave her a look of mock horror.

'Just two names, Orac. One you already have, but we'd like you to pay particular attention to him — Henry Arnott. And a new name — Alfie Brown.'

'And what part do we think Mr Brown plays in this drama?' asked Orac.

'That of the next victim, or so he believes. He knows all the other victims and has been exploring with all of them. That is a first. We are interviewing him now. Jackman believes he could be the link that will lead us to the identity of the killer.'

'Well, at least he's still alive,' remarked Orac. 'You can talk to him and maybe hit upon what's driving this murderer.' She took the memo from Marie. 'I'll certainly see what I can find out from here.'

Marie turned to go. It was good to have Orac back. She made you feel safe. She turned back. 'Orac? When this important stuff is out of the way, could you check out anything you can find about an old airfield at Randleby, near Fenchester? I want to know who owns the land and who is responsible for it. It seems that anyone who asks questions about the place gets warned off.'

Orac frowned. 'But wasn't that one of the places you listed as being the site of a disappearance? Aaron Smith was taken from there, as I recall.'

'It is.'

'Well, Marie, the good thing about computers is that they have an infinite capacity for multi-tasking. I'll start searching now and we'll see what comes back. I'll ring you.'

Marie thanked her and left. Orac seemed to be back to her old self — one less thing for Marie to worry about. It dawned on her that if it wasn't for this horrendous case, her life was looking pretty good. Her old nemesis had been put away for life, and a very attractive man had asked her out. Added to that, Orac was home again, Jackman was settled with Laura, and Max had turned into Dad of the Year. If Gary were to meet someone and Robbie get a little more settled, life would be just about perfect.

She realised it was the first time in years that she had felt this way. Her grief at losing her husband so young had left her emotionally numb. She would never forget him, not a day would pass when she didn't think of him, but suddenly it felt as though the shadows were lifting.

She wandered into the CID room, to be met by an anxious-looking Gary.

'I've been puzzling over that bloody airfield, Sarge, and wondering how come someone knew you were going there. After all, it was only John, Ralph, you and me that talked about it, wasn't it? How come you were met by a welcoming party?'

'I've been wondering that myself,' she said. 'But the boss wants us to shelve that for the time being and concentrate on young Crazy Hazy.'

'Oh, I totally agree, he's our priority, but it's been nagging away in the back of my mind.'

They heard Robbie's desk phone ringing.

'I'll take that,' said Marie, and hurried over.

Stella sounded pretty hyped up. Marie grabbed a pen and a memo pad. 'Say that again, Stella. The Pea-house? Where's that?'

A few moments later, she was hanging up and running to Jackman's office. 'Boss! Stella has something for us! An abandoned warehouse that wasn't on the list. She's absolutely sure no one has checked it, and she's just had a message on her Facebook site that has registered alarm bells. The mother of one of her UE friends lost her dog and she's been out looking for it. She heard the noise of whining from inside the old warehouse but can't get in. Her son, who's away, posted an SOS to Stella to see if any UEs were in the vicinity and could help her get inside.'

'Oh my! Where is this place?'

'Stella's given me directions. It's out on an area of farmland that stretches down to the river near Updyke about six or seven miles outside Saltern.' She looked at him eagerly. 'Shall I notify uniform?'

'See if anyone's in the area, but you and I need to go. It could turn out to be the lost dog, but what if . . . ?'

He was already on his feet. 'We'll take my car. Come on.'

* * *

He didn't need to ask Marie if she was as keyed up as he was. 'If it is him, I pray we get there in time.'

'Uniform are sending a car, ETA around ten minutes.' Marie looked at her watch, then raised an eyebrow. 'But at the speed you're driving, we should get there first.'

'What do we know about the Pea-house?' he asked.

'I just googled it. Updyke used to be a thriving community surrounded by pea-growing farms. It was a factory where they sorted and packed peas for export. It fell into disuse years back since different crops are grown there now. It's completely abandoned.'

'Just the sort of place the Magician would like.' He put his foot down.

They arrived a few minutes later and were met by a distraught-looking woman in walking boots, jeans and a Berghaus jacket.

'I only wanted one of my boy's friends to help me, I never meant for the police to be called! Honestly!'

Jackman held up his hands. 'It's fine. You're not in trouble, okay? It was our decision to come. Now, what's your name?'

'Pauline Seabrook, sir.'

'Okay, now tell me what you heard.'

'Whimpering, sir, whining. It has to be my Iggy, he's a right terror. He's a Jack Russell, and it's not the first time he's got in somewhere and couldn't get out.' She paused. 'But the sounds stopped about fifteen minutes ago, and now I'm really worried.'

No more than I am, thought Jackman. 'Okay, Marie, let's find a way in. You stay here, Mrs Seabrook. There'll be another car here shortly, tell them to come and find us.'

He and Marie ran along the side of the big old warehouse, looking for a way in.

'This place is huge!' yelled Marie, loping along ahead of him. 'Where's the main entrance?'

They turned a corner and came upon the remains of what must have been the driveway into the factory. It was overgrown and littered with junk, a graveyard for dumped factory equipment and rusting old vehicles.

'This way!' Marie called out. 'There are big double doors.'

He caught her up. 'And it's been opened recently.' They made out scuffs and footmarks through the mud and the weeds that had grown up around the doors. He put his shoulder to one of them, but it held firm. 'Locked, damn it!'

'Hang on.' Marie pointed to a narrow personnel door located a little further along. 'Try this one.'

It caved in on the second attempt, and Jackman almost fell through into a big open foyer.

The stench of damp hit them. They saw at once that the place was treacherous.

'Tread carefully, Marie! This is a death trap.' He glanced at the main doors but there was no key. Whoever had used the door had locked it and taken the key with them.

They stood for a moment, listening, wondering where to start first.

'I hate to say this . . .' Marie nodded towards a rickety staircase, 'but knowing his MO, the only way is up!'

She was right. 'Just be very careful, Marie. No accidents out here, okay?'

It was not easy. Several times he wondered how the Magician could have manhandled his victim up these hazardous steps, but the footprints and drag marks told Jackman he had.

Someone had been here recently, and he was pretty sure it wasn't a group of explorers.

'There's one more floor.' Marie had stopped to work out the next stage of the ascent. As she did so, they heard a sound.

They stopped still and listened.

'That's no Jack Russell,' whispered Marie.

'God, no, it isn't!' Jackman passed her and ran up the final stairs, with Marie at his heels. He knew what he was going to find, but it was still a shock when he stared upwards and saw the figure of Crazy Hazy, swinging slowly in the half-light above.

'Ring it in! Ambulance, Marie. Now!' Jackman leapt forward to where the loose end of the rope had been secured and started to untie the knots, cursing as he fumbled. The knot started to give, and he braced himself to take the dead weight of Keith Hazell, as he began to gently lower him from the rafters.

'On their way! And a police crew are here already, on the stairs, from the sound of it.' Marie positioned herself beneath the hanged man, ready to ease him down to the floor without injuring him further.

She was trying to avoid looking at the lad's face, and Jackman didn't blame her. He swallowed hard. From the look of him, they might just have got to him before he died, but he wasn't sure how much of a life the kid would have left.

'We've got you, Keith! We've got you! Hold on in there. You're safe now.' He wondered if this was really true. He'd had a brief look at the young man's eyes and recalled Rory's words about pressure building up. He doubted that Keith could see them at all.

Two police constables rushed in. One ran to assist Marie and the other helped Jackman with the rope.

'He's down,' Marie gasped as she eased him onto his side. 'But, oh, Jackman, he's in a very bad way.'

Jackman pulled out his phone and asked to be connected with ambulance control. 'I need to know what to do to help him!' he yelled. 'Or we're going to lose him!'

It turned out there was little they could do other than try to keep him warm and leave him in the recovery position. Keith needed professional help, not first aid. The next fifteen minutes were a nightmare of uncertainly.

Then, finally, the ambulance was blue-lighting Keith Hazell to Greenborough. Jackman and Marie watched it go, flying down the long straight drove to the main road.

'Poor kid,' she said in a hushed voice. 'I really don't fancy his chances, do you?'

'From what the Prof told me earlier, no, I don't.' He straightened up. 'Well, we'd better get going. We will have to get forensics out — again.'

'Rory's going to love us. But at least he doesn't have to cut anyone down this time.' Marie looked down and wrinkled her nose. 'Talking of which, I need a shower and a change of clothes. Crazy Hazy was in a bit of a mess, wasn't he?'

'Ah, that's not your new perfume then. Look, take my car. I'll wait here and do what has to be done. Uniform can drop me back. It'll be a good while before I get it all organised.'

She took his keys from him. 'Okay. I'll bring Ruth up to speed, shall I?'

'Please, Marie, and get the others organised. I'll keep in touch.'

'Any plastic bags in your car, sir?' she asked hopefully.

'In the boot, there's a roll of them.'

'Good.' She took off her jacket and rolled it up. 'This took the worst. I'll bag it and boot it and sit on another bag so I won't mess up your car.'

He smiled. 'It's had worse in it. Not much, I admit. Now, off you go.'

Just as she was about to leave, she pointed to the patrol car. 'Seems we're using a new breed of police dog these days.'

There, curled up on the front seat, lay a small Jack Russell. Jackman laughed. 'Iggy, I presume?'

'I'll tell Mrs Seabrook that he's in police custody. See you later.'

He watched her go, wondering if Keith Hazell had been the last on the list. Would they have to go through this again and again before they caught the Magician? It was a depressing thought.

CHAPTER THIRTY-ONE

Marie showered at the station. She always kept a change of clothes in her locker, so she was soon good to go again. She notified the super and then returned to the CID room, where Gary was waiting for her.

'Sarge! I've just heard from John about that airfield. Can I talk to you somewhere private?'

Marie nodded. 'The boss won't mind if we nick his office for five minutes, he's tied up out at the Pea-house.'

'I heard you managed to get that young explorer down just in time.'

She sighed. 'I'm not sure if he'll make it, Gary. God knows how long he'd been up there. You should have seen the state of him. Poor little sod.'

They went into the office. 'I'm sorry you had to see it, Marie, but thank heavens you got there when you did. You might just have saved his life. He's young, and the young can be remarkably resilient.'

Marie shrugged. 'Okay. The airfield.'

'The main thing, Marie, is that it's not what we thought, and I'm certain it has nothing to do with the Magician. It must have been pure bad luck that they chose the airfield, but it stirred up all sorts of problems.' They sat down at

Jackman's magnificent desk. 'There *is* a secret to that place, but it's a very old one — very old indeed.'

'Get on with it, Gary!'

He chuckled. 'John, as it happens, got on very well with Sidney, and so the old man decided to tell him his story. He swore John to secrecy . . .'

'And? Patience isn't my strongest point, Gary Pritchard, and it's wearing dangerously thin.'

He flashed her a wicked grin. 'It *was* an RAF base, and the story involves an aircraft that crashed there, just towards the end of the war. Old Sidney was a farmhand working the land when it came down, and he—'

There was a loud rap at the door. It was Berry Hopkins, the office manager. 'Sergeant Evans! Professor Rory Wilkinson on your desk phone. Says it's urgent.'

'Damn! Stay right where you are, Gary.' Marie hurried out.

'My dear Sergeant! Good news, for once! We have DNA! That debacle at the control tower finally yielded some evidence. Your killer was in a hurry, no doubt thrown by the appearance of the gorgeous DI Jackman and that lovely young detective he had in tow. At some point, your man cut himself — not surprising, as the place was knee-deep in broken glass. He got some blood on the Asquith lad's clothing — result, you find me a suspect, and I have a beautiful double-helix belonging solely to your killer.'

'So, I take it you've found no matches on our system,' she said.

'None, but at least we do have admissible evidence. Come on, Sergeant, I expected rounds of applause!'

Marie smiled. 'Sorry. I'm thrilled, really I am.'

'Mmm, alright then, but I'm not sure if you deserve the second bit of news.'

'There's more?'

'Cardiff just called from that pea warehouse. She'd only been there ten minutes and she found something. She's such an asset, that one. I'm so pleased she's going to stay . . .'

What is it with people today? Marie thought. *Why can't they just say what they have to say?* 'Yes, I'm sure she is, Rory. And?'

'Oh yes, well, your lovely inspector noticed that this Magician person had put a lot of care and attention into getting everything right when he hung up that last victim. Cardiff put up an extending ladder and found that he had sanded down the rafter to allow the rope to slide over easily. She found two perfect prints.'

'That's brilliant!'

'Good. That's the reaction I hoped for. Oh, and wood is *wonderful* for fingerprints. Being porous, it preserves the print so much better than a manmade surface. Evidently, he either didn't think we'd bother to check right up in the rafters, or he believed that we'd just pull the rope down and check that. Whatever, he didn't put on those cursed gloves. *And* he reckoned without the intrepid Cardiff!'

'This is the best news we've had, Rory. Have you told Jackman?' she asked.

'Cardiff passed on the good news. Now, I'll have the prints very soon. Shall we check them, or would you like that happy task?'

'I'll take them directly to Orac as soon as you have them, Rory, so IT can check for a match.'

'Fine by me. I'll call you as soon as I have them. The good thing about patent prints over latent ones — that is, visible rather than invisible — is that you can collect them using photography. We might need to improve the quality of the images but it's a simple process, and in any case, we probably won't need it.'

She thanked him again and hung up. Would the killer be on the system? Could they be that lucky? Things were finally beginning to look better.

She turned away, but her phone rang again. She picked it up expecting Jackman, but it was Orac.

'We need to talk, Marie.'

'Have you got a link for us? So soon?' asked Marie incredulously.

'I have, er, some thoughts, shall we say. Can you come down?'

'On my way, Orac.'

All the way down the stairs, Marie kept jumping from one supposition to another. The airfield? The Magician? And why had Orac sounded so troubled? Marie broke into a run.

Orac appeared distracted and anxious.

'You haven't had bad news, have you?' Marie asked. 'Your sister?'

'No, no, nothing like that,' Orac said dismissively. 'It's where this search is going. I don't like it. I need more time, because this is something I dare not second guess or make assumptions about, but I think that by this evening at the latest, I'll be able to tell you what links these deaths. Will you promise to wait at the station until you've heard from me?'

Marie frowned, puzzled. Orac had spoken with such urgency. She agreed to stay around.

'Thank you. I think your Alfie Brown is going to be able to fill in one or two gaps in my data. You said you were interviewing him. Is he still here?'

'I'm not sure. Robbie was the one meeting him. I'll ask.'

'I'd really like to talk to him,' said Orac. 'As soon as possible.'

Marie called Robbie.

'Marie? Where are you?' He sounded puzzled.

'I'm down in IT. Tell me, did you bring Alfie Brown to the station to interview him? Is he still here? Orac needs to talk to him.'

'Yes,' Robbie said. 'I thought it was safest, all things considered. He's downstairs, but to be honest, Marie, he's not the best person to get anything out of. Poor guy is pretty frightened. He's convinced that the Magician is coming for him and he doesn't feel safe even here.'

'Could you bring him down to IT, Rob? He might be of some help to Orac.' She ended the call. 'Robbie is bringing him now. Is there anything I can do?'

'Not yet, Marie. Just give me a little more time, okay? You can leave Alfie with me and I'll ring up when we've finished. This could take a while.'

Marie frowned. 'You really think he can provide the information we need?'

'I'm sure of it.'

When Alfie Brown arrived, Marie understood what Robbie had meant. The young man was a bundle of nerves, almost incapable of standing or sitting still. Oddly, he seemed to take to Orac, and after a few minutes she indicated for Marie and Robbie to leave.

'I'm not sure that this is correct procedure,' said Robbie, 'but already Orac seems to be getting on a whole lot better than me.'

'Don't worry about procedure. She'll let us know when she's through and we can collect him.' Marie decided not to say more. Orac had said she would tell her specifically, so she would wait for her call.

Once back upstairs, she looked around for Gary, hoping to hear more about the airfield mystery, but he was nowhere to be seen. She called across to the office manager. 'Berry? Where's Gary?'

'He said he was popping out for a while, Sarge, but wouldn't be long.'

Marie sighed. Once again, the airfield would have to wait, which was a shame because she needed a distraction to stop her worrying about what Orac might have found. From the way she looked, she had discovered something really bad.

* * *

Still out at the Pea-house, Jackman was just about to hand over to uniform when his mobile rang. It was Laura. He still felt a little start of pleasure when he saw her name on his screen.

'Hello, sweetheart. I just thought I'd let you know that I still haven't been able to talk to Cally Prothero.'

Jackman stiffened. This wasn't what he wanted to hear. 'That's worrying.'

'Henry seemed quite distressed, actually. He said he was wondering if she was reacting badly to the drugs the hospital prescribed. He was thinking of taking her back and getting her checked over. It is possible. Some people react badly to sedatives.'

'So, she was still sleeping?'

'More or less,' said Laura. 'He told me he had taken her a cup of tea and asked her to ring me, but she seemed too lethargic to even make the call. I recommended that she stop taking the tablets and that he phone the hospital and talk to someone about them. I also reminded him that shock can have a delayed effect. Some people just want to sleep all the time to block out their memories.'

'Sounds like good advice.' He paused. 'He didn't give you any cause for concern, did he, Laura? As in that he was lying to you?'

'Not at all. Why, darling? What are you thinking?'

He wasn't sure. And he wasn't sure of Henry Arnott. Either the man was exactly what he seemed — perfectly genuine and in love with Cally, as Marie had suggested — or he was a bloody good liar. 'Probably nothing, but it worries me that we haven't made actual contact with Cally herself.'

'Shall I call round when I finish here?' Laura asked.

'No! Absolutely not, Laura. If anyone's going, it'll be me. I'm honestly not sure about that man and I don't want you going anywhere near him on your own.'

'That was a bit forceful, my love.' She sounded rather amused. 'But I appreciate what you're saying, so I'll stick to ringing up. Don't worry.'

'I mean it, Laura. He's still a suspect, not high on our list, I admit, but . . . He just bothers me.'

'I hear you, Jackman, honestly. I won't be making any house calls, I promise.'

Jackman ended the call and rang Marie to say he was on his way back. She sounded preoccupied but promised to fill him in on his return. Hearing that did nothing to ease his growing apprehension. He sensed a mounting tension. He'd felt it before, and it always heralded some crisis in a case.

* * *

It wasn't until around eight thirty in the evening that Orac called. An uncle had collected Alfie Brown and taken him to stay with him for a while, as the young man had flatly refused to go back home. Everyone else had left, except Robbie, who, having kicked this case off in the first place, felt obliged to see it through.

All three of them went down to the basement and found Orac alone. She sat with her hands together as if in prayer. She looked terrible. 'The first thing I have to tell you is that there's another victim. It isn't Alfie Brown, as he supposed, but his cousin, Stevie Brown, another urban explorer.'

Jackman sat rigid, waiting for what was to come.

'I have his address and I know you'll get someone straight round there, but I suspect your killer has already abducted him.' She spoke in a monotone, flat and emotionless. 'He is the last. There will be no more deaths at this man's hand.'

'Then we have to find this Stevie, and make sure he doesn't become the final victim!' Robbie said.

'You will, DC Melton.' She handed him the address. 'Get your colleagues round there by all means, but then I have to tell you what I've discovered.' She looked from one to the other. 'Please, just sit down and listen.'

Marie could sense Robbie's impatience, so she sent him outside to ring uniform. As soon as he was back, they all pulled up chairs and waited.

'After I returned and began working on this investigation, I started to think about my quest to find my sister and some questions arose. The timing, for one thing. You needed my help, and I wasn't here, and I felt bad about that.' She smiled ruefully at Marie. 'But that wasn't even the half of it.' She stared down at her hands, now folded in her lap.

'To my shame, I was stupid enough to be lured out of the country. I was effectively removed from here because these killings could not have taken place if I had been part of the investigation.'

Marie let out a long sigh. 'I really hope it's not what I'm thinking.'

Orac met her gaze. 'It probably is. When I saw the forensic photos of the young men's bodies *in situ*, I knew they were the key to the whole thing, but it wasn't until I managed to find what bound the victims together that I knew for sure.'

'You know who the Magician is?' Jackman leaned forward. 'Orac! If you do, we have to get out there and find him!'

'My dear Inspector, I can most likely tell you exactly where you'll find him, if you will just allow me a few more minutes. I can save you rushing around and getting nowhere,' she faltered, 'even if doing so will break my heart.'

Marie's heart went to Orac. 'It's Dara, isn't it? Can you tell us why? Why is he doing this?'

Orac's sigh seemed to come from her very soul. 'Yes. Dara. My dear friend, my partner. The man who not only saved my life but traced my sister for me. You see, his only son died while exploring an abandoned building. I've only just found the details, because Dara has never spoken about his boy's death. His name was Lars, which I did know. He had become addicted to urban exploration. He went out alone one night, fell through a high ceiling and got his left foot trapped. He died, suspended upside down, but remained undiscovered for several days because he hadn't told anyone where he was going.'

'So his father is targeting other urban explorers?' asked Robbie, wide-eyed.

'Five young men, who were a major influence on Lars and led to his becoming such an avid explorer. I believe that Dara blames them for his son's horrific death and he's made them pay. Sackcloth and ashes, in penitence for their part in his boy's death.'

Jackman let out a long, low breath. 'But this Dara is a silent hero who fought undercover for his country. You knew him so well, you trusted him. How did he turn into a killer?'

'Love, Inspector Jackman. That's the answer to your question.' Orac looked at him sadly. 'Suppose you had a precious son or a daughter? Just think about it. Dara and I lived life on the edge. We both saw insanity on a grand scale while we did the work that we did. And never forget we were trained to kill. It was part of your life. But, we all have a breaking point, Inspector, and Dara is only human, albeit a broken one.'

From Jackman's expression, Marie saw that he was weighing up a murderer who tortured and killed young men, with a hero who had saved Orac's life. She knew he understood in part, as she did, but there was no forgetting what he had done. Marie had nothing but admiration for Orac. This must be tearing her apart. She would have laid down her life for him, yet she was handing him over to the police because that was the right thing to do.

Marie held out her hand to Orac. 'What you've told us took great courage.'

Orac took her hand and squeezed it tightly.

She let it go and took a deep shaky breath. 'Now to the facts.' She swallowed and picked up a sheaf of printouts. 'Some of this I accessed using searches already collated by Philip and Leon, along with some of my own. I also have information from the coroner's report on the death by misadventure of Lars Peter Quinnell — Quinnell being one of the names Dara took after leaving the job. I always knew him as Dara Quinn. Other facts come from my personal knowledge of Dara himself. For instance, his training taught him how to carry a wounded comrade out of the line of fire and to safety, meaning that he could easily have carried those explorers back to his car. He was always strong and very agile.'

'Did the military teach him those pressure-point techniques too?' asked Jackman.

'Not to my knowledge. It wasn't used in basic training, but I've seen him use them, and I know he is capable of felling someone in an instant. I saw a man drop like a stone once, giving us a chance to get away from a bad situation.'

'Did he practice martial arts, Orac?' asked Marie, thinking of what her black-belt friend from the Kuk Sool Wan dojang had told her.

She nodded. 'He did — well, we both did but he was way ahead of me, and he meditated a lot. He had a deeply spiritual side.'

This was hard to equate with the horror Marie had witnessed in the bell tower on Hallows Fen, but she wasn't going to contradict Orac.

'Dara must have found the names of Lars's urbex friends — those he blamed for his son's death — from a log that Lars kept on his computer, along with hundreds of photographs. This electronic diary was mentioned at the inquest, because they were trying to ascertain whether he had gone out alone or with others. One of his friends, Stevie Brown, was present at the coroner's court as a witness. He admitted that it had been he who got Lars into urban exploration in the first place, and he was proud of the fact that Lars had become such an enthusiastic explorer. He said he was very good at it and usually very careful. He was shocked when he discovered that Lars had gone out alone, and even more surprised that he had told no one where he was going. He said it was totally out of character, and he could only imagine that he'd done it in response to a dare from another explorer.'

'A very costly dare,' murmured Jackman.

'Indeed,' said Orac quietly. 'I found photographs. Look.' She handed them a couple of images of a good-looking young man with longish fair hair, a slightly crooked nose and a ready smile. 'Lars. He wasn't yet twenty-one when he died.'

'So sad,' Marie said softly.

Jackman handed her back the photographs. 'Orac? Where is he going to take this Stevie Brown?'

She looked at him, her lenses masking all expression. 'Back to where Lars died.'

'How do you know?' asked Robbie.

'Because I know Dara. It will be a fitting end to it all. Dara likes things to be properly done. No loose ends. He's obsessive like that.'

'The laundered clothes delivered to Rory Wilkinson,' mused Jackman. 'Like the belongings of a fallen soldier being sent home.'

'Only he knew they'd be classed as evidence, so he sent them direct to the Home Office pathologist. No drama, no fuss,' added Marie.

'We should get organised, sir,' said Robbie urgently. 'The Magician — Dara Quinn — could be on his way already.'

Orac shook her head. 'I don't think so, Officer Melton. I took the liberty of ringing Professor Wilkinson and asked if it was possible that all the victims were "hanged" at, or near, a specific time. He agrees that it's more than likely that each victim was actually strung up at around midnight.' She paused. 'The approximate time Lars fell through the ceiling.'

'Dara will be that specific?' queried Jackman.

'Without a doubt,' said Orac.

'Where is this place?' asked Marie.

'The old airfield at Randleby, in the ruin of the control tower.'

Marie gasped in disbelief. 'But we were assured that Randleby has no connection with this case!'

'I beg to differ. It has everything to do with it,' Orac stated. 'It was the beginning of this whole thing and was to be the end of it.'

'But we checked the history of Randleby.' Robbie's voice rose. 'We've scoured every newspaper, every online site, every bit of local history and even talked to the local police at Fenchester. There has been no mention whatsoever of a boy ever dying there.'

'You are quite right,' Orac said. 'Because the government issued a gagging order restricting the broadcasting of any information pertaining to Lars Quinnell's death.'

'Ah, the old secret,' whispered Marie. 'Whatever that is.'

'It isn't connected to Dara, Marie.' Orac looked at her. 'I'll be able to tell you more about that later, but for legal reasons the location of the body was kept secret.'

So, what the hell was so important about that miserable plot of land? Marie desperately wanted to know. She would just have to wait. They might have up to three hours to organise a massive operation if they were to save Stevie Brown. She glanced at Jackman and he nodded slightly.

'We have work to do, Orac. We can't assume he'll wait, we have to get there as soon as possible' He smiled sadly at her. 'Thank you. Your decision must have come at a tremendous cost to you. But if it's any consolation, you've done the right thing.'

'Then why does it feel as if I've stabbed my best friend in the back?'

'You couldn't have lived with the alternative, Orac.' Marie laid a hand on her shoulder. 'It's just not in you to allow a young man to die, or for the loved ones of those other innocent young men to have no closure.'

Orac sighed. 'Do you know what the final nail in the coffin was?'

Marie shook her head.

'The Book of Kells. He told me he was in Dublin, and he was going to Trinity College Library because he'd never seen the manuscript. He forgot, Marie. I have a very good memory. He saw it years ago.' Orac stood up. 'I'm going to ask one favour, Jackman. I want to come with you. I need to talk to him.'

Jackman opened his mouth, apparently about to protest, then stopped. 'Alright. But we have to go now.'

Orac swallowed and muttered her thanks. Jackman hurried out. Marie waited while Orac went to her locker and retrieved her jacket. 'Okay, my friend, let's go.'

CHAPTER THIRTY-TWO

Jackman had warned Ruth Crooke that there might be a breakthrough that evening regarding the Magician case, and she had decided to work on in her office and wait. In preparation, she had alerted uniform to the possibility of an incident, so as soon as he had notified her, she set the wheels in motion. Now that they knew the killer was ex-military, she also asked for an armed tactical unit to be on standby in case of a possible situation involving firearms.

It was decided to get to Randleby as speedily as possible and to conceal themselves in the hangars and stores. They would take down Dara Quinn and secure his hostage before he could get into the old control tower building. They were fully aware that this would be no easy feat given Quinn's background, but Jackman was pretty certain that he wouldn't want to deliberately injure any innocent police officers.

As soon as Ruth Crooke was given the location, she passed the information up the chain and requested someone who had knowledge of Randleby Airfield to make quite sure that they were not hindered in any way — a man's life could be jeopardised if this happened. Assured of a clear passage, the operation was to go ahead as planned.

Robbie, Ruth and the uniformed operation commander travelled in one vehicle, along with a trained negotiator, while Marie and Orac rode with Jackman. The journey passed in silence. Jackman could only imagine what was going through Orac's mind.

He first realised that something wasn't right when they approached the perimeters of the airfield and found the gates unlocked and wide open. Then he saw a big 4x4, parked on a flat expanse of hardstanding between one of the hangars and the battered remains of the control tower. There had been no attempt to conceal the vehicle.

'I was wrong,' breathed Orac. 'He came early.'

This changed everything.

Jackman's radio broke into his thoughts. It was Ruth, wanting to talk to him immediately.

He jumped from the car and raced back to Ruth's vehicle.

'Do we know if he's armed?' she asked.

'No. But Orac said he rarely carried or used a gun, even when working. He preferred other methods. Now she's certain that his only interest is in the five young men who led his son into the pastime that killed him.'

She turned to the uniformed superintendent beside her. 'We need a situation report on exactly who is in that airfield and where they are.'

He nodded. 'We'll surround the main area and I'll have teams check out the two nearest hangars and the control tower. That place is dangerous, it's little more than a ruin, so we need to take great care in there.'

'You need to take great care, full stop,' added Jackman. 'Quinn was a highly trained professional. He could be armed, and we have no idea about his mental state.'

'He's killed three men, critically injured another and abducted a fifth. I would suggest that his mental health isn't up to much,' Ruth said bitterly.

'That goes without saying, Super. I was thinking more of how he'll react when he sees a police cordon around the place where his son died.'

This was a bit strong, but she took it well. 'DI Jackman is right. Tell your officers that this is a delicate situation and not to underestimate Quinn at any cost.'

Superintendent Fuller nodded. 'I've briefed them already. They are all aware that this is a possibly volatile situation. Now, I need to get this moving, especially if there's someone at risk in there.'

He left the vehicle and gathered his officers together. Soon, one by one, they peeled off from the assembly and slipped through the gates. Jackman, Ruth and Robbie returned to his car. They waited, silent, tense.

Suddenly Orac's phone vibrated.

She pressed the speaker button and they listened.

'Oh, Ciara, why didn't you stay in Ireland and let me finish this? You should have just gone to Dublin like I asked.'

'And why didn't you talk to me before you started all this, Dara? I was your closest friend. I would have helped you.'

'It was too late for that, Ciara, and don't use the past tense. You still are my closest friend. I don't blame you for any of this. I know you too well, that's why I spent months scouring Ireland to find your sister for you. All I needed was for you to be gone for a week, so I could complete my mission.'

'You were never in Dublin, were you? You were here, hunting those young men.'

'I would have joined you afterwards, I swear. But you came home.'

Dara Quinn sounded frighteningly calm, considering that he must have seen that he was surrounded by police officers. 'Ask him about Stevie,' Jackman whispered urgently. He had to know if the young man was dead or alive. It would make a difference to how the situation was handled.

'Where are you, Dara?' Orac asked. 'Are you alone?'

He laughed, a short bark. 'You know exactly where I am, my dear friend. And no, I'm not alone.' Another little laugh. 'Although my companion isn't very good company right now.'

'Have you killed him too, Dara?' asked Orac, her tone even.

'Let's say the process has begun, albeit a little ahead of time. I knew that as soon as you made the connection, you and your friends would be here *en masse*. Sadly, I was forced to bring it forward.'

That meant that Stevie Brown was now suspended by one foot high up in a dangerous building. But he wasn't dead, unless Quinn had completely changed his methods. Jackman needed to cling to that supposition.

'So come down, Dara. Please. I desperately need to talk to you,' Orac pleaded. 'For the sake of everything we went through, I need to see you.'

'Then you come up here to me, Ciara. I won't hurt you, you know that. If you want to talk, that's the only way it can happen.'

Orac stared up at the ruined control tower. 'Okay, I'll come.' She ended the call.

Jackman grasped her arm. 'No! You can't.'

She turned those disconcerting eyes on him. 'I have to. He won't hurt me. I know it.'

'You thought he'd wait until midnight, but he didn't,' Jackman said urgently. 'You can't afford to be wrong about this too.'

'I'm not. That was just a simple change of plan, not a change of heart. Dara would never, ever hurt me.'

'I can't allow you to do this, Orac.'

Gently, she took his fingers and released them, one by one. 'You mean well, and I know you're thinking of my safety, but the only way he'll come down from up there is if he is carried down, dead. I have to see him before it's too late. Jackman, I'd be blind if it weren't for him! He saved my life more than once. I don't for one moment condone what he's done, but neither can I rewrite the past. He was a brave man and a loyal friend, and I have to say goodbye. I *have* to.'

The silence that followed her words seemed interminable, until Jackman said, 'Then we come too, and that's final. If you go, we go, and if he as much as breathes on you, Ruth

317

has an armed tactical unit standing by. I'd be prepared to swear I thought he had a gun.'

She didn't respond. Instead, she pushed her phone back into her pocket and began to walk towards the gates. 'He'll be up there.' She pointed to the highest point of the derelict tower.

Jackman turned to Ruth. 'Can you get some lights on this place? I'll go with her and take Marie. Robbie and the negotiator can follow, with a couple of uniformed officers.' He didn't wait for a reply but turned to Robbie. 'I want you to hang back and if there is the *slightest* indication that he has a firearm, call Ruth immediately.'

'And I'll activate the tactical unit.' Ruth's face held unusual warmth and concern. 'You take great care. I want you all back safely, understand?'

Jackman looked up at the crumbling ruin and took a deep breath. 'We'll be back, Ruth.' He turned to Marie. 'Ready?'

'Ready.'

* * *

With Jackman leading the way, they were almost at the entrance when Marie noticed that Orac was struggling. She took her arm. 'What's the problem?'

'Partial night blindness,' Orac said in a clipped, matter-of-fact manner.

'Okay, I'll get ahead of you. Keep hold of my jacket.'

After this, they made good progress across the rubble-strewn area. Soon they were at the outer door and, just as Jackman pushed it open, the control tower was illuminated. The bright white light of the halogen lamps made everything look unreal. She seemed to have stepped into some strange other world, the light too bright and the shadow too black.

'This way.' Jackman had the beam of his powerful torch directed towards a concrete stairwell.

The ground floor was more or less intact, although filthy, littered with broken glass, pieces of crumbling brick and plaster and the twisted metal from some old window frames. Marie suspected that the first and second floors would have been worst affected by the passage of time and the constant winds off the sea.

She was soon proved right. As they emerged onto the next floor, they all stopped. A blast of cold night air signalled that one corner had gone completely.

'Okay, everyone,' Jackman called back. 'Take great care from now on. Watch every step. The stairs are covered in crap, so tread warily.'

The temporary lights set up by uniform were penetrating deeper inside the collapsed part of the old building. It made moving forward easier but also created areas of dense blackness that intensified the surreal, almost cinematic effect. Marie kept a close eye on Orac. She was clearly unhappy in this odd half-dark, half-brilliant glare but she moved on, doggedly.

Finally, they stepped out onto the third floor. It resembled the pictures she'd seen of bombed-out buildings after the war. One whole wall had disappeared and part of the second had crumbled into heaps of rubble.

They stood and gazed around them, trying to take in where they were and, more to the point, where were Dara Quinn and his hostage?

Then they did see him, and they all gasped. Quinn was lit up by the outside lights as if in the spotlight of some theatrical production.

Above them were the skeletal remains of part of the metal framework of the observation gallery on the very top of the tower. Most of the ceiling had collapsed, although some rafters, joists and platform-like areas remained.

Dara Quinn was perched high up, sitting on a wooden beam that was still attached to one of the existing walls. He sat quite still, and Marie noted that he was holding a length of rope tightly wound around one hand.

Nothing moved — with one exception. To Quinn's left, suspended by his left ankle and securely attached to the other end of the rope, was the gagged and writhing body of Stevie Brown.

The rope, passed over an exposed roof joist, was not tied off or secured. Quinn had looped it through a piece of metal bracket, but it was only held fast by his own hand.

Marie looked down and saw that the hanged man had been positioned over a gaping hole that went straight down to the ground floor. If Dara did release his grip, Stevie Brown would fall head-first down the three floors onto concrete.

No one spoke. The only sound, other than the faint whistle of the wind, were the muffled cries of Dara Quinn's final victim.

Jackman turned and held out his hand to Orac. He stepped back beside Marie and whispered to her, 'This is her time. Ours comes immediately afterwards.'

Marie nodded, but kept within reach of Orac, should her impaired vision cause her to make a wrong move in this strange light.

For a time, she and Quinn stared at each other in silence. Then Orac said, 'Grainne? Did you only look for her in order to get me out of England?'

A soft sigh wafted down to them. 'No, Ciara. I've been trying to find your sister for years. I've made countless trips to Ireland, all fruitless, until recently. It wasn't until I realised what I had to do for my son that it suddenly came to me that it would be best that you weren't around for a while.' He paused. 'The timing couldn't have been better. I'd just managed to trace Grainne, or Louisa Kennedy as she is now, but there were a few last pieces of the jigsaw to put in place. I left those for you. I thought it was fitting that you actually discovered her for yourself.' Another pause. 'It was to be my parting gift to you, with love.'

Marie was having difficulty connecting the use of the word "love" with those horrific deaths.

'Thank you,' Orac whispered. 'I will always be grateful to you for that. As I will for everything you did for me in the past. But, Dara, you can't kill that boy, you just can't.'

'I have to. I promised Lars.'

'Your son died in a tragic accident, doing something he enjoyed. No one forced him to become an explorer. He loved it. This young man shouldn't die because your son made a terrible mistake in going out alone. Please, Dara, tie off that rope and come down. This isn't how I want our friendship to end.'

The conversation moved back and forth, with neither party backing down. Marie sensed Robbie hovering at the top of the stairwell behind her. She took a careful step back to get within earshot. 'Robbie,' she hissed. 'Fire service, quick. Get a safety net across the ground floor, beneath that hole. Now!'

Robbie disappeared while Jackman nodded in approval. Marie just hoped that Trumpton could organise it fast. At any moment, Quinn could decide to release that rope.

Orac kept begging Quinn to free the boy. Marie's eyes moved to the gagged figure swinging above her, wondering how long he could hold on. It took a while before she realised that Orac had been very slowly edging towards a narrow stone staircase that led up to where Dara still sat on his rafter.

'Orac,' she whispered. 'No. Stay where you are.'

Orac paused for a few moments, eyeing the stairs, no doubt calculating her route up. At some time, they must have had a bannister rail, but it had gone, and one side was completely open. The treads were no more than eighteen inches wide and in places they were chipped and worn. But worst of all, they went nowhere. They stopped just shy of the wooden rafter, after which there was nothing but empty space. Marie thought with horror of Orac's poor vision.

Marie suddenly picked up a change in Quinn's voice. He was asking Orac to leave and to take the police with her. At that point, Jackman moved forward.

'He'll not come down, Orac. It's time a professional negotiator spoke with him.'

Orac remained silent, and, as Jackman turned to beckon the trained officer to approach, she dived towards the stairs.

Without thinking, Marie followed. She heard Quinn calling down, begging her to go back, but Orac climbed on.

Marie was amazed at how fast Orac moved, despite her poor vision. She had to stop her. Marie was certain that Quinn intended to let Stevie fall, then throw himself down after him, and she was pretty sure that Orac knew it too. But was it Orac's intention to stop him — or join him?

'Orac!' cried Marie. 'Ciara! Stop! You can't do this! Think of your sister! Dara has given you your sister back, so accept his gift. Do as he asks. Please!'

There was nothing more she could do. Then, to her relief, Orac stopped climbing. Marie saw her shiver and hastened forward to hold her steady. Slowly, inch by inch, they edged back down the cracked and pitted stairs. Marie heard a voice above her whisper, 'Thank you.' She paused and looked up, but no one was there.

In the days that followed, she often wondered if she had really heard the dull thud of Dara's body hitting the concrete hardstanding, or if she had just imagined it.

The second they were back on solid ground, Jackman dashed past her and started up the stairs.

'Go careful, sir!' she yelled after him. 'They're treacherous.'

'He hasn't secured that rope properly!' Jackman shouted back. 'And I don't know if your safety net is in place yet! If that kid doesn't stop flailing around, the rope will give!'

She shouted at the panic-stricken Stevie Brown, 'Keep calm! Keep as still as you can, Stevie. Help is on its way! Stay still, for God's sake!'

Miraculously, he responded. He stopped kicking and managed to steady the rope. 'Good man. Just stay like that for a bit longer.'

Jackman had almost made it to the rafter when Stevie renewed his struggles, and this time the rope came loose.

Stevie Brown plummeted towards the ground.

Marie felt the draught as he fell.

'No!' screamed Jackman.

There was a long moment of silence, and then she heard voices drifting up to them from two floors below. 'We've got him! He's safe!'

Marie brushed away tears and turned her attention to Jackman, who was trying to pick his way back down to where she and Orac stood waiting. At one point he slipped, gasped, then regained his balance. A shower of tiny pieces of stone cascaded down around them. Being bigger and heavier, Jackman's descent was hazardous in the extreme.

At last, he was standing beside them. 'I'm so sorry, Orac,' he said softly.

There was nothing more to say.

'Let's get you out of here,' said Jackman to the grief-stricken woman. 'Take with you the knowledge that you saved that young man's life.'

When they reached the ground floor, Orac said, 'I want to go to him.'

Marie and Jackman shared a look, and then, in silence, they walked around to where Dara lay.

Surrounded by a spreading pool of dark blood, one of his legs was twisted behind him unnaturally. Marie and Jackman stood back, allowing Orac to approach him alone. She sank down at his side, took his lifeless hand in hers and began talking very softly.

They turned away. A lump formed in Marie's throat and tears welled up in her eyes. Yes, he was a killer, and maybe it was for the best that he had ended his life, but he had risked his own life to save Orac and preserve her sight. He had pledged his life to his country and served it well, and his loyalty had damaged him beyond repair.

Marie whispered, 'It's sad, isn't it? The world will see him as a monster, and all the good he did, all his bravery, will be forgotten.'

'Not by everyone.' Jackman nodded towards Orac.

Maybe that was enough.

EPILOGUE

Tonight, the Golden Compass at Randleby was playing host to a number of very diverse guests. Gary Pritchard, who had organised this occasion, had commandeered one of the two bars for the whole evening. When they had all eaten, he stood by the bar and tapped his glass for silence.

'I thought it might be appropriate for us all to get together so we can hear the true story of the mystery of Randleby Airfield, and what the future holds for it.'

Marie was sitting between her mother, Rhiannon, and DS Ralph Enderby. She was enjoying herself immensely. A years-long shroud of darkness had lifted, and life was looking good.

The whole team were in attendance, plus Rory, accompanied by both Spike and Cardiff Erin. Robbie and Ella sat with Stella and her husband, Tom, and next to them were Will and Lisa Sheringham along with several other urbexers, including Ray Zachara and Emily Butters. Cally Prothero and Henry Arnott were with them. It turned out that Cally's oddly drugged demeanour had been caused by a bad reaction to the medication the hospital had prescribed her. Henry had taken her back and insisted that they examine her thoroughly. Marie had been right all along. Henry truly did care for Cally and, judging by the way she kept touching him, she felt the same. Marie smiled to herself. Hopefully, it would serve to dampen Robbie Melton's ardour and bring his attention back to the beautiful Ella.

A few people coughed, and silence fell over the assembly. Gary introduced his old friend, John Beard.

'I was told some of this story by an actual eye-witness,' he began, 'an old fenlander now in his nineties, who is still sharp as a tack. But first of all, you need to know a bit of fen history to appreciate what I'm about to say.' You could have heard a pin drop in that bar.

'Because of our close proximity to Germany, our position on the East Coast, and with such flat terrain, Lincolnshire had more airfields than any other county in England. The majority of our Second World War bombers took off from here, and we became known as "Bomber County." Most of you know this already, but what you might not know is that more aircraft also crashed here than anywhere else. It is thought that a couple of thousand aircraft came down in our fields.'

This was an astounding figure, and there was a general murmur of surprise.

'The other thing that you might not realise is that some planes hit the ground at such speed that they completely buried themselves. The soil closed in on top of them, and the combination of oil, earth and a lack of air preserved them like time capsules. Maybe ten per cent of the planes that crashed here are still beneath the ground.'

'There's a memorial not far from where I live,' said Ray Zachara. 'A Lancaster bomber is still under the field where the memorial was erected. It's the resting place of five men, I believe. I thought that was a one-off, a kind of fluke.'

'Not at all,' John said. 'I've contacted an aviation heritage centre and they confirmed that there's a group of people who spend their free time hunting for these planes. Apparently, so long as they know that the crew all jumped, they get a licence from the MOD to excavate the aircraft. They take them to museums and put them on show in aviation centres. They call themselves "wreckologists," and are a recognised recovery group and a member of the British Aviation Archaeological Council.'

'How do they know whether the crew bailed out?' asked Stella.

'Records. Even in wartime, they did their best to document those who died or who were presumed missing. The MOD rarely gives permission to excavate a site where they believe there are remains — those are considered war graves, and then there is the Protection of Military Remains Act 1986.'

'And that's what happened here at Randleby?' asked Robbie excitedly.

'Absolutely.' John smiled. 'And old Sidney Packer saw it come down. He says that by the time he got to the crash site, the field looked like a battleground, but there was no plane! He knew it was a German bomber, but it had just vanished. Then Sidney realised that a single airman had bailed out. He found him with his parachute tangled in a tree. With a few other farm hands, they cut him free and held him until a vehicle was dispatched from RAF Randleby to pick him up. Sidney said he'd heard of planes burying themselves but had never actually seen it before then. He said it was the strangest thing he's ever seen.'

'So, why wasn't it common knowledge?' asked Marie. 'Why is Sidney Packer the only one who seems to know about it?'

'Because the military stepped in?' chanced Jackman.

'Almost immediately,' said John. 'And in a very short time, RAF Randleby ceased to exist. The locals were sworn to secrecy as a matter of national security and as it was a time of war, they took it very seriously indeed. A lot of families were later relocated, leaving no one but Sidney to tell the tale. He wanted to get it off his chest before he died. He had heard that some of the restrictions were soon to be lifted and some details were finally to be made public.'

'What details, exactly?' Rory looked enthralled.

John looked across the room to where Superintendent Ruth Crooke sat nursing a small dry sherry. 'Would you do the honours, Superintendent?'

Ruth stood up. 'We all knew that there was a lot of clandestine activity taking place there, and we were definitely not made welcome when we asked permission to investigate the area. But there has been an official statement made.' She cleared her throat. 'It has been acknowledged that a German Second World War bomber, a Dornier 17, crashed into the field adjoining the runway at Randleby. There was one survivor. As the other two crew members died in the aircraft, it was designated a war grave and was not to be disturbed. Their names were registered with the German authorities. After some tests, they have now estimated the depth at which the bomber is lying, and the field will once again be used for shallow planting. The rest of the airfield will be demolished, and the area will be cultivated as a wildlife park. Work is to begin immediately.' Ruth pursed her lips. 'As you may realise, that is far from the whole story. The rest is unconfirmed, and I suggest that once heard, you consign the whole thing to the back burner.'

All eyes were upon her, intrigued.

'There are two rumours. The first is that there was a fourth man on that flight, someone of very high standing who was delivering information vital to the war effort. If what he was carrying was ever dug up, or if it was known that he was heading for England, it could have meant a disaster for our campaign and, later, may have given rise to questions that the MOD preferred not to answer. So, RAF Randleby was effectively erased.'

'Surely any paperwork would have decayed over time?' said Kevin Stoner.

'Strangely,' Rory said, 'a lot of paperwork has been found intact after years underground. I've been told that when airmen bailed out, they purposely left all paperwork behind believing it would be destroyed on impact. Mostly it was, but if a plane did as John here described, I can well believe that everything inside could have been preserved.'

'The second rumour,' continued Ruth, 'is that the fourth man was an eminent scientist who was defecting, and that he was carrying other important documents.'

'I'd have thought they could have dug it up and disposed of all evidence, no matter which of those two scenarios was true,' suggested Max.

'There was a war on, son, it was chaos.' John shrugged. 'But there were still regulations to follow. It was easier to cover it up and allow the world to forget.'

John's story over, the company chatted amongst themselves. Ralph turned to Marie. 'I've got a bit of news that might interest you.'

She noticed the sparkle in his eyes and wondered what was coming.

'A friend of mine who runs a site clearance company has been hired by the MOD to clear the existing structures and haul it all out for disposal.' He smiled at her. 'He's giving me a certain time when one of his trucks will be pulling into a lay-by for a short break. Should you happen to be there, and just happen to have a trailer with you, a certain old motorcycle might accidentally fall off the back of said lorry.' He winked at her.

'You wicked man! How did you arrange that?' Marie almost jumped up and down. 'I'd given up on that old bike. Now I'll be able to get it restored!' She leaned forward and kissed his cheek. 'I love you!'

For a moment there was an odd look in his eyes. Then he seemed to recover himself. 'It was worth the fifty quid then?'

She hugged him.

Jackman gave her a quizzical look. 'Doesn't have anything to do with a certain Norton, does it?' he asked. 'I haven't seen you look so elated since they locked up Alistair Ashcroft!'

'Can't say,' she replied. 'Military secret, you know.'

Jackman came over and sat with them. 'So, it's all over at last.' He looked serious for a moment. 'Before we came out tonight, I heard that Stevie Brown is none the worse for his horrible experience. He has some ankle problems, and mentally he's pretty stressed out, but hopefully it's nothing permanent.'

'And the other lad, the one you saved after hours of being hanged upside down?' asked Ralph. 'Did he survive?'

'It will be a long haul, and there's no guarantee he will make it, Ralph. He had brain haemorrhages and what they hope is temporary loss of vision, so it's too early to say.'

'Poor kid. What did Quinn accuse him of?'

'Putting pressure on Lars to go out exploring on a regular basis — that's all we can think of. Like the other urbexers. They either encouraged him, befriended him, or fired him up to do more and more extreme exploring. Nothing that any other kid wouldn't have done on finding another like-minded soul. Such a terrible waste.'

And a waste of his own life too, thought Marie, her earlier effervescence evaporating. Orac wasn't here. Marie hadn't expected her to be. She'd already explored the mystery of Randleby on her computer and was certainly not up for an evening with a bunch of excited coppers and explorers. They had talked several times, once about the fact that Dara Quinn had been staying in Heron Court, in a flat close to Orac's, for the whole time he was carrying out his killings. But mostly they talked about Orac's sister and what she should do. She still wasn't a hundred per cent certain, but she *was* drafting that letter to leave with Grainne's solicitor. It was good enough for now. The only thing that worried Marie was that Orac seemed to be slipping back into a private world of her own, and she hoped it wouldn't end with her shutting Marie out. They had developed a bond over these past few weeks, and Marie hoped that it would be a lasting one. It was early days, of course, and Orac was still grieving, but Marie was watching out for her and would continue to do so. Orac had so few friends, and this particular one was determined to be there for her, no matter what.

Her upbeat mood began to return. Her mother was beaming at her, winking towards Ralph and giving her a thumbs-up. Marie threw Rhiannon a mock frown, and then burst into laughter.

From the moment they consigned Alistair Ashcroft to prison for life, Marie had started to feel free. The feeling was growing. There would be other terrible cases, because that was what her job was all about, but right now, looking around and seeing the people she loved and cared about all enjoying themselves, Marie Evans felt bloody good!

THE END

ALSO BY JOY ELLIS

NIKKI GALENA SERIES
Book 1: *Crime on the Fens*
Book 2: *Shadow over the Fens*
Book 3: *Hunted on the Fens*
Book 4: *Killer on the Fens*
Book 5: *Stalker on the Fens*
Book 6: *Captive on the Fens*
Book 7: *Buried on the Fens*
Book 8: *Thieves on the Fens*
Book 9: *Fire on the Fens*
Book 10: *Darkness on the Fens*
Book 11: *Hidden on the Fens*
Book 12: *Secrets on the Fens*

JACKMAN & EVANS
Book 1: *The Murderer's Son*
Book 2: *Their Lost Daughters*
Book 3: *The Fourth Friend*
Book 4: *The Guilty Ones*
Book 5: *The Stolen Boys*
Book 6: *The Patient Man*
Book 7: *They Disappeared*

DETECTIVE MATT BALLARD
Book 1: *Beware the Past*
Book 2: *Five Bloody Hearts*
Book 3: *The Dying Light*

STANDALONES
Guide Star

Thank you for reading this book.

If you enjoyed it please leave feedback on Amazon or Goodreads, and if there is anything we missed or you have a question about, then please get in touch. We appreciate you choosing our book.

Founded in 2014 in Shoreditch, London, we at Joffe Books pride ourselves on our history of innovative publishing. We were thrilled to be shortlisted for Independent Publisher of the Year at the British Book Awards.

www.joffebooks.com

Join our mailing list to be the first to hear about Joy Ellis's next mystery, coming soon!